THE SCARLETT BELL
SERIAL KILLER
SERIES
BOOKS 1-5

DAN PADAVONA

Copyright Information

Published by Dan Padavona

Visit our website at www.danpadavona.com

Scarlett Bell Books 1-5

Scarlett Bell Books 1-5

Scarlett Bell Books 1-5

MIND OF A KILLER

CHAPTER ONE

The horror movie credits rolled as Kacy Deering took one more sip of gin and pulled Braden's arm off her shoulder. Braden touched her bare thigh and she swatted his hand, softening the gesture with a smile.

"Not now."

"Come on, Kacy."

"What if the Walshes come home?"

The television volume was low so it wouldn't disturb five-year-old Chase upstairs. The hands on the grandfather clock edged closer to eleven. Though the Walshes weren't due back until midnight, Kacy remembered them returning an hour early the last time she babysat. A few minutes earlier and they would have caught Braden sneaking down the driveway in the dark.

The boy moved his hand back to her thigh. She grabbed his wrists with a playful giggle.

"Stop."

He sighed.

5

"Fine. Be that way."

"It's not like I don't want to."

"Yeah, yeah. But never tonight, always next time."

He pushed himself off the leather sofa and snatched his sweatshirt. Yanking it over his head, he ripped the keys from his pocket. That was another thing. His Charger was parked in the driveway. Old Clyde Sullivan next door wouldn't notice the car due to the bordering oaks and privacy fence, but he'd hear the thumping bass of the car stereo and see the headlights burning holes into the garage. And if the Walshes happened to pull up…

Kacy brushed the hair from her eyes and folded her arms.

"I'm sorry," she said, looking down at the floor.

"It's not a problem."

The way he glared at the door indicated it most certainly was a problem.

"Call me in the morning. I'll make it up to you soon. I promise."

Braden nodded. Then he was gone into the June night.

Through the closed door she heard the engine gun, followed by music blasting. Something pinged off the undercarriage, probably a rock. Then nothing. Worrying again about Mr. Sullivan, Kacy parted the curtains and stared across the property. Thick foliage cloaked the Sullivan's house.

Just the dark night.

The quiet of the sprawling Dutch Colonial pressed down when she closed the curtains, strangely deafening. Kacy rubbed goosebumps off her arms and turned on the news. Anything to break the silence.

Thump.

She was about to flop onto the couch when the noise scared her. Couldn't discern if it came from upstairs or outside.

"Chase? You awake?"

She turned off the television and listened. No pitter-patter of feet crossing the upstairs hall, no toilet flush or water running.

She called the boy's name again and shrugged when no reply came. Running her eyes across the living room, her heart leaped as she eyed the half-empty bottle of gin on the end table.

"Shit," she said, quickly snatching the bottle and stuffing it into her backpack, wondering how she could be so careless.

Kacy's feet slapped the polished hardwood as she carried their glasses into the kitchen. While she waited for the sink to fill she breathed against her hand. No scent of alcohol. She scrubbed the glasses clean, dried and put them away in the cupboard, the busy work settling her mind. She felt foolish for getting jumpy after watching a horror movie as if she were in middle school again.

Back in the living room she packed her windbreaker and wrapped it around the bottle. Evidence concealed. Now she only had to wait for the Walshes to come home, fingers crossed that the neighbors didn't hear Braden leave.

Thump.

Louder this time, too heavy for a child's footsteps.

Suddenly she was terrified of the Dutch Colonial's hidden corridors, of the night scraping at the windows and how every shadow looked deformed and monstrous.

She padded to the staircase and peered up. Darkness

swallowed the second-floor landing.

"Chase? You didn't fall, did you? Chase?"

Little more than a whisper emanated from her dry throat.

Kacy grabbed her phone. Fingers squeezed the case as she held the banister and placed one foot on the bottom stair. Braden would be home in a few minutes. She contemplated calling him, then decided she couldn't deal with him making fun of her for being afraid.

She flicked the wall switch. Now she viewed the top of the stairway. A fire lily accented the landing, its red petals open like gaping mouths.

Halfway up the stairs she stopped and listened. Perhaps the sound had been the bathroom door slamming.

But the bathroom and bedroom doors were open when Kacy reached the landing, all rooms spilling black shadows into the hallway like blood in the moonlight. She didn't like the twin quarter-moon windows. Like Halloween pumpkin eyes.

Her heart was a trip hammer. It climbed into her throat and constricted her lungs. Kacy knew she was being foolish. Her mind refused to stop racing.

Houses made strange sounds sometimes, but never this loud.

She swiped at the phone and pulled up her contacts. Wanted to phone her mother. And say what? That a bump in the night turned her into a frightened toddler?

Kacy took another measured step down the hall. The floor was chilly on her feet. From this angle, the boy's bed was impossible to see. She carefully edged toward his room, frightened when the floorboards squeaked.

Chase's bedroom was only steps away, yet it seemed

so far. Miles away. If only she could break the ice off her legs and move faster. The plan was already firm in her mind—she would go inside, close and lock the door, curl up beside the boy and wait until the Walshes came home. Which should be any minute now.

The floorboards groaned while she was still. Wasn't her. Who—

The light switch flicked off a split second before the landing went black.

A gloved hand covered Kacy's mouth. Suffocated her scream and dragged it under. A slice of moonlight flared across the knife's surface before the intruder raked the blade across her throat.

A terrible burning. Tearing. Choking.

Then she was one with the darkness. Tumbling into the depthless black.

CHAPTER TWO

The shrill of the phone ringing pulled Scarlett Bell out of a deep sleep. The nightmare was back, worse than it had been in years.

Reaching for the phone, she knocked the sleeping pills off the table and spilled her water. It poured onto the carpet as she cursed and righted the glass.

"Bell," she said, turning on the lamp.

"You awake yet?"

She wasn't sure who it was until Neil Gardy's trademark snicker tickled her ear. The laugh was something close to Muttley, a cartoon dog from her childhood, and always managed to lighten her mood. The clock read four, the first grays of predawn bubbling out of the Atlantic and touching the windows.

"I am now."

Grabbing the first thing she saw which passed for a rag, she dropped her t-shirt on the spill and stomped down. The cotton wicked the water and touched the sole of her foot.

"How soon can you be at Dulles?"

Her adrenaline ratcheted up.

"Uh...I don't know." Scarlett fumbled through the fallen items on the floor and retrieved her wallet and FBI badge. At thirty-two, she was the Behavior Analysis Unit's youngest agent. "Six-thirty if I hurry."

"Make it six."

Opening the sliding glass door, she let the thick humidity caress her skin. The Potomac sparkled below her walk-out deck, the salty taste of the Atlantic on the wind. Inside, she hurriedly stuffed three days worth of shirts and pants into an overnight bag, still no idea how long she'd be away or why she needed to leave.

"What's the rush?"

"Someone murdered a teenage girl in the Finger Lakes."

"New York."

"Right. Tiny village called Coral Lake. Ever hear of it?"

With a huff, Bell realized she'd need socks and underwear and started unloading her dresser drawer.

"Can't say that I have. I don't get it, though. One murdered girl shouldn't require BAU assistance."

"Normally it wouldn't," he said. She heard a zipper, probably Gardy sealing his suitcase, ready to bolt and waiting for her to get moving. "It's not pretty. The girl was babysitting. Our unknown subject slit the girl's throat and chopped her into pieces."

"Jesus." Jillian popped back into her head. The memories always did when a young person was murdered. "Tell me the kids weren't..."

"Only one kid in the house. And, no. He didn't touch the boy. Only the babysitter. Maybe he didn't know the

11

boy was there. Somehow the kid slept through the whole ordeal."

Bell released her breath. Being a sound sleeper might have kept the child alive.

"One more thing." A pause, as if he didn't want to tell her something. It wasn't like Gardy to pull punches. "He scalped her."

"He what?"

"Scalped the skin and hair off her head and took it with him, along with her clothes." She let the bag drop and fell down on the bed. Her head spun. "You still with me?"

"I'm here," she said, forcing herself into a sitting position as she switched the phone to her other ear. "That's unique to say the least. What does CODIS say? Any similar murders in New York over the last few years?"

"Nothing like that, no. Which tells me one thing. He's new to this."

"And just getting started."

"Exactly. If he's this violent on the first kill, imagine when he escalates." Bell didn't want to imagine. "But we've got to hit the ground running. The murder occurred Friday night so we're already a day-and-a-half behind."

"Why the delay?"

"I don't think the local sheriff knew what he had on his hands. He didn't consider the serial killer possibility. Good thing he realizes he's in over his head. The crime scene techs have been over everything, but the house is undisturbed. Minus the body parts, of course. But the scene gets a little more stale with each lost second, which is why we need to be on that flight."

She did the math in her head. If she settled for a

granola bar for breakfast, she could shower and be out the door in forty-five minutes. Then there was the traffic around D.C. to deal with, always a potential fly in the ointment. At least it was a Sunday morning and not a workday.

"Okay, I'll be there by six."

"Before six."

"But you said—"

"Up and at 'em, sunshine. See you in a few."

Typical Gardy. He always wanted things done five minutes ago. Gardy was one of the BAU's most respected agents, a prime candidate for Deputy Director of CIRG, the Critical Incident Response Group. It couldn't happen soon enough as far as Bell was concerned. Anyone was a fitting replacement for Don Weber and his religious devotion to statistics. Bell appreciated someone needed to fight the higher-ups, and statistical proof validating BAU's crime-solving methodology was critical for funding, but did he need to treat everyone like a number?

After showering she raked the brush through her straight, blonde hair. It touched the tops of her shoulders, the longest her hair had been since senior year at George Mason. In the mirror, her emerald eyes appeared to glow under the LED lighting, almost cat-like.

In the quiet of the bathroom the memory of her dream returned. She was nine-years-old again, as was the case each time the dream returned. Fate lent her another opportunity to warn her friend. Don't let Jillian walk home alone. Stay away from the creek. The water was dangerous, and someone had seen a stranger along the banks.

During sleepovers Jillian was always afraid of the dark. When the lights went out Bell would croon like a ghost until Jillian yelped and turned the lights back on. Then the door would open and Mrs. Rossi would be angry, warning Jillian she would wake the neighbors. Then one day someone stole Jillian away and turned the lights off forever.

The abduction and murder remained an open sore for Bell, a wound that would never heal.

Shaking herself out of her thoughts, Bell hurried to the bedroom and dressed, snatched the granola bar out of the cupboard when she finished.

She was packed and running for the door, the .40 caliber Glock-22 holstered, when she remembered the sleeping pills. They rattled in the bottle as she unzipped the overnight bag and stuffed them inside with her clothes, a subtle reminder to make an appointment with her therapist, Dr. Morford, when she returned. Whenever that might be.

The viciousness of the murderer simultaneously terrified and invigorated her, as did the prospect of getting inside his head. Somewhere to the north, the killer walked among his unknowing neighbors, breathing the same air, waiting for an internal alarm to sound and propel him to kill again. Bell's stomach tingled with the excitement of the hunt.

One final glance around the apartment to ensure the oven burners were off and the windows locked, and she shut the door.

She could already see the sun growing out of the horizon when she reached the highway, the distant ocean bloody and frothing.

CHAPTER THREE

The flight into Syracuse was turbulent, the plane dropping and tilting in roller coaster undulations. Gardy looked a little green beside Bell. He kept eyeing the vomit bag.

"So tell me more about the sheriff," Bell said.

She wanted to keep him talking and take his mind off the bumpy ride. The window light brought out flecks of gray in Gardy's eyebrows and short, brown hair.

"Sheriff Lerner. Less than a year on the job and it shows. He's part of a disturbing trend—politicians without law enforcement backgrounds who know a thing or two about winning elections, but not so much about law enforcement."

"You think that's why he didn't call for help sooner?"

"You mean he wanted the spotlight for solving the case on his own."

Gardy paused when the plane tilted, and for a frozen moment Bell felt sure he was about to snatch the bag from the seat compartment and yawn his breakfast. Thankfully the plane steadied.

"No. I don't think he understood the gravity of the situation. In his mind, it was the girl's boyfriend or a former lover with a jealous streak."

"Tell me about the boyfriend."

"Braden Goodrich, age 17. No criminal record, exemplary grades, star attackman on the lacrosse team and headed to Syracuse University."

"Doesn't sound like our target."

"Doesn't mean he didn't do it, either."

Gardy waved at the female flight attendant, who winked and produced a can of ginger ale. He winked back as she handed him the can, and the girl disappeared to the back of the plane with a hint of rosiness on her cheeks.

"Suave."

"I try."

Bell wondered if Gardy really tried. The special agent was in his middle-forties now, unmarried and without a steady girlfriend. Though Bell had only worked beside Gardy for a year, she understood the special agent was married to his job, an admirable trait that would leave him lost and alone when he eventually retired.

"You should ask the girl for her number."

He cocked an eyebrow and grinned.

"Ask for her *number*? That is so yesterday. I'm surprised you didn't suggest I ask what sign she was."

"Sign?"

"You know. Pisces, Capricorn. Her Horoscope sign, ya dig?"

Bell shook her head.

"I don't dig. Must have been before my time, old man."

The plane dipped again, and this time Gardy

snatched the bag and stuffed it into his jacket.

"Better safe than sorry." Gardy sipped the drink, then burped into his hand and sighed in relief. "Maybe I'll keep it. These things make great sandwich bags."

She pulled the case file from his open briefcase and spread the photos across her lap. The pretty flight attendant strolled back to Gardy, saw the pictures and quickly retreated to her station.

"Thanks a lot."

"Sorry about that. Don't worry. You'll see her when we disembark. Plenty of time to find out if she's really a Capricorn."

His Muttley laugh told her the nausea was gone as she turned her attention to the pictures, more gory and disturbing than she'd feared. At the bottom of the stack was a year-old photograph of Kacy Deering. The perfect lighting and canned smile marked it as a yearbook photo, a hint of mischievousness in the teenager's eyes. Bell wondered what Kacy's parents must be going through.

The Syracuse airport was tiny and vacant compared to Dulles, the building undergoing a remodel. The dusty air made Bell cough as they carried their bags through the terminal.

Sheriff Lerner was waiting for them outside, his Dodge Ram running curbside. Summer heat glistened the sheriff's brow. He had the stooped appearance of a man who'd been sedentary for too much of his life, belly drooping over belt, knees weary and failing.

"Agents Gardy and Bell?"

Gardy tilted his ID badge, plainly visible around his neck, as was Bell's. He held out his hand and Lerner took it. The sheriff's eyes passed disinterestedly over Bell, dismissing her as though she were Gardy's child on take-your-kid-to-work day.

"Thanks for meeting us."

"Figured it would be quicker if you followed me. The highway won't get you to Coral Lake, but I know a few shortcuts that will. I trust the flight was okay?"

"Not so much."

They followed the sheriff's truck in a rented Accord. The air conditioning was frigid, and the scent of cigarette smoke was burned into the seats. Gardy saw Bell scrunch her nose and nodded.

"Yeah, it's against the rules to smoke in these things," he said, one hand on the steering wheel, eyes shifting between the road and Bell. "It's the maintenance workers. They're always taking drags on their breaks, then they crawl inside the vehicle and bring the stench with them."

It took a half-hour to reach the village of Coral Lake. The water was the first thing to grab Bell's attention. Deeper blue than a clear sky in January. She couldn't take her eyes off all that blue. Foaming waves crested and broke in the wake of a speedboat. Several boats were out on the water, one man casting a fishing line, a couple floating in a canoe. Beside a long pier in the center of town, people lined up for a boat tour.

The village was small and quaint and bursting with money. Interspersed among the eateries were antique shops and pricey clothing stores. The sheriff's brakes flared and Gardy stopped behind him, allowing a parade of affluent-looking villagers to cross the intersection. Across the street, a woman wearing a Bluetooth earpiece exited a Lilly Pulitzer store carrying two shopping bags. Outside a brick homemade ice cream shop, an older man and a young boy accepted ice cream cones through the window, the younger boy tilting the cone and hurriedly licking the melt.

It hardly seemed possible for an active serial killer to be stalking this otherwise idyllic slice of life.

Soon the village center faded in the mirrors, and the sheriff turned onto Coral Hill. Upscale homes amid a dotting of mansions popped out of the trees as the serpentine road curled up a gentle incline. Bell's questions about how the killer butchered Kacy Deering without attracting attention were answered by the designed seclusion of Coral Hill. Privacy fences girded the properties, and most of the homes were set deep into the trees. Another layer of isolation.

Lerner's truck turned up a stone driveway and parked outside a white, looming Dutch Colonial with blue shutters and quarter-moon windows cut into the second story.

Bell leaned her arm out the window.

"Can you see the neighbor's house?"

"No. You'd think this was the only house on the street."

Thumbs in his belt loops, Lerner stood on the porch. A fist-sized chunk of glass was missing on the left side of the Walsh's door. A yellow rope of police tape blocked the entryway and swayed like a jump rope.

Yanking down the tape, Lerner stood aside for the special agents.

"As you can see, the perpetrator broke the glass to gain entry, though nobody heard. The closest neighbor is Clyde Sullivan," Lerner said, gesturing at a dense stand of elms and birch. "If you look close you can see his garage through the trees."

Gardy slipped off his sunglasses.

19

"Close enough to hear glass shatter."

"Sure, except Mr. Sullivan don't hear too well these days. You could park a semi in his driveway and yank the air horn for an hour before he'd notice."

"Hmm."

Lerner shifted uneasily when the conversation stopped. He didn't know what to do with his hands, which he switched between belt loops and pockets as the special agents glared at him. Then his eyes widened with understanding.

"Oh, yes. You'll be wanting to view the crime scene now. Let me show—"

"That won't be necessary, Sheriff," Bell said, striding past Lerner.

The sheriff glanced at Gardy, a desperate plea for the special agent to intervene.

"She's the boss," Gardy said, smiling. "No worries, Sheriff. We'll take it from here."

CHAPTER FOUR

The interior of the house was chilly from air-conditioned air spilling down the walls. In the foyer, summer heat bled through the broken pane and forced the cooling system to work overtime. The downstairs lighting was a study in contrast, sunshine beaming through the windows while shadows crawled from the corners.

The foyer opened to a sprawling living room, replete with a grandfather clock, gas fireplace, and ceilings which seemed to stretch to the sky. A 60-inch television hung on the wall. To the left was a kitchen accented by a long island. The stairway stood off the foyer.

Bell sat on the couch and jotted down her observations onto a notepad. Taking notes on her phone was more convenient, but Bell strongly believed in the connection between hand and mind when it came to processing information. Behind her, Gardy's footsteps echoed through the downstairs like water drops in a cavern. Though the preliminary investigation indicated no signs of forced entry besides the obvious pane break, the older agent checked each window and door as he scanned for anything the sheriff's department missed. And based on their assessment of Lerner, Bell wouldn't have been surprised to learn they missed plenty.

It was quiet for a while, just the hollow footsteps and the old house slumbering. A hand touched her shoulder and she jumped. Hadn't noticed Gardy coming up behind her.

"Sorry. Didn't mean to sneak up on you." Peering over her shoulder, he glanced at her scribbles. "You need more time before we do the walk-through?"

Bell clicked the pen several times in thought, then she shook her head.

"No, I'm ready."

"Then let's—"

"I need to do this alone, Gardy. Just the first walk-through, then we'll look together."

He opened his mouth to argue and thought better of it. A year together had taught him not to argue or question how she got inside the mind of a killer.

"Then I guess I'll walk the perimeter, check out the backyard."

He waited for affirmation but she was deep in thought, already putting herself in the killer's shoes, seeing the house as he saw it. Gardy sighed and walked away. She never heard the door shut.

Bell tucked the folder and notepad under her arm and climbed the staircase. A cherry wood banister ran the length of the stairs, and a flowering plant bloomed on the second landing.

She took each step slowly, picturing the killer moving in her place. Silent. Stalking. Watching Kacy Deering from the shadows.

That was the first piece of conflicting narrative. Why didn't she hear him shatter the window?

She might have been listening to music. God knows kids turn the volume up to dangerous levels these days, but the investigators didn't find earphones on the landing. Just her phone. And all those body parts. Bell knew he took her clothes as trophies, a way to live out his fantasies. Keep the girl alive in his mind while her parents mourned. Where was he? Close. Not a drifter. A local. Someone everyone knew. Someone who knew Kacy.

A chill touched her on the landing. It wasn't the air conditioning.

A macabre blood spray covered the walls on the second floor, the floorboards black and stained beneath the attack.

Bell's fingers trembled. She could barely hold the folder as she knelt down and spread the photographs across the hardwood. Her breaths flew in-and-out as she studied the pictures, the grisly scene made all too real now that she was at the murder scene.

This was where it happened. Where the killer butchered Kacy.

Chase's bedroom door leaned open. A few toys lay scattered across the floor. Five-year-olds were notoriously heavy sleepers, yet she couldn't believe the boy slept while Kacy screamed outside his doorway. It didn't make sense.

Unless Kacy didn't scream.

Which meant the killer approached from behind. Took her by surprise.

Careful not to mar the evidence, she stood beside the blood splatter, facing Chase's door as Kacy surely had. Perhaps the teenager heard something upstairs, thought it was the boy and came to check on him. Only it wasn't the boy.

Her neck hairs prickled as if someone was behind her.

Bell spun around to an empty hallway. Twin beams of sunlight blazed through the quarter-moon windows. She let out a breath and removed her hand from the Glock's hilt.

The bathroom was to her right, the master bedroom one door down, with a spare room tucked into the corner behind the rail. All the doors hung open.

Stooping down, she lifted Kacy's yearbook photo and ran her eyes over the girl's face. By now she'd memorized every angle and curve, the exact arc of the teen's smile, the way one eyebrow arched as though she was in on a joke. When Bell finished, she imagined the teenager standing alone in the hallway moments before the murder. Pictured her outside Chase's doorway, back turned to where Bell now stood.

"Where did you watch her from?"

Her voice trembled and cracked.

A wall switch was affixed between the bathroom and bedroom doors. She flipped it up and evened out the harsh beams through the window.

Bell stepped inside the bathroom and closed the door to a sliver opening. Squinting, she craned her neck but couldn't see the murder scene. The door handle was closest to Chase's room, making it impossible for the killer to observe Kacy without ducking his head out. Perhaps the killer hid in secluded darkness before he struck. She didn't think so. No, he'd want to watch the girl, fantasize over the murder first, a twisted foreplay.

The master bedroom offered a better viewing angle of

the blood stain, but even with the door cracked open, chandelier lighting flooded inside, casting a spotlight on anyone spying into the hallway. This wasn't the killer's hiding spot.

That left the spare room.

She knew this was the room the minute she stepped inside. Felt his presence like transient heat after the fire burned out. From this vantage point she could hide in shadow and see Chase's door, the chandelier light falling short of the threshold. Taking nothing for granted, she walked the room, hurriedly snapping photos on her phone. Her nerves were hot wires. For the first time since the investigation began, Bell felt she'd picked up his trail. The room appeared undisturbed. One bed stood in the far corner with the bedspread tight as concrete. Unless guests were in town, nobody slept here. A cherry wood dresser stood opposite the bed. She dutifully checked the insides and found nothing.

He might have hidden in the large walk-in closet. This is almost as big as my bedroom, she thought. Empty shelves. A lonely close hanger.

She got down on all fours, the thick pile carpet soft on her knees as she searched for anything that might belong to the killer. Although she found nothing, Bell made it a point to ensure the crime scene techs swept the closet.

Convinced there was nothing else to find, she headed for the doorway. Something caught her eye. An imperfection on the door frame at eye level. A hole.

Initially it looked like a bad patch job after the removal of a hook-and-eye latch. She bent close and turned a penlight on the frame. The splintered shavings told her he'd used a sharp object, almost certainly his knife, to cut into the wood. Bell pictured him alone in the dark. Glaring at the unknowing girl. Anxiously plunging the knife tip into the frame, spinning the weapon with a powerful grip until the blade whittled in.

Her hands were sweaty. The killer *knew* she was on his trail. The sensation was so sudden and powerful that she sprinted across the room and pulled back the blinds. Lerner's truck sat below, the heavyset sheriff leaning against the grille with his arms folded. Her footfalls echoed as she ran down the hallway to Chase's bedroom. Stepping over the spilled toys, she drew back his blinds and peered into the backyard. Nobody in the yard. The trees swayed as though laughing.

"What are you doing?"

She screamed and spun around to Gardy in the doorway. Mottled light turned his face into a picket fence.

"Easy now. You okay?"

Bell willed her breathing to slow.

"Yeah…yeah, I am. Grab Lerner. I know where he watched her."

CHAPTER FIVE

The vents blow stale, warm air across his face. The van won't cool anymore. The heat makes him nauseous, trickles salty wetness down his forehead.

Inside, everything smells of copper piping and grease like the after-hours scent of a fast food restaurant. Nervous, he plays with the radio dial. It's the news, someone talking about the stock market. Not talking about the murder.

Everyone in the village talks about him, but they don't know he's the killer. Yesterday he replaced the Fenton's water heater, and Mrs. Fenton couldn't stop jabbering over Kacy Deering and the horrible monster who killed her. It was enough to make him laugh inside. Frightened him that she might see the smile creep into his eyes and crawl out of him like a black widow.

He's learned to be patient, and he must be. They are looking for him now. Everyone is. But *they* are, especially.

His gaze falls on the blue Accord. There's a small dent above the rear wheel well. It's not their car, but a rental. These must be the agents, for who else would accompany the sheriff to the Walsh house? His neighbors gossip, and

27

when they talk he learns things. It's a small village, Coral Lake. Everyone knew the agents had arrived as soon as they drove into the main square, hugging close to Sheriff Lerner's Dodge Ram like obedient mutts, passing so close to his front door that he could have personally greeted them from his front stoop.

A trickle of panic runs down his back. Kacy is alone now. Unprotected.

She won't run away, but someone might try to steal her from him. The agents will certainly try.

Last evening he heard a hiker move through the woods and pass close to his personal space. Kacy's new home. He could hear the hiker stomp through brush, the firecracker pops of sticks snapping. The knife was in his hand, its blade sharp and still carrying the girl's scent. He was ready to defend his home, to protect Kacy, before the footsteps receded down the hill and he released his breath.

The sun is a molten glare on the windshield. He grips the steering wheel, squeezes with held breath, knuckles white. He strains until his face reddens, then releases.

The warmth of relaxation caresses his body. It begins at his scalp and works through his arms and legs. A pins-and-needles sensation.

He is brave to be here in full view. Anyone can see the van, but they don't suspect his intentions.

His tension released, he closes his eyes and imagines the shed. One light bulb affixed to the ceiling, powered by a solar panel. Pine scents from surrounding trees coloring the musty mattress smell. Their sanctuary. No one can hurt them there.

He doesn't like to remember the leather straps affixed to the cot and hopes he never has to use them. He doesn't think he will. Kacy accepts him now and may one day learn to love him after she recognizes how he protects her. Yet the straps are a necessary reminder that, if she is disloyal, punishment will be necessary.

The female agent's shadow passes over the upstairs window in the Walsh house. The spare room. She must feel his presence by now, senses him behind corners and in every shadow. She fears him. This makes him smile. He cannot see her face because the house is much darker than the midday sun. Only the hint of a silhouette. A specter in the glass. The male agent enters the house. Earlier he observed the agent paw around the property and considered entering the house while the man was in the backyard. It would have been so easy to kill the sheriff. Leave him bleeding behind the truck. Then he would edge the front door open, careful not to step upon broken glass and give himself away. Ascend the stairs.

Movement in the driveway catches his eye. Then he sees her and his heart freezes. The female agent.

She is more beautiful than he dreamed. Blonde hair that catches the light. Soft, red lips. He watches her move animatedly between the sheriff and the male agent, can't hear what she's saying but knows it's about him. And Kacy.

He thinks the beautiful agent deserves the opportunity to meet Kacy in person, to come live with them and understand his only desire is to keep them safe.

"Why did I ever agree to let such a disgusting boy into my home?"

The woman's voice makes him jump. His neck burns red where the seatbelt bites and pulls him down.

Pulse racing, he ensures the windows are still rolled

up. Prays nobody heard the voice.

In the mirror, he spies the long metal trunk in the back of the van. Chains hooked to each side because it slides easily. She shouldn't be able to talk inside the trunk, and this troubles him. At least she cannot hurt him anymore, not locked away. Does she know about Kacy?

"Answer me, filthy child."

He opens his mouth to answer and nothing comes out. His throat is too dry. Heart climbs into his voice box and pounds.

His eyes lock on the mirrored image of the trunk. Somehow he feels safer watching the trunk through the mirror, as though spinning around to look directly at the case will cause the chains to snap apart and the top to fly open. Releasing her fury upon the world.

"M...mother."

No reply. The tension rises inside the van.

"What do you want? Well, just don't sit there with your tongue tied into knots. Say something. Or are you too simple to speak?"

He checks the side mirrors. None of the neighbors are on the road. Yet she is too loud. Someone will hear.

"Answer me!"

He swallows. For a moment, he sees the male agent's head shoot up and look in his direction. They shouldn't be able to see him through the tinted windows from this far away.

After a pause, the male agent rejoins the conversation.

As static pops from the AM radio, he begins to speak, shy and fearful initially before his confidence grows. Though she may scream, he holds the power now.

He tells Mother of his job and the many people he

meets every day. Yes, he speaks freely with them, no longer feels the need to cower in the presence of others. The village respects him. He does not share with her his secret activities. She won't approve and will yell again, and then the agents will hear.

When she doesn't snap back at him, he continues with more conviction. He has a girlfriend. Yes, really. She is a very pretty girl, kind of heart and loyal. The words aren't out of his mouth for more than a moment before he regrets them, wishes to pull them back. He braces himself, expecting Mother to demand he introduce Kacy to her.

Kacy. He must remember not to speak her name aloud, lest Mother learn her identity and seek her out.

At that moment, the female agent climbs into the Accord. While Mother tells him to continue, to tell her more about his new girlfriend, he waits for the male agent to join the woman. He doesn't. Instead, he pulls himself up into Sheriff Lerner's truck. The Ram's engine growls, brake lights burning like hateful eyes. Like Mother's eyes.

A cloud of dust kicks up as the truck speeds down Coral Hill. It winds around curves, and then he cannot see it anymore.

Now it is just the beautiful woman in the Accord. Alone in the driveway where he'd waited in darkness with the house key.

He clears his throat.

"And there is another woman, Mother."

Yes, another woman. The beautiful agent. She could learn to love him, too.

CHAPTER SIX

Gardy and Bell split up to save time on their interviews. While Bell headed to the Deering house, Lerner drove Gardy into the village center.

Bathed in sunlight, the Coral Lake Suites stood on the lake shore, radiant and stately. There was no lobby to speak of in the boutique resort, just a hallway which led to three first-floor suites. Guests picked up keys at a sister resort down the road, Lerner had told him before wandering across the street to the cafe. An elevator gave access to the second and third floors. The Walshes were checked into 301.

The elevator stopped on the second floor, and an older woman in flip-flops and a sunbonnet stepped inside and pressed the button for the lowest floor. When the car moved again, she smiled and put a hand over her mouth.

"Oh, dear. I thought it was going down."

"No worries. It'll get you there eventually."

Her eyes fluttered about the elevator, the woman obviously uncomfortable locked inside an elevator car with a complete stranger until she noticed his badge.

"You must be the agent everyone is talking about."

"Ma'am?"

"The FBI person."

He snickered.

"Agent Gardy. And I'm not alone."

"Two agents?"

"Yes."

"My goodness. Two secret agents in Coral Lake. It doesn't seem possible."

"We're not secret agents, ma'am," Gardy said, trying hard not to double over laughing. Already he could feel his chest tickle. "My partner and I work for the Behavior Analysis Unit."

The woman gasped.

"You mean like that show on television? The one where they hunt for serial killers every week?"

Gardy's shoulders shook.

"Something like that, yes."

"Candice Squires," she said, offering her hand.

"Neil Gardy. But I suppose you can see that from this unfortunate badge."

She waved her curiosity away and shook her head.

"I'm terribly sorry for being nosy. It's just that..." She looked down, the light gone from her eyes. "It's so awful what happened to that girl. She was a senior in high school, her whole life ahead of her. Who would do such a thing?"

The elevator door opened on the third floor. Knowing the woman wasn't done talking, Gardy held the door open. He hoped she wouldn't keep him here too long. Gardy's Aunt Loraine could trap you at the doorway for hours on end, firing conversation starters when you touched the doorknob.

"Did you know Kacy Deering, ma'am?"

"No, I can't say I did, but in a village this small you know everyone's names."

Her eyes fell upon Gardy's ring finger and realized he was single. For goodness' sake, he thought. She's profiling me.

"You know…" Her lips curled into a grin, eyes full of life again as she fished through her purse. She produced a wallet-size photo of a pretty woman with flowing auburn curls. "My niece, Jenna."

Gardy shifted his feet.

"Isn't she pretty?"

"I…uh…"

"She's a real estate agent right here in Coral Lake. Oh, my. She's an agent, just like you."

Polite laughter.

"What a coincidence."

Get me the hell out of here.

"I should give you her number. Wait just a second, I know it's in here somewhere."

He could see room 301. Just a few steps away if he could escape the elevator. The woman rummaged through her pocketbook again. She really was his Aunt Loraine.

"It's not necessary, ma'am. I'll be leaving town soon."

The woman sighed.

"Look at me making a fool of myself, trying to play matchmaker. It's just that Jenna's so successful and pretty, but lousy with relationships just like my sister. Jenna's a good girl. She finally left that deadbeat husband of hers. The divorce hasn't gone through yet, but—"

"I really should go. Hey, it's such a beautiful afternoon. I bet you have a big day planned at the lake."

She beamed.

"Why, yes. I'm meeting Trish and Irena at the Bluefish Grill, then we're going on the boat cruise before Evelyn meets us at…"

"It was nice meeting you. And good luck to your niece."

He could still hear her talking as the elevator closed and the car began its painfully slow descent to the first floor.

Gardy raised his hand to knock on 301 and stopped. He took a breath and steeled himself, remembering the Walshes lives had turned upside-down.

A pretty black woman with long braids opened the door on the first knock.

"Lyra Walsh? I'm Special Agent Gardy."

"Yes, Mr. Gardy. We've been expecting you. Come in, please."

Gardy tried not to whistle. He figured a room like this ran five or six hundred a night as she led him inside. A sliding glass door took up most of the back wall and led out to a balcony, beyond which the lake sparkled and swelled. In the center of the room, a young boy sat on the floor with a parent's iPhone, tilting the phone and drumming his thumbs, lost inside a game.

"Nathan? The agent is here."

The bathroom sink shut off, and Nathan Walsh came into the main room towel drying his face. His skin was lighter than Lyra's, almost almond, hair cropped short. Nathan's gray slacks were designer, probably worth more than Gardy's entire wardrobe.

"Agent Gardy?"

Nathan shook his hand.

"Thank you for seeing me on short notice."

"Of course. Please have a seat."

Nathan sank into a cushioned armchair and pinched the bridge of his nose. Gardy sat across from him on the couch.

"My apologies for not answering the door," the man said. "I've been fighting a migraine since morning."

"Mr. Walsh, your family has been through a lot, and I don't want to take up all of your time."

"No need to apologize, Agent Gardy." He put his arm around Lyra, who stood by his side. "As you can see I have my whole family together, and for that I'm thankful."

Lyra pursed her lips.

"I wish we could say the same for the Deerings. Chase, why don't you play your game in the bedroom so we can talk."

Gardy watched the boy walk into the bedroom, shoulders slumped and feet dragging.

"I'm sorry, Mr. Gardy," Lyra said, waiting for the door to close. "This has been hard on all of us. Chase just wants to go home and have his bedroom back."

"I'm sure he does. Mr. Walsh, are you certain your son never heard anything?"

"Yes. Except for the upheaval, Chase is acting perfectly normal. He has no idea what happened."

"I see. How well did you know Kacy Deering?"

Nathan shared a look with his wife.

"We've known her for about two years. Is that right?"

Lyra nodded.

"We met Kacy through the United Methodist Church on Grant Street. Chase was three then." Lyra glanced at the bedroom door and ensured the boy wasn't eavesdropping.

"She came recommended as a babysitter, and we'd used her ever since."

"Did she have any enemies?"

"I wouldn't know," Lyra said. "But then again she was a teenager, and sometimes kids develop rivalries."

"What about at church? Did you ever notice anyone pay too much attention to Kacy?"

"Not that I can recall."

Nathan rubbed the top of his head.

"We've been over all of this with the sheriff."

"I realize that, Mr. Walsh, but I want to be thorough. Finding out who did this is my only priority."

Lyra massaged Nathan's shoulders.

"Kacy was a nice girl. Dependable. And she was good with Chase."

"Kacy's boyfriend was inside your house Friday night. She brought alcohol."

Lyra glanced down at Nathan. His head tilted up and their eyes met.

"We suspected as much," Lyra said. "Kacy understood she wasn't to have friends over or drink when she babysat, but Nathan and I were teenagers once, too. She'd been with the Goodrich boy for a long time, at least since we moved to Coral Lake two years ago. You don't suspect he was...involved, do you?"

"We're looking into all possibilities."

"I can't imagine he'd do such a thing."

"What about friends and family? Does anyone have access to your house?"

Nathan moved Lyra's hands off his shoulders and rested his head against the chair.

"You mean extra keys?"

"Yes."

"The killer broke the front door window, Agent Gardy. He didn't need a key."

"I understand, but it's important we cover all bases." Nathan exhaled.

"Yes, a few people have keys. For one, there's my brother, Kendall."

"Where is Kendall now?"

"Kalamazoo. He hasn't been to Coral Lake in over a year."

"Where can I reach your brother?"

Nathan rolled his eyes and opened his wallet. When he found his brother's business card, he handed it to Gardy, who copied the name and address and handed the card back.

"Thank you. Who else?"

"Well, there's Clyde Sullivan next door. He keeps an eye on the house when we go south for the winter."

It occurred to Gardy the Walshes were young to be snowbirds. Nathan recognized the question on Gardy's face.

"I consult for technology firms, mostly small startups, but I'm sure you've looked into my background already. I set my own hours and work from anywhere, a nice luxury when it's five below zero. Coral Lake might look like paradise, Agent Gardy, but check back in the middle of January."

"What about Chase? Doesn't he have school?"

"We home-school our son. It makes sense since we travel so often, and Lyra taught elementary school before my consulting work took off."

Gardy leaned forward on his knees and studied his

shoes for a moment.

"I need to ask you something else, and I hope you won't take it the wrong way."

When he looked up Nathan was glaring at him.

"Then ask your question, Agent Gardy."

"Can you think of anyone who would want to hurt you or your family?"

"No, I cannot." Challenge filled his eyes. "Are you suggesting someone might hurt us because we are black?"

Gardy noticed Coral Lake was predominantly white, but nothing suggested racist undertones existed in the affluent town.

"Please, Mr. Walsh. That's not what I meant at all."

Lyra went back to rubbing the tension out of Nathan's shoulders. Nathan glared out the window.

"But it crossed your mind. Coral Lake has never been much for diversity, a blind man could see as much. And sure, the good townsfolk manage to misplace our invitations whenever the rich and famous hold their soirees. But this isn't 1960s Mississippi. We are as much a part of the community as anyone."

"I agree," Lyra said, moving to sit upon the armrest. She held Nathan's hand. "Whoever perpetrated this vicious act, I can assure you he wasn't aiming for us."

CHAPTER SEVEN

The ashtray was a graveyard of shriveled cigarette butts. Stephanie Deering's kitchen sink overflowed with dishes, the counter dabbed by sauce and what appeared to be a chunk of fat. Sitting across from Bell at the kitchen table, Stephanie's hands trembled as she stacked a pile of spilled bills. She had Kacy's eyes and facial features, Bell thought. Time and a smoking addiction had parched and shriveled her skin, colored the tips of her fingers yellow. She wore a bathrobe over an old pair of sweatpants.

"They won't leave you alone, you know?"

Bell waved the smoke from her eyes and coughed into her hand as Deering fired up another cigarette. The tip glowed red and angry, then receded.

"Who won't leave you alone?"

"Creditors. Nothing but a bunch of vultures."

Bell knew from Lerner's briefing the father had left them two years ago and the Deerings had money problems.

"How often did Kacy's father contact her?"

Stephanie rolled her eyes.

"Christmas. Birthdays. That's about it. Couldn't be

bothered the rest of the year."

"Is he still in Sacramento?"

"Far as I know. He wouldn't tell me if he moved, the son-of-a-bitch."

Bell glanced down at Lerner's notes.

"It says here you were working while Kacy babysat."

"Story of my life. Soon as I finish at the restaurant, I waitress at Marilyn's for another eight hours."

"Marilyn's. That's out on route 20, right?"

"That's right. About five miles out of town."

"How did Kacy get to the Walsh's?"

"She walked. It's only five-minutes away."

"Right, but afterward she'd have to walk in the dark."

Stephanie pounded the table. The stack of bills toppled over and spread out like the loser's hand in a game of poker. Fire flared in the woman's eyes.

"You think I wanted her walking home alone? You've seen that hill. Nothing but blind curves and no shoulder to speak of. I did what I could, Agent Bell." Stephanie picked up the bills and shook them. "Two jobs, and the rest of the time I cook and sleep. Someone had to pay the bills and save for college because you can bet her father wouldn't have helped."

A tear crawled out of her eye. She swiped it away.

"I'm sorry. None of this is your problem. I realize you're just trying to find who did this. Would you do that, agent? Would you find who hurt my girl?"

Bell reached across the table and touched her arm, a small gesture to let the woman know she sympathized.

"We'll find him, Mrs. Deering. I promise."

Stephanie sniffed and produced a ragged tissue. She stamped the cigarette out and slid the ashtray away.

"I'm sorry. It hits me at the strangest times, you know? Sometimes it's just the way the light moves across the kitchen, and I think it's time for Kacy to wake up and I'd better grab her before it gets too late. And then I remember."

Another tissue was in Stephanie's hands. She sniffled.

Bell closed her notebook and put down the pen. It seemed to put Stephanie at ease.

"If you want to take a break—"

"No. Please continue. I want you to find who did this. I want you to find him and put a bullet in his head."

"I'll do everything I can to find him, Mrs. Deering. Let's talk about school."

"Sure."

"Did Kacy have enemies?"

"Not Kacy. Never. Don't get me wrong. She wasn't one of the popular girls, but she never had a problem with any of them."

"No fights, no drama?"

"Nothing like that. I don't think the in-crowd knew she existed."

Bell could relate. She'd floated through high school like a ghost, clinging to a tight-knit group of friends, barely acknowledged by the various cliques.

"What about boys?"

Stephanie smiled wistfully, eyes turning misty again.

"She was...is...a very pretty girl, my Kacy. Lots of boys were interested. Not that I was home much, but when I was the phone rang off the hook, always some boy looking for her."

Bell sat forward and held Stephanie's eyes.

"Did any boy pay your daughter an unusual amount

of attention, perhaps too much?"

"Well, she was with Braden. Lots of boys tried and tried, but she was happy dating Braden."

Stephanie's brow wrinkled. She paused, lips moving as if working out a problem in her head.

"Mrs. Deering?"

"Now that you mention it there was one boy who took things too far."

Grabbing the pen, Bell reopened the notebook.

"What was the boy's name?"

"Ethan, I think." Stephanie nodded. "Yes, Ethan Lancaster."

"When you say he took things too far, what exactly do you mean?"

"Let me think for a moment. This was two years ago when Kacy was only a sophomore. He was an older boy, a senior, but he'd failed a grade way back. He used to call Kacy several times a day. Likely more than that, because sometimes I'd pick up the phone and there'd just be silence on the other end."

"Did Kacy ever tell him to stop?"

"At first, I think she was flattered. The idea of an older boy and all, and this was before she dated Braden. But the calls kept coming, and that worried Kacy. And me, of course. He wouldn't take no for an answer."

Hurriedly scribbling notes, Bell glanced up.

"Mrs. Deering, at any point did Kacy think someone was following her?"

"Ethan broke into her bedroom one night."

Bell froze.

"Broke in? Did he hurt Kacy?"

"No. I caught him before he...I don't want to think

about what he intended."

"Your daughter's room is on the second floor. How did he get up that high?"

"There's a lattice running up the back of the house," Stephanie said, pushing up from her chair. Bell followed her across the kitchen where they peered along the backside of the little two-story. A vining plant, dead and wilted, snaked through the lattice. "See what I mean?"

"I see it. I hardly think it would support my weight. How big was Ethan?"

"Bigger than you. Heavier, too. What you do is climb a few feet and stand on the window sill. Otherwise, the lattice will snap. From there you grab the lower roof and pull yourself up if you have strong arms. Or if you're light like me."

Craning her neck, Bell looked up the side of the house. The climb appeared awfully steep.

"Sounds like you've done this before."

"Agent Bell, I'm coming and going so often I can't count the number of times I've locked myself out of the house."

Bell wanted to get a better look at the lattice and window from the backyard. She filed a mental note to do so when the interview finished. They returned to the table. Stephanie slumped into her chair.

"Back to Ethan. Did he break the window?"

"No. It was summer and Kacy left her window open, which I told her not to do on account of the weatherman calling for storms. Still, he needed to pop the screen out of the window. That's how I heard him."

"Please tell me you called the sheriff."

"Wasn't anything they could do. It was dark, and I

never got a good look at his face. Besides, if you think Sheriff Lerner is a waste of space, you should have known Sheriff Myers. What a piece of work."

"Did they question Ethan?"

"Oh, sure. They sent a deputy to the Lancaster's house. The boy claimed he was in bed sick that night, and the father vouched for him. You can always tell a Lancaster is lying when their lips move."

After the interview finished, Bell photographed the lattice and searched for additional entry points. In the hot interior of the rental car, Bell sat in silence. The wind ran up and over the windshield and made a whistling noise. She recalled no mention of Ethan Lancaster in Lerner's briefing, which struck her as odd.

Bell turned the key and rolled down the windows when the engine fired. Her clothes smelled like an ashtray and she wanted a shower.

Before she took the car out of gear, she dialed Gardy. The special agent was just leaving the Coral Lake Suites when he answered.

"We have a problem, Gardy."

"Yeah?"

"Kacy had a stalker."

CHAPTER EIGHT

Gardy was waiting in the village common with Sheriff Lerner when Bell pulled the car curbside. The shoppers strolling the sidewalk all stared at her. They knew who she was, and it reminded them of the danger hiding within the village.

Lerner, who'd carried a dejected disposition from the moment he met them at the airport, suddenly beamed.

"Yeah, I know all about Ethan Lancaster. He worked with Norwood Construction until recently before the guy up and broke the foreman's nose over some petty bullshit. Ethan is a hothead and a violent one at that. About a week afterward we nailed him on a DUI. It's one thing after another with that guy. I've been saying it's only a matter of time before he does something crazy, but I never expected anything like this."

"Slow down," Gardy said. "It's a helluva leap to go from bar fights and climbing through a girl's window to hacking her into pieces."

"Is it a leap? I thought that's how these serial killers get started. Committing sex crimes and the like."

Bell shook the windblown hair from her eyes and lowered her voice as a middle-aged couple passed.

"Except he didn't rape her."

"Well, I might not know much about profiling, but I guarantee you Ethan Lancaster did this."

The sheriff's office was a brick building with white columns running up the front. By the time they arrived, Deputy Crandall, a young and muscular man with short stubble popping out of his face, said Ethan Lancaster was already on his way.

The tiny office was cramped with desks, making it a challenge to weave toward the back. The interrogation room was gloomy and held a small table with two plastic chairs on the left end and one on the right.

Ethan took longer to arrive than expected. A half-hour later Deputy Crandall led Ethan into the room. The man sat across from Bell and Gardy, rocking back on his chair and chewing on a wad of gum. There was a chip missing from a front tooth, otherwise Bell thought women might have found Ethan attractive. The beginnings of a beard circled his round face, hair tied on top of his head. A man bun, she laughed to herself. What kind of bad boy sports a man bun? The younger man looked strong, physique thick and pudgy, muscles crafted from hard labor rather than a gym membership. Physically he fit the rough profile she'd shaped in her head. The human body was built to survive trauma. Bones were hard, muscle tendons tough and resilient. It took strength to chop a body into pieces.

The deputy waited for Gardy's signal, then stepped outside the door.

Gardy nodded at Bell to begin.

"Thank you for coming in, Ethan. I'm Agent Bell, and

this is Agent Gardy."

She reached across the table to shake his hand. He glanced at it and kept rocking back, a derisive grin on his face. Bell pulled her hand back and flipped open Ethan's folder.

"You're a busy man. In the last year alone, an assault, a DUI, and two separate charges for public intoxication."

He leered.

"The assault was bullshit. Guy swung on me first."

She shuffled through the papers, shaking her head in wonder. It seemed Ethan couldn't stay out of trouble.

"Tell me more about the assault."

"It was a fight."

"Okay, the fight."

Ethan rocked forward. The metal chair legs clonked down on the floor.

"Gerry gave me shit about not working an extra hour. We were falling behind on a roofing job, which was his fault for taking on too many jobs in the first place. Told him I was busy, that I had shit to do and couldn't stay. Gerry said either I worked the extra hour and finished the job or he'd fire me, so I told him I'd sue his ass. You can't force someone to work extra hours without paying them. I mean, this is America. Right?"

"Then what happened?"

"Gerry got up in my face and acted tough, said he'd throw my ass off the site himself if I ever talked to him like that again. I told him to try. By then the rest of the guys had come over to watch the shit-show. Guess Gerry felt he needed to prove his manhood now that we had an audience. He shoved me, I shoved him. You know how it goes. I guess it got a little out of hand with the both of us screaming. I don't even remember hitting him. I mean, one minute he's yelling in my face, and the next he's on his back, nose all crooked and bleeding, and I got two guys on my arms pulling me away."

"You said he hit you first," said Gardy, sharing a glance with Bell.

"If I said that's what happened, then that's what happened."

"Ethan," Bell said, resting her elbows on the table and propping her chin up with her hands. "Is it common for you to hit someone and not remember?"

Ethan's eyes darted between Bell and Gardy.

"I get mad sometimes is all."

"So it's possible you've hurt someone in the past and don't even remember doing it."

Ethan's fingers curled and uncurled in his lap, clenching into fists, knuckles white.

"I see what you're doing. Trying to put words in my mouth. If this is about that bitch, you can forget it."

"What bitch?"

Ethan was almost shouting now. He rose a few inches off the chair and leaned aggressively across the table.

"Kacy Deering. Who else would we be talking about? I mean, that's why I'm here, right? Because you think I was the one who did it."

The door opened. Deputy Crandall met Gardy's eyes, and the special agent raised a hand to say the situation was under control. Crandall nodded and returned to his post, glaring at Ethan until the door closed.

"Two years ago you broke into Kacy's bedroom."

"You can't prove that."

"Are you denying it happened? The mother says she

saw your face."

Bell didn't blink over the lie. For the first time since the interview began, Ethan looked visibly rattled. Not surprising as for two years he'd believed it was too dark for Stephanie Deering to see.

"You got it all wrong."

"Good. That's why we're here, Ethan. Not to accuse anyone, but to clear up misconceptions and set the record straight." She flipped to a blank page and clicked her pen. "Why don't you tell us what really happened?"

The tension fell out of Ethan's shoulders. He seemed to shrink several inches as he slouched down in the chair.

"First of all, I didn't break into Kacy's bedroom. She invited me."

"Were you and Kacy lovers?"

"I wasn't dating her if that's what you mean. Look, it wasn't any secret that Kacy liked to play around. And when she did, she liked it dangerous."

Gardy glanced sidelong at Bell and led with the next question.

"How do you mean?"

"Like sneaking guys into her room when her mother was down the hall."

"You say you didn't break into the room, but the mother heard you knock the screen out of its tracks."

Ethan squinted up at the ceiling for a moment, then vigorously shook his head.

"No, no, no. Definitely not what happened. Kacy lifted the screen and let me inside. The thing is it was dark, and her nightstand was right up against the window. I kicked over a picture frame before my eyes adjusted."

"Then what?"

Ethan smirked.

"Use your imagination."

"I don't have much of an imagination, Ethan, so I prefer you humor me."

Sitting back and stretching out his legs, Ethan locked his fingers behind his head.

"We got in bed."

"Did you have sexual intercourse with Kacy Deering?"

"We would have. She was into it, and it got pretty hot in there. That's when we heard her mother running down the hall. Now, I figured Kacy was gonna tell me to hide. Maybe under the bed or such. But the bitch screams rape, for Christ's sake. I swear that's how it went down."

"You didn't force yourself on Kacy?"

"I'm not bragging, Agent Gardy, but I don't need to rape a girl to get action. I damn near broke my neck climbing out that window in the dark. I had to swing from the lattice over to the porch roof, and I almost lost it trying to slide down the rail. Then I'm running through the yard and staying in the shadows, and all this time I can hear her whore mother screaming she's gonna call the cops."

The room was quiet for a moment. The fluorescent lights buzzed and flickered. Bell watched Ethan fidget, a clue he might not be telling the whole truth.

"That must have made you angry as hell," Bell said. "Kacy throwing you under the bus like that."

Ethan paused, measuring carefully what he said next.

"I wasn't happy but I moved on. Lots of fish in the sea, as the saying goes."

"That seems a little hard to believe. If you'll indulge me for a moment..." Bell flipped through the notes from

Stephanie Deering's interview. "The mother remembers you called Kacy several times a day."

More squirming.

"I take it you have a problem hearing the word 'no.'"

The young man worked his jaw back-and-forth. They could hear his teeth grind.

"The only problem I have is putting up with bullshit lies. Like Kacy pretending she didn't invite me into her room. Bitch only did it to save her ass. Yeah, maybe I called her a few times."

"Maybe more than a few times?"

"You got proof of that?"

"Where were you Friday night?"

A wolfish grin formed on Ethan's face. It showed too many teeth.

"Drinking beer with my old man."

"Out in public where someone saw you?"

"Nah, just at his place. Thirty-two Pleasant Street, about half-a-mile from here as the crow flies. Now that's a silly saying, isn't it? As the crow flies. Makes you wonder who starts this shit."

Gardy picked up his phone.

"If I were to call your father now…"

"Yeah, he'd vouch for me. Bet that puts a serious crank in your shorts, me having an alibi and all."

After Ethan left, Sheriff Lerner made a call to Corey Lancaster. He leaned against his desk, arms folded. Bell and Gardy sat across from him as the final vestiges of daylight burned at the window.

"His story checks out. Corey Lancaster claims his son was with him Friday night until two in the morning. Of course, the apple doesn't fall far from the tree. The father might be lying."

Bell didn't think so. To the sheriff's consternation, she ruled out Ethan as the murderer. Besides, Braden Goodrich had arrived.

Though she knew Kacy's boyfriend didn't fit the profile, they went through with the interview. The boy was visibly distraught and cried repeatedly, blaming himself for not staying with Kacy.

"I was gonna go back and drive her home," he said, wiping his eyes on the collar of his shirt. "I figured I'd drive around for a little bit and wait for her up the road."

"Did you call Kacy?"

"No...no, I didn't."

She already knew he hadn't called but wanted to confirm the boy was being honest. The phone history showed no calls from Braden that evening.

"But you worried over Kacy walking home in the dark. Why didn't you call?"

He dropped his eyes. Shrugged once and shook his head.

"Because I was mad."

"You were upset with Kacy?"

"It's stupid, okay? I thought she wanted...I mean..."

"You thought she wanted to have sex with you."

"Well, yeah."

"And you became angry when she didn't want to."

He shifted in his seat, looked off into a shadowed corner.

"I wasn't angry. Just hurt." He choked on his words and fell silent. "I can't believe she's gone."

Bell ran through the rest of her questions. She knew full well Braden Goodrich had nothing to do with Kacy's murder.

On their way back to the hotel, Gardy and Bell ate fish sandwiches on the pier. Dusk settled over the village and slashed streaks of magenta across the blue lake waters. The last tour boat of the evening left port. Shop owners turned off the lights and locked doors.

"You feel that?"

Gardy looked at her, confused.

"It's fear," she said, continuing.

The setting sun took the villagers' resolve with it, dragging it into the ground. The few people remaining on the street hustled to their cars with lowered heads and hands cupping arms, wearily glancing up now-and-then as if expecting someone to leap out of the shadows.

"Makes you wonder if the village will ever be the same."

Gardy sighed.

"We both know that answer. Before Friday, nobody could conceive something this horrible was possible. Maybe in New York City or Rochester or Buffalo. Not in Coral Lake."

The breeze off the water was chilling. It would take another month before the cold breath of winter disappeared from its depths. Bell rubbed goosebumps off her arms.

"Maybe we should go someplace warmer."

They found a bench in the village park. Cut in silhouette, a mother duck led a train of ducklings across the water. The tour boat was nothing but a blinking light on the horizon.

"So it doesn't appear Ethan Lancaster is our guy," Gardy said, watching the boat vanish. "That is if we believe the father."

"He doesn't fit the profile, regardless."

"No, he doesn't."

"Our guy is a loner. He might go out for a drink, but I guarantee he sits at the end of the bar away from everyone else. I don't see him holding an office job. Too many people would look at him. So if he happens to work in an office, he has a corner cubicle."

Gardy stuck his hands into his pockets and jiggled his legs to stay warm.

"You believe he watched Kacy for a long time, months perhaps. So I agree."

"He was likely abused as a child. No siblings and a one-parent household. The unknown subject needed space to hide and construct his own fantasies of dominating and controlling others."

"That ties back to why he stole Kacy's clothes."

"And scalping her, though that was rather unexpected."

"What do you think that represents?"

"I don't think the clothes and hair are necessarily trophies, at least not in the way these guys usually think. No, I feel he's keeping her alive. For himself. And that tells me she was special to him."

At the clicking of heels, Bell lowered her voice as a woman strode along the sidewalk.

"Somehow he knew her."

"In a village this small it's not hard to believe," said Gardy. "But that doesn't explain how she was special to him. A neighbor, perhaps?"

Keys jingled with desperate intensity as the woman looked over her shoulder. Her eyes locked on Gardy's and Bell's shadows, then she whipped open the car door and drove off without turning on her headlights.

"Yes, possibly a neighbor. Except Lerner interviewed the Deering's neighbors and nobody fit the profile. Loner, strong."

"Then not a neighbor. He saw her in a different setting. We could go round and round for hours and never get close to an answer. Look around. In daylight, I could sit on this bench and watch a hundred girls walk through the park."

"Right," she snickered. "And ask them if they were a Pisces."

"I'm just saying. If you were really obsessed with someone, you wouldn't have to go far to watch them every day in this village. It's supposed to hit 80 degrees by Saturday. I bet half the town will be in the park."

Bell leaned forward, elbows on knees.

"We missed something at the Walsh house."

"Between the crime scene techs, deputies, and our walk-through, I think we covered all the bases."

Bell rubbed at her temples and closed her eyes.

"No. Something isn't right about the break-in. I want to look again."

"Okay, but it can wait until tomorrow. It won't do us any good to paw around in the dark."

No, she thought. It can't wait until tomorrow. I need to figure out what I missed.

In the end, she decided he was right.

But time had already run out for them.

CHAPTER NINE

Angela Thiele hated this part of her job. The employee parking spaces stood at the back of the lot, away from the lamps and the pharmacy's brightness.

The paper bag was in her hand, filled with blood pressure medication for Mrs. Ives. It crinkled and brushed her legs as she walked, her shoes clonking against the blacktop. She could see her father's Nissan Rogue under a clump of trees, the vehicle's white glow barely visible, and she chided herself for parking in the shadows during the heat of the day so the sun wouldn't bake the interior. What difference would it make? Her deliveries didn't begin until after dark, and closing time was midnight. Now the mosquitoes nipped at her, the air uncomfortably cool without a jacket.

The shifting wind brought music from the village square as she passed between two cars. She had to turn sideways to squeeze through, the bag of medicine held above her head as she danced between the parked vehicles. It felt strange that nobody was in the parking lot except her. No customers. No employees taking a smoke break. Scary, like strolling through a graveyard at midnight.

The parking lot opened to a vast, desert-like empty space. It was ridiculous Mr. Ripple made the employees park this far from the store. The lot was never more than quarter-full during peak hours. What would be the harm in allowing her to park near the lamp lights? She would be sure to bring it up to him before she left for school in August. If he became angry, it would be no skin off her back. This was just a summer job. Next year she'd be sure to apply at the marina. Anywhere but the pharmacy.

The keys jangled in Angela's hand as she approached the Rogue. She needed to weave between Karla's Jeep and Ron's Volkswagen to reach her father's vehicle. Close now. Only a few more seconds alone in the dark.

She saw the van parked beside the Rogue. It was too close. The sides brushed up against her driver side door. Her first worry—how would she explain it to her father if the van scratched the exterior? Then her worry turned to irritation. Even if the Rogue was unscathed, she'd have a helluva time squeezing into the driver's seat. She might need to crawl in through the passenger side and shimmy over the gearshift. If she ripped her skirt doing so, she'd take her keys and rip a long, sharp line down the side of the shitty van. Whose van was it, anyway? It wasn't Ripple's. Angela didn't know what kind of vehicle he drove, but she bet her life he eschewed the employee parking rules and pulled up close to the pharmacy.

When she reached the Rogue's bumper she peered down the tunnel formed by the van and her father's vehicle. It was a tight squeeze for sure, but she thought there was just enough room to wiggle through and pry open the door. If her door clipped the side of the van, tough shit. That's what you get for parking too close.

She edged sideways past the van and took in its shabby appearance. Rust pockmarked the sides. The bulk leaned slightly to the right, something wrong with the undercarriage or whatever held vehicles upright. She didn't know much about how vehicles were built and didn't particularly care as long as they got her where she needed to go.

Halfway to her door, she noticed a long, metal box through the van's windows. It was probably filled with tools, yet its presence made her skin prickle. It looked too much like a casket.

The way forward constricted. The van was angled slightly to the right. Too tight. But the door was so close she could reach out and touch it with the tips of her fingers.

Stubbornly, she pushed forward. And stopped.

The van trapped her against the Rogue, pressing against her skirted thighs. A nervous giggle and Angela reversed course, admitting defeat. This wasn't such a good idea. Better to try the passenger door.

Except she couldn't move.

The ridiculous predicament might have made her laugh had she not been alone in the dark, the pharmacy on the other side of the lot seeming a million miles away. Panic rose in her throat. She thought of calling for help but didn't want the indignation of someone finding her in this predicament. No, she could get herself out of this. She needed to stay calm and think things through.

Angela stepped sideways. The rusty van scraped at her thigh and seemed to bite down. The girl yelped and shoved her hands against the van's bulk, hoping she could force her way backward and buy herself a fraction of wiggle room. When that failed, she gripped the top of the van and struggled to pull herself up. Her legs writhed between the vehicles, their cold exteriors like dead hands against her flesh. Struggling only worsened her situation. The two vehicles crunched the bulge of one kneecap, the pain excruciating. She yelped and twisted toward the back door until her body popped free.

She bent over to touch the throbbing knee and froze. She wasn't alone in the parking lot.

As she clutched the keys and limped out from between the vehicles, the man's silhouette filled the tunnel. Before she could react, the pipe wrench came down on her head.

The night spun. She crumpled to the pavement. Fingers brushed against her father's Rogue as a powerful hand gripped under her arms and dragged.

To the van. Eyes fluttered as unconsciousness pulled her down and down.

The door slid open.

And then there was only darkness.

CHAPTER TEN

The alarm tore Bell out of a dream. She glanced at the window, through which morning light shone brightly. Rubbing the sleep out of her eyes, she checked her phone and found two missed calls from Gardy and a message.

Where the heck are you? Call me.

Her hands were jittery as she rolled through her phone settings. Bell's mother used to tell her she could sleep through a tornado, but lately the slightest noise awakened her and often left her anxious and unable to close her eyes for the rest of the night. The settings confirmed the ringer was off. She certainly hadn't turned the phone off. Damn Apple.

She started texting Gardy when he knocked on the door. Throwing the sheets back, she climbed from the bed and rushed to the door. The mirror stopped her as she touched the lock. She wasn't dressed to answer the door. The nightshirt barely made it past her hips.

"Bell, you okay?"

Her answer came out as a croak. She cleared her throat.

61

"Just a second."

She pulled on a pair of sweatpants and brushed her fingers through the rat's nest atop her head. Not exactly presentable, but it would have to do.

When she pulled open the door his eyes were averted toward something interesting on the rug. Clearly he expected her to be less than decent.

"It's okay. Come in."

Gardy cautiously rolled his eyes back to the doorway until he verified she was clothed. He raised his hands as if to say, *why in the hell won't you answer your phone?*

"I know, I know. My ringer was off. Don't ask me how." She sat on the edge of the bed, the sheets and blankets a rumpled mess. "What's going on?"

"Our target might have struck again last night."

"Oh, Jesus. Where was the body?"

"No, there isn't a body. Not yet anyway. Let's hope it's just a coincidence, but I have my doubts."

She chewed a nail as he sat on the ottoman, elbows on knees, looking down. He rarely met her eyes when he was nervous.

"Then I take it we have a missing person."

"Another teenage girl. The sheriff's office took a call about an hour ago from the parents of Angela Thiele. She hasn't been seen since halfway through her shift at Brockhart's Pharmacy yesterday evening, and she was due to get off work at midnight."

"Wait. The parents are just reporting this now? What took so long?"

"Apparently she sleeps in late after work, not too different from some people I know." He shot her a meaningful glare. "So nobody thought twice when she didn't come down for breakfast. The father was the first to notice his Nissan Rogue wasn't in the driveway when he went outside to grab the garbage cans. Even then they figured she'd spent the night at a girlfriend's house."

Bell was up now and digging through her bag for something to wear.

"What time did the pharmacy say she left?"

"Lerner pulled the manager out of bed an hour ago. Guy named Derrick Ripple. He said Thiele went out for a delivery run around nine o'clock and that was the last he saw of her. Apparently he'd overheard the girl telling a coworker she was thinking about quitting, so Ripple figured she'd blown off the delivery."

"Idiot."

"Lerner said as much about the guy. Regardless, the sheriff's department found the Rogue at the back of the lot where the employees are supposed to park. The side door is all scuffed up, maybe a sign of a struggle. They're testing for DNA now."

Bell grabbed a change of clothes and headed for the bathroom, leaving the door half-open so they could continue speaking.

"You think it's the same guy? Kacy's killer, I mean?"

Gardy exhaled.

"If it's the same guy, he struck awfully fast again. That in itself is unusual. It's a different pattern, too."

She spat toothpaste and leaned her head through the doorway.

"Maybe not a new pattern at all. Perhaps he thought the lot was too risky to kill the girl, so he needed to take her somewhere."

"Which is why we have to figure out where he took

her...if this is our guy."

Bell didn't need to reply. It was the same person who killed Kacy Deering. Gardy knew it, too.

A half-hour later they were inside the sheriff's office. The parents were there. Bell estimated they were both around forty-five-years-old. The father had a thick mat of black hair and wore a golf shirt and khakis. The mother's clothes suggested she was ready to work in the garden before the panic began. She leaned her head against her husband's shoulder, eyes flashing around the room like birds trapped in a greenhouse. After they interviewed the parents, Gardy and Bell sat in chairs across from Lerner. The sheriff sat behind his desk. Bell caught the hint of a quiver when Lerner moved his hands, the sheriff obviously overwhelmed.

Lerner removed his hat and rubbed at his forehead. "What do we do now?"

"We keep rattling the bushes," Gardy said. "Brockhart's is close to the village square, isn't it?"

"About a block-and-a-half away."

"Then chances are somebody saw the guy's vehicle. Call in anyone off work today and canvas the neighborhood. Talk to Angela's coworkers. Ask if anyone saw an unusual vehicle hanging around the lot, something that didn't fit."

Bell tapped the pen against her cheek, thinking.

"In particular, focus on vans seen in the area. See if that rings a bell with anyone. We're dealing with an abduction now, and while it's not impossible the unknown subject drives a car, he likely used a van."

Lerner blinked.

"That makes sense. Would be easier to catch the girl

and throw her inside."

"Not only that, but it gives him a greater sense of isolation and solitude, and I believe that's very important to him. In the meantime, hold the Thieles a little longer and get Stephanie Deering to come in. There has to be a common relation between them, someone who knew Kacy and Angela."

Lerner slapped his hands on his desk.

"I'll call Crandall and get him in early."

When they were out of earshot Bell leaned close to Gardy.

"I still want to look at the Walsh house."

"You sure? The priority is finding the link between Kacy and Angela. You said so, yourself."

"I missed something important, Gardy. The sooner I figure out what it is, the better. It's our best chance to find Angela."

"First we need to check out the area around the pharmacy. Talk to people. This will take most of the day."

"I understand. When we have a moment."

With a shared glance, she and Gardy agreed to revisit the Walsh house after they exhausted their remaining options.

Bell noticed the Thieles staring. She nodded back at them, a promise to do her best and bring their child home alive. They dropped their eyes to the floor.

CHAPTER ELEVEN

The bare bulb casts harsh light inside the tight confines of the shed. When Hodge moves the shadows are elongated, grotesque. It makes him edgy, makes him clutch his hair and yank. His hands come away with a clump which he brushes on his jeans.

Inside the shed, the heat builds, humidity bleeding rivulets of sweat down his neck, soaking his shirt and producing a greasy vinegar stench. The sun will soon set judging by the long shadows cutting among the trees. It will be warm tonight. The full heat of summer has arrived in Coral Lake. Winter no longer sleeps in the shadows. He should shower, he thinks. He should clean himself so he is presentable to the women. It is true they are under his control, but decency is important. The problem is the shower is in his home inside the village, and he can't leave them alone.

The girl is asleep on the cot. Her wrists are bound behind her back by rope, knees drawn to her stomach. When she breathes her chest swells and recedes, a gentle lake tide he wishes to touch and swim within. There will be time for that. They have the rest of their lives together.

Sharing the cot is Kacy, the girl he continues to hide from Mother.

He isn't insane, Hodge tells himself, understanding the mannequin isn't flesh and bone. When he runs his nailed fingers over the mannequin's skin, it is stiff and cool to the touch. Dressed in Kacy's clothes, the pelt fixed upon its head, the life-size doll *is* Kacy. Squinting, he observes her chest and wills the flesh to expand and contract as does the other girl's.

He reaches out, desires to touch the new girl's skin. She has slept a long time. Occasionally the girl mutters and squirms, legs running dog-like in her sleep. Apprehension grips him. The new girl will love him as Kacy does. Yet she is deep in a dream now and will be frightened by the sudden touch.

Her skin is tan and young and perfect. He can no longer help himself.

Hands poised over her breast. A trickle of spittle crawling from the corner of his mouth.

A scream comes out of the forest. He backs away. Eyes move between Kacy and the sleeping girl. If they hear, neither reacts. They continue to sleep side-by-side. Sisters. No, more than sisters. They share a bond linked inextricably to him.

Still no reaction from the girls.

Careful not to wake them, he shuffles to the entryway. Cracks the door open and squints. Though the day grows long, the outside world is brighter than the shed. He can see the van beyond a stand of trees. The small clearing in which the shed resides is vacant. Overgrown grass ripples in the wind.

Hodge begins to shut the door when the shrill voice rings out again. Shouting his name.

Eyes lock on the van. Silently, he pleads for her to be quiet before she draws attention. But she won't stop. Keeps yelling his name, voice warbling on the edge of hoarseness.

He closes the door and stands with his back pressed against the frame. Breaths heave in-and-out as he watches them sleep. Mother's yells are frenzied and grow in volume until he is sure his ears will bleed. Cannot understand why the girls haven't awakened.

Finally it is too much for him to handle, and he throws open the door. The shed rattles with his fury. Heedless of the girls, he slams the door shut and stalks toward the van. Hands clutch ears and try to smother the infernal screams.

He comes upon the van and yanks on the sliding door. Meets resistance as Mother's yells echo inside. Locked. He'd forgotten it was locked.

Head darting around the forest, he fishes the keys from his pocket. Inserts the key into the locking mechanism and twists. An empty popping sound.

Hodge wrenches the door open and climbs inside. He is enraged by her, yet confused. He gave her the gift of perpetual, immutable sleep, and she will not sleep, will not be quiet or allow him to live in peace.

From his back pocket, he removes the knife. Touches the edge to his thumb and draws blood.

He will teach Mother to be silent again. To obey.

The trunk rattles and bucks, shaking the van. She knows what he intends.

She screams his name, tries to intimidate and recapture dominance over him. He is evolved and beyond her.

He fumbles with the locks and throws the trunk open.

CHAPTER TWELVE

Something shook the cot. A loud thump.

Angela's eyes opened to the dingy shed. Her vision was blurry, eyelids crusted shut by sleep and tears. She didn't know where she was and became confused by the cramped confines. Around her rose the thick, hot scent of baked wood.

Then she recalled the nighttime walk through the parking lot. The shadowed man blocking her escape route.

Remembering him striking her with the wrench brought pain. Angela's head throbbed and turned her thoughts cloudy.

She'd recognized the man. What was his name? Hodge. Her parents hired him to install insulation in the basement. She didn't know much about home repair, but she found it curious that the job dragged out for multiple days, Hodge always finding some new problem which required him to return. She didn't like being alone in the house with him. The way he leered at her from the corner of his eye. He didn't think she noticed, but a girl senses eyes on her.

The memory of the abduction pulled her up from sleep's depths into a new nightmare. She twisted on the filthy mattress. Rope cut into her wrists.

Someone shouted. She couldn't tell where it came from. The way it echoed told her she was somewhere outside, perhaps in the wilderness.

Angela struggled to turn herself over and heard yelling again. She was about to scream for help when the truth came to her. The voice belonged to Hodge. Who was he yelling at?

She wiggled her wrists and fought to pull her hands through the bindings. Sweat poured down her arms and made the rope slick. This was good, she thought. It might be enough to free her hands.

Yet he'd bound her good. The fight hurt Angela and made it feel as though she might dislocate her wrists.

When she turned over, the mannequin face stared back at her with dead eyes. She cried out. Swallowing the next scream and praying Hodge hadn't heard, she wiggled backward to the edge of the cot, away from the glaring monstrosity. To Angela's horror, the mannequin wore a teen girl's clothing—a halter top and cut-off jean shorts with manufactured rips down the thighs. Affixed to its head was a pelt of dark hair. A wig, she thought, until she noticed the smear of dried blood along the doll's scalp. She almost screamed again as her tears flowed.

Angela swung her legs into the air and used momentum to sit up. She couldn't peel her eyes away from the mannequin-thing. It seemed to watch her, inviting her to stay here forever, wherever here was. It struck her the clothes and hair must be Kacy Deering's, and then there was nothing she could do to prevent herself from crying out, delirious. She dropped forward and buried her mouth against the dirty bed. Let it suffocate her screams until she couldn't cry anymore.

Her shoulders shook as she pulled herself into a sitting position. She struggled to compose her thoughts and buried the roiling panic trying to confuse her. Angela twisted her head so she couldn't see the mannequin-thing anymore, but she felt its eyes on her back as she stood up. Her legs buckled.

The wall saved her. She slumped against the side of the shed until feeling returned to her legs. Looking down, she saw scraped flesh across her thighs and purplish bruising on her kneecaps.

It was quiet outside the shed. She couldn't hear Hodge anymore.

Which meant whoever he was yelling at might have disabled him.

Or he'd heard Angela and was coming back to the shed.

The door latch was low to the ground. Angela needed to bend at the knees and squat, facing away from the door. She groped behind her for the latch and cursed the ropes, then found the mechanism with her fingers. Pulled up and found it locked. This couldn't be. It had to be unlocked. She wasn't meant to die here. She pushed down until the latch screeched and popped. Quietly, she wedged her fingers between the door and frame and inched it open. Nobody was coming.

The sun was almost down when she shuffled through the entryway. She heard birds and tasted the sweet freshness of natural air.

Her legs almost failed her as she stepped outside.

Then she found her footing and moved faster with no idea where she was or where she was going. Everything looked the same around the clearing. Trees and overgrowth. Taloned shadows reaching toward her, growing as the light faded.

She walked faster, cutting between trees until she found the van. She froze in place. The side door was thrown open, but she didn't see Hodge. Careful of where she stepped, she slipped through the forest, cutting away from the van. Even if he'd left the keys in the ignition, she couldn't drive with her hands tied behind her back. She still didn't know where she was when it occurred to her the van must be on some sort of driveway or path. And that meant a road must be near.

Crouching down, she peered toward the van until she noticed the worn track leading down an incline. She climbed over a stump and spotted the road at the bottom of the hill. Below the road, amid the relics of daylight, Coral Lake shimmered in the valley bowl. She knew where she was now. Civilization was close.

Angela was past the van and struggling through the forest when she heard him coming. He screamed with insanity, berating Angela for leaving him, yelling something about betrayal. She didn't dare look behind. He was close. She heard him stomp through the overgrowth.

She broke out of the forest and cried for help as the earth swallowed the sun, and darkness dripped from the sky.

Hodge smashed through the trees. Right behind her.

CHAPTER THIRTEEN

"What the hell were you thinking?"

Bell brought her fist down on the hood of Sheriff Lerner's truck. Lerner jumped and stammered.

"Please try to understand. Nathan and Lyra Walsh just want to put their lives back together."

"They're staying at a boutique resort through the weekend. They could have waited another day. What was the rush?"

Gardy stepped between them and placed his hands on Bell's shoulders. Their eyes locked, Bell's bloodshot and burning with fury.

"There's nothing we can do about it now," said Gardy. "No reason we can't do another walk-through, make sure we covered all the bases."

She bulled past Gardy. The sheriff took a step backward and bumped into the Ram's door.

"Please," Lerner said, hands raised, trying to mollify the special agent before she bit his head off. "Try to see things from their perspective. It's just a piece of glass."

He gestured at the new pane in the door. Bell slapped

her palm against her forehead.

"It's a crucial piece of evidence."

She took another step forward, and Lerner slid along the side of the truck until he leaned back over the cab.

"Now, calm down. There's a perfectly good reason for fixing the door. The weatherman is calling for storms overnight, and the Walshes can't exactly have rain pouring through a missing pane."

Again Gardy moved to intervene, this time clutching Bell's arms and walking her away from the sheriff.

"Get off me, Gardy!"

"Then get yourself under control."

"I'm perfectly under control."

She looked over her shoulder at the entryway, saw a fireball of setting sun reflecting in the glass. That's when it clicked.

Bell tugged free of her partner's grip and stomped up the steps. The new glass, shimmering and perfect, not a hint of dust or a child's fingerprints, stood out from the others. Even so, she swung around and pointed at the repaired pane.

"Is this the piece?"

"Yes," Lerner said, cautiously shuffling into the yard. "As I said, it's no big deal—"

Pulling the sleeve of her jacket over her hand, Bell whacked the pane with the outside of her fist. The new pane shattered and tinkled down in the foyer.

"What...I can't believe...Agent Gardy, do something before she wrecks the house."

Gardy scowled as he crossed the yard, his shoes making swishing noises through the grass.

"She's not gonna wreck the house." When he clonked

up the stairs to Bell's side, he raised his eyebrows. "You aren't gonna wreck the house, right?"

It was clear to Bell Gardy was trying to diffuse the situation with humor. The glint in her partner's eyes told her he was on the same page. Behind them, Lerner paced back-and-forth. His hands clawed at his face while he muttered about lunatic agents and how he would explain this to the Walshes.

Using her sleeve, Bell knocked away the remaining jagged pieces and reached her arm through the opening. She groped for the door handle and came up several inches short.

"Hold on. My arms are longer than yours."

She stood aside for Gardy, who pushed his arm through the missing pane. He grunted, straining to reach the handle. With his arm at full extension, his fingers fell short of the mark by a few inches.

Now Lerner climbed the steps and stared incredulously at the agents.

"Are the two of you satisfied?"

"Smile, Sheriff. Thanks to Agent Bell and her somewhat unconventional techniques, we're several steps closer to catching the killer."

"How is that?"

"Unless our murderer's arms stretch to his ankles, there's no way he could have put his hand through and unlocked the door."

"Meaning?"

Bell folded her arms and leaned against the rail.

"The killer was inside the house the whole time. How in the hell did I miss it?"

Lerner's eyes traveled between the opening and the

handle.

"Wait just a second. Let me try."

The agents moved aside as the sheriff waddled forward. He had a confident look in his eyes, a certainty he'd prove the woman wrong. The agents shared a grin as he struggled to reach the lock. He was red-faced and out of breath when he finally pulled his arm back.

"I guess I owe the two of you an apology. Let me get this straight. The killer was already inside the house while the Goodrich boy visited Kacy Deering."

Gardy nodded.

"No doubt he figured Braden Goodrich would give him a fight, so he waited for the boy to leave before he made his move."

"And smashed the pane after the fact to make it look like a break-in. Jesus. I can't believe we didn't see it."

"Which also explains why Kacy didn't hear the killer break into the house," said Bell, pumping with adrenaline now that the puzzle pieces fit together. "He was already upstairs."

A sudden gust nearly stole Lerner's hat. The leaves rattled like dead things.

Gardy descended the stairs and gave the front of the house one last look.

"No other signs of forced entry. I can examine the sides and back, but I won't find anything different from yesterday."

Bell followed Gardy to the sidewalk, the sheriff trailing behind.

"Gardy, who did the Walshes say had keys to the house?"

"Two people. The neighbor, Clyde Sullivan."

"He ain't our guy," said Lerner.

"And the brother who lives in Kalamazoo."

Bell shook her head and paced a trench into the lawn.

"That can't be right, Gardy. They forgot someone."

"I'll give Nathan Walsh a call."

Gardy walked a few paces away. She couldn't eavesdrop on the conversation with Lerner rambling continuous apologies, but Gardy wore a grin when he returned.

"About two years ago Walsh hired a local contractor to redo the basement. A guy named Alan Hodge."

"I know Hodge," Lerner said. "He corners the market on contracting work in Coral Lake."

"They gave him a house key, which he returned, but he could have copied it in the meantime."

The wheels spun faster in Bell's head.

She brought the phone to her ear and listened as it rang and rang.

"Bell?"

She held Gardy's eyes and placed her finger over her lips. Just before she gave up, a voice answered on the other end. Tired, haggard.

"Hello?"

"Mrs. Deering?"

"Hold on…yes…who is this?"

Something toppled over. Deering cursed under her breath. It was clear the woman was three sheets to the wind or hungover.

"Mrs. Deering, this is Agent Bell."

"Agent…Agent Bell. What time is it?"

"Please, Mrs. Deering. I have one quick question to ask. It won't take a moment."

An exasperated groan.

"Fine. Ask away."

"Have you had any repairs done to your house over the last two years?"

"Repairs? What's this about?"

"Think hard."

It was quiet on the other end. Bell wondered if Deering had fallen asleep.

"No, not that I can recall."

Bell's stomach sank. It had to be the handyman. She was sure.

"Are you absolutely certain?"

More silence. Deering coughed, a thick, mucus-filled hack that made Bell cringe.

"I'm sure. No, the only thing we did was remodel the basement, but it wasn't a repair. I wanted someplace for Kacy and her friends to—"

"Who did the remodel?"

Gardy and Lerner watched Bell, who held up a finger.

When Deering said it was Alan Hodge, Bell snapped her finger and mouthed the handyman's name at Gardy. Already Gardy had his own phone to his ear. She could overhear him trying to find someone at Quantico to run a background check on Hodge.

Bell thanked Deering and ended the call, cutting her off as the woman's questions became frantic. Even in her state of confusion, Deering had seemed to figure out Hodge was a suspect.

"Gee, I don't know about this." Lerner rubbed behind his neck. "Alan Hodge works for half the families in Coral Lake."

"Tell me more about Hodge. Is he a large man?"

"I suppose so. I mean he's maybe an inch or two taller than me."

"But strong."

"Thick, I guess you would say. The guy spends his days carrying washers and dryers down basement stairs."

"And he lives alone. No wife or kids."

"Are you asking me or telling me? Seems like you already have all the answers."

"Sorry, Sheriff. Truthfully, profiles are just theories. They aren't foolproof, and there isn't any guarantee Hodge is our man."

Yet her gut told her otherwise. She hadn't seen a photograph of Hodge, but the picture she'd worked up in her head sent goosebumps down her arms.

Remodels took weeks to complete, sometimes months. A lot of time to observe a teenage girl. That's how the obsession began.

"Understood. To answer your question, yes, Hodge is unmarried. No girlfriend as far as I know, but I can ask around."

"Probably unnecessary. Listen, we think the reason he scalped Kacy and took her clothes is so he can keep her alive, be able to play with her as long as he wants."

Lerner's mouth twisted as if he'd bitten down on something sour.

"But she's dead."

"Yes, but a part of his mind believes otherwise, even though he consciously recognizes it's all fantasy."

"You told us this during the first briefing. I don't see how this helps. The evidence is purely circumstantial, nothing a judge would issue a warrant over without some way to tie him to the scene."

Over Lerner's shoulder, Bell could see Gardy talking into his phone, hand over his other ear to block out the wind.

"It's important because the person who murdered Kacy, be it Hodge or someone else, needs privacy."

"As I confirmed, Hodge lives alone."

"What's his address?"

"Canal Street, right in the center of the village where they're setting up for the strawberry festival. Christ, his house was a stone's throw from us yesterday."

Part of the profile fractured in Bell's head. No, it wasn't likely Hodge kept Kacy's remains in his house. Though he could easily conceal the clothes and hair in a bag, Hodge would want more seclusion. Too many people strolling Canal Street, shopping and glancing through his windows as they passed. It sounded like everyone in town knew him. Plus, and this thought made Bell cringe, the remains would begin to stink and attract attention.

She was about to ask Lerner another question when Gardy walked over, the phone back in his pocket.

"So Alan Hodge grew up in two different foster homes, the first in the northeastern corner of Pennsylvania, the last in Irondequoit outside Rochester. Nothing out of the ordinary we found about the Pennsylvania location. An older couple raised Hodge until he was five, but they gave him up after the father died and the mother fell ill."

An abusive childhood stood center in Bell's pattern. Although multiple foster homes pointed at a disjointed upbringing, it didn't imply maltreatment.

"What about the next family?"

"Not a family. One woman: Rhonda Winston. Turns out the police were called to her house on three separate occasions for suspected abuse, but none of the charges stuck. The catch is Winston was arrested for heroin possession after Hodge turned eighteen and moved. While the officers searched the premises, they discovered a cramped crawlspace in the basement with a dirty cot shoved inside. A couple of children's toys, as well."

"My God."

"Bell, there were leather straps on the side of the cot. Looked like she tied the boy down and locked him inside the crawlspace."

The image came unbidden to her. The filthy cot, probably dotted with vermin droppings. A bare bulb swinging like a hangman. Darkness. His mother's abusive screams. Insanity.

Even Lerner slumped his shoulders as though struck. Bell sifted through the scope of the abuse. Was he beaten? Molested? The background fit. Explained how Hodge's fantasies began and why he needed to be alone with the victim.

"It's him. It has to be Hodge."

"There's something else." Apprehension crawled on centipede legs down Bell's spine. "Rhonda Winston went missing two weeks ago."

"He killed the mother."

"We don't know that."

Yet they did. It was plain on Gardy's face as they walked back to the vehicles. Bell was right about the killer just getting started, except Kacy Deering was his second victim.

"Sheriff," Gardy said, climbing into the Accord. "Call the station and dig up anything you can on Alan Hodge. Bell's right about the need for privacy. Does he have a shop or warehouse he works out of?"

"Good question. I'll have Crandall check the village records."

"Do that, and get back to me as soon as you find something."

"Where are you going?"

"Hodge's house."

Gardy shifted into drive. The sheriff yelled something over the engine noise about not having a warrant. Bell's hands trembled as the Accord hugged the curves of Coral Hill.

CHAPTER FOURTEEN

"It can't be in the center of the village. Hodge has to work in privacy."

The road flew at the windshield as Bell clutched her phone and waited for Lerner to reply. She heard the sheriff shuffe papers, then fingers clacked away on a keyboard.

The village was lit in orange as the sun descended into Coral Lake. The car lurched to a stop at a red light.

"Just go through," she mouthed to Gardy. But he couldn't. A train of pedestrians was crossing in front of him. "Come on, Sheriff. There has to be something."

Lerner's voice warbled through the speaker.

"Nothing yet, but...hold on, I've got Crandall on the other line."

Bell watched the houses move by slower now. Gardy had turned off the main road onto Canal Street. A scattering of modest and upscale homes lined the road. Lawns were well kept, the landscaping manicured. Hodge's home was the third property from the corner. It was a small, white two-story, so nondescript it appeared to hide in plain sight. A short concrete walkway led to a set of gray stairs. A screened-in porch fronted the door. Through the screen's haze Bell could see a rocking chair, table, and what appeared to be the remnants of an old washing machine.

The car hadn't come to a complete stop when Bell threw open the door. Gardy snagged her shirt before she could jump.

"Will you slow down?"

"We both know it's Hodge."

"And we don't have a warrant, not even probable cause to search the house."

She threw Gardy's hand off her shoulder.

"He might be killing her right now. I'll take my chances on—"

Lerner's voice cut her off. She'd forgotten about him.

"Repeat, Sheriff."

"Agent Bell, I just got off the phone with Deputy Crandall. He says Hodge owns land on the west side of the lake. A half-mile north of the Jepsen-Burns interchange. There are about four square miles of undeveloped land, mostly used by the locals for nature walks and hiking. Hodge's property sits about a hundred yards above the lake."

She scrolled through a GPS map until she found the interchange. She followed the map northward and saw the forest. Her heart drummed harder.

"I see it."

"Good. Because we can move on him now. One of Angela Thiele's coworkers recognized Hodge's van at the pharmacy last night. Says she only noticed because he was parked in the employee's section, right up against Thiele's Rogue."

"To prevent her from opening the door."

"Right. The girl went inside to tell Angela how close the van was to her father's vehicle, just in case Hodge scratched it, but Angela was already gone."

A shiver rolled through Bell. There was a good chance Angela was already inside Hodge's van when the coworker noticed. It was a small measure of luck he hadn't captured the other girl, too.

"Someone recognized Hodge's van parked beside Angela at the pharmacy last night," she said to Gardy.

Gardy cocked his head out the window and examined the empty driveway.

"That qualifies as probable cause in my book. I don't see his van, though."

"He's not here, Gardy. Hodge owns undeveloped land on the west side of the lake."

"Do we have an address?"

"Working on that right now."

Setting the GPS to the approximate coordinates of Hodge's forestland, Bell pressed start and read the directions.

"We're sending two cars to his place on Canal Street," Lerner said. She'd sent his voice through the car speakers so they could both listen.

"That's fine, Sheriff," said Gardy, wheeling the Accord around. "But I seriously doubt he's here."

"I'll have my men check the house regardless and meet you on the west side of the lake. I already put a bulletin out for Hodge's van."

"Good work, Sheriff. We'll be there in five."

Gardy took the corner hard into the village center. Darkness descended on the village as the Accord motored toward the west side of the lake.

CHAPTER FIFTEEN

The footsteps were right behind Angela as she struggled down the hill. She thought she could outrun Hodge, but he was faster than she believed possible as he hurtled down the hill on momentum.

He tackled her in the grass, and the ropes sprang apart. Her hands free, she jumped to her feet before he collapsed down on her.

His fingers grasped her hair, and she spun and slapped his hands away. She backed up and lost her footing. Struck the ground. Her vision went blurry as the air whistled out of her lungs.

He pounced on her, all girth and muscle. One hand gripped her neck as the other cocked back in a fist. She bridged hard and jabbed her fingers into his eyes.

Still straddling her stomach, Hodge yelled and grasped his face. Angela bridged again and twisted, and this time Hodge rolled off. As she climbed to her feet and ran for the road, he blindly swiped his hand out and clutched her ankle. She screamed and fell. The road was so close. Only fifty feet away. If anyone drove past, they'd see the struggle and come to her aid. But there was nobody. Just the empty clearing and the growing darkness. And Hodge's insane bellowing.

Angela felt herself dragged backward. He still had one hand around her ankle. The other massaged his eyes. He was too strong. No way she could kick free.

Instead, she allowed Hodge to drag her, and when he was close, she kicked her free foot into his groin and toppled him.

The bastard refused to release his grip. She yelled for help and slammed the back of her other foot down on his hand. And again. This time his hand opened, and she scurried away as he lay curled on the ground.

Angela willed her legs to work. Her knees kept folding when she tried to stand. He came after her on all fours. Called her *traitor*. Promised she would pay for turning on him, for abandoning Kacy.

The starlit lake was just below the road. The water called to her. So many fond memories were tied to the lake. Boating with her parents when she was a child. Skipping school on the first warm day of spring with Terri, letting the sun bake their bikini-clad bodies. The timeline of her life was tied to watching the sun rise and set over this lake.

She couldn't die here. Wouldn't allow him to take her life.

So she crawled faster as he closed the distance between them. The ground cut into her bare knees, scraped at her palms.

A strange mantra played around in her head. If she could make it to the lake, everything would be okay. Hope buoyed when she heard the approaching engine.

She was a few feet from the road when his hands

closed around her neck.

CHAPTER SIXTEEN

Bell unbuckled the seatbelt and leaned forward. A loaded spring ready to explode. Gardy sneaked a glance at her, but the tree-lined road accelerated at the windshield and forced him to focus on driving.

In the headlight beams she saw the trail branch off to the right.

"There! I see it."

He slammed the brakes and fishtailed the Accord. The path came up on them too fast, forcing Gardy to back up and yank hard on the steering wheel to make the turn.

The car jounced over rocks and miniature hillocks as it climbed. Trees leaned over the trail. In the dark they appeared as deformed beasts, their branches claws that would rake Bell's eyes out when she exited the vehicle.

Lerner's voice came through the speakers. The sheriff was halfway to the village and would reach their location in fifteen minutes.

Bell rolled down the window and leaned her head out. She searched for any indication of Hodge's lair. It had to be here somewhere. This was where he took the girls.

"We'll find her," Gardy said.

The Accord hugged a hard curve. The spike strips vaulted out of the ground.

Gardy braked too late. The jagged teeth tore into the tires with shotgun pops. Momentum jerked the back end of the car toward the forest. Then they shot sideways down the incline. The trees rushing at them. Gardy pulling on the wheel.

The driver side barreled into the trees. An awful crunch of metal and glass.

Gardy's head struck the window and ricocheted. She watched his eyes roll back into his skull as the seatbelt clutched his shoulder and neck.

It was quiet now. The radio was dead. Night sounds swelled around the vehicle.

Bell tried to rouse him, but Gardy didn't respond. She didn't dare touch him. Worried over spinal injuries. His neck lolled over against a backdrop of crumpled glass. To her relief he breathed.

Her door was jammed. She needed to force it open with her shoulder, but when she stepped down it felt as if someone drove a lance through her knee.

Bell's legs buckled. She leaned on all fours. Bloody drool trickled off her lips, and she swiped it away with her hand.

Trembling, she struggled to her feet and limped a few inches at a time until her knee reluctantly agreed to support her weight. She walked in absolute darkness and searched for the trail.

"I'm coming back for you," she promised the man in the car. "I'll get help."

Gardy didn't respond. She watched him in silhouette,

slumped over and lifeless, a marionette propped up by the seatbelt. It killed her to leave him, but she had to find Angela.

She flicked on her handheld radio to dead silence. Broken. When that failed she used her phone to dial the sheriff's number. It took several rings before he answered.

"Lerner?"

"That you, Agent Bell?"

"I need an ambulance. Agent Gardy's hurt."

He stammered over the growl of his engine. If she used her imagination, she thought she heard the Ram's motor on the ridge. He couldn't be more than ten minutes away.

"Shit. Okay, stay calm. Are you injured?"

"I'm fine. Just get help for Gardy."

She'd wandered up the trail for over a minute when she saw the wooden bulk of the shed growing out of the earth. She threw herself inside the shadow of an elm tree.

It was dark inside the shed, no hint of light bleeding around the door. Her hand moved to her hip and removed the Glock-22.

She was breathing too fast. Getting lightheaded. The night seemed to swallow everything except the shed as she cautiously approached.

With her back against the wall, she reached for the door latch. Counted to three while muttering a prayer inside her head.

Bell whipped open the door and spun into the entryway, gun raised. The dark rolled out to greet her. Darkness and a carrion scent.

She turned on the flashlight and saw the girl on the cot. A teenager. Stiff. Rigor mortis already setting in. Her heart fell before she inched forward and saw it was a mannequin. In the gloom it looked real. The little girl inside her worried the mannequin would suddenly sit up.

Swiping the light around, she stared at the blood-smeared pelt atop its head. Kacy. Her stomach turned.

Leather straps hung off the cot. Hodge had recreated his nightmarish childhood.

The shed was otherwise empty. Just the cot and a single bulb affixed to the ceiling. Wires ran through the roof, undoubtedly to a solar panel. A generator would make too much noise and attract attention.

So where were Angela and Hodge?

A flare of hope told her Angela escaped and Hodge was in pursuit. If so they could be anywhere in the forest. Bell forced herself to admit she needed help. The area was too large to canvas by herself, and her knee seemed to be held together by frayed strings.

In the corner lay a toolbox. Peeking her head through the entryway, she confirmed the clearing was empty and closed the door.

Bell opened the toolbox and removed the top compartment. Beneath lay a stack of photographs. She thumbed through the candid pictures of Kacy and Angela, some apparently taken inside the girls' homes while Hodge worked. And another girl, a pretty teen Bell didn't recognize. His next target.

She closed the shed. The forest thickened behind the shed where Hodge's land ended. The trail led back to the road and lake. Somewhere along the way was the Accord. And Gardy.

Fireflies ignited the air as she walked, keeping to the grass in case Hodge was watching the trail. Help was late in arriving. Bell should have heard Lerner's truck by now.

A cool wind blew off the lake, whipping at her face and making it difficult to discern noises. Whispering another promise to help Gardy, she made it back to the road and knelt amid an overgrowth of weed and grasses.

His footsteps approached before she swung around with the gun.

Hodge struck her from behind and sent her reeling. She fell forward as he drove his weight down on her back. The overgrowth claimed the gun and hid it from Bell as she desperately groped through the darkness.

His hands clutched her neck and squeezed. Reaching up, she grabbed the back of his head and tried to flip him over. Hodge was too strong. He muscled his neck backward and broke her grip, then he rose and crashed down on her spine, driving the air from her lungs.

She coughed and sucked the night air into her chest. Bell ran her legs along the ground and attempted to squirm out from underneath. His hands closed around her neck again. The thick meat of his fingertips dug into her windpipe while he thrust down on the small of her back.

Then he clutched her by the hair and drove her face into the dirt. Ripped her head up and smashed it down again.

Blood poured from her nose. She tasted it on her lips.

He lifted her head and drove it into the ground again, this time grinding her face into the earth.

Toying with her.

She strained her back trying to rise. His weight was fully upon her, making it impossible to throw him off.

The terrain spun when he resumed choking her. A terrible wheeze came from her throat when she tried to inhale. Her vision failed as she started to lose consciousness.

He crept higher up her back. Increasing his leverage, she knew. Bell used the opportunity to crawl onto her knees.

She would die if she didn't free herself in the next few seconds. Unable to breathe, she felt the fight drain out of her. She bent forward and whipped her head back. It struck Hodge's face flush. His grip weakened, yet he continued to strangle her. Bell cracked her head against his face again, and Hodge fell backward holding his nose.

Blood gushed between his fingers as Bell croaked and coughed. She couldn't suck the air back into her lungs quickly enough.

Pins-and-needles coursed through her arms as she struggled onto all fours. He rose behind her as she forced herself to crawl into the road.

The macadam dug into her knees. Ahead, the lake sloshed against the shoreline. She imagined the sheriff's truck coming around the bend and cutting her in half as she continued to crawl. Her will to survive kept her from fainting, wouldn't allow her to stop.

Hodge caught her in the road. He booted Bell in the ribs and crumpled her. She curled up as he kicked her again, the impact driving spikes of pain through her ribcage. She swiped at his leg, but he had her by the hair now. Pulling her across the blacktop. Dragging her over the gravel shoulder toward the water.

Bell felt the rocky shoreline scrape her back before she knew where she was. Hodge stood over her, ripping the hair from her scalp and leering. He flung her into the shallows where something sharp and rusted sliced into her shoulder. The blade of an abandoned outboard motor.

She saw a darker pool well up through the ripples. Her blood. It poured out of the open wound.

He clutched her from behind. The muscles of his forearms closed over her windpipe in a headlock. She whipped her head backward, but he was ready this time and moved his bloodied face away. He grabbed her by the hair and shoved her face underwater. Her hands slid across slick stones and plunged into the mud.

Bell's legs flailed as he drowned her. She closed her hand over a rock, searching for something large enough. The fist-sized stone was smooth and round. It kept slipping from her hands as she tried to grasp hold. Water filled her lungs. She wretched as he yanked her head back by the hair, coughing out muddy lake water.

When Hodge shoved her head under she swung back with the rock. She struck his face, but there was no leverage behind the blow. The rock glanced harmlessly off his cheek and dropped from her hand as she imagined him laughing.

He pushed Bell's face into the muddy lake bottom. Muck filled her mouth and eyes, her legs coming to rest behind him as her life teetered.

Hodge tugged Bell out of the water and sat on the small of her back. Clutching her chin from behind with both hands, he leaned back and strained to snap her neck. Her spine shrieked with pain.

The agony flared her senses, her body breaking.

When Hodge leaned farther backward he lost his grip, his slick fingers sliding off her chin. She twisted beneath him, drove her palm up, and struck his shattered nose. A sound like twigs snapping.

Stunned, Hodge stumbled backward. He quickly

shook the cobwebs out and came at her.

Bell flipped over and scissored her legs around his neck as he leaned down. His eyes went wide as her thighs clamped together. Straining, squeezing until her legs shook.

He went down to one knee, and she thought she had him. Then he pushed up and lifted Bell's entire body off the ground. Clutching her hips, he tried to throw her down.

She refused to let go. Veins stood out down his neck and arms. He beat his fists against her thighs. Lifted her higher.

He almost had her over his head when she jerked her back and twisted. A crackle as the torque snapped his neck.

Hodge went limp. They crashed to the ground together. Bell landed on Hodge's legs.

She rolled off and lay on her back. Hodge's eyes were open but blank. The man appeared to be stargazing, except his chest no longer moved.

Carefully, she moved her palm over his face and thought this is the part of the movie when the killer suddenly opens his eyes and sits up.

Thankfully, he didn't. Bell was too exhausted to defend herself if he did.

She tried to crawl into a sitting position and collapsed. Her shirt was soaked with blood, the shoulder wound shooting waves of hot pain down her arm.

A moment later, she heard the motor approach. Lerner to the rescue. Bell's eyes squinted shut. Through tears, she began to laugh.

CHAPTER SEVENTEEN

Gardy was somewhere near the lake shore. The starlight was sharp, the moon coloring the water an eerie blue-gray.

He'd come awake minutes ago and stumbled through the trees before he shook the dust out of his brain and realized he was lost. The girl's cry snapped him awake, and he followed the voice, calling out to her every minute until he zeroed in on her location.

He was somewhere south of Hodge's property when he saw Angela Thiele splayed over the rocks. Her legs extended into the lake up to her knees. Waves rolled over her stomach and splashed her face. She cried harder when she saw him. It wasn't until then he realized how terrifying he must have looked. A helmet of blood-soaked hair, a leaking gash on his forehead, eyes glowing in the moonlight. His badge was on crooked. At least that was an easy fix.

Realizing who he was, the girl calmed.

Gardy didn't know much about lakes or if tide played a factor, but it was plain the waves were getting higher as the wind gusted toward the shoreline. Soon the water would be over Angela's head.

"Don't worry, Angela. You're safe now. I'll get you back to your parents. Are you injured?"

She shook her head. That was a good sign. He prompted the girl to move her arms, then her legs. Not paralyzed, just exhausted and in a state of shock.

Everything hurt when he knelt down. He slipped one arm under her neck, the other beneath her knees, and scooped her up. Water poured off her body as he carried her up the shoreline and toward the road. He almost missed the two silhouettes strewn across the shore a quarter-mile away. Jesus, Bell.

He walked in Bell's direction, the girl waterlogged and limp as a rag doll in his arms, when he heard the ghost screams. Coming closer. Tired and confused, he took a while to figure out the wailing ghost was an ambulance siren, then the truck's headlights flared over the hill and lit his face. Gently setting the girl down, he waved his arms until the sheriff swerved in his direction and stopped along the shoulder.

The look on Lerner's face was one of abject horror as he climbed down from the cab. The ambulance came to a stop behind Lerner's truck as Gardy leaned over, hands on knees.

A female paramedic with blue eyes and a lion's mane of blonde hair tried to stop Gardy as he limped past.

"Agent?"

Gardy looked over his shoulder at Lerner.

"I'll live. Take care of the girl. I'm going after Bell."

***

Bell's eyes shot open at the sound of footsteps. Thinking it was Hodge, her hand instinctively moved to her hip for the missing gun.

She saw Gardy and gasped. The shock of his bloodied forehead didn't last long before her eyes turned cross.

"Just like you to show up in the nick of time and save the day."

He dropped to one knee, saw Hodge's crumpled form and reached for his gun. She snickered, though doing so quickly reminded her how much she hurt.

"Don't worry, Superman, I already defeated the villain."

A beam of red light rotated over their heads. She could hear Lerner's voice and two others, probably emergency workers. As he ran his eyes over her wounds, he stopped on the empty holster.

"And you lost your gun again, I see. Weber will be thrilled."

"Weber can...ow!"

She flinched when he touched her shoulder. Gardy issued a sharp whistle that momentarily deafened her. He waved someone forward, and she heard footsteps approaching.

The sudden memory of why they were on Hodge's property jolted her. She tried to sit up. Gardy blocked her from doing so.

"Where's the girl? Is Angela alive?

"She's fine, Bell." She held his eyes and searched for a flicker of dishonesty. "I swear to you. She's in the ambulance by now. You'll meet her at the hospital."

"I don't need to go the hospital. Help me up."

"You do and you will," Gardy said as the blonde paramedic stooped beside him. He met the woman's eyes and cocked his head at Bell. "She's stubborn, this one. Good luck."

The woman took one look at Bell's shoulder and winced.

"Ma'am, I need you to remain still. I'm going to cut away the fabric and dress that wound."

Bell rolled her eyes.

"You know how much I paid for this shirt?" She saw Gardy raise an eyebrow and scowled. "Fine. It was on the Target clearance rack. Still nice, though and...ouch! Are you sure you need to do that?"

Placing gauze over the wound, the woman pressed down.

"Just to stop the bleeding. With how long you've been bleeding, I'm surprised you're conscious."

"Feel free to put her under," Gardy said. The paramedic didn't seem to hear him. "I'm a little jealous of that injury, Bell."

Bell glared at him and sucked air through her teeth when the pressure increased.

"What the hell are you talking about?"

"That'll leave a nice little scar. You can't buy street cred like that."

CHAPTER EIGHTEEN

An endless ocean of blue flowed outside the plane's windows. Bell stretched her aching legs and leaned the seat back, muttering a silent prayer of thanks that the return trip to Dulles had remained smooth. Gardy sat in the next seat and sifted through the case notes, a thick eye-patch-looking bandage affixed to his forehead that made him look like a pirate with bad aim.

The flight attendant was a male this time, and to Bell's boundless amusement, he paid Gardy an uncanny amount of attention. He brought the agent another tea when Bell elbowed him.

"Bet he's a Pisces."

"I bet you should shut up."

The flight attendant gave them a curious glance. Bell grinned.

"Don't worry. Inside joke."

She reached for her iPad and groaned, forgetting the shoulder.

"Serves you right for making fun of him. He's just being friendly."

"He's being more than friendly, Gardy. You see, this is why you can't get a date. Women throw you signals all the time and they go straight over your head. Besides, I wasn't making fun of him. That would be rude." She shifted the ice pack on her shoulder. "I was making fun of you."

Bell's stomach dropped when the plane unexpectedly began its descent. She blew the hair from her eyes.

"Maybe I should fly back to Coral Lake," she said.

Gardy unfolded a pair of reading glasses and set them on the end of his nose, jotting something down as he watched her from the corner of his eye.

"Need a vacation?"

"My parents are coming for the week."

"That's wonderful. You didn't tell me your parents were visiting. When do I get to say hello?"

"I'll let them know how excited you are to meet them. Hey, I've got a great idea. Maybe they can stay at your place."

"The bachelor pad? That would kill my swagger, Special Agent Bell." When she didn't laugh, he put down the pen and peered at her through the tops of his eyes. "Okay, what's bugging you?"

Bell shook her head and stared out the window.

"They're okay, but I can't deal with the *I-told-you-so* lectures right now."

"How do you mean?"

"That I'd just get hurt working this crazy job. This *man's* job. Dad always figured me for an exciting career in the retail industry. Or maybe I'd be a fashion designer."

"Nothing wrong with fashion design."

"Didn't say there was. My college roommate makes

six figures in fashion design. I can't wait until Mom and Dad see my shoulder. Wouldn't be surprised if they end up in Weber's office Monday morning and berate him for putting their precious daughter in danger. My parents are good people, but their expertise is in running my life."

Gardy removed another folder from his briefcase and thumbed through a series of notes and photographs.

"You tend to exaggerate when things don't go your way. I'm positive it's not as bad as it sounds."

"Well, you say that now, but wait until they try to fix us up."

Gardy coughed into his hand. The male flight attendant was quick to ensure he was okay.

The plane was ten minutes from arrival when Bell glanced over and saw the photograph.

Logan Wolf.

She'd recognize the deep-set, black eyes anywhere. They seemed to penetrate her mind.

"New evidence?"

Gardy flipped to a map of the United States. A scattering of dots indicated where Wolf was recently seen.

"Tough to say. There was a murder outside of Melbourne, Florida last week. A drifter. Officially, it's an unsolved murder, but the MO looks like Wolf's work."

Victim's throat slashed with a sack over his head. Seven such murders in the last year alone.

She wondered if anyone would ever find Logan Wolf, the former BAU-agent-turned-serial-killer. A master profiler, Wolf returned home from work one night in July of 2013 and butchered his wife. Throat slashed. Sack over her head. There was never an explanation. Wolf simply vanished.

Bell shivered. The perfect killer. Impossible to catch.

"Oh, we'll catch him," Gardy said, reading her face. "He might cover his tracks better than the Alan Hodges of the world, but he can't hide forever."

"He's been doing a good job so far."

Gardy slid the folder into his briefcase and locked it away.

Bell didn't look forward to landing. She could have stayed in the air for another month. Between her parents and Weber, Bell didn't relish facing the new week. After the Deputy Director saw their injuries and figured out she'd lost her gun, he'd have a conniption.

Gardy closed his eyes. Bell was about to do the same when the male flight attendant smiled and handed her a business card. She turned it over and grinned. When the attendant disappeared toward the back of the plane, Bell slipped the card into Gardy's pocket.

His eyes sprang open and glanced down at his open pocket.

"What was that?"

"Smile, Gardy. He gave you his phone number."

Scarlett Bell Books 1-5

BLOOD STORM

CHAPTER NINETEEN

Cars hurtle past Clarice, their taillights painting red streaks across her eyes. Stereos thump bass, and she can feel it in her chest. In the distance, the neon lights of countless tourist shops burn brightly.

She has walked for almost an hour now. Lost and afraid. Feet ache. The discount heels aren't helping matters.

The late summer heat is a second skin she can't peel off. It weighs her down. Slumps her back and makes her knees heavy.

As she passes a vacant storefront, she sees her reflection in the glass—the dark, curly hair matted to her head as the sweat pours off in buckets.

The sun is below the ground now, the blues and magentas of gloaming rapidly draining to black. She sneaks a glance over her shoulder but no one is following. Just her mind playing tricks on her, turning every shadow malevolent.

She abandoned her car after the temperature light

spiked and steam rolled out of the hood. Of course, the phone is dead. Damn battery drains if she looks at it wrong.

Clarice stumbles through the wrong side of Sunset Island and thinks she knows where she is. If she is correct about her location, the boardwalk is only five blocks away. There the lights will be bright, the streets lined with vacationing families. Safety. Someone will help her.

The faraway blinking lights become a beacon. They pull her forward and make her legs not so weary. She will be all right.

A dark sedan slows to a stop, and a man leans his head through the passenger window. Another man sits behind the wheel. She considers asking them for a ride before she notices the passenger leering at her. A catcall. For a second, Clarice thinks she hears the door latch opening, then the car spins its screeching tires and jets up the road.

She brushes the sweat off her forehead and moves off the sidewalk and into the grass. Slips off her shoes. Ahead lies a vacant parking lot of shattered glass and oil residue, but she takes advantage of the grass while she can, the soft carpet heaven under her feet.

Clarice is almost to the parking lot when she hears the big truck motor crawl up from behind. She walks a little faster, and the truck keeps pace. It's a rusted, shabby Ford F-150. A dark color she can't make out in the failing light. It follows along, falling behind then jerking forward. Her heart is in her throat when the motor guns and the truck disappears into the night.

Except that it doesn't disappear. After she slips her shoes on and hurries across the parking lot, she sees the truck pulled to the side of the road. The engine is off, the dead-eye taillights extinguished. She looks for a side street, an alternative route that avoids the truck. There is none. It's either go forward or turn around and risk the rundown section of Sunset Island again.

As Clarice approaches the truck she doesn't see the driver. The windows are tinted but she can see a vague outline of the steering column. She breathes faster when she is even with the bumper, head on a swivel. A row of houses sprout up around her. Though many are derelict with sagging porches and broken windows, she takes solace that the worst of the resort city is behind her.

She is almost to the end of the block when she sees the man behind the hedgerow. He watches her approach, then steps back into the shadow and vanishes. It could be anyone, she thinks. A homeowner. Someone who might call a tow truck or drive her to the boardwalk. Her intuition tells her otherwise. It's the truck driver. She senses him.

The darkness is almost complete when she stops. Perhaps the best course of action is to turn around and wait until she is sure the man is gone.

No, he will still be here no matter how late the hour is when she returns.

She veers off the sidewalk before she reaches the hedgerow, intending to cross the street, when the shadow breaks out from the bushes. He'd been standing beside her the whole time without her noticing.

Before she can scream, he covers her mouth and clamps a forearm over her chest. As she flails in his grip the man drags her into the bushes. Thorns reach out and tear her skin. Clarice bites down on his hand, the only defense she can think of, and the man hisses.

Then anguish as he strikes her in the back of the neck. A club of some sort. She pitches forward onto her knees and he clubs her again. The world spins as she splays out on her stomach. She feels a hot trickle of blood on the back of her head and neck and knows she must remain conscious if she is to survive.

Clutching at clumps of grass, she drags herself forward. Across the lawn of the unlit residence. Somewhere a box air conditioner rattles, and another vehicle passes. Nobody sees or bothers to help.

He follows her. She sees his shadow enveloping her own, a predator stalking wounded prey.

The man grunts and brings the club down on her head again. Her eyes flutter shut.

She can feel his hand around her ankle, grass and stone under her stomach as he drags her deeper into the darkness.

And then she feels nothing at all.

CHAPTER TWENTY

Lightning stroked across the sky as Special Agent Scarlett Bell gripped the steering wheel and fought to keep the Accord in its lane. Her partner, Neil Gardy, sat in the next seat, one eye on the darkening sky and the other on the case briefing.

She wasn't dressed for South Carolina heat. The pant suit itched and made her dread what it would feel like on the beach. What she wouldn't have done to pull her blonde hair back in a ponytail, trade the suit for shorts and a tank, and spend the afternoon in the hotel pool.

"That hurricane isn't headed this way, is it?"

Gardy checked his phone.

"Nope. The National Hurricane Center predicts landfall over Central Georgia in the next 24 hours."

"Still, that's a little close for comfort."

They'd attended a conference in Savannah and received a call about a dismembered body on Sunset Island, South Carolina, a narrow strip of land which curled into the Atlantic and drew tourists from as far away as Maine and Quebec. The barrier island barely jutted above sea level, a sitting duck in a storm surge. Were it not for the traffic the drive would have taken only a half-hour.

A sudden gust of wind pulled the car out of its lane into oncoming cars. A chorus of horns squawked as Bell righted the vehicle.

Breathing heavily, both eyes glued to the road, she wondered why he'd insisted on renting another Accord.

"Boy, I'd love to drive an SUV right now. One of those over-sized monsters that stand up to hurricanes, tornadoes, and New Jersey drivers."

Gardy gave his trademark snicker, the one that reminded her of Muttley, the cartoon dog. He sneered at her and flipped between grisly photographs of a murdered woman.

"I tried, but they were out. Besides, nothing stands up to New Jersey drivers."

"I think you wanted the Accord. It was all part of your evil plan. Do you own stock in Honda?"

As fast as the storm had formed, it split apart and died. Typical southeastern summer weather. One second a raging typhoon soaked you to the bone, the next it was sunny.

And perpetually humid. Even with the windows rolled up and the air conditioner on, Bell couldn't stop sweating.

They were five minutes from where the body had been found on the beach. A woman, dismembered and buried in the sand.

"Our contact is Detective Joe McKenna," Gardy said, closing up the folder and cracking the window open. He looked a little green. "He's leading the investigation."

Gardy burped into his hand. Bell glanced at her

partner.

"Don't tell me you're carsick."

"I shouldn't read while the car is moving."

"I'll slow down."

"No, just get us there. I'll feel better once I get out and walk."

Getting there proved to be problematic. The train of vehicles nearly came to a stop, edging forward, bumper-to-bumper as horns honked. Welcome to paradise. Bell saw the toll booths a half-mile up the road. Only two booths, hardly enough to handle peak season traffic.

Bell tapped a drumbeat on the steering wheel.

"You know what this reminds me of?"

"The traffic? I'd say D.C. during the morning rush. Or Beirut."

"No, the case. You remember the Cleveland Torso Murderer?"

"Vaguely. That was the 1930s, right? Something close to twenty dismembered bodies, but they never found the killer. A little before my time."

"You sure about that?"

He snickered again, and as she glanced over she detected fewer flecks of gray dotting his dark, brown hair.

"Agent Gardy, are you coloring your hair?"

"What? No...I...uh..."

"Uh-huh."

He craned his neck out the window as if a secret route existed around the traffic.

"It's been almost two hours since they found the body," he said, checking his watch. "By the time we get there—"

"I know, I know. I'm trying."

After several minutes of vehicles cutting each other off and drivers shouting lewd insults, they broke free of the glut. The way forward opened to a thoroughfare lined by palm trees and stores painted in bright pastel tones, as the Atlantic sloshed to both sides of the road. For a while, Bell felt a strange sense of vertigo as if she stood upon a monstrous ship, the suggestion of movement beneath as the sun sparkled off the water. She didn't drive so much as the ocean pulled her forward.

The spell broke when the island widened and the thoroughfare dumped them into the heart of the tourist district. Surf shops and seafood restaurants. A few boutique hotels nestled between ice cream stands and arcades. The license plates represented the entire east coast and some from as far away as California and Texas. The largest hotels grew against a tropical blue sky. The ocean thrashed behind the concrete structures.

Gardy's color improved the moment they stepped out of the car, and he immediately slipped on a pair of sunglasses as the glare intensified.

"Feeling better now?"

"Much better, thanks. But I should probably drive on the way back."

She tossed him the keys. He caught them one-handed and slipped them into his pocket.

"Show off."

Bell saw the crowd massing around the scene when they reached the beach. Yellow police tape stretched between roadblocks and flapped in the wind, the barrier holding back a curious throng. A few people held their phones over their heads and snapped photographs while a row of police officers urged them back.

A tall officer with cropped black hair held up his hand when Gardy and Bell approached. Gardy flashed his badge, and the cop nodded and waved them through.

Halfway between the looky-loos and the body, a middle-aged detective in a white Polo shirt jogged forward to meet them.

"You must be the agents from the Behavioral Analysis Unit."

"I'm Agent Gardy, and this is Agent Bell."

"Joe McKenna," the detective said, shaking Gardy's hand first, then Bell's. "Glad you could come on short notice. How was traffic on the way in?"

"Stop-and-go."

"You're lucky," McKenna said, walking. "This time of year, it's a lot more stop than go. Anyhow, thanks for giving us a hand. This caught us off guard, and frankly, we don't know what we're up against."

Bell glanced at the crowd and pulled out her phone in case the killer was among the onlookers. Gardy saw her taking photos and gave her a thumbs-up.

A freshly excavated hole lay twenty yards from the water. A pale hand poked into the sun.

Three crime scene techs in white suits finished collecting evidence and packed up their gear. Baggies covered their shoes. Bell wondered how they could walk on the sand dressed like that.

"Around one o'clock this afternoon we received a call about a human hand buried in the sand. A nine-year-old girl was digging around and found it. Fortunately, she didn't find the rest of the body."

Bell grimaced.

"I hope the kid is okay."

"The mother noticed what it was and pulled the girl away before she saw too much. To be perfectly honest, the mother is the one who'll probably end up with nightmares."

"Do we have an ID on the vic?"

"Nothing yet, but I'm confident we'll find out soon. Carlton Yates is the best ME in South Carolina."

A female officer leaned in and said something to McKenna.

"That's fine, Suarez. I'll have the agents examine the body, then we'll clean the scene up." The female officer angled toward the onlookers as McKenna walked beside the agents. "Second body we've found like this, both dismembered, though the last was five years ago. The mayor is having a shit-fit. Not exactly good for the tourist trade when someone's kid digs up body parts. Whatever insight you can lend is most appreciated."

Bell knelt down and covered her mouth. The smell was terrible, a salty carrion stench that steamed out of the hole. Tiny crabs skittered over the scattered body parts, which were roughly arranged to resemble a human.

"Was the previous body found on the beach? The one from five years ago?"

"No. That one was found at a construction site five blocks south of the beach. Assuming it's the same guy, is it normal for a killer to go inactive for five years?"

Bell glanced up at McKenna.

"It's not unheard of. Serial killers change their patterns for reasons we don't fully understand. Some target the same type of victim for years, often a woman who reminds him of someone important from his childhood, then completely shift gears for no apparent reason and track different women. Some kill on a set schedule, others need an outside trigger to set them off. In short, they make their own rules."

"To complicate things further," Gardy said, slipping on a pair of latex gloves. "Maybe the unknown subject spent time in prison. It's not uncommon for a serial killer to have a rap sheet of lesser crimes. The five-year lull might be a clue. I'll have Quantico run a search on anyone from this area who was incarcerated during that time frame."

McKenna nodded absently.

After Bell put on gloves, Gardy manipulated the body. He slipped his hands under the upper torso and tilted it. A dark purple bruise tattooed the woman's neck.

"Blunt force trauma to the back of the neck."

"We saw that, too," McKenna said, wiping his sunglasses on his shirt. "Looks like he struck her with a bat or a rock."

The body was organized like a mad god's doll parts. Four faint purplish tints marked the ankle.

"He dragged her by the ankle," said Bell. "Detective, did the techs dust the ankle for prints?"

"Yeah, but the sand mucked everything up. When we get the body to the coroner's office, we'll take a closer look. They found a blade of grass though."

"Which suggests the body was dumped here."

"That seems likely. We didn't find blood or signs of a struggle nearby, but this stretch of beach is four miles long. Too much area to cover."

The wind gusted and dragged sand across the body. The officers shielded their eyes as children splashed through building waves, oblivious to the macabre scene playing out behind the barricades.

Bell examined the woman's right hand.

"Detective, did you notice the missing forefinger?"

"I meant to ask you about that. We couldn't decide if it was lost in the dismemberment or—"

"No. He took it with him."

CHAPTER TWENTY-ONE

Darkness slides across the plate-glass windows fronting the Island Mart. The sun is down, and the aisles are empty of shoppers as the crowds flock to clubs and take night walks on the beach. The store is a ghost that whispers memories of squealing shopping cart wheels and intercom squawks. All that remains is the contemporary pop drivel pumping out of the speakers.

Derek Longo reaches into a loaded shopping cart and stocks snack treats on the shelves. Pudding and chips. Mixed nuts and Jello. The man's frame is portly and soft, his head bald. Dark circles ring his eyes. Not from exhaustion. The circles are always there, a permanent tattoo.

He likes the night shift. Only a few customers visit after nine o'clock, usually kids with fake IDs trying to buy beer. One assistant store manager, who he rarely encounters, runs the store overnight. She's in the back office cruising the Internet and pretending to work. She leaves him alone, just the way he wants it.

He doesn't like being around other people. They

make his skin itch. If he spends too much time in a crowd, he breaks out in hives, red welts which burn and swell. Once a group of college students came into the Island Mart after midnight and made nuisances of themselves, yelling across the store, drunkenly giggling and knocking items off the shelves. They found Longo in the bread aisle and wouldn't stop asking him idiotic questions. How long does it take to bake the bread, and does he bake it himself? Does he prefer white or multi-grain? Can you make a peanut butter and jelly sandwich with gluten-free ingredients?

What he wouldn't have paid to skewer them on meat hooks.

They saw the hot splotches burning his neck and arms and snickered. Whispered and pointed as though he was a freak show. When they were gone, he stole a tube of hydrocortisone cream and slipped into the bathroom where he covered his body until the itching ceased.

He pushes the memory away and pulls a step ladder over to the shelves. Two younger workers, both fat girls without college educations, appear at the end of the aisle and look in his direction. One says something into the other's ear, and they both giggle and hurry away.

Longo's nickname is Nosferatu, for he only works the night shift and his complexion is preternaturally pale for a coastal southerner. They all laugh at him. He knows this and doesn't care.

He finishes stacking the pudding and turns to the Jello cups. His lunch box is beside him. Gray with metal latches. It looks like something a mother buys her son when the boy outgrows cartoon and superhero lunch pails.

Ensuring the aisle is empty, he runs his hand along the edges of the pail. He senses her inside. Her finger, wrapped in a freezer bag and blanketed with ice. The ham sandwich will surely freeze because of this, but he doesn't care.

It is dangerous bringing a part of her to work. The risk excites him, makes him touch the front of his jeans when he's sure nobody is looking.

He cannot be without her. Freezing the body part slows the decaying process. Eventually it will rot, no matter how long he keeps the finger on ice. Then he will need to say goodbye, and parting will hurt.

He lifts the lunch box and carefully places it on the shelf. Slides it into the shadows where the fluorescent lights fail to reach. No one to ask questions as he resumes the monotonous work.

The cart is almost empty when the automatic doors slide open at the front of the store. A visitor at this time of the night is rarely good news. Probably someone looking to cause trouble like the college students. Longo instinctively ducks his head though there is nowhere to hide in the antiseptic glow. His pulse races as footsteps approach. Maybe he should retreat to the back until the intruder leaves.

Longo is halfway down the rows when he sees her. She is beautiful, skin soft and flawless. Black hair, darker than midnight, curls down to her shoulders. Her eyes are a striking green. Green like the Caribbean. Her ample chest is barely contained by a black halter top.

She enters Longo's aisle, and he turns his shoulders so his face is hidden. She puffs an exasperated sigh and retreats, unfamiliar with the store layout, and heads toward the rear of the store. He hears her move down one aisle and up the next.

Her footsteps quicken. Longo knows she's found what she was looking for.

Carefully, he glides to the end cap. He can be quiet when he needs to be.

Peeks around the cheese snacks and snaps his head back when she turns. She saw him, he thinks.

The woman goes still. No footsteps. His breath quickens. If the woman saw him spying, she might tell the manager. At the front of the store, a female cashier talks on her phone.

The patter of sneakers against the recently mopped floor resumes, and he slips out of hiding.

The rows are empty. He can hear her although the woman remains hidden from view.

He walks, silent as a cat. Checks each aisle. No sign of her.

A look over his shoulder confirms the assistant manager is still in her office, the cashier at checkout. Nobody watches.

He finds the woman in the pharmacy, stooped over on one knee and reading a bottle of Tylenol. She touches her forehead and groans. Spins around and sees him.

He quickly averts his eyes and turns to the shelves. Rearranges the protein powder containers.

He feels her eyes. Senses the quickening of her heart.

The itch begins on his forearm, then the welts spread across his stomach. Longo winces and bites his tongue. Fights the urge to drop the containers and scratch bloody streaks into his flesh.

"Are you okay?"

The woman's voice freezes him.

"Sir?"

He cannot turn his head. Throat too dry to answer.

Longo twists his head slightly, just enough so the supple outline of her figure touches the corner of his eye. He nods slowly and feigns arranging the powders again.

She steps forward and pauses.

His longing to scratch the festering hives grows. The welts are everywhere now. His legs, buttocks. The bottoms of his feet and between his thighs.

When he is certain she will speak to him again, she unexpectedly veers around another end cap and gives him a wide berth. Hurries to the checkout lanes and away from Longo. He chews his tongue until the taste of copper fills his mouth.

Voices echo through the nearly empty store as the cashier greets the woman. Soon she will pay for her item and disappear, and he will never see her again.

He moves from one aisle to the next until he crouches beside the candy rack of an empty checkout lane. Hershey bars, Skittles, Starburst fill his vision. He smells the sugar bleeding through the paper. The security cameras capture his every move but he doesn't care. She is the one. The woman he needs.

Longo spies her from behind the rack. Can see the Nike sneakers and bare ankles. His eyes crawl up her capris. She twists her head as though she senses him. He ducks behind the candy and knows her glare is fixed on his hiding spot.

The cashier thanks her, and now the sweat bubbles out of his pores because he hears the crinkle of the bag, jangle of keys. She is leaving.

If he follows her out the front door the cashier will know. The girl will demand Longo tell her where he is going or threaten to report his truancy. Where should he tell the girl he is going? Maybe to his truck. He forgot something. No, that won't do. Regardless of what he tells the cashier, he can't walk through the sliding doors. The beautiful woman will notice him following.

The loading door behind the building.

He bursts out of hiding and runs down the aisle toward the back. By now the woman must be in the parking lot. He imagines the car chirping as she clicks the key fob. The sign above the double doors reads *Employees Only*. He shoves the doors open and hurries through the loading area. Weaves between stacks of unopened boxes sleeping on pallets.

Longo muscles open the jammed exit door and stumbles into the warm night. The corner of the building is farther away than he remembers. He needs to run again though he is out of breath.

Her car backs up, the brake lights red. His F-150 is parked nearby. Momentarily, he panics and thinks he forgot his keys. He feels them in the front pocket chewing into his thigh.

Then he climbs into the cab and fires the engine. He won't let her get away.

CHAPTER TWENTY-TWO

Gardy eyed Bell as though she'd sprouted an extra head when she removed a pizza slice from the hotel refrigerator.

"What? Don't you like cold pizza?"

"I do, but I wouldn't stick hot pizza into a refrigerator just to make it cold."

"Cold pizza is my super power. Deal with it."

He shook his head and tore a hot slice of tomatoes-and-peppers pie from the box. Bell sat cross-legged on the floor beside Gardy and leaned her back against the bed. The cutoff jean shorts and tank felt like heaven compared to the pant suit.

The news was on. Some television weatherman with an obvious toupee stood along the Georgia coast while his jacket snapped in the wind. Bell scowled.

"Once, just once, I'd love for a stop sign to fly by and clock one of these idiots in the head."

Gardy peeked over his reading glasses at her.

"Has anyone ever said you have a violent streak? Maybe I should go back to my room."

"Stay and eat. A growing boy needs his pizza. Anyway, it's not like those reporters are saving lives. It's all for attention."

"Right, for ratings. Everyone knows that. No harm, no foul."

"But," she said, pointing at him. "Every once in a blue moon, one of these bozos gets too close to the storm, and the emergency workers, who should be focused on saving innocent lives, are called in to rescue the reporter caught in the storm. They're nuisances."

Gardy held an argument on the tip of his tongue until he saw the weatherman unnecessarily balancing on the edge of a pier while waves smashed over his knees.

The latest forecast showed Hurricane Ana reaching category-three before it smashed into the Southern Georgia coast the following morning. The outer bands would affect Sunset Island, and already distant lightning interrupted the dark through the window.

Gardy chewed his food without further comment. She caught him staring past the television, apparently transfixed by the shade of white paint covering the wall.

"You're quiet tonight. Something bugging you?"

He reached over the bed and grabbed another slice.

"Got off the phone with Weber before I came over."

Don Weber, the Deputy Director of CIRG, put Gardy in the doghouse after the Alan Hodge case in June. Hodge killed a teenage girl and nearly murdered another in Coral Lake, New York. Though Bell and Gardy stopped Hodge, Gardy totaled a vehicle in pursuit and nearly killed them in the crash.

"That doesn't sound good."

"Let's say he made it clear what our role is on this

case."

"To stop a lunatic from killing anyone else. What other purpose could we play?"

Gardy exhaled.

"We're consultants to the Sunset Island Police Department and nothing else. We lend our opinion, help them find this guy, but it's up to them to take him down."

Bell tucked her feet under her thighs and sat taller.

"Is this about Coral Lake? Sheriff Lerner all but laid the case in our hands."

"True, but don't forget Lerner is a politician first, not a sheriff."

"So he wanted the glory, and now he's in Weber's ear trying to say we stole the case from him. What an asshole."

He shrugged.

"Did you expect anything less?"

"Nope. That's one thing. What else has Weber's shorts in a knot?"

"More of the same. Logan Wolf is a hot media topic again."

Bell shivered. Elusive as a phantom, Wolf was the former BAU agent who murdered his wife and became the nation's most notorious serial killer. Gardy was determined to capture Wolf.

"But you aren't leading the task force on Wolf."

"True, but I'm the senior profiler with Blottman retired. I haven't cracked the code on Wolf, and ostensibly I'm the reason we can't find the psycho."

The irony wasn't lost upon Bell that Gardy often deferred to her when profiling serial killers. Weber not caring for Bell's opinion didn't surprise her. Bell wasn't on his radar. The Don Webers of the world wouldn't be happy until all female agents were relegated to desk jobs or secretarial positions.

Gardy clapped his hands together.

"Forget all of that. Let's talk about the profile. What do we know about the unknown subject?"

Bell pointed the remote at the television and turned the volume down. The ceiling vents hissed cool air.

"Based on the evidence, I'd say the profile is similar to the Hodge case. Our target is disorganized and was abused as a child. He's white and in his thirties or forties, has poor social skills, and probably works alone. Remember Hodge was a private contractor."

"Right, which isolated him from office settings and allowed him to find potential victims."

"Their poor social skills and disorganized natures often mean the unknown subjects have unreliable transportation."

"Not with Hodge."

"No, but it's something to consider. The inability to communicate freely with others often forces the subject to hunt close to home. These guys travel little, don't leave their comfort zones."

"A local. The mayor will love that."

Bell swallowed her diatribe on politicians. When she glanced at the television, the weatherman showed Hurricane Ana veering north over the next 24 hours.

"You notice that, Gardy? Maybe we should check another channel."

Gardy held out his hand, and she gave him the remote. He flicked to the next news channel and saw a similar track displayed.

"That's not optimal."

"It's getting closer."

"So it will come down like cats and dogs tomorrow. Nothing we can do about the situation. Good thing they got the body out of the sand before the rains came in."

He handed the remote back to Bell, who flicked off the television and slumped against the bed. She caught herself picking lint off her t-shirt, a nervous habit. Tracking a serial killer was difficult enough without torrential downpours and flooding bringing the island to a standstill.

"Tell me more about Clarice Hopkins."

The ME had identified the woman by fingerprint and relayed the information to Detective McKenna, who called Gardy.

Gardy reached into his folder and brought out a print of the woman's driver's license. She was pretty, Bell thought, though a rough life had cut deep lines into her face. She had long, flowing black hair and blue-green eyes, an unusual and striking combination. There was a hint of derision in her stare. Anger and exhaustion.

"Hopkins was thirty-eight and originally from Beckley, West Virginia. She moved to Sunset Island nine years ago and worked various low-paying jobs. A lot of office temp work. McKenna said she'd received an eviction notice from her landlord. Hopkins was two months behind on her rent."

"So she was struggling with money."

"Uh-huh."

"How far away from the dump site did they find her car?"

"About three miles."

"So her car breaks down on the wrong side of town, and she can't call for help because the bargain basement phone won't hold a charge. Then what?"

Gardy squinted his eyes and looked at the ceiling.

"She starts walking."

"Because she doesn't dare ask anyone for a ride. Not in that section of the city."

"But it's a long walk to the boardwalk."

"Not necessarily. If she hustled she could make it in an hour. Beats the alternative of waiting for sunset when you're in the wrong section of town. Let's look at the map."

Paging through his briefcase, Gardy removed a street map and laid it out on the carpet. They both leaned over the map and nearly collided heads.

"Sorry," he said, sheepishly moving to the side.

She smelled his cologne and freshly shampooed hair. Bell cleared her throat.

"My fault."

A red dot marked where the car was found. A second marking showed where the police excavated her body.

"Keep in mind," he said as she ran her finger along the streets connecting the two points. "He could have killed her anywhere and dumped the body at the beach."

Bell shook her head.

"It's possible, but if we follow the logic that our guy stays close to home, it's more likely the murder and burial are all within a few miles of each other. Somebody had to notice Hopkins walking. You see a pretty woman walking alone at night down those streets, you're bound to wonder what she's up to."

"The police canvassed the area. So far nobody saw her."

Bell reached for another slice of pizza and knew she'd pay for it at three in the morning. She ate too much when she was anxious.

"Our target can't hide in plain sight for long. He'll make a mistake, and when he does, we'll catch him." She saw Gardy glance down at his knees. "Hey, why so glum? This better not be about Weber again. Be real, Gardy. It's not like he can fire you over Coral Lake."

"No, but if this case doesn't go well, I won't be a part of the BAU much longer."

CHAPTER TWENTY-THREE

The red light reflects bloody tones off the wet pavement. The power lines swing like jump ropes as the wind builds and the rain falls in buckets.

His is the only vehicle on the road except the red Volvo. Longo knows to keep his distance. He wishes for traffic between the F-150 and the Volvo, something to distract the woman from the headlights following a hundred yards behind her.

He considers cutting down a side street and decides it is a bad idea. Too much risk. He won't be able to live with himself if he lets her get away.

The Volvo is stopped at a red light up the road. The synchronized lights turn green simultaneously, but he sits on the brake and allows her to push ahead. She can't move fast in these conditions. He can afford to be patient.

When her taillights are pinpricks he checks the mirrors, sees the open road, and hits the gas. The truck lurches forward like an unleashed predator, kicks up water and sends waves cresting toward the gutters. Out of the corner of his eye, he spies his house. Sees the hedges girding the walkway. A tingle moves through his stomach. This is where he murdered the woman. Dragged her into the basement and chopped her into pieces.

How he wishes to bring the new woman here.

By now the police must have found the body. He doesn't own a television, has no interest in reading newspapers or listening to the radio. He prefers quiet when he drives. It helps him think and plan.

The F-150's engine roars as he stomps the accelerator. He closes in on the Volvo and is only a block behind the woman when she turns toward the beach.

Knowing he is too close, he hangs back until the car clears the corner, then he presses the gas and reaches the intersection. Another car is on the road a few hundred yards behind. Its headlights are blurry in the rain. He stops in the middle of the road and waits at the intersection, watching the Volvo weave around parked cars. The street is narrow, the population dense. Too many eyes.

Longo considers whether he should follow the Volvo through the neighborhood when the car honks at his bumper and flashes its beams twice. An urge to throw open the door and stride to the driver's window overcomes him. He imagines the driver's eyes when Longo removes the knife from his pocket. Fingers curl around the steering wheel and squeeze until it hurts. Another series of honks.

He turns and follows the Volvo as the driver curses him through the window.

A few minutes later, he can smell the sea as the Volvo's brake lights ignite two blocks ahead. The car stops, then cautiously advances through standing water. The flooding is sufficient to stall her car, and he wonders what he will do if that happens. He could offer her a ride. It would be easy to club the woman and drag her body into the truck. Take her back to his house. Even if he didn't knock her unconscious, she'd be helpless to escape his truck. The passenger door handle is broken. The door only opens from the outside.

The Volvo turns again, and they leave the overpopulated neighborhood behind. The houses are larger now, the space between properties growing. By the time she pulls into the beach house, there are no other houses in sight.

The rain abates, and the ocean thunders. He cannot see it in the dark, can only hear the sea slamming against the shoreline.

Longo kills the headlights and engine. He is far enough away that she can't see him in the dark. Around him in the newly developed community grow huge mounds of dirt. A flat slab of leveled terrain marks where construction will take place. It will be months before anyone lives here.

The private solitude sends a tingling sensation down his back.

The car door slams, and the Volvo chirps when she engages the locks. His eyes follow her silhouette along a winding, landscaped path. She climbs the stoop and punches a code into the digital lock. The door opens and she is gone.

Longo climbs down from the cab and leaves the door open a crack. Steps over the curb and walks through the wet grass, the mud making sucking noises beneath his shoes. The roar is deafening. Ocean and wind. Power.

Nobody bears witness when he enters the yard and stands amid the dark. The ocean grows in volume, and a salty spray carries to his face. Her mailbox reads Gwen Devereux.

A noise brings his head around. A cat. The feline advances and stops several feet away, tail curling and uncurling. Longo ignores the cat until it is emboldened enough to paw forward and rub against his shin. The animal's fur is wet. The cat purrs, craving his attention.

He considers kicking it away but senses the cat belongs to the woman. Instead, he bends to rub the cat behind its ears, hand stopping beneath its collar. It would be so easy to snap the animal's neck and leave the carcass on her doorstep. He imagines the woman's horror when she answers the doorbell.

The idyllic seclusion of the beautiful woman's house changes Longo's thinking. There is no reason to kill Devereux and take her back to his house. He will murder the woman and stay here. Eat her food and let the waves put him to sleep at night. No snooping neighbors to notice.

As long as he keeps her body in the house, he will not require a small piece of her. No memento this time—

The finger.

His heart hammers.

He forgot the lunch box. It's still in the store. Where did he leave it?

In the snack aisle, he remembers. Tucked behind the food containers.

Longo stumbles, glances around in the dark and wonders how he could be so careless and forgetful. He feels eyes in the dark watching him. They seem to be everywhere, looking down from the heavens and out of the copse.

He backs away from the house, furious with himself.

Furious and frightened. Someone will find the finger. The manager has fired him by now for abandoning his shift. He can't simply march into work and paw through the snack containers, searching for the lunch box. There will be too many questions. He needs to leave town. Yes, he must leave before they find him. And go where? He has no savings. The derelict house is his only equity.

His head spins. Can't put thoughts together.

Longo runs for the truck.

They're coming for him now.

CHAPTER TWENTY-FOUR

The briefing room inside the Sunset Island Police Department could have seated an entire football team. Dawn had barely cracked, but inside the briefing room it looked like high noon. Bright floodlights beamed from the ceiling, enough to give Bell the beginnings of a migraine.

Speaking in front of crowds always put butterflies in Bell's stomach, and they were beating their wings vehemently while she scanned her notes. A baker's dozen of officers faced the podium from their seats, murmuring and trading jokes while they waited for the meeting to begin.

William Tanner, the Chief of Police, stood at the front of the room beside Detective McKenna and Gardy. Tanner was tall and possessed a long face with drooping eyes, a sad dog appearance.

She watched Gardy nodding as they spoke, his eyes occasionally drifting to her place beside the podium. He winked, a promise she could handle this. A few of the officers, including a heavyset man in the back row, watched her skeptically. Bell noted there was only one female officer among the thirteen present.

"If I can have your attention," McKenna said, tapping the microphone. The talking abruptly ceased. "Special Agents Gardy and Bell from the Behavioral Analysis Unit were kind enough to join us this morning. They traveled a long way to get here, so I trust you'll afford them the same respect you do me."

Laughter.

"Okay, maybe a little more respect than that. The agents are here to lend their expertise and help us find a killer. So I will get this briefing underway and turn the microphone over to Agent Bell."

The officers glanced at each other and traded whispers. Bell felt the butterflies crawl into her chest and cleared her throat.

"Good morning, everyone. Agent Gardy and I wish to thank Chief Tanner and Detective McKenna for allowing us to speak with you today. As you all know by now, the body of Clarice Hopkins was discovered yesterday at approximately..."

Bell's voice seemed to drift away from her. The officers were losing interest already, some moving their eyes to their laps, where they doodled on notepads or checked their phones. She realized she wasn't telling them anything they didn't know but was nonetheless struck by their lack of decorum. The female officer, a young, stocky woman with a buzz cut—Suarez, the officer Bell saw at the beach—leaned over and said something to the heavyset troublemaker in the back row. They shared a grin.

"Our target, or the unknown subject as we commonly refer to him, is between thirty-five and forty-five and the product of an abusive upbringing. He is highly uncomfortable around crowds…"

It occurred to Bell she was also uncomfortable in front of crowds, at least when required to speak. She wiped her sweaty palms on her pants and cleared her throat again. The silence from the back of the room was disinterested and hostile.

"…and his unreliable mode of transportation forces him to hunt within a confined radius."

"I don't see how this helps us capture Tom Thumb."

More laughter. It was the troublemaker who'd spoken.

"Tom…Thumb?"

"The killer. You just described half the population of Sunset Island. Maybe you enjoyed the boardwalk, but once you get outside the tourist zone, the entire city is nothing but degenerates and rundown houses. And now we have a growing gang element to deal with. If I were a travel agent, I'd tell every customer to check out Hilton Head or Myrtle Beach. It's only a matter of time before Sunset Island's issues spread to the boardwalk, and then we'll have a bigger problem."

Nods of agreement and conversation followed.

"Gentlemen, please," McKenna said, raising his arms. "And ladies."

"Speak for yourself," the female officer growled, and this got the entire room laughing.

"Let's allow Agent Bell to complete her profile."

She'd lost them completely if she ever had their attention at all. As they continued to talk over McKenna, Bell glared at Gardy, who raised his eyebrows. Neither the police chief nor the lead detective held sway over the officers.

Bell yanked the microphone off the stand and brought it close to her mouth.

"Excuse me."

Her proximity to the microphone caused a well-timed shriek of feedback. Several of the officers ducked and covered their ears. The room's cacophony dropped to a few lingering whispers.

"Thank you. The officer in the back. What did you say your name was?"

The heavyset man glanced around the room as if he wasn't sure Bell meant him. Then he shrugged at the female officer beside him.

"Rivera."

"Officer Rivera, you referred to the killer by a name. Can you repeat it for the rest of us?"

"Tom Thumb."

She glanced at Gardy, who shook his head to show this was news to him. The police chief palmed his forehead. It was Detective McKenna who approached Bell and leaned his head over the microphone.

"I apologize on behalf of the department. Apparently, we have a few creative officers in our midst. Tom Thumb is their nickname for the killer."

Bell narrowed her eyes.

"I don't get it. The killer stole a finger, not a thumb."

"Take good notes," the female officer said. "Officer Rivera just predicted his next trophy."

The room found the joke funny. Bell didn't.

"What you call him privately is your own business." Bell strode forward until she stood a few feet from the officers. She didn't need the microphone, which dangled from her left hand. Somehow her voice sounded louder without amplification. It seemed to carry from the heavens as it bounced down from the ceiling. Her eyes shot a hard warning across the room and landed on Officer Rivera, who shifted in his seat. "However, if your pet name escapes this room and makes it to the media, you will undermine our efforts and turn this investigation into a laughingstock. And that is something the FBI will not take kindly to."

She waited until the only sound in the room was her own breathing.

"Are we clear?"

They were.

The rest of Bell's briefing was met with rapt attention. When the profile was finished, she turned the microphone over to Gardy and McKenna, who fielded questions for several minutes. Bell's adrenaline thrummed at peak levels. She crossed her ankles to keep her legs from trembling, pleased by the new climate of cooperation in the room and wondering where she'd summoned the courage from.

The meeting was about to wrap up when McKenna's phone buzzed. He held up a finger and stepped away. Seated at the front of the room, Bell didn't think much of the interruption until Chief Tanner's phone rang. Now a low murmur ran through the crowd as the officers checked their phones. The noise built into an excited clamor, which didn't end until Tanner pocketed his phone and grabbed the microphone.

Tanner hadn't yet spoken when Gardy leaned into her.

"We've got a problem."

"Now what?"

"The National Hurricane Center issued their new

forecast. Ana is headed right for us."

CHAPTER TWENTY-FIVE

A pall of overcast hangs from the sky as Longo slumps low in his seat. The truck is parked in the middle of the lot, hiding in plain sight.

Rubbing the sleep from his eyes, he hears heels click against blacktop and ducks down. A woman pushes a shopping cart past the truck, and then she is gone. He must be patient. He checks the clock and sees it is ten. Dolores, the store manager, is about to go on break.

Right on schedule, the glass doors slide open and Dolores strides through, hurrying to her car. She will be gone for a half-hour. This is Longo's only chance to slip into the store unnoticed and retrieve the lunch box.

A notepad lies upon the passenger seat. Gwen Devereux's work address, which he discovered using a Google search at the public library, is scribbled on the top sheet. He turns the pad face-down.

Pulling a baseball cap over his head, he exits the truck and shuffles toward the entryway. Waits until a man and woman enter together and slips behind the couple, head lowered as he follows them past the checkout lines. They veer toward the produce aisle, and suddenly Longo is exposed. He keeps his head down and turns when he sees Rick Youngsly, the produce manager, walk toward him. If Youngsly recognizes him he gives no sign.

At the end of the produce aisle, Longo turns and stops. Two stock boys replenish an end cap. He doesn't know their names, but they've seen his face before. As they turn in his direction, he swerves into the toy aisle. Walks forward. Hears the familiar voices of coworkers.

The snack aisle appears, and he rushes forward to find a fat woman in flip-flops pawing through the pudding and Jello cups. He stops beside the pretzels and feigns interest as she continues to browse. It takes an unbearably long time before she moves on.

Longo reaches the middle of the aisle as the woman turns the corner. He catches her glancing back before she vanishes. He checks to ensure no one watches, then he shoves the snack containers aside. Yet he can't find the lunch box. His heart hammers. It was here. He moves a few paces and tries again, wrecking the neat stacks of jello and pudding cups.

Voices bring his head around. A man holding a child's hand waddles toward him. The boy points to the snack he wants, and the man shakes his head and says the sugar will make the boy's teeth fall out. Yet they continue to browse. The man sees Longo and squints, pulls the crying boy away and shoots accusatory stares over his shoulder.

When they are gone Longo shoves his hand inside the stacks and into the shadows. Feels nothing hidden behind. Then he remembers being on a ladder. Yes, the lunch box was farther up, too far to reach standing on his toes. He knows where the step ladder is kept, but he can't go into the back without being seen. Instead, he climbs onto the lower shelf. The frame whines under his weight. It won't hold him for long.

He shoves the snacks aside, and the lunch box is not there. This can't be.

Cups rain down and crack open as he becomes frantic. Someone took it. That's the only explanation.

He stumbles backward and bumps into the shelves of potato chips. His head swims.

Glancing to each side, Longo feels the walls closing in. The store seems brighter as though a hundred spotlights shine upon him.

"Hey, what are you doing?"

A stock boy with glasses and a moonscape of acne sees him. Longo turns his head and walks away when the boy approaches. More shouts from behind, followed by a call for security.

He rounds the end cap and runs shoulder-first into a woman carrying a cake. The dessert falls from her arms and splatters as she tumbles against the shelves. Angry voices from those who saw pursue him down the aisle.

He runs, heedless of anyone who gets in his way. People with alarmed faces move aside as he muscles between overstuffed shopping carts. Longo fights through the jam, sees the exit doors and runs faster. The checkout workers point and yell. They think he stole something. Did they see his face?

He collides with one of the automatic doors and rattles the glass. The door jitters as it slides open. He squeezes through and angles for the truck, for safety, dodging a vehicle which screeches to a halt in the fire lane.

A curtain of rain slices between the truck and the Island Mart as if God aids his escape. He climbs into the cab and turns out of the parking lot before the pursuit catches him.

CHAPTER TWENTY-SIX

The Sunset Cafe sat in a nook between Barnes and Noble and a movie theater complex. It was normally overrun by the lunch crowd at this time of day, but today it was empty except for the forty-something man working behind the counter, and even he eyed the clock with anxious desperation.

Gardy struggled to pull the door shut after he and Bell pushed inside. Though they'd only been out of the car for a few seconds, their hair was wet and water poured off their windbreakers.

While Gardy pulled out a chair near the window, Bell wiped the rain from her face at the counter.

The man wiped his hands with a towel and smiled. "What can I get you?"

"I'll take a hot herbal tea, please. What do you want, Gardy? My treat today."

Gardy glanced up from his phone and asked for black coffee.

Bell guessed the man behind the counter owned the cafe as he was the only person present despite the peak hour. He ran his finger down a ledger, silently moving his lips and adding figures in his head. His honey-brown, curly hair was tied back in a ponytail, and he wore thick-lensed glasses that slid down his nose. The cafe smelled of dark-roast coffee and pastries. Running her eyes over the display, Bell promised herself she'd behave.

"Good thing I have insurance."

She glanced up.

"Good thing, indeed. I'm surprised you're open. You didn't want to make a run for the border?"

"Risk and reward," he said, winking. "On one hand, this is the only cafe open on the block. On the other hand, time is ticking against me."

Thunder roared in agreement.

"Will you leave the island?"

He leaned his arms on the counter and stared thoughtfully at the wall.

"I guess not. I have a condo two miles inland, so I'm not worried about the storm surge. It's the city that concerns me. Once that water comes ashore there's nothing to hold it back." He handed her the drinks. "What about you?"

"We're here for the duration. Hey, we can take these to go if you want to close early. It might not be a bad idea."

"No worries. Take your time. I need to finish the books before I lock the doors."

Bell pulled out a chair across from Gardy. He raised the coffee and nodded. Bell sipped the tea and singed most of the flesh off her lips, then decided discretion was the better part of valor and let it cool.

He sipped his coffee and moved his eyes between Bell and his phone, never holding his gaze for more than a second.

"The fiasco at the police department. That was on me."

The memory of how the officers acted made her cheeks burn.

"It didn't seem like they wanted us there."

He bobbed his head a few times and watched the trees sway outside the window.

"It's the cops, not McKenna or the chief. The same old unnecessary turf war — they think we're here to steal the case and swoop in for the glory."

"I don't see how that makes it your fault."

Gardy gulped his coffee and exhaled.

"McKenna pulled me aside beforehand and told me to expect resistance. I should have said something to you."

"It wouldn't have made a difference."

"At least you would have known what you were in for. Anyway, as you already guessed, none of those cops put much faith in what we do. Profiling. That fat cop who gave you trouble?"

"Rivera."

"Yeah, him. He's sort of the circus ringleader, and he puts profiling right up there with crystal gazing and tarot cards. I don't blame him for having doubts. Despite the research, most of what we do is more art than science. But he should have shown you respect, and I should have stood up for you. Sorry about that."

Bell tapped her finger on the table and watched the proprietor work. Gardy noticed her lost in thought and folded his arms on the table.

"Bell?"

She shook the cobwebs free and looked at him.

"Yeah."

"Seems like something else is bugging you."

She raised her eyebrows.

"Are you profiling me, Agent Gardy?"

He snickered.

"Guess I can't turn it off. But you didn't answer my question, which in itself suggests guilt."

She shrugged and slumped back in her chair, thoughtlessly running her finger along the side of the cup.

"Remember when I told you my parents were coming to visit?"

"On the flight back from Coral Lake, yes."

"I kinda threw them out."

He leaned forward.

"Whoa. What happened?"

Bell blew the hair off her face.

"Things finally came to a head. My injuries were the catalysts, but it brought out all of their angst over me working with the BAU. We fought over it for a few days. It got nasty over dinner one night, and Dad said women weren't cut out for law enforcement."

Gardy winced.

"That led to a lot of shouting and arguing about traditional jobs for women." Bell put air quotes around *traditional jobs*. "I was pretty worked up by then, and I said things I shouldn't have said. Then I threw them out. Told them if they can't respect me working with the BAU they needed to leave."

"Ouch. I hope you worked things out."

Bell shrugged. She felt tears building behind her eyes and angrily pushed them back.

"That was six weeks ago. I haven't heard from them

since."

"Be the bigger person. Call them. They're wrong, Bell, but they're still your parents."

A Ryan Adams song played over the speakers. Bell was thankful the music shielded their conversation from the proprietor. A renegade tear crawled from the corner of her eye and flowed across her cheeks. She let it mingle with her rain-soaked hair.

"Enough about my parents. Back to the present. This storm is royally screwing our case."

"You mean Tom Thumb."

"Don't start with that nonsense."

Gardy grinned.

"It is kinda catchy."

"Sure, if you're into dismemberment."

"The way I see it, Ana puts everything into a holding pattern. The killer isn't likely to hunt new victims in the middle of a category-four hurricane."

"Maybe, maybe not. Think about the possibilities. The hurricane will take down communication lines. Cell towers and such. What better time to—"

Gardy held up a finger when his phone buzzed.

She drank her tea while he talked. The liquid had cooled below molten levels but was hot enough to warm her chest. His eyes lit up, and he snapped his fingers.

Bell mouthed, "What is it?"

He held her eyes as he spoke on the phone.

"Yeah…okay…give me the address." He pulled a pen and notepad from his pocket. "Fulmer Parkway…got it. We'll be there in ten minutes."

She gathered up her bag as he ended the call.

"Where are we going?"

"To someplace called the Island Mart. Someone found a severed finger."

CHAPTER TWENTY-SEVEN

The horizon was black when Gwen Devereux tilted the Venetian blinds and peeked out the window. The last she'd heard, the hurricane was expected to strike Georgia and spread bands of thunderstorms and heavy rain over Sunset Island. So maybe that was why the sky looked so dark and the palm trees were swaying as though frightened.

Gwen owned DesignForce, a rapidly expanding web design firm she hoped would turn its first profit next quarter. Now she wondered what would happen if a catastrophic storm struck the island and wiped out her business. Her worries didn't help the headache she'd battled since last evening. Making matters worse, Oscar hadn't come home this morning. Normally this wouldn't concern Gwen, for the cat sometimes hunted the beach for two or three days before returning to her door. But the weather worried her. Unlike many people who believed animals possessed a sixth sense for predicting natural disasters, Gwen was pragmatic. The cat didn't know a storm was coming any better than she did.

She sat in front of her computer and nervously slid the mouse around. Thunder groaned over the sea.

As she clicked on the latest forecast, Cheri glided over in a rolling chair.

"Did you hear?"

"Hear what?"

"Ana. The hurricane is heading for Sunset Island."

"That can't be. I checked and…"

The website refreshed, and she saw the massive storm spinning off the Atlantic seaboard. The new track catapulted the storm straight over Sunset Island. Gwen pressed her hands against the sides of her head, ruffling the black, curly locks.

"Oh, this isn't good."

Cheri swung her feet onto Gwen's desk and sat back.

"Depends on how you handle the situation. Me? I'm hopping into the car and driving to Atlanta. At least I intend to if the big boss woman lets me leave early. There's nothing better than a hurricane party with no hurricane to deal with."

"Yeah, yeah," Gwen said distractedly, refreshing the screen as if doing so would change the forecast. "Of course, you can leave early."

Cheri, whose short blonde hair was styled into a bob, reminded Gwen of Gwyneth Paltrow. Cheri was the firm's best designer, even better than Gwen when she set her mind to her work. But she was easily distracted, changed discussion topics and boyfriends as often as she did shoes.

"And what are you planning to do, my friend? Please tell me you don't intend to ride out a killer hurricane."

Gwen had considered exactly that, except the beach house wasn't an ideal place to hole up in a storm this strong.

"I'm not sure yet."

Cheri swung her legs off the desk and scooted forward with the chair, resting her head in her hands.

"You know, you could come with?"

"Sounds dangerous."

"Think about it. You and me together. The Atlanta club scene would never be the same."

Gwen's lips curled up. A few days with Cheri in Atlanta sounded a ton better than the alternative.

"Let me think on it."

"Okay, but don't think for too long. If we want to beat the traffic off the island, we need to get going."

Rain slapped against the window and made Gwen jump. The storm decided her. It was too risky to stay.

Gwen grabbed her keys and stuffed them into her bag.

"You sold me."

"Yay!"

"But I'm not leaving without Oscar."

"Gwen, cats are smarter than people. He'll find shelter. Don't worry."

Gwen looked out the window, considering. Already she observed a line of cars massing at the bridge. The traffic would only worsen with each passing minute.

"I can go home and be back in an hour."

"That's too long."

Gwen sighed.

"Look, either I grab Oscar and leave in an hour, or I ride it out. I couldn't live with myself if something bad happened."

"Fine."

The disappointment was clear on Cheri's face.

"Tell you what. If I'm not back in an hour, go without me. I'll meet you in Atlanta."

Cheri squinted doubtfully.

"I don't know about this. Doesn't sound like a smart plan."

"I promise I'll be fine. Even if I get stuck in traffic, I'll make it off the island before the storm hits. Besides, storms always miss us. You'll see."

Cheri dragged her feet and slumped her shoulders as they walked out of the office. When they reached the elevator, Gwen felt a pang of worry. What if lightning struck and the power went out while they were inside? The doors opened and Cheri entered. The woman turned and faced Gwen, who stood undecided at the threshold.

"Well, are you coming?"

Gwen entered before she could talk herself out of it.

The elevator descended two floors and chimed at the main level. When the doors slid apart, Gwen clutched her bag and hurried out as if fleeing from a haunted house. Cheri quickened her pace to keep up.

There was a bald man wearing a gray janitor's uniform in the lobby. He faced away from them and stared down at the trash receptacle as if uncertain how to remove the bag. Gwen didn't recall seeing the man before, but the firm which owned the office building recently changed cleaning services.

"Is that the new guy?" Cheri asked.

"I'm not sure."

Something about the man was familiar. She tried to recall where she'd seen him, but her head throbbed and urged her to escape the lobby lights.

The wind nearly threw Gwen down when they

stepped onto the sidewalk. Commerce Street, usually overrun with traffic at midday, was an empty tomb. Cheri bent low and turned her head as a spray of rain caught them.

"I'm parked in the garage," Cheri said, shouting over the wind and pointing across the street. "Meet me at the Sunoco next to the bridge. One hour, Gwen."

Gwen nodded and clutched her bag to her body. The storm groped at her, tried to lift Gwen off her feet.

She was halfway down the sidewalk when she looked back at the office building. The janitor, the man she swore she recognized, was staring at her through the window.

CHAPTER TWENTY-EIGHT

The wipers slice through the waterfall streaming down his windshield, and more water replaces the flow. Longo hunches over the steering wheel and peers into the storm. He can barely discern the development, but last night's memory pulls him through and tells him where to turn before the street signs become visible.

Gwen Devereux's Volvo is parked in the driveway when he stops along the curb. He sits inside his truck for a moment and watches. The lights are on in the living room. He watches her shadow pass over the curtains and swerve toward the back of the house. She will leave soon, he knows. He overheard her discussion with the blonde woman about leaving the island. As expected, nobody gave him a second glance when he arrived dressed as a janitor. Then the news about the hurricane broke, and the office building cleared out and left him alone with the women.

The storm whips at him when he steps from the truck. It shrieks over the ocean and unleashes an army of waves against the unsuspecting beach. Besides Devereux, he is the only living soul in the development. Everyone else in town flees. As he moves into a stand of trees and watches from the shadows, another wish comes to him unbidden. What if the blonde woman comes to the Devereux's home? He never considered killing two women at the same time. The idea excites him.

Longo touches the knife inside his jacket pocket. Runs his thumb down the blade and feels a trickle of blood warm his hand.

He surveys the surroundings, taking nothing for granted, and confirms no one watches. Then he slides the knife from his pocket. Curls his fingers around the hilt and squeezes.

Movement in the shadows catches his eye before he steps into the yard. The woman's cat has found him again. Remembering Longo, the animal is no longer cautious. The cat rubs against his shin and purrs, innocent eyes glancing in expectation.

But he has other ideas for the cat.

CHAPTER TWENTY-NINE

Gwen Devereux's travel bag lay open on the bed as she rushed back-and-forth in the bedroom. Convinced she'd packed enough clothes for three days, she zipped the bag shut and cursed. Toothbrush, toothpaste, deodorant. In her haste, she'd forgotten them.

Rain sprayed the bedroom window. Beyond the pane, whitecaps turned the sea into a frothy monster. It was halfway up the beach. She'd never seen it rise this far.

As she rushed to the bathroom cabinet she heard a truck motor. Odd. She thought nobody was left in the development. Then the motor vanished under the storm, and she wondered if she'd imagined the sound.

After packing the toiletries, she hurried to the back door and threw it open. The salty ocean spray met her immediately and soaked her front. Calling for Oscar with growing desperation, she glanced around the beach. An impenetrable haze swallowed everything, making it impossible to see. Braving the storm, she stepped onto the deck and called again. Oscar would find shelter, she tried to convince herself. Maybe Cheri was right about cats being smarter than humans when it came to evading Mother Nature. Was she willing to get herself killed over the cat? A part of Gwen begged her to stay. She couldn't live with herself if Oscar was terrified and pawing at the back door minutes after she fled the development.

Her eyes drifted over the windows as she turned toward the door. No chance the glass would hold up, even if the storm surge didn't crash through the kitchen. The supplies for boarding the windows sat in the garage, planks she never thought she'd need. It was too late now.

She threw the door shut and battled against the wind until it clicked into place. The phone rang as she toweled her hair dry. It was Cheri.

"Where are you?"

"I'm almost ready to leave."

"Did you find Oscar?"

Gwen slid into a kitchen chair and rubbed her temples.

"No. I'm still looking."

"You have to leave now. We're under a state of emergency with mandatory evacuations along the coast. That means you."

"I know. Let me try one more time."

"Gwen."

"I swear I'll leave right after. Wait for me at the Sunoco. I'm coming."

Cheri's protests cut off. Nothing but silence on the other end.

"Cheri?"

Bursts of truncated conversation came through the receiver as the connection wavered. Gwen caught syllables she couldn't make sense out of. Then the line went dead.

Great. Ana had taken down a cell tower.

Gwen clicked the phone off and sat with her head between her knees. Damn this migraine. Were it not for the storm she would have driven to the emergency room and demand a shot of Sumatriptan.

The memory hit her when she stood up. She knew where she'd seen the janitor. Stacking shelves at the Island Mart last night. She'd caught him staring at her. It was an odd coincidence, to say the least, but not strange a person needed to work two low-paying jobs to make ends meet. And maybe that was the reason he'd stared at her through the window. Recognition. She felt a little foolish for getting the creeps.

Gwen put the thought aside and went to the front door.

She was about to call for Oscar again when she saw something sticking out of the ground in the front yard. The rain pulled a veil across her vision. Hands cupped to elbows, she edged down the stoop and saw the cat's head and paws jutting out of the ground. Its neck lolled to one side, swollen and distended, tongue snaking between open fangs. She bit down on her hand and sobbed as her brain slowly processed the horrific scene.

Then she saw him standing in the rain. She knew who he was as soon as she saw the gray janitor's uniform.

He strode across the lawn as she screamed and turned for the house. A moment after she threw the lock, his body collided with the front door.

CHAPTER THIRTY

Detective McKenna was already on scene with two additional officers when Bell and Gardy arrived at the Island Mart. The officers wore navy blue Sunset Island PD rain slickers beaded with water droplets. A woman Bell guessed was the store manager stood among the officers, her dirty-blonde hair unkempt and frizzy as if she'd recently run in from the rain. The woman's clothes stunk of cigarette smoke.

Gardy nodded at McKenna.

"What have we got?"

McKenna walked into the store as he spoke, the others following.

"About three hours ago, a shopper found a lunch box in the snack aisle. The box was pushed toward the back of the shelves as if it had been forgotten. He figured it belonged to a worker, so he turned it in at the customer service desk."

"Do we know who the lunch box belongs to?"

"A local guy named Derek Longo. He works the overnight shift."

"*Worked* the overnight shift," the manager said. "I fired him this morning."

"By the way, this is the store manager, Dolores Storey. She found the finger."

Storey nodded, folding her arms as if she couldn't shake the gooseflesh bubbling off her skin.

"I didn't open the box until an hour ago. Had no reason to, but it was…leaking water and smelled bad. As soon as I saw what was inside I phoned the police."

McKenna stepped around a woman hustling bottled water into a cart.

"So here's what we know. Derek Longo abandoned his shift sometime after midnight this morning. Didn't say a word to anyone, just walked off the job. The Island Mart only had one cashier working at that time of night."

"Renee Wood," Storey added.

"Right. Wood wouldn't have noticed except she heard Longo's truck start. Guy drives a 1998 F-150, black. It makes a lot of noise, so it was next to impossible not to hear him leave. Nobody saw Longo for the rest of the night. But get this. Two hours ago, one of the stock boys claims Longo was inside the store and acting strangely."

Bell swerved around two men arguing over a loaf of bread.

"Acting strange how?"

"Says Longo had a paranoid look on his face and ran over some woman outside of the bakery. Then he sprinted through the front entrance and knocked one of the automatic doors off its hinges."

"He was after the lunch box."

"That's my guess. By then it was already at the customer service desk."

McKenna pushed open a pair of double doors at the back of the store. Walking beside Gardy, Bell saw a small warehouse with crates and boxes upon pallets. McKenna and the manager took a sharp right down a dark hallway and into the security office. A thin, mustached man with greasy hair sat before a row of monitors. He wore a blue security uniform with a radio affixed to his hip but didn't carry a weapon.

"This is the head of security, Evan Thames."

By way of McKenna's introduction, Thames shook Gardy's hand, then Bell's. His palms were moist and scabby.

Bell wiped her hand on her pant leg and gestured at the gray lunch box next to the video console.

"I take it the finger is our vic's?"

"We sent it to the lab for testing, but I think we all know where the finger came from. In the meantime, we sent two cars to Longo's address on Edgewood Boulevard. He wasn't home, but our guys entered the premises and found blood splatter in the basement. It'll take time to match the blood to Clarice Hopkins."

Bell looked sympathetically at the store manager.

"Mrs. Storey, what can you tell us about Derek Longo?"

Storey dropped onto a metal folding chair and stared down at her lap.

"Derek worked with us for about seven months. He preferred the night shift from eight-until-four. I was the one who read his application and made the call to hire him."

"Do you know if he has family in the area? Friends he might stay with? A girlfriend?"

Storey shrugged.

"Can't imagine Derek with a girlfriend. If you even glance at him, his face breaks out and his neck turns red. He's a strange one."

"Breaks out. As in hives?"

"Yeah, I guess so. Derek seemed uncomfortable around people, which is probably why he wanted to work overnights. As the detective pointed out, we have one cashier, an assistant manager on the night shift, and one person to stock the shelves. That was Derek. For what it's worth, I always made a point to invite him to store picnics, to make him more comfortable around his coworkers, but he never came."

Gardy, who remained quiet until now, leaned against the video console, tapping his phone against his chin.

"The question I have is why Longo suddenly abandoned his shift in the middle of the night. Something set him off."

Bell glanced at Gardy.

"We need to view the security footage from Longo's shift."

Thames slid his rolling chair in front of the controls and folded his arms.

"They can't force you to show them the footage, Mrs. Storey. Not without a warrant."

The store manager hissed through her teeth.

"This isn't the time to worry about warrants, Evan. Show them the footage."

"You're sure about this?"

"Just do it."

Thames spun around in a huff, shaking his head.

"Derek was on shift for over four hours. How much

do you really need to see?"

"Start ten minutes before midnight," said Gardy.

"Fine."

Thames typed the information into the computer, and the monitors flickered. It took a moment for Bell to realize the footage, which displayed multiple views of the store over several monitors, wasn't live. The only discernible difference was the lack of people inside the store on the replay.

Gardy leaned over the security guard's shoulder and pointed at the monitor.

"Does the system play the footage back at a faster speed?"

"Sure, I can choose multiple speeds."

When Thames clicked the mouse the footage appeared the same, then Bell noticed shadows in the lower portion of the frame moving unusually fast. Several seconds later, Longo entered the screen pushing a shopping cart. He disappeared from one screen and reappeared in another as the various views followed his progress through the Island Mart.

"Pause it there," Bell said, kneeling beside Gardy.

Gardy nodded.

"Check out the shopping cart. You can see the lunch box. Start it again."

McKenna squinted at the monitor as Longo removed the lunch box and ran his fingers along the side, almost caressing it. The video advanced and Longo shoved the lunch box onto the shelf while he stocked the snack aisle.

"He'll risk getting caught to keep the trophy with him at all times. What would make him forget the lunch box? It doesn't seem possible."

Longo restocked the shelves at triple-speed. Bell was about to tell Thames to speed up the footage when Longo suddenly stopped and crept to the end cap.

"There," Gardy said, pointing at the monitor. "He notices someone. Who's he looking at? The cashier? Pause it."

Thames froze the footage, and Bell's eyes traveled over the monitors until she saw the woman. She was mid-stride near the bread aisle and angling toward the back of the store.

"Detective, do you have a photograph of Clarice Hopkins on you?"

McKenna opened his iPad and swiped a finger across the screen.

"Right here," McKenna said, enlarging the picture of the first murder victim.

Bell glanced between the photograph and the video monitor.

"The resemblance is undeniable."

McKenna tilted the iPad so Gardy could compare.

"Same hair color and style," Gardy said, moving his eyes back-and-forth. "Similar facial features, though the woman on the monitor appears younger. Can you zoom in on her face?"

Thames drew a box around the woman's face and clicked the mouse. The closeup was blurry and pixelated, obscuring her identity.

"That's as good as I can get it."

"Try a different camera."

"What you see is what you get. She's only visible on camera three."

At Gardy's instruction, Thames unfroze the video.

The woman appeared to jump from monitor-to-monitor as multiple cameras followed her progress through the store. Longo crept behind, stalking the woman. Watching the madman hiding amid the aisles, creeping closer to the shopper, sent a chill down Bell's spine. As if she watched a horror movie, a part of her wanted to shout at the screen and warn the woman.

After grabbing a medicine bottle, the woman hurried to the counter. Bell bit her lip in frustration. The security camera near the pharmacy was close enough to get a reasonable view of the woman's face, but she kept her back to the camera the entire time.

A few seconds later, the view switched to the checkout.

"Please tell me she paid with a credit card," McKenna said, bending over the monitor.

When the woman pulled cash from her wallet, McKenna cursed and spun around, hands on hips.

While she paid, Longo bolted toward the back of the store and passed between four monitors before smashing through the double doors. He'd gone after her. Did Longo abduct the woman?

After Thames restarted the footage, Bell shouted at the security guard to go back a few frames. There. The woman's face was captured by the camera at the front of the Island Mart. Bell's face leaned inches from the monitor now.

"Zoom in again." The security guard drew another box, and the woman's face filled the monitor. "We got her. Can you print it?"

Thames nodded, and a few seconds later, the printer hummed and spit out the photo.

Gardy grabbed the picture and handed it to McKenna.

"I need this woman identified. Can you get her picture on the news?"

"Sure. We'll set up a hotline number. "

"I like our chances," Bell said, shrugging into her windbreaker. "With the hurricane coming people will watch the news."

"Until the power goes out."

"Which is why we need to move on this now."

"I'm on it."

Gardy placed his hand on the security guard's shoulder.

"There's the fire lane. Don't you have an angle on the parking lot?"

Thames shook his head.

"Sorry, this is all I have."

Bell and Gardy shared a glance. They could have identified the woman by her license plate.

When they came back through the store the aisles were vacant, the shoppers having purchased their supplies and fled. Sunset Island was a ghost town.

Gardy rushed to catch up to Bell.

"Slow down. We'll find her."

"It needs to happen fast, Gardy. Longo took her."

CHAPTER THIRTY-ONE

Gwen ran for the phone first. Found it on the kitchen table as the front door rattled against the intruder's force. She dialed 911 and immediately looked for something to defend herself with. A steak knife lay on the counter, and she grabbed it as the receiver crackled in her ear.

The call disconnected at the same time the front window shattered. She heard him crawl over the pane as the storm winds hunted through the living room, whipping the curtains into a lunatic frenzy.

Indecision paralyzed her. He'd cut her off from ascending the stairs, leaving the hurricane's building fury as the only option.

She grabbed the doorknob and pulled. A freight train of winds slammed the door open and threw her against the wall. The kitchen was a confusion of loose papers and driving rain as she fought the force driving her backward.

Longo's hand closed on her shoulder. She screamed and turned, slashing the knife against his chest. A thin ribbon of blood colored his shirt as he retreated toward the refrigerator. She came at him with the knife again, and he brought something from behind his back.

The club struck Gwen on the side of her head. Her knees buckled, and as she battled to stand, the weapon thundered down on her neck.

She collapsed on the kitchen floor. Legs and arms flat and outstretched. Eyelids fluttering as the storm peppered her body with soaking rains.

She felt him clutch her ankle. He dragged her through the hallway and to the staircase. Then he bent and lifted her into his arms and slung her rag doll body over his shoulder.

Gwen was unconscious when he tossed her onto the bed.

CHAPTER THIRTY-TWO

Somehow Longo's house was exactly as Bell envisioned and yet completely different. The brown siding sagged over the crumbling foundation like a decaying tooth, and a lightning-bolt fissure ran across the living room window. The interior presented a sparse organization she hadn't expected, the table bare and the wood floor recently swept.

The power was off. Ana turned afternoon into the darkest of midnights. Flashlights knifed through the darkness and swept around corners as the officers continued their search. Occasionally a beam slashed across Bell's face and temporarily blinded her. The confusion and dark made it seem like they were inside a haunted house, groping blindly at the walls and searching for an escape.

The stairs squealed underfoot as they climbed. Ancient flower print wallpaper covered the walls. A faded rectangular outline marked where a picture once hung.

The bedroom stood upstairs at the end of a long corridor. They passed the bathroom, then a spare room, empty except for an old mattress tipped against the back wall. The closet door stood open. Gardy aimed his flashlight and confirmed the boogeyman owner wasn't inside.

Though the officers had cleared the house, Gardy and Bell approached the room with guns drawn. Her mouth was dry as they swung into the room, Gardy first with his gun aimed left, then Bell sweeping the Glock right. The windowpane rattled, and Bell swung her gun toward the sound. The wind wanted to come inside.

Bell breathed again and lowered her weapon. Gardy caught her looking and shot her a nervous smile. She could hear the officers' footsteps downstairs, their disembodied voices muffled. They seemed a million miles away.

A worn shirt and jeans were strewn across the bedspread. To Bell, it appeared Longo had left in a hurry.

The pillows were yellowed with age, the sheet threadbare along the edges and fraying. Beside the bed stood a nightstand with a picture on it. Gardy had already picked up the photograph.

"Look at this. It's him, don't you think?"

The picture's color was faded and bleeding, the corners curling beneath the glass. The boy in the picture looked about five-years-old. He squinted and shielded his eyes from a harsh sun. Comparing the beady eyes and pudgy facial features with a recent photograph of Longo obtained by Detective McKenna, Bell saw the resemblance.

"That's Longo. I wonder who the woman is. The mother, I think."

Above the child stood a stern woman in her forties or fifties. Her eyes were caught halfway between the photographer and the boy, as if she expected him to misbehave the moment she looked away. A vintage, overly modest dress which oddly looked made in the 1930s fell to her ankles. Bell got the impression the woman's grimace was permanently etched on her face. What struck her most was the long, dark curls falling down to her shoulder.

"Look at the hair, Gardy."

He angled the picture so it caught the light.

"Just like Longo's targets."

Though the woman's mouth was drawn and twisted with derision, the long, slender face and high cheekbones were a fair match for Clarice Hopkins and the mystery woman from the Island Mart.

The closet wasn't organized so much as it was barren. Three shirts hung from hangers, eerily moving on their own as the storm shook the old house. The dresser held a few changes of clothes. Two of the drawers were empty.

Bell felt a measure of comfort when they joined the officers downstairs. She couldn't put a finger on why the house felt so creepy to her. It seemed to hold secrets in its walls, as though it was hostile, a conspirator to the crimes it witnessed.

Those feelings of comfort evaporated when they descended into the basement. The death scent was the first thing to hit her. Then the blood splatter on the concrete walls and the bare, crumbling floor. A bloodstained knife lay on a worktable alongside a spool of rope and a discolored gag. The crime scene techs were still working. She didn't want to get in their way.

Though Bell collected little tangible evidence which would help her catch Longo, she felt closer to picking up Longo's trail. A sixth sense.

McKenna spun around at their approach. It seemed Bell and Gardy weren't the only ones feeling spooked.

"I'm keeping two officers on the scene just in case Longo comes home. Otherwise, we're wrapping up operations here. Let's hope the woman's photo gets traction with the media. In the meantime, we'll reconvene at the station and ride out the storm."

"Detective, we have a description of Longo's truck and his license plate. I think Agent Gardy and I should look for him."

McKenna narrowed his eyes at Bell.

"I don't recommend you try. The low-lying roads are flooded, and the full brunt of the storm hasn't reached us yet."

"He's close, Detective. Our profile says he hunts in a small radius."

The detective glanced at Gardy, who shrugged as if to say once Bell made a decision there was no convincing her otherwise. McKenna blew air through his lips.

"Okay, but Officer Repasky will take you in the police truck. That rental won't hold up to hurricane winds."

Bell winked at Gardy.

"You see? I told you we shouldn't have rented another Accord."

CHAPTER THIRTY-THREE

The beach house makes a strange grating noise when the wind blows. Like an old door creaking open. The storm doesn't frighten Longo. He is barely aware of its presence. A petulant dog yapping at his heels. He has everything he wants. Solitude. A beautiful home. The woman asleep on the bed.

Gwen. She looks like a Gwen, he thinks.

Her breaths are so shallow it is difficult to know if she is alive. He bends over her body and hears the gentle susurrus of her breathing. Longo holds no fear of her suddenly lashing out, not with her ankles and wrists bound by rope.

A banging noise brings his head around. A loose shutter flaps against the house. He will need to fix it when the weather clears.

"Gwen."

Longo chokes on her name. It comes out hoarse.

He says her name again, but she doesn't stir.

Gwen looks peaceful. If she stayed this way, he would allow her to live. They could have a wonderful life together, the two of them by the sea. But deep in his heart, where the harsh realities of life fester and ooze, he knows it cannot be. There will be pleading and screams. She will fight him and try to escape, and he will be forced to still her heart. Yes, his original plan to preserve an entire body on ice will work. Then they can have a long and peaceful relationship.

Content in knowing she is sleeping soundly, he explores his new home. In the hallway, his shoes make the floorboards whine. The bathroom is small and clean and features a shower stall. The feminine mauve color doesn't bother him, and he thinks he will keep the style as is.

Plush carpeting covers the stairs. Makes his footsteps silent.

The shattered living room window lets in swirls of rain. Grabbing a blanket off the couch, he covers the television and drapes the end over the antique coffee table.

He crosses to the kitchen when something crashes upstairs.

Longo takes the stairs two at a time and finds Gwen writhing on the floor. She'd fallen off the bed and smashed a glass nightstand. The corner caught her back, and a red splotch soaks through the back of her shirt as she moans.

Too much noise. It confuses him, makes heat flare on his cheeks.

The moaning and thrashing continue. When he demands she stop yelling, Gwen suddenly notices him in the room and screams. Her cries are piercing. Like fingernails on a chalkboard.

At this moment, he understands what he must do. Killing her is inevitable. She will never learn to obey or be comfortable in their relationship.

From his back pocket, Longo removes the club.

She sees what he intends and instinctively turns to her stomach, helpless to defend herself with her wrists bound behind her back.

He strikes the top of Gwen's shoulders. She cries and pleads.

All he wants is for her to be quiet.

Longo curses and brings the club down on the back of her head. Gwen's legs twitch and go still.

For a long time, he stands above her broken body and listens to the storm. A high-pitch whistling noise slides over the roof. Somewhere over the ocean, thunder booms.

Then Longo hears a buzzing sound as the lights flicker off.

The power is dead.

CHAPTER THIRTY-FOUR

Officer Gerald Repasky wore a lampshade mustache and spoke with a southern drawl. Repasky looked directly at Gardy in the shotgun seat while he talked, making Bell nervous the officer would lose control of the vehicle.

A wire cage separated the front seat from the back, Bell the prisoner on this trip. Apparently other officers rode in the back, for the floor was littered by an empty potato chips bag and a half-drank bottle of Pepsi, which buzzed with fizz as it rolled between the cage and door.

The wipers sloshed through an endless curtain of rain. Bell could barely see the buildings as Repasky drove away from the beach and into the derelict section of the island.

"That was the old IBM plant," Repasky said, pointing to a sprawling gray building which took up half of the block. "A few years ago the city tried to convert it into apartments, but the idea didn't take. Now it's just an empty building kids tell scary stories about. They're right. Driving by gives me the willies."

Bell kept searching for the elusive black F-150. She knew the odds of finding it were slim, but Longo had to be close.

A Denny's billboard lay on its side. Pieces of the sign blew around in the street.

"And that was the high school before they moved it out past the bridge. South Carolina state football champions in 1997." He displayed his fist, adorned by a gaudy ring. "I played linebacker. Second on the team in tackles my senior year."

He went into his brief collegiate career when another piece of signage smashed against the windshield. Repasky did the worst thing possible, slamming the brakes, and the next thing Bell knew the tires hydroplaned, the truck fishtailing down the road at over thirty mph.

Repasky cranked the wheel into the skid until he gained control of the vehicle. Then they drove forward at a slower speed, Repasky decidedly less talkative and white-knuckling the steering wheel.

Gardy's face was pale, his right hand glued to the *Oh, Jesus* handle and his left arm braced against the dash.

"I think I'm going to be sick."

Bell leaned forward.

"Focus on your breathing. You're fine."

Repasky shot an over-the-shoulder glance at Bell.

"Maybe this isn't such a good idea. Why don't we go back to the station?"

Bell noticed a piece of sign lodged in one of the windshield wipers.

"Another ten minutes. If we don't see the truck by then, we'll head back."

Repasky sighed.

"Okay, you're the boss. But I don't see how we'll find him in this weather. You want me to keep going straight?"

"Actually, I think we should turn around. The woman from the Island Mart didn't live in this area of town."

Repasky's eyes found hers in the mirror.

"How can you tell?"

"She wore a designer shirt and jeans. That's a good indicator she lived on the upscale side of the island."

"But not a guarantee."

"No. Until we know differently, we play the percentages."

The officer executed a U-turn and took them back toward the resort district, where they came upon an intersection with a dead traffic light that danced and swung with the building storm. Repasky turned right, and they proceeded down a narrow street which Bell doubted could accommodate a second truck driving in the opposite direction. But that wasn't a problem. The police truck was the only vehicle on the road.

Repasky grabbed his radio and asked dispatch about the road conditions near the beach development. The dispatcher confirmed the flooding was worse near the beach.

The storm drains were clogged with debris and overwhelmed. The water was halfway up the tires. The truck churned ahead, Bell leaning forward expectantly as Gardy scanned driveways for Longo's F-150.

They were almost to the beach when the storm exploded. Rain shot horizontally at the windshield, blinding Repasky. A stop sign broke off the post and whacked the grille.

Gardy gave Bell a nervous snicker.

"That's what you get for wishing the weatherman got decapitated."

"I never said I wanted to see him decapitated—"

The wind struck the side of the vehicle and lifted the truck off the ground. They crashed down on the tires as Repasky shouted over the roar of rolling thunder. Then the truck slid sideways as if driven by the fury of a vengeful god. Bell couldn't see anything but rain.

The front of the truck tipped. Bell had the sensation of falling off the end of the world, the truck teetering over a black chasm. She gripped the cage as the front end slammed down.

They were in a ditch, the rear wheels spinning. Repasky threw the transmission between drive and reverse. It made no difference. They were stuck in the middle of a hurricane with water rising over the hood.

Repasky shouted into the radio. If dispatch replied it was impossible to hear over the storm.

"Bell," Gardy said, staring wide-eyed at the water leaking through the window.

"Get us out of here, Repasky."

The officer stomped the gas.

"I can't. She ain't going anywhere."

The water was up to Gardy's ankles and rising fast. The agent forced his door open as the wind tried to rip him from the cab.

"Climb out. We need to find shelter."

Bell hit the ground with Repasky behind her. Then the full force of Ana slammed them to the earth.

CHAPTER THIRTY-FIVE

Gwen was sprawled on the bedroom carpet when she awoke, the fibers itching her face and making her eyes water. The light in the room was all wrong. Gray and mottled with moving shadows.

A vise was around her head. Squeezing.

She lifted her arms to touch the back of her head and found her wrists bound. Ankles bound, too.

She remembered the man. Twisting onto her side, she looked around the room and didn't see him. Just the empty bedroom, the nightstand shattered and in a clump. Squirming across the floor awakened more pain when the wound across her back tore.

Where is he?

She listened but didn't hear the man. Couldn't sense him anymore as though a heat source had been removed from the room.

All around her the house groaned as the storm bulled off the Atlantic. The walls made a splintering noise. It was a matter of time before the hurricane ripped the house apart. She wondered when the ocean would ascend the beach and barrel through the kitchen.

Hot pain shot from her neck into her skull. Gwen winced and felt her body drifting toward unconsciousness as the floor pitched and spun. She fought to stay awake, but the tide of exhaustion dragged her under.

When she turned over, Gwen felt her wrists slide against the bindings. Had the ropes loosened? Blood seeped down from her back and slicked her wrists. She pulled one arm and then the other, the ropes clutching just below her hands. If she yanked too hard she'd dislocate her wrists.

She kept working the wrists back-and-forth, listening for the man. Another tug and her hands popped out of their bindings.

Free.

A prickling sensation on the back of her neck told Gwen he was behind her. She looked toward the bedroom door, and the entryway was empty.

The ropes around her ankles were tighter. Tied in multiple knots. It would take time to undo all those knots, time she didn't have. A thump came from below. He was somewhere in the living room.

The first knot unraveled, and she got to work on the second when the stairs groaned. She went silent. Waiting. Breaths coming fast as her inner radar fought to home in on his position.

Nothing. The groan might have been the wind pushing at the walls.

The second knot fought her. He'd wrenched it tight, and she snapped a nail to the quick as she wrangled the ropes apart.

One more.

The third knot proved to be the weakest. It pulled apart, and the pressure relief on her ankles was heaven. Standing was a challenge. Gwen gripped the mattress and pulled. Arms shaking, she almost crashed to the floor and drew his attention. After she climbed to her feet, she remained still until the room stopped spinning.

Each step across the floor caused Gwen's stomach to drop out from under her. The carpet was soft, a faithful friend which quieted her steps and guided her to the window.

She barely recognized the development. The road sign lay on its side. A spray of shingles fanned out a hundred yards or more as the palms bent toward the earth.

An otherworldly force pushed at the back of the house and shook the walls. The ocean. Nature was about to reclaim her land.

Leaning on the sill, she estimated the distance from the window to the porch roof. It was five feet sideways and several yards down. A death wish.

Yet she had no choice. It was jump or face the maniac without a weapon.

She slid the pane open a crack. The wind whistled through the opening, a shriek the man must have heard.

Slid the window up another few inches and felt the pressure in the room release. Like prying the lid off a sealed jar.

And that's when she heard his footsteps cross the living room and ascend the stairs.

Gwen tore the screen off its tracks and climbed through the window.

CHAPTER THIRTY-SIX

The new high school was a modern brick structure that stood a half-mile beyond the bridge. An expanse of windows along the front of the school looked out upon the rapidly intensifying hurricane. All that glass made Cheri nervous, and she backed into the cafeteria, putting another wall between her and the windows in case they imploded.

"Why don't you come inside with the others?"

Cheri jumped, not hearing Brenda sneak up behind her. The high school served as a shelter for those fleeing their homes, and Brenda, a stout woman in her late-fifties, was one of the city workers overseeing the operation.

"I want to be here when my friend arrives."

Brenda gave a doubtful nod and turned toward the gymnasium where the majority of the refugees convened. It wasn't likely anyone was out driving during the peak of the storm.

Cheri checked her phone again. She'd texted Gwen three times since their call cut off. Had any of the messages gone through?

She'd waited at the Sunoco until the wind frightened

her. Though Cheri was tempted to abandon the island and drive to Atlanta, a growing worry something was wrong, that Gwen was in danger, kept her rooted to Sunset Island. Now she was trapped inside the shelter with no hope of fleeing the storm. Ana caught her.

Cheri nervously rubbed her hands in the back of the cafeteria. A small group of people clustered near the front with their eyes focused on a television broadcasting the local news. An emergency message scrolled along the bottom of the screen.

She checked her messages when something on the television caught the corner of her eye. Something that shouldn't be yet was. Cheri fumbled the phone and snatched it before it fell to the floor. Gwen's picture was on the television. The image was grainy and blurred around the edges, obviously obtained from a security video, but Cheri knew it was Gwen. Which made no sense because Gwen wasn't in trouble with the law. Cheri had just seen her.

Cheri rose on trembling legs and shambled toward the television. She shushed two people talking, and they stared at her as Cheri stood before the screen as if she'd seen a phantom.

"Do you know that woman?"

She didn't know which of the men spoke.

"Miss?"

Below Gwen's picture was a phone number. A hotline number to the Sunset Beach Police Department. And a hotline number meant trouble. Something terrible was happening.

She started entering the number when it vanished from the television, but her memory was sharp, fine-tuned by panic and concern for Gwen.

To her relief, the call went through. A moment later, a female answered.

CHAPTER THIRTY-SEVEN

Bell's eyes flickered open in confusion. She lay on the floor among a row of chairs, many of which were overturned. There were four rows arranged symmetrically to face a center where a table, covered by a white cloth, stood as a focal point. A flower arrangement served as a centerpiece for the table, and high above hung long, cylindrical lights. It took her a few blinks before she realized she was in an interfaith church, though she didn't recall how she got there.

Outside, the hurricane roared. It shook the walls, an angry monster who wanted to eat. The lights swung over her head, making her think this might not be the best place to rest.

Below her lay a purple carpet which did little to cushion her back. Her clothes were soaked through and pasted against her skin.

Someone moaned.

She turned her head and saw Gardy leaning over Repasky. The officer's eyes were closed to slits, teeth gritted.

"Keep your leg still. Try not to move."

Gardy noticed her and crawled over.

"Good, I thought we'd lost you."

He brushed the hair from her cheek.

A stinging pain brought her hand to the side of her head. It came away with blood.

"What happened?"

He told her she'd lost consciousness after being struck in the head by debris. Bell groaned.

"Please tell me it wasn't a stop sign."

Gardy snickered.

"Only you could make a joke at a time like this. For the record, it was a tree branch."

"A big one?"

"Big enough to maintain your street cred."

A water droplet wet her forehead. The roof was leaking. She sat up on her elbows and rolled a kink out of her neck.

"What happened to Repasky?"

Gardy lowered his voice.

"It doesn't look good. I think the leg is broken."

"I can hear you, you know?" Repasky was on his side, propped up on one elbow and clutching his injured leg. "A break is a break. You make it sound like you'll need to put me down."

"Nothing that drastic. The question is how do we get you out of here."

"No rush. We'll wait out the storm. We're in God's house, Agent Gardy. Nothing bad will happen to us—"

The shriek of wood and nails tearing apart came from above, and a section of roof shot skyward. A torrent of rain poured through the opening, and the wind followed, stalking inside the church.

A stack of hymns shot into the air and rotated in the miniature cyclone as Bell and Gardy crawled toward the fallen officer. She shouted at Gardy, but the wind ripped her voice away and pulled it into the heavens. He put a hand to his ear, and she pointed across the room at a set of doors. The restrooms. Gardy nodded and lifted Repasky under one shoulder as Bell propped him up from the other side. Together they supported Repasky, who hopped on one leg as the hymns shredded and flapped around them.

The officer slumped against the wall when they staggered into the restroom. Bell gathered they were inside the women's room by the soft pinks accenting the facility.

"This is a helluva way to go out," Repasky said. "Dying in the women's bathroom."

Bell tapped the walls.

"We should be okay. The plumbing adds support to the walls, and there are no windows."

Despite Bell's confidence, Gardy radioed dispatch and reported Repasky's injury. Gardy talked to the dispatcher for a moment before McKenna jumped in on the conversation.

"We can't reach you. Ana drove the Atlantic across the lower half of the island. You're cut off until the storm lets up."

"How long before that happens?"

They heard McKenna shuffling papers.

"According to the National Weather Service, you're looking at hurricane-force winds for the next thirty to forty-five minutes. After that you've got another three hours of tropical storm conditions and a tornado threat."

"We can hold the fort for a few more hours."

"You do that, and I promise we'll get someone out to your location as soon as Mother Nature lets us. In the meantime…"

Bell recognized the female dispatcher's voice in the background. She couldn't make out their conversation, only bits and pieces. Something about a person named Devereux.

"Agent Gardy, you still there?"

"Copy. We're here."

"We got a positive ID on the woman in the security footage."

Bell sat forward. An electric charge moved through her body.

"Gwen Devereux, One Atlantic Way. A phone call came in from a woman who claims she works with Devereux." More background chatter. "We've got confirmation, Agent Gardy. Suarez just found her on Google. She runs a firm called DesignForce on Sunset Island. I'm looking at her picture right now."

After the call ended Gardy knelt and kept knocking the back of his head against the wall.

"She's right around the corner. I don't know what to do."

Bell couldn't believe what she heard.

"What we do is go after her. Atlantic Way is less than a mile away."

"How do you propose we do that? Those are one-hundred-mile-per-hour winds out there, and we don't have a vehicle."

"Yes, we do."

Gardy glanced back at Repasky and said, "Sit still." Then the agent jumped up and chased after Bell. She yanked open the door. The church was in shambles, the chairs tossed around the room while a waterfall of rain poured through the roof.

"Don't even think about it," he said, standing a few feet behind her.

Bell stared through the window at the automotive repair shop across the street.

CHAPTER THIRTY-EIGHT

The full brunt of Ana ripped at Gwen as she lay flat inside the copse. All around her, trees swayed and snapped with shotgun blasts. The ocean crashed mere feet from the copse, the storm having swallowed the beach. Now it took aim on the development and Sunset Island beyond.

Gwen felt the storm shred her back as she gripped a sapling and prayed for the storm to end. The wind dug beneath her with bony fingers and lifted her body off the earth. Now she extended from the tree, a human kite caught in the wind. She screamed when a wave surged over her legs, the fury of a thousand jet engines blaring into her ears.

Daring to raise her head, she saw her house still upright as Ana turned the shingles into confetti. Her car stood in the driveway, useless without keys, and the next nearest residence was a block away.

Even if the hurricane abated, she didn't think she could run to safety. Though she'd survived the jump to the porch roof, landing on the ground jammed her hip. She'd limped into the copse and fallen flat moments before the worst of the hurricane struck, all the while keeping her eyes on the house, knowing the man was inside. She wished the storm would claim the house and drag the man into the sea.

A piece of bark gashed her forehead as the storm felled another tree a few feet away.

Gwen closed her eyes. All she wanted was to fall asleep and leave her life in God's hands. If this was the way she was meant to go, she accepted her fate. She wanted the nightmare to end. It seemed Ana's wrath would never relent.

Until it did.

The change was subtle at first, the wind receding by twenty mph. Gwen barely perceived the change amid the tropical downpour, but the trees no longer bent earthward.

Trembling, teeth chattering, her flesh grated by countless razors, Gwen propped herself up on her hands and caught her breath. Clumps of mud dripped from her hair, and something sharp pierced her side. She pinched the glass shard between her fingers and pulled. Cried out. The glass came out bloodstained. Debris in the form of insulation, snapped branches, shingles, and glass lay around her as if a bomb had exploded.

Her body protested her attempt to stand, but she bit back the pain and stood panting against a stout palm that survived the massacre. She put one foot in front of the other, felt the storm try to wrestle her back to the earth, steadied herself, and kept walking. Lightning flashed and was immediately counter-punched by a blast of thunder.

Halfway out of the copse, Gwen heard him coming. Footsteps snapped branches. She turned and saw his vacant eyes as he pushed through the debris.

Gwen screamed as he lunged for her.

CHAPTER THIRTY-NINE

Entering the repair shop was the easy part. The plate glass fronting the building had imploded, the door cockeyed and swinging on one hinge.

How they fought their way across the road, Bell barely remembered. The flooded road tried to sweep Bell off her feet and whisk her into the Atlantic. She remembered clutching Gardy's elbow, the agent screaming in her ear to turn back as pieces from the interfaith center's roof rained down around them.

The Jeep Grand Cherokee was parked in front of the shop. The passenger side window was smashed in, safety glass sparkling on the seat. Otherwise, the SUV appeared unscathed. Inside the shop, Bell found the keys hanging off a hook behind the counter.

"Stealing a Jeep? I don't like this, Bell."

Bell pointed to a big oak tipping over. When it fell, it would crush the Jeep.

"We're doing the owner a favor."

"Yeah, you keep telling yourself that. What about Repasky? He's alone."

Half of the church's roof was gone, and the wind intended to take the rest.

"I don't like leaving him any more than you do. He's safe inside the bathroom."

"And if the ocean reaches the church?"

Bell shook her head.

She climbed into the driver seat before he protested. Gingerly sitting on glass pellets, Gardy yanked the seatbelt across his chest and shot her a *you've reached a whole new level of crazy* stare. The motor gunned, a good sign. Bell backed out of the parking space and weaved the vehicle between broken glass and a huge chunk of palm. Gardy's teeth gritted as the Jeep plunged into the flooded roadway.

The water level eclipsed the tires. It flowed like a rapid out of its banks and pulled the vehicle to the side as Bell battled to push the Jeep forward. They moved against the flow for the length of the street, but the ocean had completely engulfed the intersecting road, blocking their only path to Atlantic Way.

"Take it as a sign from heaven. Turn around while we still can."

She hit the accelerator and splashed forward. The water level climbed above the grille, and it moved fast enough to sweep them downstream at highways speeds. Driving through the flood was a stunt the criminally insane wouldn't pull.

"Bell!"

"I've got this."

A moment before the front end dipped into raging waters, Bell pulled right on the steering wheel and took them over the curb. They climbed a sloped yard toward a sprawling brick mansion, the Jeep jouncing crazily as

Gardy braced his arms against the dash.

"Bell!"

"Hang on. I know what I'm doing."

The Jeep's tires spun divots of mud, then caught as Bell engaged the all-wheel drive. The SUV shot forward and nearly blasted through the front door before she spun the wheel. She wondered if the owners were home and if they'd find humor in surviving a category-four hurricane only to have a pair of FBI agents drive a stolen Jeep through their living room.

They swerved around the side of the house and cut through the backyard, narrowly missing the solarium. Bell thought she saw the face of an alarmed woman in the glass as Gardy cursed and asked her if she'd lost her mind.

The Jeep rounded the house and started down the opposite side of the yard. They evaded the worst of the flood, and Bell noticed the Atlantic Way intersection off to her right. But the yard sloped treacherously on this side of the mansion, and as the ground fell out from beneath the wheels, Bell experienced vertigo, the sensation of plummeting on a rollercoaster.

"Brakes, brakes!"

The brakes did her less good than Gardy's yelling. The terrain tore away like baby back ribs off the bone, and she didn't so much drive the Jeep as hang onto the steering wheel for dear life while they hurtled toward the unforgiving macadam.

The front tires bounced off the road. Bell's teeth clicked together, and her neck snapped against the seat back as the vehicle fishtailed. She straightened the wheel before the water ripped them backward.

Gardy's face was white, breath flying in-and-out. As

she angled toward Atlantic Way, Bell saw Gardy glare at her. He said nothing, and somehow that made it worse. She knew he was furious though his anger was temporarily cloaked by sheer terror. It mattered not. She navigated the flooded roadway and cut a path toward Gwen Devereux.

In the mayhem, she never noticed the wind letting up. A few breaks of blue cut into the battleship-gray sky. The storm still shoved the Jeep like it was a child's toy, yet the worst was behind them. They were going to make it.

"Okay, slow down now. The house is somewhere around the bend."

Bell's hands shook as she nodded at Gardy. It hardly seemed possible anyone lived at the end of Atlantic Way. To the left, the ocean stormed up the beach. On the other side of the road lay empty plots and undeveloped land, all submerged in standing water. She dodged a tree blocking their lane, then the road twisted and concluded at a dead end.

A copse stood to their left, the trees twisted and mangled, the ground littered with debris. The beach house was behind the tree line. A black F-150 was parked along the curb.

"Stop here," said Gardy. "That's Longo's truck."

Bell stepped out of the Jeep. Thinking the same thing, they were careful to nudge the doors shut and avoid attracting attention.

Sticking to the truck's blind spot, Bell approached the F-150's driver side, with Gardy a few steps back and angling to the right. Both had their guns drawn. The truck's windows were tinted, but Bell could see the inside panel. Her mouth was dry when she swung around the door.

The cab was empty.

They climbed over the curb and sloshed through the mud, using the copse as a shield. Gardy, hair soaked and hanging against his head like leeches, led Bell forward.

A thump beyond the trees brought Gardy and Bell to a halt.

They locked eyes a moment before Gwen Devereux screamed.

CHAPTER FORTY

Bell circled behind the beach house while Gardy approached the front stoop. The wind tunneled between the copse and the home, ripping Bell backward as she fought toward the back door. Half of the deck was gone. The ocean was almost past the steps. The back door hung open and banged against the house.

She stood with her back to the wall, gun raised and heart hammering. Counting to three in her head, she swung into the entryway.

"Freeze!"

Longo stood behind Gwen, clutching her waist with one arm, the opposite hand holding a knife to her throat. He blinked as though he couldn't process Bell being here.

"Don't...don't come any closer. I'll kill her."

She believed he would. He swallowed hard and darted his eyes between Gwen and Bell, a rat caught in a trap. Or a hungry rat leering over smaller prey.

"You don't want to do that, Derek."

He blinked again, surprised she knew his name. His eyes turned confused and swiveled erratically. At any moment, Longo might swipe the blade across Gwen's throat. Despite her accurate profile of Longo, she didn't know how he'd react in the heat of the moment.

Gwen shivered. Her clothes were drenched and bloodstained. The woman's face looked unnaturally gray.

Bell took a breath, then another. She needed to think this through.

Over his shoulder, she spied the hallway and the front door. She hoped Gardy was already inside the house. At the angle Longo stood, he'd spot the door opening and probably kill Gwen in panic before either Gardy or Bell fired a shot.

An idea occurred to her.

"Put the gun down," Longo said. A trickle of drool curled down his lip.

Bell took a small step sideways. Just enough to change his line of vision, force him to turn his head away from the front door.

"Put it down or I'll cut her."

"Okay, Derek. I'm putting the gun down."

Gwen shook her head and uttered, "No."

As Bell carefully knelt, she maintained eye contact with Longo. This was a helluva risk. Nothing prevented him from slicing Gwen's throat when Bell dropped her weapon, nor could Bell defend herself if Longo attacked her next. His tongue ran across scabby lips as she gently placed the gun on the floor. He held his breath. Bell removed her hand from the Glock, and Longo inhaled sharply.

Bell's knees felt weak as she stood up. A smile formed in his eyes.

"There you go, Derek. Why don't you let her go

now?"

He shook his head.

Where was Gardy?

Bell's eyes tracked automatically to the hallway. Longo noticed and swung his head around. The blade pressed hard against Gwen's throat, folding her skin over the edge. He might panic and mistakenly cut the woman.

"I'm right here, Derek."

He turned back to Bell but shot paranoid glances over his shoulder, unconvinced the hallway was empty.

"That's right. It's just the three of us." She allowed for several seconds of quiet. Ocean water trickled over the kitchen threshold while the back door continued to slam against the house. "But it could be just the two of us."

She had his full attention now. Her clothes were soaked through, and when she shrugged out of her jacket, the white blouse left little to the imagination. Longo's tongue flicked out again. Lizard-like.

"I know why you like her." Bell jerked her eyes at Gwen. "She reminds you of someone, doesn't she?"

Longo didn't reply. Just stared. An empty shell, a cipher craving something unattainable to fill his nothingness.

"Your mother?"

Bell needed to be careful. This was dangerous territory. He looked like kindling about to catch fire.

"What I don't understand, Derek, is why you want to be with a woman who reminds you of someone who treated you poorly."

His fingers tightened around the hilt.

"Stay calm, Derek. Look at me. Don't you realize you're allowing your mother to win again? She hurt you, didn't she? Controlled your life and never let you breathe. But that part of your life is behind you. You call the shots now. Just you, Derek. But if you hurt her, you'll go to jail. You don't want that. That freedom you waited for your whole life will disappear forever. Why go back to letting others rule over you?"

Longo's grip relaxed. Gwen slumped against his body now. If he let go, she'd crumble.

Not daring to look over his shoulder, Bell relied on her peripheral vision to observe the hallway. The path to the front doorway was cloaked in shadow.

"Forget your mother. She can't control you anymore. Instead, look at me. I think you'll agree I look nothing like her. Wouldn't you rather be with someone like me? Someone young, someone who never hurt you?"

The corner of his eye twitched. She watched his teeth grinding behind closed lips.

"I promise you this. The moment you let go of your mother's memory and choose me, you'll gain the power you always craved. Real power."

A darker presence interrupted the shadowed hallway. Gardy caught her eye and slid along the wall, mere steps from the kitchen and directly behind Longo. No way the madman could see the agent approach.

The problem was Gardy couldn't shoot. Not with Gwen and Bell directly aligned with Longo.

Bell breathed deeply. Willed herself not to look at Gardy and give him away. With every inch the agent gained on the killer, Bell feared the floor would squeak or Longo would sense Gardy's presence.

Gardy was poised beside the refrigerator now, the faint outline of his shadow drawn along the wall.

"Let your mother go and take me, Derek. Until you do, you'll never be free."

As she said it, Bell swiped her foot against the Glock and kicked it across the kitchen.

Longo grinned.

He let go of Gwen and lunged at Bell with the knife. Bell dropped to the floor as gunfire exploded.

Three shots pierced Longo's back and formed ragged holes as they exited his chest. Red sprayed the walls and splattered Bell's face.

Her ears rang from the blasts when Longo's dead weight hit the floor inches from her head. Gwen lay on her side, sobbing. Gardy checked the woman first, then dropped to one knee beside Bell. He kept the Glock fixed on Longo, whose back hitched as he drew in jagged, slushy breaths. Gardy tore a piece of cloth off the killer's shirt and pressed it to the open wound on Gwen's back.

Gwen looked at Bell. The woman closed her eyes.

CHAPTER FORTY-ONE

Bell sat behind her desk at Quantico, nervously drumming her feet despite the lack of music. Phones rang in neighboring offices, and she heard the voices of fellow agents congeal together like traffic on a distant highway.

The clock read five minutes until noon. She had half a mind to grab her bag and take an early lunch, but that would leave Gardy alone with Weber and only postpone the inevitable.

Her phone rang. Two sharp blips that caused Bell to jump in her seat. She picked up the phone, and Weber's administrative assistant told Bell he was ready for her.

Gardy was already seated in one of two chairs facing Weber's desk. The agent's eyes lifted off his lap momentarily and met Bell's. He gave an almost imperceptible shake of his head, a signal that Bell shouldn't say anything.

It was no secret that Don Weber, Deputy Director of the Critical Incident Response Group, set his eyes a few rungs up the ladder. The silver-haired, sharp-featured fifty-one-year-old would be Director of the FBI within a few years. Now he licked his thumb and forefinger and paged through Gardy's report, staring at the paper as if the special agents weren't there. He stopped on one particular page and hissed through his teeth.

Bell didn't know where to fix her eyes. Staring at the report might be akin to snooping, yet she didn't wish to see the pallor and defeat on Gardy's face. So she gazed at the various plaques adorning the walls, staring at the diplomas and awards but not seeing them. The walls might have been blank white.

Weber flipped another page and slapped it down. He would fire Bell, but she didn't care anymore. She risked her life to take murderers off the street and opened the door for new nightmares to haunt her. And for what? So a politician could critique her every step and threaten her job on a whim?

It was Gardy she worried about. Her partner, the most talented agent she'd encountered during her brief career, was married to the job. The irony was Gardy should have been sitting in Weber's chair. No one in the BAU was more qualified to be Deputy Director of CIRG, and there wasn't a field agent who didn't pray he'd take Weber's place.

Bell felt Weber's glare before she brought her eyes back to him. His hands were folded on the desk, jaw working from side-to-side as if contemplating who to condemn first.

"Don, I—"

"Save it, Agent Gardy." Gardy seemed to shrink a few inches in his chair. "You'll have your chance to speak later."

This was too much. Bell opened her mouth, but

Gardy warned her with his eyes to let it go.

"Neither of you deserve to represent the BAU."

He looked from Gardy to Bell as if daring either to protest. Spreading the papers across his desk, he sighed.

"I got off the phone with the Sunset Island Police Department an hour ago."

Another pregnant pause. For God's sake, if he wanted to fire her he should get it over with.

"To say you're both lucky would be an understatement. Detective McKenna was particularly pleased with your contribution to the case, and he confirmed the hurricane cut off the lower third of the island, leaving the two of you as the only options to pursue Derek Longo."

Weber threw up his hands.

"But stealing a private vehicle and nearly crashing through a residence?"

Bell sat forward.

"It was the only way around the flood—"

"I'm well aware of that, Agent Bell. There's no excuse for risking multiple lives, including yours and your partner's. You're damn fortunate you weren't charged with trespassing after stealing keys from a repair shop. And it seems the owner of the Jeep Grand Cherokee couldn't be happier that his vehicle was utilized to save Gwen Devereux and apprehend a killer. Apparently the guy refuses to wash the mud off the grille. Says it's like a badge of honor. I believe he used the term *street cred*."

Bell bit hard on her tongue to keep from laughing. Gardy faked an itch and covered his mouth with his hand.

Weber sat back in his chair with his fingers interlocked behind his head.

"Why are you still here?"

Gardy glanced at Bell.

"I don't understand. What happens now?"

Weber looked as if he chewed something sour. He gathered the papers together and slid the report across the table.

"What happens now, Agent Gardy, is you tighten up this report and resubmit by 0900 hours tomorrow morning. And this time choose your descriptions a little more carefully. Try not to make the BAU look like a clown car hurtling into a crowd of innocent bystanders."

Gardy slipped the report under his arm.

"And the second you're finished, you're to start on this."

Weber opened a drawer and produced a second folder. He handed it to Gardy, who opened the folder and scanned the documents. Bell saw Logan Wolf's name.

"Director Weber?"

Weber looked at Bell, annoyed she was still in his office. To this point he'd focused his vitriol on Gardy. He aimed his anger at her.

"Yes, Agent Bell?"

"Does this mean Agent Gardy and I are to continue working together?"

The Deputy Director's eyes were sharp when they fixed on Bell.

"For now, yes. I'm tasking the two of you with capturing Logan Wolf and ending this media frenzy once-and-for-all. Should you fail, the both of you will be scrubbing barnacles off ships at the marine fishery."

CHAPTER FORTY-TWO

At summer's end, the Chesapeake Bay is home to Ruddy Ducks, Sanderlings, and the Northern Gannet. On a quiet afternoon, should you stumble upon a slice of beach not overrun with tourists, you might encounter all three species plus a diverse number of other birds.

Bell broke the lease on her apartment and purchased a condo on the coast. It meant an extra half-hour commuting to Quantico, but she couldn't have made a wiser decision.

Thirty minutes before sunrise every morning, she rose early and ran along the water. Except for the occasional fisherman or person walking their dog, the beach was empty. Peaceful. She loved the feel of wet sand on the soles of her feet, the cool shock of the water when the tide rolled over her ankles.

Since moving to the coast Bell no longer required sleeping pills, and her sessions with Dr. Morford improved. The nightmares of Jillian Rossi's abduction rarely came to her these days, nor did the prevailing dream of a murderer chasing nine-year-old Bell along the creek. She hoped her childhood friend was finally at peace.

Learning Derek Longo's mother mentally and sexually abused her son came as no surprise. Young Derek was eventually removed from his home and placed with a great uncle shortly after his eighth birthday, but by then it was too late. The damage had been done, the first steps already taken down a dark pathway into madness.

The first week of September, when the summer heat slackened and the first Canadian geese of the season appeared, Bell received a phone call from Gwen Devereux. The conversation was awkward initially, Bell unsure what to say to the woman. Instead, she let Gwen talk, and slowly Bell was drawn into the conversation. Gwen was rebuilding along the South Carolina coast.

"Aren't you worried about hurricanes?"

Bell heard Gwen smiling through the phone.

"Storms don't frighten me, Agent Bell. Why cower from thunder when we can laugh in the rain?"

And yet storms had a frightening way of springing up unexpectedly. At any given time, between twenty-five and fifty serial killers were active in the United States.

Bell stood at the counter, slicing scallions as the black bass fillet seared in the pan. The sliding glass door to the third-story porch was open to the screen, allowing the salty ocean air to mingle with the succulent smells inside the kitchen. All was silent along the beach except for the gulls and the waves.

She tossed the scallions into a bowl and mixed in extra virgin olive oil, lime juice, and cilantro. When the mixture was to her liking, inspiration hit, and she shifted items in the food pantry until she located the poppy seeds. The perfect addition.

The bass was plated and topped, her mouth watering

from the smells, when the doorbell rang.

Bell peered through the peephole and was surprised to see a FedEx deliveryman outside her door. He was young for a deliveryman, in his mid-twenties at most.

She opened the door and he handed her an envelope. She scanned the return address and frowned. The letter had come from someplace called Red Falls, New York. The sender's name, William Friend, immediately struck her as fraudulent.

The man was halfway to the steps when she called him back.

"Are you certain this is for me?"

"You're Scarlett Bell, ma'am?"

"Yes."

He looked at her confused. She pointed at the sender's name.

"What I mean is I don't recognize the sender."

"It's probably from a marketing firm. I'm sorry to admit we deliver plenty of those. Do you want to return the letter?"

Bell held the envelope to her face and studied the name and address.

"No. I'm sorry for holding you up."

"Not at all. Have yourself a nice day."

She kept looking at the envelope as she shut the door and sat at the table. The food was getting cold, but Bell didn't think she could eat. Not until she read the letter.

She yanked the tab and tore the package open. The letter was nestled between two pieces of cardboard. She fished it out and read.

Dear Scarlett,

I trust life beside the sea has cleansed you of the nightmares. But not all dreams can be washed away by nature, nurture, or sleeping pills.

You spent your whole life running, Scarlett. Understand the monsters never stop chasing, and sooner or later you must catch your breath.

I can help you face the monsters, dear Scarlett.

One day soon, I should hope to know you better. We have so much to learn from each other.

Sincerely,
Logan Wolf

KILL SHOT

CHAPTER FORTY-THREE

The inside of the trunk is dark, save for the pinprick of circular light dotting his forehead. The trunk smells of spent fuel and old tires, the stench part of his skin.

The heat grows stifling. Makes it difficult to breathe. Outside, the California sky is a picturesque reflection of the Pacific. Students dart in erratic parabolas, and a crow squawks and picks at spilled french fries on the sidewalk.

He slides the muzzle through a drilled hole, and everything goes black inside the trunk. He places his eye to the scope and scans the students convening outside the James Arts and Sciences Building.

Four points intersect upon a circle in the scope. Perfection.

Most of the students disperse as two girls with backpacks hurry past the car. They can't see him, don't realize he conceals himself mere yards from them.

One student remains. Seated at the top of the concrete stairs, the boy leans against the building. He wears headphones, a backpack laid upon the ground beside him. His hair is brown and curly, skin tanned, a pair of sunglasses wrapped around his face as he checks his phone.

Inside the trunk, the shooter feels nauseous. Skin clammy like something dark and gelatinous crawled over his body. The scope frames the boy. From here, the shooter can almost see the boy's eyes and smell the oily vape scent on his sweatshirt.

A smirk spreads across the shooter's face. He imagines the boy in his dorm room shooting digital adversaries during a *Call of Duty* marathon.

This is not a game. The boy is about to find out.

The gunman's heart races. Makes his head swim and feel unnaturally light, as though it might float away if he opens the trunk. He knows this is bad. He must calm himself and make his heart rate slow.

He breathes deeply. Exhales.

Checks the scope again. Finger twitches on the trigger. The sitting target hasn't moved.

The time of truth arrives. If he doesn't go through with the shot, he never will. He'll return to his home as a nobody, another failure who doesn't follow through with plans and promises.

The shooter prepared for this day and spent months practicing. His aim is exemplary.

Across the parking lot, a vehicle with a loud motor approaches. Music thumps through the windows. The rock-and-roll guitars rattle his chest.

He times the beat. Waits for the bass kick. Squeezes the trigger.

The rifle bucks against his shoulder.

He swings the scope across the quad, then back to the

boy who sits in place. Did he miss? He couldn't have missed from this range.

He scans the sidewalk and sees a blonde girl remove her earbuds and glance around in alarm. To her, it might have been a vehicle backfiring or someone setting off a firecracker. When the blast does not come again, she cautiously sticks the earbuds in and looks around one more time before moving on.

The gunman watches the boy slump over as though asleep. Blood trickles out of the hole in his stomach.

Red hate courses through the shooter's veins. Nobody notices the dead boy. The world is a desensitized animal that deserves to be put down.

Slowly, the shooter cracks the trunk open. The lot is empty of people. Vacant and lifeless.

He slips out of the trunk and ducks beneath the car tops, then slides behind the wheel and cranks the engine.

The air conditioner blows hot air against his face as he backs the car out of its parking space. He is halfway across the lot when the first scream shatters the day.

CHAPTER FORTY-FOUR

The sun was down, and the purple-blues of dusk tinted the darkening sky over the Chesapeake Bay.

An ocean breeze played through the screen door as Special Agent Scarlett Bell sat at the kitchen table, her partner, Neil Gardy, leaning over the letter. Gardy wore latex gloves. His forefinger and thumb clutched the corner of the note.

Two hours had passed since the FedEx delivery boy handed the envelope to Bell. She'd had no idea who the sender, who referred to himself on the return address as William Friend, truly was. Nothing could have prepared her for the shock of learning the letter came from the nation's most notorious murderer, Logan Wolf, a former Behavior Analysis Unit special agent who butchered his wife and became a serial killer. For five years, Wolf had eluded the FBI, including his former BAU colleagues charged with tracking him down.

"Here, slip these on," Gardy said, handing her an extra pair of gloves.

"But I've already touched the letter. My prints are all

over the envelope."

"Humor me."

Bell read the letter again, as frightened and confused as she'd been after she tore the envelope open.

Dear Scarlett,

I trust life beside the sea has cleansed you of the nightmares. But not all dreams can be washed away by nature, nurture, or sleeping pills.

You spent your whole life running, Scarlett. Understand the monsters never stop chasing, and sooner or later you must catch your breath.

I can help you face the monsters, dear Scarlett.

One day soon, I should hope to know you better. We have so much to learn from each other.

Sincerely,
Logan Wolf

"He seems to know a lot about you, Bell. What's this about nightmares and sleeping pills?"

During her first year as a BAU special agent, Bell didn't divulge her childhood trauma to Gardy. She brushed the blonde hair away from her face and set the letter down. The time came to be truthful with her partner.

"When I was nine-years-old, my best friend was abducted and murdered."

He watched her silently, eyes inquisitive as if seeing her for the first time. In his middle-forties, her dark-haired partner was among the most experienced and respected field agents in the BAU.

"Her name was Jillian. For about two years we were inseparable. The neighborhood kids claimed they'd seen a stranger down by the creek, but we played there a lot and never saw anything. It felt like those urban legends kids tell each other. They wanted to scare us. The creek was a shortcut between our house and Jillian's, so when she left after dinner, I didn't think much of it when Jillian headed toward the water."

Bell was quiet for a time. Living by the ocean seemed to wash away the old nightmares, lent her a peace she hadn't experienced in the twenty-three years since Jillian's murder. Now the old feelings were back, the sense of dread she couldn't shake.

"Mrs. Rossi called my mother after Jillian didn't come home. I realized what had happened as soon as I heard Mom's voice in the kitchen. It was almost deja vu. As if I'd recognized all along something bad would happen to Jillian."

She slid the letter across the table. It came to rest, harsh and glaring beneath the kitchen light.

"You were a kid, Bell. Don't blame yourself."

Bell shrugged and rested her chin on her palm, eyes tilted warily at the note as if it were a sleeping tarantula.

"They found her body dumped along the creek bed. I didn't want to believe it was true. The calling hours were more like a weird dream than something real. The body in the casket didn't look like Jillian. It was someone else. A mistake. A few weeks later the nightmares started. In the dream she was at my house, ready to leave, and I tried to tell her not to walk by the creek. Kids saw a stranger and it was too dangerous. But the words wouldn't come out. Other times I dreamed the stranger chased me along the creek. I always woke up when he grabbed me. That nightmare won't die."

She didn't tell him Jillian's death was her impetus for becoming a BAU agent—the unwavering stare across the table told her Gardy already knew—nor did she divulge the nightmares were so frequent she no longer recalled if the abductor had truly chased nine-year-old Bell or if she'd only dreamed it happened. A year of therapy and hypnosis with Dr. Morford yielded no conclusive answer.

He picked up the letter and leaned it toward her.

"How could Logan Wolf know any of this?"

Bell shook her head. A serial killer had uncovered her address and intimate details about her life.

Gardy carefully slipped the letter into a plastic bag and zipped it shut.

"We don't have a choice. We need to bring this to Weber."

Bell bristled. The Deputy Director of the Criminal Incident Response Group was the last person Bell wanted involved with the case. He despised Bell, didn't trust female agents. Now he'd learn her secrets and use them against her.

"In the meantime, I want an agent watching your condo at all times."

"What? No. That isn't necessary, Gardy."

He closed his eyes and inhaled.

"It *is* necessary. This isn't a run-of-the-mill criminal we're talking about. This is Logan Wolf. And he knows where you live."

"He won't come after me."

Gardy turned the letter in Bell's direction.

"Oh? So this is just fan mail, I assume."

"The vibe I get isn't that he wants to hurt me."

"I hope you aren't buying this *dear Scarlett* nonsense."

"Of course, not. He's trying to put a scare into me. Considering everything he learned about me, he probably found out we're tasked with capturing him."

"All the more reason to take one of us out of action. We're not doing things your way this time, Bell. A killer like Logan Wolf. It's way too dangerous."

Bell slouched in her seat. In one fell swoop, Wolf had stolen her idyllic home and dredged up her worst nightmares.

Gardy's phone rang. He held her eyes as he answered.

Indignant and frustrated, Bell rose from her chair and padded to the refrigerator. The fish dinner was plated inside and covered with plastic wrap. She picked at the cold meal, wondering how this evening could have gone so wrong. The wind through the screen ruffled Bell's hair and suddenly made her feel vulnerable. She crossed the living room and shut the sliding glass door. The ocean sounds disappeared.

"That was Weber," Gardy said as he pocketed his phone.

Had Gardy told Weber about Wolf?

"There was a murder at an arts and sciences university called Vida College. Ever heard of it?"

Bell cupped her elbows with her hands and rubbed away the chill.

"It's just outside of Los Angeles, isn't it?"

"You know your universities."

"A friend of mine went there for dance. What are we looking at?"

"A male student was shot in the head. Appears to be a

sniper situation."

"Jesus."

"Yep. The college requests BAU assistance. Plane leaves Dulles at 11:35."

Bell looked at the clock. That gave her a half-hour to pack and another hour for the commute.

"Okay, I'll meet you at the terminal at—"

"Oh, no. I'm not leaving you alone."

She huffed.

"This is crazy, Gardy."

"Is it? Just because Wolf sent a letter doesn't mean he isn't in the area."

Bell walked to the window and looked down at the beach. Footprints trailed along the water.

"You're overreacting."

Gardy folded his arms and leaned against the table.

"Maybe so, but I'm not leaving until you're safely out the door. And since I need to stop at my apartment, too." He glanced at his watch. "That gives you fifteen minutes."

"Fifteen minutes? That's not enough time."

He rolled his eyes.

"Women."

"Excuse me?"

Gardy gave his Muttley-the-cartoon-dog snicker, amused by the incredulity twisting her face.

"The clock is ticking."

She stomped to the bedroom and threw a few changes of clothes into her travel bag. In the bathroom, she grabbed toiletries and the bottle of sleeping pills. On the way out of the bedroom, she flicked off the light and stood in darkness for a moment. Still and quiet. She could see Gardy's shadow on the kitchen floor as his worry blanketed the room.

He led the way to the parking lot. Night settled over the coast, the sickle moon sharp.

Bell took one look at the minivan and chuckled.

"What?"

"A Honda Odyssey?"

"So?"

"What are you, a soccer mom?"

He clicked the key fob. The minivan chirped and flashed its taillights.

"It's functional and roomy."

She recalled the Accords they'd rented on their last two cases.

"I knew it. You really do own stock in Honda."

"Are you getting in or not?"

The overnight bag thrown over her shoulder, Bell opened the door and climbed in.

"If you hand me a bag of Capri Sun, I'll kick your ass."

CHAPTER FORTY-FIVE

The Vida College Dean of Students, Dana Steinman, walked briskly across the quad toward the white-and-gray-faced Arts and Sciences building. Bell and Gardy flanked Steinman. The students cut a wide berth around the trio.

"Nobody expects something like this to happen here," Steinman said. Bell saw her purposely look away from the blood-stained slab of concrete above the steps. "I'm getting pressure from parents to close the school, and we're only a few weeks from midterms. This is a small liberal arts college. How is this possible? We don't experience the political discourse you expect at a larger university."

Bell turned sideways to avoid three students who stared at their phones while they walked.

"Has that been a problem at Vida College? Political discourse?"

"Last April a fringe group called the White Wall shouted down students attending the spring diversity festival. No physical violence. Just a lot of posturing."

Gardy climbed the steps and knelt beside the red splotch of concrete.

"Seems strange such a group is allowed on campus."

"We don't allow hate speech on campus, Agent Gardy," Steinman said, her glare sharp. "Frankly, their view of the world makes me sick, but so far they've done nothing more than attend rallies and make themselves seen."

High atop the steps, Bell overlooked the quad. The air felt searing as if the devil breathed between the buildings. She expected campus protests and students rallying together. Instead, everyone walked with their heads down and scurried from one building to the next as if they feared another shot would slice through the momentary peace.

"But the White Wall might be involved," said Bell.

Despite the warm end to summer, Steinman rubbed the chill off her arms.

"The thought occurred to me. The boy the shooter targeted, Eugene Buettner, volunteered at the Cultural Diversity Center."

"Was he particularly outspoken?"

"If by outspoken you mean did he advocate for minority students at Vida College, then yes. Students should express themselves freely without fear of backlash."

"Dean Steinman, has a member of the White Wall ever pushed the limit on what the college finds acceptable? Maybe he or she runs a private website. An inflammatory manifesto out of the college's jurisdiction."

Steinman thought for a moment.

"No, not that I know of, but I'll make it a point to have our IT department look into their activities."

Gardy snapped a series of photographs on his phone and turned to survey the quad.

"What about campus security? Have they zeroes in on

where the shot was fired from?"

"I'm afraid our security department is rather small
and unequipped to deal with an investigation of this
magnitude, which is why we lean on the village police for
support. Speaking of which, here comes Detective Ames
now."

An African American woman in a beige suit hurried
up the steps. She wore a scowl as the wind tossed her curly
hair around.

"Sorry I took so long. Traffic is a bear. You must be
Agents Gardy and Bell."

Ames shook both of their hands and nodded at
Steinman.

"Cheryl," said Steinman, moving aside to make space
for the detective. "Our office is swamped, and I should get
back."

"Of course."

"Call if you need anything. Agents Gardy and Bell,
thank you for affording us your expertise. Please let me
know what you find."

They watched the dean judiciously descend the steps.
Her heels clicked and echoed off the walls, a lonely sound.

Gardy turned to the detective.

"What can you tell us about the White Wall?"

Ames appeared as if she wanted to spit.

"Misguided degenerates, each and every one of them.
Their leader is a senior named Kyle Hostetler. We rang
him up last year for speeding through a residential area,
but otherwise, he's squeaky clean."

"You don't think he is, though."

"Nothing sticks to him. Agent Gardy, he believes
people of my race shouldn't hold power because we don't

have adequate mental facilities. Idiots like Kyle Hostetler are what's wrong with the world. Take the diversity festival last year. The students organized a rally but complained members of the White Wall physically impeded them from taking part. Hostetler was there the entire time, and several people witnessed him organizing his minions, yet Hostetler managed to vanish when the trouble started."

Bell leaned against the wall, arms folded.

"That's interesting. The dean claimed no violence took place."

Ames laughed without mirth.

"Depends on your definition of violence. Is hostility violence? How about intimidation? It's easy to paint statistics in a better light by subjectively altering definitions."

"Sounds like the college turns its head away from problems."

"It's not that the college doesn't do enough to curtail intimidation, but they brush incidents under the rug to maintain their image."

The steps became crowded as multiple classes dismissed. A brunette female squinted at the sun and pulled out her earbuds. She hesitated when she saw Bell.

"I hope you find the monster who did this."

Bell squeezed past Gardy and moved closer to the girl.

"We'll do our best. Did you notice anything yesterday?"

"Yeah. I was across campus. I work in the student center at the cafe. I heard the blast, but I figured it was a car backfiring."

"Did you know Eugene Buettner?"

"Sure. I mean...not personally, but he was active on campus."

"Did he have problems with members of the White Wall?"

The girl shifted her feet.

"I'm not sure. I hope you kick them off campus. It was a matter of time before they turned violent."

The girl pulled a knit beanie over her head and blended in with the departing crowd.

Bell joined Gardy, who surveyed the environment. The theater and literature buildings bordered the quad, and two dorms stood further down the walkway. The dorms interested Bell most. Plenty of open windows with good views of the stairs. Yet a gun blast would attract attention if fired from the dorm.

Detective Ames seemed to sense Bell's theory.

"We canvased both residence dorms. Most everyone heard the gunshot but said it came from farther away."

Partially shielded by a small grove of trees, a parking lot butted up against the end of the quad.

"Now, that's a possibility," Gardy said, bringing binoculars to his eyes.

Bell nodded.

"Good sight line on Buettner's location, plus the trees offer concealment."

The detective's phone rang. She walked a few steps away as Bell ran her eyes between the parking lot and the stairs. A minute later, Ames pocketed her phone and returned.

"That was the ME. Now is a good time to discuss the autopsy report. I'm headed to the coroner's office if you want to follow me."

"We'll check out the parking lot and meet you there," said Gardy.

Ames nodded and hurried across the quad.

CHAPTER FORTY-SIX

The County Coroner's Office is a rectangular, beige chunk of concrete that looks as if a brick fell from the sky and landed at the edge of Milanville, California. Inside, the examination room is long and blindingly bright, the floor plan broken up by silver tables.

The ME, Paul Canon, was busy working on the Buettner boy when Gardy and Bell arrived with Detective Ames. Canon's hair was snow-gray, bald on top, and he sported a pencil mustache which appeared straight out of a black-and-white mystery. He moved in slow, precise steps as he rounded the table and passed a circular dish to Gardy.

"The bullet went through the stomach and lodged in Buettner's spine."

Gardy whistled.

"That's a 0.50 caliber BMG round. Our shooter means business."

He handed the dish to Ames, who studied the bullet under the light with Bell. Though Bell didn't touch the round, she noted its size—large enough to stretch across her palm. A miniaturized missile.

Ames raised her eyebrows.

"Yikes. What's he shooting, an M80?"

"A Barrett M82 sniper rifle fired this round, to be specific."

Bell and Ames gaped at him.

"I'm a bit of an enthusiast," said Gardy. "But I don't own one myself."

"What's the range on the M82?"

Gardy took the dish from Ames and handed it back to the ME.

"It's not the range so much as the damage. An M82 in the hands of a capable shooter will take down communications equipment, disable aircraft, and punch holes in an armored vehicle."

"So he's not using it to hunt deer."

"Not unless the deer is driving a Chieftain tank."

They stared at him again. He opened his mouth and Ames said, "I know, you're an enthusiast."

The day was hot and arid when they came outside after the autopsy.

Ames placed her hands on the small of her back and stretched.

"Based on the evidence, what do we know about our shooter?"

In the distance, downtown shimmered like a mirage in the heat.

"The killer lacks empathy for others," said Bell. "That much is clear from the murder and the weapon used. In our experience, shooters are similar to other serial killers who tend to be loners. He's never had power during his life, and now he exerts control over his world through violence."

"Rage built inside this guy for a long time," said Gardy as Ames swung her eyes to him. "Yet he didn't act until now. Something set him off."

"What's our next step?"

"I'd like to get Kyle Hostetler into the interview room," said Bell.

Ames grinned.

"I like your way of thinking, Agent Bell. I've been waiting to nail his ass to the wall for four years."

"In the meantime, run a ballistics check on the round and see what comes back."

"Already on it."

The sun was in their eyes when they turned to their vehicles curbside. A rifle shot exploded. Bell hit the ground as Gardy covered the detective. Ames dragged the radio to her mouth and called for backup as the day went eerily silent.

"Stay down," Gardy said.

He motioned the others to crawl toward the rented Subaru Outback.

When they made it to the Outback, they sat with their backs to the door, guns drawn as a stream of cars passed. No further shots came. Shortly after, the wail of approaching sirens screamed from the center of the village.

Bell crept out, using the grille as a shield.

"Get back."

Gardy glared at her, but Bell swung the gun around the corner and saw no shortage of hiding places.

A stand of trees in a park across the street. A vacant building with two broken windows. A five-story apartment complex, and a train of parked cars along a side street.

Feeling exposed, she ducked next to Ames and Gardy.

The detective's voice quivered when she spoke.

"Thank God, he missed."

Bell wasn't so sure.

"He didn't miss. The shooter sent us a message."

CHAPTER FORTY-SEVEN

William Meeks pulls the black, cut-out circle of aluminum out of the hole in the trunk. A spotlight of sunshine beams through the opening and cuts the darkness.

The shooter doesn't know whether to laugh or panic, and what emanates from his chest is a choked giggle that sounds frighteningly loud in the confines of the trunk. He can't believe he fired at the officers. Wonders where he summoned the courage. He thinks they're local cops, but two of them might be FBI.

The plan is perfect. The entire Milanville Police Department is en route to the County Coroner's Building on the other side of the village. Downtown belongs to him now.

He brings his eye to the scope and centers on a young woman breastfeeding on a park bench. A boy with facial piercings rides a skateboard down the sidewalk, and an elderly man stumbles out of the boy's way. The man resumes sweeping the sidewalk in front of a flower shop after the boy passes.

Sitting ducks. All of them.

Light and shadows shift on the street as a cloud drifts overhead. The wind carries a strange myriad of scents into the trunk—baked concrete, flowers, exhaust fumes. He chews his nails. Knows it is a filthy habit, but he can't stay calm.

A Mexican couple pushes a pair of strollers down the sidewalk. The scope centers on one carriage, then the next. He imagines the outrage and terror that will follow if he pulls the trigger. Such an act will prove he knows no boundary. No one is safe.

Meeks recalls the long days spent in the mountains. Target practice honed his aim, made it razor sharp. Yet it couldn't replicate aiming the scope at a living person, didn't capture the intensity of knowing a good Samaritan with a gun might shoot back.

This is what a professional athlete feels, he thinks. To hit a one-hundred mph fastball while thousands of people scream. Grab the football and run over a weaker player with the television camera fixed on you. It's a good pressure. Separates the men from the boys.

He swings the M82 toward a grassy island set in the medium. A balding father sits on a park bench with his toddler son. The boy holds a cheap model airplane and repeatedly flies it across his vision. Meeks imagines the pretend propeller sound, focuses the scope on the child's exposed belly and touches the trigger.

The trunk becomes hot again. Not stifling, but uncomfortable. He exhales and puts the rifle down. Opens the laptop beside him and scans the latest news. The Vida College shooting dominates the headlines. As he pages through the articles, he realizes the police and media are no closer to finding him than they were when he killed the

Buettner boy. No news yet of the shot fired toward the officers, but the media will pick up the story soon.

He minimizes the web browser and checks the GPS program. Studies his position and escape route. Knows where to drive if the operation goes south.

The din of voices brings his head around as he closes the laptop. A movie lets out, and dozens of people stream from the Milanville Cineplex down the street.

Two women laugh beside the car. He didn't see them coming.

Quickly, he removes the muzzle and fumbles in the dark for the round piece of aluminum. Covers the hole and blankets the trunk in darkness. Waits patiently as they scuffle along the sidewalk, moving away from the car.

He doesn't like that they approached the car without him knowing. Only being able to see in one direction makes him edgy, turns the interior of the trunk a shade hotter and makes it difficult to breathe. His fingers are sweaty. He should install a fan and run the power off the cigarette lighter.

Meeks can't wait much longer. He pops the aluminum plug out and puts his nose to the opening. Breathes the fresh air. His pulse returns to normal.

Movement on the sidewalk causes Meeks to scoot toward the back of the trunk and bring the muzzle up.

Peering through the scope, he spies a white businessman with a Bluetooth ear-piece strutting past the movie theater. This is the man the shooter seeks. A representative of consumerism and profiteering.

He reminds Meeks of the pudgy, graying banker who denied his loan. One year from profitability, and now this. This is how the world works. You come from nothing, are treated like a nobody, and the world ensures you stay in your box. Wrapped in a neat little package so people of privilege can kick you down the street and toss you in the garbage when they're finished.

The man sneers while he speaks. People look at him oddly as he struts past, seemingly speaking to ghosts.

The snide businessman's progress takes him behind a mailbox and a line of parked cars. Meeks curses and chews his lip, tastes the copper trickle down his tongue. It takes several seconds before the man emerges from cover. Meeks will lose his angle if he doesn't act.

The angle isn't right. Trees planted along the sidewalk obscure the shot.

He breathes. Waits.

The moment comes.

Meeks pulls the trigger.

The sound after the blast is akin to a jet plane shooting into the heavens. A murderous Doppler effect.

The businessman's chest explodes in a shower of red, the force hurling him against a plate-glass window. The panicked screams begin as the man flops down into a seated position, legs splayed stupidly as though he decided to rest there a while. He isn't dead yet. Unlike the movies where death is as instantaneous as the final credits, it will take a while for the man to die. The man's chin drops to his chest. He looks at the gaping hole, unable to lift his arms as the blood pumps and pumps.

Most of the bystanders drop to the pavement or seek shelter inside stores. They are not safe behind a thin layer of glass. An elderly woman writhes in the gutter, trampled by the fleeing cowards. Her moans carry to the car, a whine like the bleating of cows.

Meeks removes the Barrett M82 from the bipod and lays the semi-automatic rifle on its side. Squishes his eye into the opening and watches people vapidly zigzag around swerving vehicles. Others climb into their own vehicles and escape the riot.

Amid the confusion, he pops the trunk open to a sliver. No one watches.

Quietly, he pushes through the gap and clicks the trunk shut.

Meeks is behind the wheel when the sirens begin.

CHAPTER FORTY-EIGHT

A call-in radio program played in the background as Gardy drove the Outback into downtown. The glare against the windshield made it difficult for Bell to read her tablet, which spilled out updates from the Milanville Police Department.

"I wish he wouldn't say that," Bell said. The caller, a self-proclaimed anti-gun activist, referred to the shooter as a nobody, a coward who didn't have the balls to fight another man face-to-face. "All he's doing is instigating the shooter."

Gardy clicked the turn signal and coasted onto Thompson Avenue.

"I doubt our shooter requires instigation. He's doing well without it."

Now the caller complained the president, senate, and congress were bought and paid for by the NRA, then called for a national uprising to overthrow the government.

Thompson emptied onto Main Street where a swarm of flashing lights swirled and colored the blacktop. There was no way to force the Outback through the massing

243

emergency vehicles. Bell pointed at an empty space along the curb.

"Pull over here."

Noticing the space at the last second, Gardy backed up and executed a flawless parallel park between two compact cars.

"Not bad," said Bell. "The old guy's still got it."

"Did you expect anything less?"

As they walked toward the crowd, the horrific scene took shape. Bell cringed. A bloody sheet covered the body on the stretcher. It almost looked like a prop from a Halloween store, too many red stains to be real. One arm, clad in a blue suit jacket and adorned with a gold watch, stuck out from beneath the sheet. Matching dress shoes poked out, angled askew from each other. A woman cried beside the stretcher. His wife, Bell figured. It hurt to look at her. Bell busied herself watching the police push the crowd back.

The crime techs assessed a portion of sidewalk secured by roadblocks and a crisscross of yellow police tape which jiggled when the wind blew. Two of the techs lined up the shot trajectory with the murder spot and pointed behind Bell and Gardy. Bell instinctively glanced over her shoulder and saw empty sidewalk and a row of brownstone apartment houses.

Bell spotted two ambulances and an armored police truck. Dozens of police officers worked the crowd, several from neighboring townships. Adding to the confusion, the media aimed cameras as reporters shouted questions and tried to muscle past the line of officers.

"There's Canon," Bell said.

The ME stood beside Detective Ames, who'd gotten

to the murder site a few minutes before Bell and Gardy. Canon noticed them and nodded once, then turned back to Ames.

Bell split off from Gardy when they reached the emergency vehicles. While Gardy talked with Ames and Canon, Bell walked Main Street. She closed her eyes and inhaled deeply, and when she released her breath, the chaos seemed to clear, lending her a calm lucidity.

Her eyes opened to an alternate view of Main Street, one in which shoppers carried bags and people milled in front of the cafe and movie theater. A bicyclist rode past, and a family played with their children on the grassy island.

All targets.

Bell took a step backward and envisioned bystanders seen through a scope. She was too close. The shooter set up farther away.

Following the curb, she walked half a block and turned around. This was the area the crime techs targeted. Several open parking spaces marked where the killer could have hidden. Inside the trunk, she theorized. Like the D.C. snipers, who killed seventeen people before they were captured.

The unknown subject's body count stood at two. She couldn't imagine another fifteen murders.

It would be uncomfortable inside the trunk. Cramped. Not much room to maneuver the Barrett M82. The killer would need to scrunch against the back of the trunk unless he removed the back seat. The muzzle would fit through a hole. If the entire village kept their eyes open, someone might spot a car with a hole drilled in the trunk.

The killer used a vehicle for concealment. No other

option made sense.

Yes, the roofs, open windows, and sidewalk afforded the shooter excellent vantage points. But someone would notice the unknown subject after he fired the gun. Among a throng of people running for their lives, it would be impossible to miss someone with a sniper rifle.

She entered his mind, rushing forth where angels fear to tread, and pictured the businessman with the dark blue suit walking down the sidewalk. Did the killer know the man? Why him and not someone else?

Bell visualized the scope targeting the businessman's chest, the four lines converging on a circle, the feel of the trigger against her finger. She sensed the cloying darkness of the shooter's seclusion.

In her mind, she pulled the trigger. The man's chest erupted with blood as the massive 0.50 caliber round punctured his heart. What level of hate did it take to kill an innocent man?

She shuddered. Felt a little sick like something crawled into her stomach and died.

LDSK. A long distance serial killer. The official definition described his character. Not a sniper, a hero who defends the public, but a serial killer who murders from a distance. And he was just getting started.

A news reporter with a camera slipped around the barricades and rushed up to her. He took Bell's picture as she glared at him.

"What do you know about the shooter, Agent Bell?"

The bastard knew her name.

"How similar is he to Derek Longo? Would you call the shooter a serial killer?"

The cops spotted the reporter and forced him back to

the sidewalk as he continued to shout questions over their shoulders.

"Is it true Alan Hodge almost murdered you in Coral Lake and that you broke his neck?"

Bell didn't look at him as she hurried toward Gardy and Ames.

Gardy raised his eyebrows at her approach.

"Find anything?"

"He's copying the DC snipers."

CHAPTER FORTY-NINE

His heart races. Pulse thrums with the cold attack of adrenaline.

William Meeks guides the black Lincoln MKS through a glut of traffic as he escapes the city center. The memory of the kill, the explosion when the 0.50 caliber bullet opened a hole in the businessman's chest, makes him light-headed. Dizzy.

The world moves at hyper-speed, and he seems to look at too many things at once—

The city buildings and interspersed apartments. Vehicles sweeping past and darting around the MKS. People talking excitedly on the corner.

About him.

Horns blare as he drives headlong into oncoming traffic. Meeks cranks the wheel and darts into his lane. His arms shake, and he can't slow his breathing. He's bitten his thumbnail down to the quick.

Yet he realizes the shootings have gone better than expected. Easy. He can kill for weeks and months, and no one can stop him.

The light turns red, and he brings the car to a stop on the edge of the crossing lane. He reaches for the radio dial when a male traffic cop with a thick mustache crosses in front of the grille. The cop locks eyes with Meeks.

Reaching across the seat for the M82, Meeks realizes the rifle is in the trunk. Nothing to defend himself with. The cop continues to stare as Meeks edges his toe onto the gas pedal. He'll run the son-of-a-bitch down if it comes to it.

Then the cop turns and waves a group of pedestrians into the crosswalk. Meeks breathes again.

When the drive resumes, he recalls the first time he shot the M82 upon the forested mountain several miles outside of Milanville. He placed a dummy fifty yards away, an easy shot for a beginner. The recoil stung his shoulder, but it wasn't as bad as he expected. The bullet shredded the dummy's abdomen, a sound like a bomb detonating beneath a pillow. Then he shot from seventy-five yards, one hundred yards. Kept moving the target into the distance until he mastered the shot.

He doesn't understand how he reached this point in his life. When Meeks was young, he spent his days in front of the television while his father worked. The mother died giving birth to Meeks, and he never thought about who she was or what life might be like had she lived. There were photographs, but they meant nothing to him. Like looking at pictures of strangers in a magazine.

Meeks didn't have friends. The gray farmhouse was six miles from town, the nearest neighbors an elderly couple a half-mile up the road.

The first time he killed an animal he was twelve. Walking the perimeter of their farmland, Meeks heard the shrill cries and parted the bushes. A fawn lay on its side, leg broken and skewed in the wrong direction. He watched it for a long time before he dropped the rock on its head. On the way home, he convinced himself it was an act of mercy. His conscience knew better.

He passed through school as the invisible man, grades a tick below average, no clubs, no sports, not a hint of trouble. Once, shortly after community college graduation, he stumbled into Mr. Davidson, his senior year English teacher and one of the few educators who made an impression on young William Meeks, at a bar outside of San Jose. Davidson politely feigned forgetting his name, snapping his fingers as though it lay on the tip of his tongue. Meeks knew the truth. Davidson had no idea who he was.

Traffic crawls to a stop at the edge of town. Horns honk as Meeks juts his head through the window, wondering what the hold up is. Not construction or an accident.

Overpopulation. Too many vehicles on the road. Throughout history, the human race was occasionally thinned by plague and natural disaster. It needs to be whittled down to a manageable number again.

The thump of hip-hop shakes the MKS before the Jeep pulls beside him. He can't see the man through the tinted windows, only his silhouette. The bass hurts his ears and sends a metronome of shock waves up his spine. Meeks stares at the man's shape and senses the driver glaring back. The window descends, and now he sees the driver. The boy is younger than Meeks expected, a hard challenge in his eyes.

Meeks brings his hand up, thumb and forefinger

extended into a faux gun, and points it at the driver. He pictures the crevice the M82 would open in the man's forehead and wishes he kept the gun in the front seat.

The light turns green, and Meeks punches the gas. Tires squeal as he shoots down the road. The Jeep accelerates until it is even with the MKS, the music louder, volume pushing the speakers to distortion. The driver has one hand on the wheel, the other on the door. Window down. An invitation to pull over and settle this.

Meeks grins and lifts his middle finger. The driver screams unintelligibly over the rap beat. The Jeep drifts in-and-out of its lane.

Looking forward, Meeks sees the line of stopped cars in the Jeep's lane and smiles. The driver notices too late and slams on the brakes. Tires squeal before the grille crushes the rear bumper of a red sedan. Meeks is laughing as he races out of the city and into suburbia. Laughs until tears stream down his cheeks. Distant mountains grow out of the land like dragon fangs.

The shootings are only the beginning. He needs more than this. Something larger.

People will remember his name forever.

CHAPTER FIFTY

Bell sat beside Gardy at a wobbly table in the Milanville Police Department's break room. Across the room, two male cops and a female officer huddled together and spoke in hushed tones, though Bell eavesdropped bits and pieces about the latest shooting.

Gardy dropped three quarters into the vending machine and punched a button, and the machine spat out a sugary pie wrapped in plastic.

Bell cocked an eyebrow.

"You're not serious about putting that into your body, are you?"

"I haven't eaten since breakfast."

"You'll get di-a-bee-tus. Haven't you listened to Wilford Brimley's warnings?"

The front door to the police station banged open when Ames brought Kyle Hostetler inside. Though the boy wasn't cuffed, the detective held a firm grip on his wrist like an angry teacher leading a misbehaving child to the principal's office. When Ames and Hostetler breezed past the doorway, Bell shared a look with Gardy and shot out of her seat.

Hostetler was alone in the interrogation room when the agents met Ames outside the door.

"No, he isn't under arrest, but he's damn well going to answer my questions."

Bell pulled Ames aside so the gawking officers at the end of the hall couldn't listen in.

"Maybe it would be better if we handled the interview."

Ames narrowed her eyes.

"I don't know about that."

"Look, you will be in the room with us, and if we miss something you can ask Hostetler anything you want. But let us have a go at him first. We haven't determined if he fits the profile."

"If your profile says asshole sociopath prick then Hostetler fits."

"Please, detective."

Ames looked between Gardy and Bell and shrugged.

"Okay. We'll do it your way, but I'm telling you Hostetler is the shooter."

The interrogation room was lit by LED flood lights, overkill for a small room. The table and six chairs, three on each side, consumed most of the space and made it a challenge to squeeze into the seats.

Hostetler sat alone in the middle seat. The detective and agents took up three seats across the table.

Initially, Bell was struck by Hostetler's hair. It was blonde and spiked, but the black roots were clear. The boy's t-shirt was white with RESIST written across the front in black letters. His neck was sunburned, and the term *redneck* crossed her mind as she opened the notebook to a blank page and clicked her pen.

The boy was cord-like. Thin yet strong. His eyes held theirs and displayed no fear.

Twenty-years-old, the boy possessed a surprisingly clean record. Except for the speeding ticket, Hostetler appeared to be an exemplary citizen.

Gardy winked at Bell. He placed full confidence in her to begin the interview.

"Hey, Kyle. Thanks for coming in."

Hostetler glared at Ames from the corner of his eye.

"Not like I had much of a choice."

"You're not under arrest, and nobody is forcing you to be here."

"It's fine. I didn't do anything wrong so ask your questions."

Bell pointed at his t-shirt.

"I like the shirt. Resist. What exactly are you resisting?"

"I know where you're going with this. You can stop right there because I'm not racist."

"That's good to know, but I never said you were. What about the White Wall? Are they racist?"

"The White Wall doesn't believe in racism. We want to keep what's ours, you see? But the government wants to give everything we've earned to illegal aliens who shouldn't even be in the country."

"But the wall in White Wall implies you wish to stop immigration. Seems rather restrictive."

Hostetler shrugged.

"It's not that immigrants are bad people. There's just too many of them. Picture America as an exclusive club. Everyone wants in, right? But if you let too many inside it gets overcrowded. At some point, you have to close the doors and tell people to go find their own club. They all end up on welfare when they get here, anyhow."

Ames chewed her lip as Bell continued.

"But that's not what's happening. Immigration hasn't stopped, and the population continues to grow. I bet that makes you angry."

"I'm not a violent person."

"You shoved students at the diversity festival."

"Did Dean Steinman tell you that? She'll do anything to get us kicked off campus. Check my record. I speak my mind, but I never hurt anyone."

Bell opened a folder and placed a picture of Eugene Buettner on the table.

"Did you know Eugene Buettner?"

Hostetler's mouth twitched.

"We had words a few times."

"At the festival?"

"Probably, yeah. We come from two different worlds. Not always going to agree. It's nothing personal."

"What did you argue about?"

"I don't remember. That was several months ago. Life moves fast."

"Did any of the White Wall members argue with Buettner?"

"Damned if I know. Just a lot of brats shouting at the tops of their lungs that day."

Bell slid the photograph in front of Hostetler.

"Eugene nearly quit school over the summer. His father was diagnosed with prostate cancer, and the mother has early onset Alzheimer's."

If Bell humanized Buettner in Hostetler's eyes, the

boy didn't show it.

"Sucks for him. We all have problems."

"He had a seven-year-old sister. How do you think she feels now that Eugene is dead?"

"She's probably sad. That doesn't have anything to do with me."

Bell flipped the page to her notes on the Buettner shooting.

"Where were you Thursday afternoon around three o'clock?"

Hostetler looked between the three people glaring at him and slowly nodded.

"Shit. You think I killed him."

"You admitted you had problems with Eugene."

"Not enough to shoot him. I don't even own a gun."

"Really? You seem like the outdoorsy type. Someone who hunts or partakes in target shooting."

"I skateboard and hike. Guns aren't my thing."

"What about the other members of the White Wall? Any of them own guns?"

"No…I mean, not that I know of."

"The college strictly bans firearms or weapons of any sort on campus."

"Yeah, and we don't keep weapons on campus. Look, we have almost twenty members. I don't know all of their hobbies or how they spend their weekends. Do you know everything your co-workers do in their spare time?"

"You haven't answered the question. Where were you Thursday around three?"

Hostetler leaned back and locked his fingers behind his head, a triumphant gleam to his smile.

"Chemistry lab. And yes, you can ask Professor

Baldwin."

"Okay, I will. I'd also like to look inside your car."

"Not without a warrant."

Bell glanced at Ames. The detective looked like her head might blow off her shoulders in a shower of sparks and fire. This probably wasn't the time to pull Ames aside and tell her Hostetler didn't fit the profile. The boy was a degenerate, but he wasn't a loner and didn't possess the hair-trigger fury required to shoot perceived enemies. Furthermore, Bell didn't require a warrant. If holes were drilled into the trunk they'd be visible from the outside. That the boy didn't want Bell snooping inside his car suggested either he possessed incriminating evidence unrelated to the case, perhaps a few joints, or he was being a pain in the ass.

Bell was about to turn the questions over to Gardy when her partner opened the folder and removed a photocopy of an M82 advertisement. He turned it face-down.

"Say, Kyle," Gardy said. "Obviously misconceptions exist regarding the White Wall."

"Obviously."

"And perhaps the fringe elements on campus, those capable of violence, contact your group from time-to-time."

"I don't know who those people are and wouldn't give them the time of day."

"Be that as it may, has anyone approached the White Wall about obtaining weapons? Guns, in particular."

Hostetler shifted in his seat. The room grew a degree warmer.

"Shouldn't I ask for a lawyer right about now?"

"You're not in trouble, Kyle."

He thought on the question, then shook his head.

"Never. As I said, we don't keep weapons—"

"Specifically, did someone request a Barrett M82?"

Gardy flipped the paper over and pushed it in front of Hostetler. The boy glared at it as though a rattlesnake coiled on the desk. His mouth moved in silence.

"What's that, Kyle? I didn't hear what you said."

"No. I don't know anything about guns." The room went uncomfortably quiet. "Can I go now?"

"Technically we can't keep you, so..."

Gardy shrugged and nodded at the door. Hostetler pushed his chair back and collided with the wall before scrambling out of the room.

As soon as the door shut Ames slapped her palms on the table and snarled.

"What the hell was that about? You let our number one suspect walk out the door."

Gardy gathered the papers and closed the folder.

"He doesn't fit the profile."

"That's ridiculous. He's a racist sociopath who—"

"The murders aren't racially motivated. Both victims are white."

"Buettner was an outspoken supporter of cultural diversity and stood up to the White Wall."

"What about the businessman? These aren't hate crimes. These are crimes of rage and opportunity."

Ames looked to Bell for support. Bell pocketed her phone.

"Gardy's right. And Hostetler has an alibi at the time of the shooting."

Ames bit her tongue.

"He knows something about the murders."

Scarlett Bell Books 1-5

CHAPTER FIFTY-ONE

Gardy's hotel room was ludicrously tidy. It didn't appear he'd checked in yet. The suitcase was tucked into the closet, the bedspread military-straight, and there were no signs of the half-drank water glasses which littered Bell's counter.

"Do you sleep in your car or something?"

Gardy grinned.

"I keep the room organized. You should try it sometime, Messy Marvin."

They'd stopped for coffee on the way back from the police department and discussed the profile again. Gardy agreed Hostetler couldn't possibly be the killer, but Bell made the call to the boy's chemistry professor to verify the alibi. It checked out.

"What bothers me most is the pace of the shootings," said Bell, falling into the lounge chair. She put her coffee cup on the table and Gardy frowned. "Two murders in two days, and I'm not counting the shot he took at us."

"He's accelerating. Whatever set him off, he won't stop until we catch him. And you should really use a coaster."

The DC snipers proved almost impossible to catch. As long as the unknown subject stayed hidden inside his trunk and carefully selected targets and escape routes, he'd remain as elusive as a phantom.

"So we should expect another murder in the next twenty-four hours."

Gardy's face was grim.

"Unless he possesses enough self-control to go underground for a while. At least until the fervor dies down. People see him on every corner, and the false alarm rate is already ridiculous. The next time he kills he runs a higher risk of being seen."

"Or someone shooting back."

"Yeah. That, too. Exactly what we need. Armed vigilantes squeezing the trigger every time someone cries wolf. I can't see him stopping. He has a taste for it now and wants to relive the first kill."

"Like chasing ghosts."

"Exactly my thought."

Bell gathered up her coffee.

"On that happy note, I think I'll head back to the room. I didn't sleep much last night."

"When was the last time you ate?"

She lifted the coffee cup.

"That's not food, Bell. You haven't eaten since breakfast, have you?"

"I'm not hungry."

"Come on. Let me take you out for dinner. We'll put the case notes away and pig out on cheeseburgers and greasy fries."

Bell's stomach lurched at the thought of heavy

comfort food forming a brick in her belly.

"Thanks, but I'll pass this time."

"Or something healthy. How about sushi or poke bowls?"

Nothing appealed to Bell. Gardy was right. She needed to eat or her body would shut down, yet she couldn't stomach food.

Against his better judgment, she retired to her room. Hers was gloomier than Gardy's, the drapes drawn with a slice of California sunshine permeating the edges. Housekeeping had made the bed, yet the bedspread was ruffled as if the blankets and sheets couldn't sit still. The overnight bag spilled clothes from the top. She noticed a pair of underwear hanging off the side and stuffed it into the bag in embarrassment. When did she become a slob?

She flopped onto the bed. Swirls were drawn into the white ceiling, making her think of wind eddies curling between mountains. Her eyelids felt heavy and wanted to close, but the case kept running inside her head, a wind-up toy she couldn't shut off.

The killer was the alpha dog now. The entire country, not just Milanville, feared him.

It wasn't enough. It would never be enough. He needed to prove his prowess again.

"On a larger scale."

Her voice was loud in the quiet hotel room. It surprised Bell, scared her a little.

The unknown subject might contact the police. Or maybe the media. She didn't expect a manifesto. No, he wanted to frighten the public, make certain they knew he was in charge.

Bell closed her eyes and felt sleep pull her into the

mattress. Each time her consciousness wavered some random thought jolted her awake.

Rubbing her eyes, she sat up and slapped the mattress. The light around the curtains had grown grayish-blue. It was almost dusk. Maybe she had slept for a while.

She shuffled to the bathroom and filled a glass with water. Drank it down in three gulps. Filled it again and took it slower this time, not wanting stomach cramps on top of insomnia.

The television remote lay on the coffee table. News about the shooter was the last thing she wanted to watch, let alone two talking heads debating the maniac's motivations. Instead, she padded to the curtains and pulled the cord. The drapes parted a few feet, enough for her to view the setting sun.

That's when she saw him.

Logan Wolf.

There. Among the trees bordering the parking lot. Staring at her with black eyes.

She stepped back from the drapes and into the shadows of the hotel room.

Blinked.

He was gone.

Bell ripped the cord until the curtains were completely open. Her breath fogged the glass as she pressed against the window and scanned the parking lot.

Nobody was there.

She stepped back from the window and saw the Glock-22 upon the dresser. Grabbing it up, she rushed to the door and unfurled the chain. Her hand was on the handle when she thought better of going after Wolf. Not alone.

Bell crept back to the window, careful to stay far enough back so Wolf couldn't see her. The parking lot was empty, save for sleeping vehicles. Darkness crawled out of the trees.

Had the serial killer been there at all?

Bell sat on the edge of the bed with her head buried in her hands. She was going crazy.

CHAPTER FIFTY-TWO

Gardy's stare was hard and unwavering. Bell sat across from her partner at a corner table, away from the crowd swarming the hotel's free breakfast buffet.

"What do you mean you *think* you saw Wolf?"

She picked at a bran muffin. The glass of orange juice sat untouched.

"It probably wasn't him. Look, I was exhausted and hadn't eaten since breakfast. It could have been anyone in the woods. One of the grounds crew, someone taking a walk. Hell, it might not have been anyone." She rubbed her eyes. "Dammit, I'm losing my mind."

Gardy put down his fork and touched her arm.

"Hey, look at me."

She did.

"You're not losing your mind. It's the letter, the case, the fight with your parents."

Bell hadn't spoken with her parents since they'd visited. She threw them out after her father espoused women weren't cut out for law enforcement.

"I don't know."

"But you should have come to me right away, Bell. If Wolf is following you—"

"How could he know where I am? It's not like the BAU advertises where their agents are headed. Oh, shit."

"What?"

"The reporter. The one hounding me after the second shooting. Gardy, he wrote about me."

Gardy pushed the waffle around with his fork. He appeared to lose his appetite, too.

"All right. It's probably nothing. You're under pressure, and as you said, you hadn't eaten. Easy to imagine seeing faces which are already in the backs of our minds. But just in case it was Wolf, I don't want you alone."

"Gardy, I still think we're overreacting."

"I'm not taking chances. You're staying in my room tonight."

She straightened her spine in surprise.

"What?"

"It's not a problem. The sofa pulls out into a sleeper, and I can—"

"Gardy, no."

"It's just for a few nights. Until we close this case."

Bell sighed.

"I don't like this. I'm a federal agent with a big honking gun. I can take care of myself."

"I know you can. That doesn't mean you walk blindly into a room without your partner watching the corners. Think about it. At the very least you'll have peace of mind. You'll sleep better."

She nodded absently. He stuffed a piece of syrupy waffle into his mouth and chewed.

"And now you're going to eat. I can't have you dragging behind me at half-speed when I take the shooter down."

Bell's eyebrows raised.

"Half-speed? Gardy, I can run laps around you."

"Prove it."

"Fine," she said, pushing back her chair.

He grinned victoriously as she joined the buffet crowd. She bit her cheek realizing he'd somehow fooled her into being hungry. Her stomach assailed her with anxious growls, and soon she loaded her plate with scrambled eggs, hash browns, a green-and-red pepper medley, and dear God, she found grits and gravy.

By the time she made it back to the table she was performing a balancing act, one hand carrying the overloaded plate, the other somehow gripping a bowl of grits and a toasted bagel.

"You know, Bell. You're allowed to make multiple trips."

"Shut it. I'm hungry."

As Bell shoveled the food into her mouth she caught him laughing.

It took a half-hour before Bell's stomach caught up to her brain. During that time, Gardy attempted to make another waffle and burned it to a crisp.

"That's what the alarm is for," Bell said. "When it beeps, the waffle is done."

"It's not so bad."

He scrunched up his lips and chewed the blackened monstrosity.

"This is why you need a girlfriend. You're not domesticated."

"The bachelor pad is spotless."

"And you eat dinners out of a box."

"Truth. Just keep your side of the hotel room clean. No underwear hanging out of the travel bag."

Her cheeks burned.

CHAPTER FIFTY-THREE

The Chief of Police, Rob Harrington, wore a graying beard and mustache over a ruddy face. Though Harrington gingerly tottered on feet which walked too many beats, his chiseled arms stretched the sleeves of his uniform.

A table served as the briefing room's focal point, and Bell was surprised to find it was a smart board when Harrington turned on the PC workstation. Floodlights were cut into the ceiling, but the room was plenty bright from late-morning sun beaming through the floor-to-ceiling windows.

Gardy had Harrington's ear off in the corner. The chief glanced in Bell's direction and nodded, then Gardy slid into the chair beside her.

Bell leaned toward her partner.

"What was that about?"

"Nothing, just going over the Hostetler interview."

Gardy didn't look at Bell when he spoke, something she found odd. He busied himself with the case notes while they waited for the meeting to begin.

Harrington manned the meeting from the head of the

table. Bell and Gardy took up two chairs on one side, while Detective Ames and three uniformed officers sat across from them. The arrangement made it seem like two different teams, a concept which bothered Bell.

Moving the mouse, Harrington clicked an icon and the smart board displayed a map of Milanville. Two red dots marked the kill sites.

Harrington led a brief round of formalities and introduced the players. The detective's hard eyes continued to fume over Hostetler.

"The anonymous tip line is up and running," Harrington said, sitting forward with his hands clasped on the table. "The phone number is plastered on the television news, so we're getting plenty of coverage. As you might expect the signal-to-noise ratio is running wild. Lots of erroneous reports, and the loonies are out in full force with their conspiracy theories. Regardless, we're manning the line twenty-four hours per day in the hope someone saw something important on the days of the shootings."

Gardy tapped his pen on the table.

"The shooter will call the tip line."

"Okay. What makes you think that?"

"He needs to interject himself into the search. Boast and show us he's the one in control."

"Additionally," said Bell. "The shooter's acceleration tells us he's at a breaking point. When the unknown subject kills civilians and contacts the department, he's demonstrating his power."

Harrington surveyed the room.

"Anyone object to the agents' profile?"

The three uniformed officers didn't budge, but Ames tossed her pen on the table.

"You already know how I feel about this, Chief. We interviewed the most likely suspect and let him walk."

Wonderful, Bell thought. The detective threw them under the bus.

Harrington switched the view and two images of the victims materialized.

"Are you certain the shootings are racially motivated? Both victims are white males."

"If Hostetler isn't the killer, he knows who is."

"We'll put that theory to the test this evening. Channel-12 is bringing in so-called experts to analyze and debate the shootings. The program will run live, including callers. To my ears, it sounds like a dog-and-pony show, but the program manager invited us to monitor the calls from their control room in the event the killer checks in."

Gardy rocked back in his chair.

"Will they allow a trace?"

"I'm working on that. She's not in favor of the idea. The lines are owned by the media, and there's a lot of hand-wringing over us monitoring their callers. But we've been good to her station in the past. We can work something out."

A tall officer with a shaved head and a face full of stubble raised his hand.

"Picard?"

"I suggest we contact campus security. If the shooter is a student, we can monitor messages originating from their network. That would bypass the television station."

"Not a bad idea except we can't confirm the shooter is a student or lives on campus. If he has an apartment, he'll use private broadband. That will take a long time to track unless Agent Gardy's connections get us national support."

"I'll call Quantico," Gardy said.

"Good. In the interim, we have our own tip line to monitor. Lots of lines cast. He's bound to bite one."

They stood when the meeting ended, the low murmur of voices rolling around the room. Bell was packed and ready to leave when Harrington approached.

"Agent Bell."

"Yes, Chief?"

"I'd like your assistance overseeing the tip line operation. We have half-a-dozen officers monitoring the calls, and frankly they don't have the experience to determine if a caller is our shooter."

Bell swung her eyes toward Gardy, who'd quietly moved to the other side of the table with the officers and Detective Ames. Was Gardy behind this?

"I'm happy to train the operators, but I feel I'm of greater benefit in the field."

"It's a matter of strategically deploying our resources. We have more than enough bodies to ferret out the shooter and take him down. You're our best profiler."

Bell bit her cheek as she nodded. Gardy was halfway out the door when she caught him.

"What the hell was that about?"

"What?"

"You know. Locking me in a call center for the duration of the case."

Gardy glanced around and lowered his voice while the others filed out of the room.

"Not for the duration of the case. Only until we find the shooter."

"Is this Harrington's plan, or did you plant the idea in his head?"

"Come on, Bell."

"Tell me the truth."

He sighed and studied the carpet.

"You're best qualified to identify the killer if he calls. And to be honest, you could use a break from fieldwork."

Her ears sizzled.

"Explain."

"The last few months have been rough. Hodge almost killed you, then you were knocked unconscious in a hurricane. Until this morning you hadn't eaten, and you're not sleeping."

She self-consciously rubbed the bags under her eyes.

"I can do my job, Gardy."

"Of course, you can."

"This is about Logan Wolf."

He pursed his lips and stared down the vacant hallway. The officers' voices were far away and unintelligible.

"I never should have told you I saw Wolf. Face it, there are only two possibilities. Either I saw him and you think I'm incapable of protecting myself, or I imagined the whole thing. Which makes me crazy."

"You're not crazy, and you're more than capable of defending yourself."

"Then talk to Harrington. Get me back in the field."

"He needs you to identify the shooter. *We* need you there."

Bell folded her arms. She didn't want to look at Gardy.

"Besides, if it really was Logan Wolf, it's a good idea to keep you around other officers."

"Stop trying to protect me, Gardy."

"I'm not. This isn't your father talking. If the situation were reversed, you'd want someone watching my back."

"Yes, and you'd refuse and be back in the field an hour later. I know how this works."

She bolted off the wall and stared straight ahead so he couldn't see her eyes well up.

"Where are you going?"

She didn't answer.

CHAPTER FIFTY-FOUR

Children giggle and shove each other around his legs. The inside of the fast food restaurant smells of grease, salt, and burned meat. The din of voices makes his head hurt.

The food is bad for Meeks, but he's too hungry to care. The scents cause his mouth to water. Pavlov's dog, unleashed and rabid.

The fat couple in front of him slide to the other end of the counter and await their meal. A pretty girl with a ponytail who looks no more than sixteen puts on an artificial smile, a trained monkey who grins on demand.

"May I help you?"

His brow is slick with sweat as he shuffles to the counter. Meeks knows he stinks. The day's excitement and cramped trunk have left ugly wet stains on the underarms of his shirt. She crinkles her nose when he reaches the counter but maintains the plastic grin. Inside his pocket is a multi-tool with a jackknife. He flicks it open with his thumb. Imagines plunging the blade through her ear. That would get rid of her smile.

"Sir?"

The girl looks uncertainly toward the back. A mustached man, probably the manager, battles to keep up with the endless stream of orders.

"I'd like a hamburger."

He doesn't remember wanting a hamburger. The words flow automatically as though he reads from a script. She turns back to him as his eyes blink. The girl tries to wear the costume smile again, but it no longer fits. She punches the order into the computer and leans over the microphone.

"One hamburger."

Moves her mouth away from the microphone.

"Anything else?"

Yes, he thinks. I'd like to open your throat and watch you twitch and bleed.

"A strawberry shake. And a large fries."

"Do you want to mega-size it?"

He doesn't know what the hell mega-size means, but it sounds good. Bigger is better. He nods slowly.

The girl glances at the manager again. He's busy berating an employee for screwing up an order. Shielding her hand from view, the girl locks eyes with a female coworker and points at Meeks, mouthing nervous words.

Meeks barely notices. He swivels around and takes in the restaurant. Over thirty people, some alone and suffering over their meals, others talking about football and the weather and other insipid topics. Families. Children crawling through tubes like rodents.

The M82 sits in the trunk. He can walk to the car and return with the rifle in seconds. Open fire on the women and children first. Let the world know how far he'll go.

"Excuse me, mister."

A middle-aged man wearing a Dodgers cap and a blue windbreaker looks at him expectantly. Meeks doesn't know what the man wants until he cocks his head to the side, a signal for Meeks to move down the counter so the man can order. Meeks proceeds to pick up his order and hears the man let out an exasperated breath.

Meeks glares at the man.

"You wanna say something?"

The man doesn't say shit.

The bag is open on the passenger seat when Meeks turns onto the thoroughfare. He stuffs handfuls of fries into his mouth and chews, washes the slop down with the shake. The sun is down, and the first stars gleam over the mountains as he cruises into suburban hill country. With Milanville behind him, Meeks opens the window and invites the fresh air inside. It blows his hair around, makes his sweat-slicked flesh tingle.

Chewing the rubbery hamburger, he thinks about the counter girl and the arrogant man in the baseball cap. If he turns the MKS around, they'll still be inside the restaurant. He can follow them, find out where they live.

He pictures shooting them from inside the trunk and feels dissatisfied. It's not personal enough.

Better to approach them. Out in the open. Revel in their terror when he aims the rifle.

The MKS coasts down a street lined with upscale homes. Bikes lay dormant on driveways. The night breeze carries the yells of children through his window. They aren't on the street. Probably playing in the backyards as death rolls through their neighborhood.

And that's when it hits him. Shoot a nameless businessman or out-of-town student and people reply, "It can't happen to me."

But kill them where they live and sleep, and they'll fear his name forever.

Meeks pulls to the curb and lets the car idle under a white alder. He pops the trunk, removes the M82, and places it on the passenger seat.

He's in dangerous territory. What if a cop drives by?

The thought sends a charge of energy through Meeks. Yes, bring the police. Bring the FBI. They'll all die at his hands.

Meeks pulls the M82 out of the dark when he spies the two teenagers.

CHAPTER FIFTY-FIVE

The dimly lit call center seated eight phone operators. Only three were currently at their posts, the others mingling in the hallway or grabbing food in the break room. The sun's glow descended behind the mountains, setting the western horizon afire.

Bell glimpsed the sunset and went back to her notes, tapping a pen against the table in thought. Upon arriving in California, she felt certain the shooter was a student. Mention of the White Wall ratcheted up her suspicions that an operative from a fringe campus group had gone rogue. Yesterday's murder in the center of town, along with the warning shot fired outside the County Coroner's Office, suggested it wasn't a student. The campus murder was one of opportunity.

That another murder hadn't occurred today didn't comfort her. It was a matter of time. A ticking bomb hidden within Milanville.

"You look like you could use a pick-me-up."

Megan handed Bell a cup of coffee and sat across from her. The female officer was a rookie with the

Milanville Police Department, fresh out of college, bright-eyed and enthusiastic.

"Oh, my God. You're a lifesaver. Thank you."

The cup warmed her hand, the aroma rich. She perked up before the steaming liquid reached her lips.

"Anything new on the shooter?"

Bell shook her head.

"Nothing yet."

"That's probably a good thing."

The call center felt like a waste of time and resources. Barely a dozen calls had come in since dinner-time, and those ran the gamut between paranoia and pranks. One caller, who sounded ten-years-old, claimed Billy the Kid was the killer. An elderly woman fretted over her neighbor, who suspiciously kept to himself and spent long evenings working in his garage. When Megan prodded for more details, she learned the woman and neighbor had a long-standing feud over the property line.

Most of the reports were false alarms as Bell predicted. Warn the community a killer is at-large, and they will see him in every shadow.

A large screen television on the wall displayed Channel-12's special on the Milanville shootings. A Berkley psychology professor named Thompson was on the screen. The audio was set low.

Bell could have screamed if Gardy were in the room. All evening she had the sensation of something important happening on the horizon. The cramped room and shriek of the telephone made matters worse.

She checked her phone and saw no messages. Dammit, Gardy.

The phone rang at Megan's station. She gulped her

coffee and held up a finger. Bell followed the officer to her station and sighed when it became apparent it was another dead end call.

"You really think he'll call? The shooter?"

Bell's shoulders slumped. No, she wasn't sure of anything.

"Yes, sometime soon. The problem is it might not be tonight. He might call a week from now for all we know."

Megan opened her mouth to ask another question when the phone rang again.

"Ugh. Well, here goes nothing."

Bell paced with the coffee cup in her hands. She froze when she heard the anxiety in Megan's reply, and then the woman was waving her hand and pointing at the phone. The shooter.

A headset was attached to the phone. Bell pulled it over her ears and leaned against the desk. The connection crackled with static, and Bell jiggled the cord until the call sounded clear.

"Can you tell me your name, sir?"

Megan's voice.

"You think you're safe in your homes, but you're not. I can reach out...reach out and take you anytime I choose."

"Am I speaking with the man who killed the student at Vida College?"

Megan met Bell's eyes in question, and Bell nodded that she was doing a good job. At the same time, she grabbed another phone and brought the receiver to her ear. Punched in the number and recognized Harold's voice at Quantico.

"I need a call traced." She needed to speak quietly so the caller wouldn't hear. Bell snapped her finger and rolled her hand, signaling Megan to keep the caller talking. It was confusing listening to the caller in one ear and Harold in the other. She gave the phone number to the agent who typed it into his terminal.

"Hold on."

"Come on, come on," she mouthed.

Megan continued to speak.

"Can you tell me where you are?"

"The girl will be the first example of what I'm capable of."

"What girl? Could you tell me her name, sir?"

"She could be any girl. Your sister, your daughter. The pretty girl next door."

Megan looked up as Bell pulled her laptop over and opened the screen. Bell fumbled the headset and caught it, the cord tangled around her ankle.

"Harold?"

"I'm working on it. Give me a second."

Several seconds later, a map of Milanville appeared on the laptop. Bell scanned the map. It took a moment for her to recognize street names. The call emanated from the western edge of the village.

Harold came back on the line.

"Bell? It's a cell phone. The closest I can get you is a two-block radius, but there's a neighborhood in the center. No name tied to the phone. He's using a burner."

"I got it, Harold."

She put the phone to her chest and wrote the coordinates on a notepad, tore the paper off and handed it to a male police officer named Yates. The officer hurried to the back of the room and relayed the information to dispatch.

"Can you narrow the radius?"

"Not from here," said Harold. "I'm calling the cell company now."

"I'll stay on the line."

The caller said something about a dog, then the line went dead.

Megan placed the receiver down and ran her hands through her hair.

"Sorry. I should have kept him longer."

"You handled him perfectly. We have his location."

Megan's face brightened as Bell dialed Gardy's number. After a few rings, he answered.

"We got him, Gardy. The Hammond Lane neighborhood on the west side of Milanville."

CHAPTER FIFTY-SIX

The air had a chilling bite for September when Colleen said goodnight to Nick. The long-haired boy smelled of cologne and sunscreen when he leaned in and kissed her lips, and this pleased her.

She wrapped her arms around his strong shoulders and kissed him back, running her tongue along his lips until he opened his mouth and accepted it. They stood together for several moments, feeling their bodies coalesce. Wary of peeping neighbors, she broke off the kiss.

He frowned.

"You sure I can't walk you home?"

Her father didn't trust the older boy and forbade his seventeen-year-old daughter from dating a college student. Allowing Nick to walk her home was an invitation for her neighbors to catch them and report back to Colleen's parents, who were out to dinner.

"You better not."

"Let me meet your parents. I'll win them over with my irresistible personality."

"Yeah, I can't see that working."

He shrugged.

"I tried, but you can't hide me forever. When can I see you again?"

"Tomorrow night."

"Can I at least call to make sure you made it home okay?"

Grinning, Colleen stood on her tiptoes and tweaked his nose.

"You better, Prince Charming. But give me fifteen minutes. I need to take out Digger."

He kissed her again, a warm peck on the forehead. Then he winked and turned down the sidewalk.

She watched him go for a while. His Corvette was parked at the end of the block and cloaked in darkness. Soon the night swallowed him.

The sidewalks were empty. Usually someone was out walking their dog or sitting on the porch. All she heard were kids playing hide-and-go-seek in the backyards.

The news stories about the shootings came uninvited to Colleen the way memories of a horror movie creep up at the edge of sleep. But she was safe in the neighborhood. The killer struck in high-profile areas like the university campus and the center of downtown.

A car gunned its motor and crawled down the lane. Colleen lowered her head and walked faster. A few seconds later it passed. She didn't recognize the car, whose dark coloration blended with the night. The vehicle stopped along the curb beyond her house, and she slowed her pace, waiting for the door to open. It didn't. The vehicle took off down the street and rounded the corner onto Linsdale.

The night took on a sharper edge and became a

dangerous thing. She jogged, arms folded, cold and scolding herself for not bringing a jacket.

Their porch light burned halfway down the block. The other houses lay dark. Dead.

Dew wicked her sneakers when she crossed the lawn. Digger barked while she jiggled the key in the lock. She shot another glance at the empty street and closed the door behind her. The dog, a beagle and terrier mix, jumped at her legs and ran in excited circles.

"Hey, buddy."

Colleen threw the deadbolt and laid the keys on the banister. Digger yipped and followed at her heels while she padded to the kitchen. She poured a kibble snack into his bowl, and the dog dived into the food before she finished. Darkness pressed against the window as she grabbed the leash and waited beside the back door. Digger looked up with a goofy smile and returned to his food. When he finished, he scampered across the kitchen and wagged his tail at her feet.

The door opened, and the night's chill followed.

"Let's make this quick. Okay, Digger?"

The dog leaped each step and ran into the yard, snout buried in the grass. Hopping from foot-to-foot to stay warm, she waited impatiently for Digger to finish his business. Across the yards, she saw the same car creep past the Henderson's house. Headlights dimmed. She waited for the vehicle to reappear on the other side of the house. It vanished.

Digger was pawing at the ground now, living up to his name and trying to root out some creature he'd sniffed out. She gently tugged his leash.

"Come on, buddy. I'm freezing my assets off out

here."

A car door opened and clicked shut outside the Henderson's house.

A stand of pines bordered the yards and concluded at a dry creek. When Colleen was younger, she pretended the pines were the redwood forest. Tonight, the trees formed at black, craggy wall that blotted out the stars and loomed over the yard like a faceless monster.

A branch snapped. Digger stopped and froze. Two faraway sirens broke the silence.

"I think we're done, Digger. Let's go inside."

The dog growled. A guttural snarl.

She tugged harder on the leash. The dog pulled against her, barking and lunging toward the trees.

Colleen heard shoes swishing through the grass before she saw the man emerge from the black. She yanked the leash as Digger pulled against her. The dog snapped at the stranger, only a dark outline against the night.

The long muzzle centered on Colleen. The blast deafened her ears a split-second before her chest burst.

And then the night went black.

CHAPTER FIFTY-SEVEN

Chief Harrington entered the call center and approached Bell.

"You sure it's our guy?"

"It's him."

He brought the radio to his ear and scanned the note for the shooter's location.

"Yeah...I want a helicopter over the Hammond Lane development on the western side of the village. And give me roadblocks on Schuyler and Linsdale. No one gets out of that neighborhood until we check every vehicle."

Chief Harrington met her eyes in question, and she raised her thumb.

"Good work, Agent Bell. Let's make sure this bastard doesn't wiggle through the net."

She followed him out of the building and across the parking lot. Along the way, Harrington barked orders into his radio. Good. They'd surround the shooter soon. Hem him in.

A siren cried across town and was immediately joined by a second. That was a mistake. She should have stressed the officers keep their sirens off until the neighborhood was blocked off. Now the shooter knew they were coming, and it was a race to trap him before he escaped. Harrington's twisted mouth told her he recognized the error.

Bell dug for her keys and remembered Gardy had the Outback.

"Hop in," Harrington said beside his cruiser.

She was almost to the passenger door when the shot echoed down from the hills. From this distance, the sound was subtle and blended with ambient noise from the village. She might have missed it had her focus not been razor-sharp, ears fine-tuned and monitoring the environment for gunfire.

The chief met her eyes over the roof. Then he shouted instructions into his radio as she slid into the passenger seat.

The ride toward the Hammond Lane development seemed to take forever. Despite the sirens and flashing lights, vehicles cut in front of the cruiser and impeded their progress. Harrington pressed the horn to clear one glut, then another formed ahead of them.

The shooter was on the move, slipping through their fingers before they snatched him.

***

His tendons are cracked whips, eyes preternaturally honed from the adrenaline pumping through his body.

Meeks giggles. A nervous, excited laugh that tickles his chest and demands release.

In his mind, he sees the girl's face. The fish-eyed panic as he aims the M82.

BOOM.

The other shootings can't compare. Up close. In the girl's own yard. The entire neighborhood heard the blast and must be in a full-fledged panic. They all fear him. This is what he wants.

He takes the MKS around the first turn and sees a police car on Schuyler. Meeks keeps the headlights off. They can't see him when he stops under a tree and watches. The cruiser angles his vehicle across one lane as another police car pulls up behind. Two cops step out of the second car and help the first officer place a roadblock across the lane. Nobody gets in or out.

Meeks drums his fingers on the wheel. The engine purrs. He feels it in his spine.

He carefully pulls the car off the curb and executes a three-point turn, but worries the brake lights will attract the officers' attention.

The only remaining option is Linsdale, which is blocked by more cop cars. Another vehicle waits at the checkpoint as an officer approaches the driver's window.

Meeks touches the M82. Runs his fingers along the muzzle.

If he maintains distance, he will win a shootout. Might kill the police before they figure out where he's firing from. But that will attract more cops, and should they close in on Meeks, the M82 will be at a disadvantage. He trained for deadly accuracy, not speed.

He backs away, a roach trapped under a glass. Scans the homes as shadows move past the windows. Take a hostage? No. Every cop in Milanville will surround the house.

One house stands out. A white two-story with a

detached garage. A for sale sign hangs in the front yard and rocks in the wind. A plate-glass window reveals an empty living room. Next door, the driveway is empty and a solitary light shines in the living room. The light is on a timer, he thinks, the owner out of town.

Meeks backs up until the MKS is even with the vacant house's driveway and turns in. Nobody watches him from the street.

He parks in front of the garage, grabs the M82, and exits the running vehicle. The garage door is locked, so he puts his sleeved elbow through one of four small windows. Reaches in and pops the lock on the garage, then pulls the MKS in.

Meeks kills the engine and pockets the keys. He shuts the garage and stands with his back to the door. Marvels at this stroke of luck.

A dark checkerboard of backyards stretches into the gloaming. He runs through the grass and cuts behind an elm tree when a dog barks. Down the road, an officer with a bullhorn orders someone to back away from the blockade.

A chain-link fence stands between Meeks and the next yard as the flashing lights of the police cars sweep red-and-blue lines across the houses. Leaning over the barrier, he lowers the rifle to the grass and immediately feels naked without it.

Meeks sticks his foot between the links and pulls himself up. His palms are slick on the dewy metal, arms trembling under his weight as he fights to drag his leg over the fence. At the top, he loses his grip and tumbles over. Crashes back-first against the lawn. The air flies out of his chest and snuffs his ability to breathe.

"Who's there?"

A woman. He lies still at the base of the fence with no cover nearby.

The neighbor's dog barks louder and yanks on its chain. Crawling up to his knees, Meeks edges along the fence, out of view of the porch.

"There's someone in the yard."

She draws an argument from a man, probably her husband, who tells her she's hearing things and needs to come inside. The woman protests and steps down from the porch. She's in the yard now. Meeks brings his eye to the M82's scope as the husband raises his voice. Finally, she relents and goes inside. The door closes.

While the way forward is clear, Meeks sprints through the darkest shadows of the yards and angles between trees. The thoroughfare into Milanville is visible beyond the neighborhood, the drone of engines like a gentle tide. Behind a ranch home, Meeks discovers two hockey goals set at opposite ends of the yard. A pair of sticks juts out from a hockey bag.

Meeks quietly unzips the bag and removes the sticks. Tosses them into the dark and slides the M82 inside. A spider crawls down his arm, and he flicks it away.

Voices travel from several houses behind. The police search the yards. Their flashlights slice through the night.

Meeks tosses the bag over his shoulder and runs for the thoroughfare.

CHAPTER FIFTY-EIGHT

Damn, it felt chilly for September. Once the sun went down, the village outskirts became an icebox.

Officer Picard skipped from one leg to the other and tried to stay warm. This was supposed to be his day off, but instead of spending the afternoon in the sun, he ended up stuck in meetings with Harrington, Ames, and those supposed experts from the Behavioral Analysis Unit. Presently, he should have been inside his warm living room. A cold beer and the ball game.

And it was all because of some sicko with a rifle.

Three vehicles impatiently waited at the roadblock with a fourth edging down the street. Their halogen lights beamed at his face and made him squint. It was going to be a long night.

Yet Picard understood their frustration. Everyone was scared. Terrified. The murderer shot a teenage girl in their neighborhood. He couldn't discern the faces inside the vehicles, not with the headlights in his eyes, but he guessed some were parents who wanted to get the hell out of the neighborhood and take their kids somewhere safe. Others had night jobs to get to. Or better places to be than a kill zone.

It seemed even colder as he approached the first vehicle. A van of some sort. That was the thing about Southern California at summer's end. It was blast-furnace-hot during the afternoon, but the cold after sundown was enough to remind him of autumns in Minnesota.

Picard swept the flashlight across the windshield and saw one man in the driver seat. Not a family. That got him worried it was the shooter.

The holstered gun lay against his hip. Picard hoped he wouldn't need his weapon tonight.

A horn honked behind the van. A man leaned his head out the window and asked Picard what the hell the hold up was.

He ignored the other driver and slowly approached the van. The man inside was heavyset and bearded. His hands stayed on the steering wheel where they belonged, and that was good. Picard didn't want trouble.

Picard made a circular motion with his hand, and the driver reached for the power window control panel. Picard hated when their hands disappeared into the dark.

The window descended with a whirring noise, and the man's hands obediently returned to the steering wheel.

"Evening, sir."

The man nodded.

"Good evening."

"Where ya headed?"

"LAX." The man stole a glance at the dashboard clock. "My flight leaves in two hours."

Picard's height allowed him to peer inside the van while he aimed the light at the seats and floor. A suitcase lay upon the back seat.

"Where are you flying to, sir?"

"New York. JFK. It's my mother's seventieth birthday tomorrow. I thought I'd better leave early. You know how the freeway is."

The man's jowls nervously quivered when he spoke.

"I sure do."

The evening chill worked in tandem with Picard's anxiety. His legs ached and became stiff. Man, how he wanted this evening to be over. Tomorrow was his only remaining day off, and by God, he intended to spend the entire day at Manhattan Beach with a cooler of beer. To hell with the shooter and the FBI. Temperatures in the eighties sounded like heaven.

"Sir, I need your license and registration."

"They're in the glove compartment."

The man reached into the dark again, the part the officer hated. Picard angled the flashlight beam around the steering wheel and followed the driver's hands. After the man slipped the license out of his wallet and handed over the registration, Picard compared the face on the license with the driver's. A perfect match, right down to the hazel eyes and jowls. Timothy Burgess. The address read forty-six Linsdale. Everything appeared in order. He barely gave the registration card a glance before handing it back to Burgess.

The van appeared clear, and this man didn't fit the agents' profile. But you could never be too careful, especially when one mistake put you face-to-face with a sniper rifle.

"I'm gonna need to check the trunk."

The second driver beeped his horn again and yelled

out his window. Picard beamed the flashlight at the man's face. An embarrassed woman sat in the passenger seat.

Burgess leaned his head out the window.

"Is that necessary? Say, don't you need a warrant for that?"

Picard did.

"Just a routine check. We can't be too careful, you understand."

The man puffed air through his lips and eyed the clock again.

"It won't take more than a few seconds."

Picard made Burgess cut the engine and take the keys out of the ignition. This provoked all three vehicles behind Burgess to honk and flash their high beams. The burst of light left red imprints on Picard's sight, and as his eyes cleared he saw a shadow move at the corner of his vision. He angled the light toward a bungalow with a long front porch. Another beep pulled his attention to the man in the vehicle behind Burgess. When he looked back at the Bungalow, all he saw was darkness.

Picard shrugged and pulled the trunk open. Nothing to see. Just an emergency kit and an extra bottle of windshield wiper solution. He bent down and looked beneath the back seat. The vehicle was clear.

He rounded the van and heard grass swish behind the Bungalow. He brought the radio to his lips and addressed Chief Harrington.

"I'm looking at a Bungalow at thirty-one Linsdale. Thought I heard someone behind the house."

"Hold up."

It was quiet while Harrington checked on the position of the search crews.

"Picard, you're probably hearing our guys. They're on that end of Linsdale near the roadblock, but we'll check it out."

The tension released in Picard's shoulders. He ended the conversation and thanked Burgess for his patience.

Then the idiot behind Burgess honked again. Picard snickered. This guy was going to get a body cavity search.

Scarlett Bell Books 1-5

CHAPTER FIFTY-NINE

The body of Colleen Sherman, age seventeen, was at the morgue when Bell rubbed her eyes. The clock hanging on the call center wall read three in the morning, and nothing good ever happened at three in the morning. Her father told her that. He had a point.

The phone calls decreased to a trickle after one. Before that, the neighborhood callers reported every growling dog as the killer. She'd spent an hour beside Chief Harrington in Colleen Sherman's neighborhood, and after Bell began to feel useless, she pawed through the backyards with the search crews, doing her damnedest to avoid Gardy's constant texts. She was exhausted, vision blurry and legs aching.

Harrington had suggested Bell call it a night upon returning, but she felt certain the killer would call and boast about his escape. Now Harrington was in his nice warm bed.

The call center was a crypt. Four officers manned the phones. Two slumped in chairs, snoring loud enough to rattle the walls.

298

Her eyelids fluttered and drifted shut, then popped open when footsteps approached.

"Sorry," she said, blinking.

Bell sat bolt upright with her hands on the chair arms. A short officer named Boden stood over her.

"Nothing to be sorry about. Don't you think you should sleep? You've had a long day."

She nodded, knowing he was right. Bell automatically reached into her pocket for the keys and remembered Gardy had them. She sighed.

"I'll drive you to the hotel."

Bell glanced around the room for an alternative. The tattered brown couch in the corner held little promise.

"I can Uber."

"It's no trouble. The boys already tore through an entire box of donuts, and whatever that sludge is inside the coffee maker isn't fit for human consumption. There's a Dunkin on the way. Besides, I saw you eyeing the sofa. You'll want to put that idea out of your mind right now unless you want to throw out your back."

Bell kept the window open while Boden drove across the village. The cool night was the only thing which kept her from drifting off. Even still, her head bobbed as if she listened to eighties metal while the officer pointed out landmarks and areas of interest. Hopefully he thought she was nodding.

The hotel doors were locked at the late hour. She rang a buzzer for entry. The door opened, and she slogged across the lobby. Apparently she made it to the elevators because the next thing Bell knew she stood before her door. The key card slid into the lock and released the mechanism before she remembered their living arrangement. The new rules. She bit her lower lip and glared at Gardy's door across the hall, then cursed herself for mentioning Logan Wolf, when truthfully she didn't know who she'd seen at the edge of the woods. Once again, an overactive imagination tossed her from the frying pan into the fire.

She opened her wallet and removed Gardy's room key. Then she edged the door open.

He'd left the bathroom light on, but it was too dark to see into the room. The air conditioner rattled and hummed, the room uncomfortably cool as she turned off the light. Bell dragged her feet to the bed and pulled back the covers. His outline was visible on the pull-out bed, curled into a ball beneath the covers with the cold air blasting his back. He groaned and turned over when the mattress springs gave her away. When he didn't stir again, she nestled into the pillow and yanked the sheet over her head.

Her brain raced in the dark. She thought about the shooter and Gardy's overprotection. So similar to her parents. Weren't they both saying in their own ways that Bell wasn't fit for law enforcement and needed someone to watch over her? The thought crawled inside her head like something primordial.

Then she fell into a dream.

CHAPTER SIXTY

Bealton, Virginia, July 8, 1995

The caw of a crow yanks her awake. Nine-year-old Scarlett turns over and watches the early morning sun move across her bedroom window.

A part of her wishes to stay in bed where it's safe.

An undefinable anxiousness pulls her from bed. She puts her clothes on and quietly enters the bathroom. Her father snores through the closed bedroom door as she runs the brush through her hair. When she's finished, she brushes her teeth and shuts the light off.

The living room is musty with the trapped humidity of night. The dining room window is open, and the translucent curtains dance like specters with the morning breeze. In the kitchen, she pours herself a bowl of Cheerios and milk, then carries breakfast into the living room where she sits in front of the television and flips the channels. Scarlett flies past the news. Sometimes the reporters talk about what happened to Jillian, as if they knew Jillian or feel the hollow loss devouring Scarlett. Settling on

301

cartoons, she mechanically eats her food and stares at the on-screen images. Watches but doesn't see. Lately feelings wash off Scarlett and vanish into the netherworld.

Scarlett's parents are still asleep when she brings the bowl to the sink and rinses half her breakfast down the drain. The television is off now, the downstairs unbearably quiet and tomb-like.

Before she knows what she's doing, Scarlett shambles out the back door to the garage where she wheels out the bicycle and straps the helmet on her head.

The bicycle is a child-size ten-speed with red-and-yellow streamers dangling off the handlebar grips. The accouterments wage war against each other, the girlish streamers in direct contrast to the pretend handlebar motor which revs when she cranks it.

Humidity clings to her as she pedals down the driveway. It's early, and the only person she sees is her math teacher, Mrs. Capuano, running the quiet streets. Scarlett says hello but her teacher doesn't hear with Nirvana rocking through her headphones.

Scarlett turns the bike down River Street. The ground mist turns the neighborhood into *Lord of the Rings*, and she half-expects to see Sam and Frodo gallop across the lawns.

The creek is audible before she can see it. The trickle grows in volume as the mist thickens, the morning fog clinging to the water as the sun fights to burn it away.

Scarlett doesn't know why she is at the creek. It is as if fate called her.

She lays the ten-speed on its side and removes the helmet. Her hair is already damp, part-sweat and part-mist, as she sits before the water. The ground is cool and wet against her legs, the air redolent of grass and wildflowers.

She watches a leaf caught in the flow catch on a stick and shoot downstream. Rocks shimmer beneath the water, and the sun turns everything flaxen and gold.

Inevitably, her thoughts turn to Jillian. Scarlett remembers their daring nighttime raid of Jeff Lombardo's tree house. They pried the flimsy lock with a crowbar and stole his baseball card collection, then held it for ransom until Lombardo agreed to drop the Neanderthal no-girls-allowed policy. It occurs to her they never took up the boy's offer to hang out inside the clubhouse.

The many sleepovers and scary bedtime stories return to her, and for the first time in the weeks since Jillian's murder, Scarlett *feels*. A tear crawls from her eye. She brushes it away and sniffs, and the creek becomes a blurred water painting. Colors and shapes. A concept or idea instead of a tangible piece of nature.

Birds thoughtlessly sing to the new day as the slowly dying mist slithers around her ankles.

That's when she sees him.

Nine-year-old Scarlett knows the man is the killer before his shadow emerges from the mist. She smells the death flowing from his pores as he staggers toward her like a monster out of an after-dark movie. The scream dies in her throat. He comes closer, his face almost perceptible behind the fog, as she scrambles backward on her feet and palms.

Scarlett jolts out of her paralysis and leaps toward the bicycle. His footsteps pound the damp earth as he tears out of the fog. The terrible squishing noises are right behind her when she lifts the bike upright and throws her leg over the seat. In one motion, her feet find the pedals while she grabs the handlebars.

Fingers swipe through her hair and catch a blonde lock. She cries out as the hair rips out of her scalp.

But she never stops pedaling, never looks back at the monster.

The tires buck when the bike picks up speed. Something jars the back rim, and the man yells. His hand caught in the spokes.

She pumps harder, hears his footsteps race behind. Closer.

His breath is on her neck.

The bike breaks out of the woods and onto River Street. Up and down the road, driveways are empty as her neighbors slumber. She cries for help. His sneakers slap the pavement. He's almost on top of her now.

Someone comes from the opposite direction, running and obscured by the sun. For a petrified instant, she thinks the killer somehow rounded the houses and came at her from the other end of the street. Then she sees it is her math teacher and drops the bike.

She half-runs, half-stumbles toward the shocked Mrs. Capuano. Falls and tears her knees open on the unforgiving blacktop. Hops up and limps into the woman's arms.

Scarlett screams in warning. The killer will murder them both.

But there is no one in the road behind her.

CHAPTER SIXTY-ONE

Bell came out of the dream with a yell. The room looked unfamiliar, cranking up her panic. Then she saw the light beneath the bathroom door and heard the shower.

She scrambled for her clothes, momentarily humiliated she slept half-naked with Gardy one bed away. When did she remove her clothes?

She gathered the pants and shirt and threw them on. The water stopped as she grabbed her shoes and socks.

"Bell?"

She froze.

While he dripped in the tub and the fan rumbled behind the door, she ferreted through her pockets and was relieved to find the keycard.

Gardy called to her again, but she was already at the hotel door as he stepped out of the shower.

She quietly shut the door and turned toward her own room. The hotel hallway smelled of eggs and pancakes, and a tray of food lay beside a neighboring door.

The door didn't open with the key card's first pass. She tried again, and the lock clicked open.

Her hand was on the handle when Gardy's door flew open. She swiveled and found him dripping in the hallway with a towel wrapped around his waist. If she weren't furious she would have laughed. He reminded her of Ferris Bueller.

"I didn't hear you wake up."

She pushed her door open.

"Go inside, Gardy. Someone will see."

"Hey, don't take off like that. We should talk."

As Gardy leaned an arm against the wall, the towel unraveled, and he snatched the edges shut before she could see anything.

"There's nothing to talk about. Everything is fine."

"Is it? Because you don't act like everything is—"

She closed the door.

Bell stood with her back against the door, arms crossed as she surveyed her pigsty hotel room. The overnight bag had tipped over and spilled clothes across the carpet. A once-used towel blocked the bathroom door open and lent her a peek at the scads of toiletries marring the counter.

He knocked on the door.

"Come on, Bell."

She felt like a total heel for closing the door in his face. He knocked again, and suddenly she became a teenage girl sulking in her bedroom while her father tried to lure her out of self-imposed incarceration. She blew the hair away from her face and rolled her eyes to the ceiling.

"Bell? Talk to me."

She threw her shoes and socks next to her bed and plodded back to the bathroom. Though Gardy didn't knock again and she never checked the peephole, Bell knew he was outside the door, standing there in a bath towel and shivering. She smirked and turned on the shower.

The water was cold at first and took a long time to warm up. She danced around the spray until the temperature reached humane levels, then she let the warmth thaw the air-conditioned ice off her body.

She reached for the body wash when the truth slammed her. The reason the shooter slipped past the roadblocks was he never drove out.

The officers were thorough and checked every parked car nearby, confirming they belonged in the neighborhood. Harrington assumed they'd arrived too late, but Bell didn't think so. They were quick enough to cut off the shooter.

For a long time last night, the idea played through Bell's mind that the shooter lived in the neighborhood and knew Colleen Sherman. It didn't feel right, didn't quite jibe. No, the shooter was an outsider, a stranger. He killed Sherman and abandoned the car after the roadblocks went up. It would have been easy to sneak through the backyards before the search crews swept through, and once he reached the thoroughfare he was a free man.

But that meant his car was still there. Somewhere.

Bell finished showering and dried. She grabbed the phone and dialed the station and got Chief Harrington on the phone.

"Yes, we'll be there in about an hour. Meeks didn't get out of the neighborhood before the roadblocks went up."

"You think he ditched his car? We checked parked vehicles."

"He's not on the street. Look for vacant houses on Linsdale, Schuyler, Hammond, and the connecting roads. Houses for sale and families on vacation. He might have found an open garage or a driveway around the back of the house."

She threw on a change of clothes and noted this was her last clean outfit. Either they wrapped the case up today or she'd spend the evening in the laundry room.

Guilt panged at Bell for not sharing her theory with Gardy first. But this was her new job, wasn't it? To hide in the call center, surrounded by cops, and unearth the killer from a safe distance.

She was almost to the elevator when Gardy caught up.

"Were you going to wait for me?"

"Up and at 'em, sunshine. Isn't that what you always say?"

She locked her gaze straight ahead as she walked. He wasn't as graceful and tripped over an empty tray on the floor, and it was a strain for her not to crack a smile as he stumbled against the wall, dropped his briefcase, and kicked a plate across the hallway.

"Will you please slow down?"

She swiveled and faced him.

"We only have an hour to get to the police station, and I want to eat."

"You haven't spoken to me since yesterday afternoon."

"I've been busy, Gardy. You know, logging phone calls and drinking day-old coffee."

He set the briefcase on the floor. A piece of lettuce clung to his pants cuff.

"You saving that for later or do you want to eat it now?"

Gardy looked down at his pants and groaned. To her

surprise, he removed the lettuce and stuffed it into his pocket.

"Yeah, I'm saving it for later."

She had to bite the inside of her cheek to keep from laughing. Damn Gardy. It infuriated her it was so hard to stay angry with him.

Bell raised her eyebrows and lolled her head toward the elevator.

"Well? Are you ready?"

"No, Bell. I'm not ready. Not until we talk this out."

She crossed her arms and studied the wallpaper.

"Fine. Talk."

"I have to be honest with you. You're acting like a twelve-year-old who didn't get her way."

The scowl she gave Gardy warned him he walked on shaky ground.

"First of all, it wasn't my call."

"Weber?"

"Right. He wanted you out of the field after I gave him the Logan Wolf letter. The sighting escalated matters further. We feel the same way about Weber, and he's overreacting, but I happen to agree with him this time."

She turned toward the elevator and he blocked her.

"Just listen for once. Wolf has your address and uncovered secrets you haven't shared with anyone else. If it was Wolf—"

"I'm not sure what I saw."

"Doesn't it make sense to lie low for a while? At least until we figure out what he wants with you? Besides, you're our best profiler, and nobody tracks these guys better. You want to be in the field. I get it. I want you there, too, and I'll get you there if you're patient. Right now I

309

need you to find this shooter for me, and that means putting in the grunt work at the call center and interrogating the traffic cams."

Bell's jaw moved back-and-forth. She nodded.

"We might not need the traffic cams."

He retrieved his briefcase and grinned.

"Because his car is somewhere in the neighborhood."

"Wait, you already knew?"

"It's a reasonable theory. We didn't have time to go door-to-door last evening, but my belief is he hid the car. Probably found a vacant home with an open garage."

Bell had to chuckle. The similarity of their thinking was uncanny.

"What's so funny?"

"Other than the lettuce hanging out of your pocket, absolutely nothing."

CHAPTER SIXTY-TWO

Textbooks and empty compact disk cases litter the floor of the Kia. Without a credit card attached to his phone, Meeks couldn't Uber across Milanville. Instead, he thumbed for a ride until a student on his way to Vida College picked him up. Now he peers out the window at the homes, which grow in size and luxury as they approach the college. The hockey bag lies at his feet. His clothes carry the cloying scents of weeds and day-old sweat. He'd slept in a nature preserve.

"How close to the college do you want to go?"

The driver's eyes stare out from behind thick lens glasses. His appearance is boyish, a face full of pimples and reddish hair that refuses to stay combed.

The boy is nervous. Terrified.

Meeks hasn't spoken a word since the boy brought him aboard, ignoring attempts at small talk.

The driver must wonder about the bag's contents. A dead body? A bomb? What Meeks carries is equally deadly in the hands of a capable shooter. And Meeks is quite capable.

"Mister?"

Meeks turns his skeletal face toward the boy. He can't recall the last time he ate.

"Here is fine."

The Kia darts into the first open spot along the curb and stops. The blinker clicks like those Newton's cradle balls that perpetually smack together.

The boy watches the bag suspiciously, then averts his eyes when Meeks catches him staring. Meeks steps from the car and throws the hockey bag over his shoulder, and the boy drives off.

He stands before a small hotel with sea-blue facing and white trim. A gated pool divides the hotel from the parking lot. In his wallet, Meeks has two hundred dollars. He doesn't expect he will require money after today.

The woman behind the counter is Mexican and speaks broken English. Two vacancies exist. Meeks chooses the top floor and pays in cash.

A family with two young girls passes him on the balcony, but he doesn't see them. Skittering catches his eye, and he crushes a roach under his sneaker.

The door opens to a small, gloomy room. Blackout curtains snuff out all light. The carpet is musty, bedspread frayed and threadbare.

He tosses the bag onto the bed and lies down, fingers interlocked behind his head, glare locked on the water-stained ceiling.

Closes his eyes. He needs to rest. Just a little while.

Meeks opens his eyes and doesn't know how long he slept. Not long, judging by the glare at the window as he throws the curtains open.

He estimates it is a little past noon as he crosses the

busy avenue. The day is hot and dry, desert-like, the sky tinged gray with smog. Two white stone columns give entry to Vida College, and he reaches a brick walkway that pierces the quad and leads toward the site of the first shooting. Students pass him on either side, seeing him but not seeing him. One boy notices Meeks' face and lowers his eyes. Meeks invokes fear. They will all fear him by sunset.

He wanders past the library and theater, feels his legs grow weary from lack of sleep as he climbs the steps of the student center. Inside, voices ring off the walls and hurt his ears. He can barely make out where he is going, the dark standing in stark contrast to the California sun. When he exits the opposite side of the building, he stops and stares. A girl with braided hair bumps into him from behind and curses Meeks for blocking the steps.

Blue and green banners, the school colors, fly outside the soccer stadium. A locked gate bars entry. Two ticket booths front the stadium and promote a six o'clock start time for a huge conference match. The stadium holds ten thousand, and Meeks expects a packed house.

On the other side of the field is a wooded area. A creek runs below the small forest, and if he follows the water toward higher ground, he'll reach the mountains.

Ten thousand people will be cramped together when the gunfire starts. No escape. He imagines how many will die, trampled in the panic.

This is his moment. Meeks returns to the hotel for the hockey bag.

CHAPTER SIXTY-THREE

A pall hung over the Milanville Police Department, a dark cloud that constricted breathing and discouraged the officers from meeting each other's eyes. Three dead in three days, the latest a teenage girl murdered steps from her home in a safe suburban neighborhood.

Bell sat in a dimly lit room and glared at the monitor until her vision blurred. The system for examining traffic cam photos was convoluted and grossly outdated. It took longer to sift through the dates and camera locations than it did to scrutinize each picture, and after two hours staring at the screen, all the vehicles looked identical.

The call center remained a dead end. Megan brought Bell coffee and kept her in the loop.

Bell couldn't believe the shooter hadn't called back. Experience with similar lulls kept her nerves on edge—this was the quiet before the storm. The shooter would strike again today.

She was about to switch back to a different camera when she saw the black car on Main Street. It was a large car with the right amount of trunk space, too far up the street to see on the Main Street camera. Instead, it appeared on the Fennel Avenue camera, the vehicle barely discernible at the top of the frame.

Something about the car drew her attention. Zooming in, she saw the empty interior, but the angle missed the license plate. The time stamp verified the picture was taken three minutes before the shooting. Otherwise, there was no reason to believe this was the killer's car, except for the way her flesh crawled when she studied the photograph.

Officer Boden was back in the office early, working a quick-turnaround shift. Bell called him over and swiveled the monitor toward him.

"Can you identify the car from this angle?"

He leaned over the desk and squinted, then turned the screen a tad to avoid the window glare.

"Looks like an MKS, but I'm not sure." He shifted his hips as though it was possible to maneuver around the two-dimensional image. "Yeah, it's an MKS. Probably several years old. Look at the front."

She did. It almost appeared the car wore a grin.

"You're a genius, Boden."

"Nah, but I know a thing or two about cars. You think that's our guy?"

She didn't want to nod emphatically, but it felt right.

"Could be. He's in the right place at the right time."

A knock on the door brought her head around as Gardy peeked inside.

"Can I borrow you for a moment?"

Bell thanked Boden, who took her place in the chair and called up additional views of Main Street.

"You ready to get back in the field?"

She glanced up-and-down the hallway.

"Seriously? Did you talk to Harrington?"

"Yeah, and Quantico. Weber isn't happy about it, but then again Weber is never happy."

Bell swallowed.

"Wow, thank you."

"Ames and I are about to head back to the neighborhood and help the officers canvas the place. I'll go door-to-door if I have to, but if we start with the vacant houses, we should be able to narrow down the search."

"I can do you one better. I think the shooter drives a Lincoln MKS."

She motioned Gardy inside and showed him the photograph of the MKS.

"How do you know this is the car?"

"Can't know for certain, but it's parked during the time of the attack, and the techs said the shot came from this direction."

"Lots of trunk space. Perfect for our guy."

"That's what I thought."

Gardy patted her shoulder, and they hurried to meet Detective Ames in the parking lot.

CHAPTER SIXTY-FOUR

The silence cloaking Linsdale felt sinister. At this time of day, Bell expected to see children riding bicycles and playing in the yards. It was dead quiet, not a soul on the street. Even the birds hushed and shrouded themselves inside the trees.

"Ames dug up a list of for-sale homes," Gardy said as he drove the Outback behind the detective's cruiser. "We'll start on the west end and work our way down, checking for people on vacation as we go."

The length of the street was thick with foliage and cloaked in shadow. Secretive, Bell thought. Easy to hide in plain sight.

They parked near the end of the road where a roadblock stood last night. From there, they walked the sidewalk while another pair of officers canvased Schuyler. As Bell studied the houses, a curtain parted, and an elderly woman poked her head through the opening. The woman pulled the curtains shut when she saw them, and her shadow traveled toward the back of the room.

"They're terrified," Ames said, referring to the

317

neighborhood.

Until they took the shooter down, the fear would only grow.

Ames bit her lip.

"I'm starting to believe you were right about Hostetler. He's not involved."

Bell looked at her.

"Why do you say that?"

"The killer shot a white suburban girl six miles from campus. It doesn't add up."

A for-sale sign leaned on the lawn of a sprawling ranch home. Boxwood lined the brick pathway to the front door, and a purple clematis climbed past the front window. They followed the driveway around the back and peered inside the empty garage.

The next vacant house pulled Bell's attention. Another real estate sign hung in the paint-chipped, white two-story's front yard. Next door, the lights were off, and a stack of envelopes bulged out of the mailbox.

"You see anything unusual?"

Gardy followed her eyes to the adjacent house.

"Two empties in a row. That solves the problem of a nosy neighbor."

Ames knocked on both doors while Gardy and Bell walked the perimeter of the for-sale home. After the detective rejoined them, they followed the driveway, which angled around the house with the garage partially hidden.

Gardy drew his weapon when the broken pane came into view. They spread to either side of the garage, Gardy on the left, Bell leading Ames to the right.

Bell held the Glock as she peeked around the corner.

And saw the black MKS inside.

It was too dark to see if anyone was in the car. She gestured at Gardy, who nodded in understanding and covered her as she bent low and crept below the windows. She grabbed the handle and tugged the door open, then rolled and shifted to the corner as Gardy darted through the car's blind spot.

The car was empty and locked. While Ames relayed the license plate number to dispatch, Bell clicked her flashlight and moved the beam across the back of the car. Her pulse thrummed as she imagined the shooter inside the trunk, the rifle aimed at her forehead.

She didn't see it at first. Then the light caught the circular imperfection, and she pressed her thumb against it. The circle popped into the trunk.

Gardy released his breath.

Hot wires ran through Bell's nerves as she gazed across the back seat and checked the floor. Everything appeared in order except for the wadded fast food bag behind the driver seat. She moved around the garage and scrutinized the backyards, picturing how it looked after sunset last night. Trees provided plenty of cover, and the only obstacle between the garage and the thoroughfare was a small chain-link fence in the distance. The shooter had slipped around the roadblocks, and nobody noticed.

"Okay, we've got a match."

Ames pocketed her phone and read the name on her notepad.

"The MKS belongs to one William Meeks, white male, age thirty-two, of Milanville, California."

Gardy was already on the phone with Quantico.

Afterward, he joined Bell behind the garage.

"Quantico is running the background check. In the

meantime, we've got an APB out on Meeks, and the department sent his picture to the television stations. We'll find this guy before nightfall."

Bell hoped Gardy was right. Because Meeks intended to strike tonight.

CHAPTER SIXTY-FIVE

Dana Steinman, Dean of Vida College, stood on the sideline and looked at the sea of blue and green in the stands. The wind pushed at her back and blew Steinman's skirt around as her heart crawled into her throat. She was used to speaking in front of crowds, well-schooled in the art of persuading donors to open their checkbooks. But ten thousand people screaming at the tops of their lungs was a new level of pressure, and she felt lightheaded as the public address announcer ran through the starting lineups.

He was almost finished, and that meant she would soon walk to the center of the pitch and deliver a speech she never imagined giving. Many of the students held signs in support of Eugene Buettner, and a long banner deriding gun violence stretched along the front rail. She prayed Kyle Hostetler and the White Wall weren't in attendance.

When she heard her name over the loudspeaker, Steinman focused on the center circle where the team captains and the senior class president, Charla Prescott, awaited the dean's arrival. Steinman's feet moved through quicksand, the long walk agonizingly slow. A smattering of cheers and boos followed at her heels. It shook her that many students blamed her for the violence, no matter how unfair the judgment.

Her hand trembled when Prescott, who sang the Star-Spangled Banner before the player announcements, gave her the microphone. Steinman cleared her throat after a squelch of feedback.

"We are here this afternoon to remember a student who believed in the power of peace and lived by that credo every day..."

The phone buzzed in her pocket, providing a momentary distraction. She paused until the memorized speech returned to her.

"I was one of many fortunate enough to know Eugene Buettner. Over the last four years, I worked closely with this young man, who believed our university could do better."

The phone buzzed again, and this time a murmur of disquiet rumbled through the stands. The clamor grew louder as she fought to get back on point.

"Please, if you will allow me to continue."

Charla Prescott leaned close and whispered into her ear.

"Check your phone, Dean Steinman. There's an alert about the shooter."

Her blood froze. Was the killer on campus?

She turned off the microphone and fished the phone from her pocket as the crowd grew deafening. Some students headed for the exits as the announcer urged the fans to stay calm and quiet their voices. The Vida College alert application displayed a photograph of a haggard-looking male with stringy hair and an emaciated face. His

skull showed through a thin layer of flesh. William Meeks.
This was the man who murdered Eugene Buettner?

The wind built, shoving her out of the circle as the
team captains walked back to their respective benches. A
lone cloud drifted over the sun and drew shadows along
the field.

"What are you going to do?"

Steinman whirled on Prescott, the girl's eyes nervous
and overwhelmed.

"I have to get everybody under control."

That was when the *kill Meeks* chants began.

***

Gardy and Bell went door-to-door on Linsdale after
Ames returned to the station to coordinate the search for
Meeks. Betsy Abernethy, a dark-haired, heavyset woman
claimed the shooter crossed her backyard, though the
husband argued otherwise. Abernethy mentioned someone
stole a hockey bag from a neighboring yard, and Bell
considered the possibility Meeks used the bag to hide the
M82.

They descended Abernethy's front stoop when
Gardy's phone rang. He plugged his opposite ear with his
hand and nodded, then snapped his finger and motioned
for Bell to give him her notepad. He jotted the information
down and thanked the caller.

"That was Ames," Gardy said, picking up his pace as
he hurried down the street toward the Outback. "A Vida
College student ID'd Meeks. Says he picked Meeks up and
dropped him off at a hotel called the Blue Sea Shell."

"Why do I know that name?"

"You must have seen it the first day. The hotel is right across the street from the university. The department is on the phone with campus security now. But there's something else. Our good buddy, Kyle Hostetler, called the police after recognizing Meeks' picture. Says Meeks approached the White Wall last year about an M82. But Hostetler swears the White Wall doesn't deal guns."

Gardy looked at Bell from the tops of his eyes, accentuating his doubt.

When they reached the car, Bell circled to the driver side.

"Toss me the keys."

"You sure you don't want me to drive?"

"With you, we get there safely. With me, we get there fast."

Gardy threw her the keys.

"Fast it is."

***

The coaches conferred with the referees on the opposite side of the field as Dean Steinman chewed her nails in the press box. Confusion ruled the stadium. Fans talked animatedly as the players from both teams milled along the sidelines and broke off into disparate groups.

Steinman's phone rang at the same time as the press booth's. She jumped, startled by the sudden noise.

"Yes?"

"Dana, this is Grant Foltz."

Foltz was the senior officer for Vida College's campus security. If he was calling her now, the news couldn't be good.

324

"We're evacuating the stadium, but we don't want to cause a panic."

"Evacuating? Is the shooter here?"

Foltz's answer cut off when the gunshot exploded out of the forest. Mayhem ruled the stadium, people screaming and shoving each other as they fought toward the aisles. In front of the press box, a circle of students struggled to flee from a woman slumped over a bleacher. Blood drizzled out of her chest and pooled on the next row.

Steinman shouted to Foltz as another shot boomed across the pitch. The press box window shattered. She fumbled the phone and dropped to the floor. She cried out when someone stepped on her leg, the press box thrown into a frenzy. People pounded on the glass and begged for entry. More crowded into the doorway, an old man in a baseball cap red-faced as the throng squeezed him against the frame.

She was certain she'd die here, crushed under the panic if the shooter didn't get her first.

CHAPTER SIXTY-SIX

Bell and Gardy exited the Outback in front of the athletics complex and ran toward the screams. Rifle fire reverberated off the buildings and came from all directions.

Gardy had been on the phone with campus security when an officer named Spacey reported gunshots at the soccer stadium. Now the agents sprinted toward the stadium as a horde of terrified people, some covered with blood, ran in the opposite direction. Bell battled against the flow, squeezing through the panicked masses as she pushed toward the entry gates.

Another explosion brought more screams.

A wide-eyed male with a gash down his forehead grabbed Bell when she ran past.

"He's killing everyone!"

The student spun away, and the flow of runners dragged him down the walkway.

They reached the stadium when Bell stopped at the fence. In the stands, a woman pointed at the forest butting up against the far side of the soccer field.

A gunshot blasted out of the trees and pierced the

metal bleachers.

"There," Bell said and pointed at the forest.

Gardy squinted and brought binoculars to his eyes. He scanned for a moment, then nodded.

"I see him."

The bipod was lodged between a large rock and a tree, the M82 poised like a black snake. Meeks' arms moved along the rifle. He was well entrenched, shielded by trees and a slight rise in the terrain.

Gardy radioed the shooter's position to law enforcement. Sirens grew in number as the police closed in on the campus.

Yet Bell didn't know how the officers would reach Meeks before he killed more people. No roads existed in the shooter's direction, and the forest dropped toward a creek and opened to a long stretch of wilderness, an escape route Meeks could follow all the way to the mountains.

A thumping sound brought Bell's head up as a helicopter passed over the complex and circled toward the forest.

The soccer players attempted to escape the shooter through the stands. They climbed over civilians and added to the riot. A shot boomed, and one of the Vida College players screamed and clutched the back of his leg. Blood spilled between his fingers.

Bell leaped the fence with Gardy on her heels. They crossed the pitch, weaving between a confusion of coaches, players, and fans who'd tumbled out of the stands. With any luck, the killer's eye was in the scope and too focused on the crowd to notice them coming. Gardy yelled into the radio as he ran. Two police cruisers and a campus security truck screeched to a halt in front of the stadium.

Bell's heart caught in her throat. She couldn't see the shooter anymore. The space between the tree and rock was empty, the dark of the forest thickening as the sun dropped behind the mountains.

She caught Gardy's eye before the agent broke through the tree line.

The chaos happened fast.

The gunshot spun Gardy around. Blood splashed off his shoulder as the agent hit the ground.

Bell had the radio in her hands. She yelled, "Man down!" and dropped to Gardy's side. He gritted his teeth and clutched the shoulder as red welled on the forest floor. She searched the hill for the shooter, who was at a disadvantage as he descended the terrain. But he was nowhere. A ghost.

Bell covered Gardy and lay flat. His eyes were closed to slits, forehead beaded with sweat.

"You're all right. Help is on the way."

"He's above the bend in the creek."

Bell raised her head and searched the creek. She saw him. Along the water, headed for the next stand of trees.

As if he sensed her glare, Meeks spun and lifted the M82. He fired up the hill and blew a chunk of bark off a nearby tree.

A warning shot meant to drive her back? No, she didn't think so. Meeks fired an accurate shot when the M82 rested on a bipod. She doubted he could shoot on the run, not from that distance.

"Drop the weapon!"

Meeks backtracked and fired. The bullet buzzed past her ear and raised the hairs on her head.

Gardy tried to roll over.

"Lay still."

He struggled again and she cursed him.

"Dammit, Gardy. Don't move."

Footsteps approached from behind. She whistled through her fingers and motioned Chief Harrington and several officers along the tree line. Unless Meeks made a run for it, the officers would hem the shooter in and force him into the clearing.

Another thunderous gun blast deafened Bell. She ducked and covered her head. Gardy's chest swelled and contracted beneath her. She worried where the bullet had clipped him and if it was lodged in his shoulder.

Swiveling onto her side, Bell removed her jacket and pressed the cloth lining onto the wound. He winced again and hurled an expletive into her ear.

Bell cautiously raised her head and immediately ducked down when Meeks fired the rifle. The bullet whistled into the hillside and erupted a chunk of earth a few feet away.

Too close.

A hundred yards to her right, the officers fanned out and entered the forest. The helicopter whirled above the creek and veered when Meeks' next shot blurred past the window. She remembered what Gardy said about the weapon, capable of taking down small aircraft.

The helicopter swooped down, and Meeks blew a hole in the tail boom. The aircraft wavered for a moment and then turned erratically toward the hilltop. Toward Bell and Gardy.

Christ, it was going to crash on top of them.

Grabbing Gardy by his uninjured arm, she pulled him up. Meeks noticed and fired past their heads.

"Up the hill!" she yelled over the helicopter.

It descended faster as the blades whipped leaves and blew dirt into her eyes.

Gardy fought up to his knees, his face pallid, eyes sunken. She had him under his arm now, dragging him along as the helicopter roared at the backs of their necks.

He found his footing and broke out of the forest a second before the landing skids clipped the treetops above their heads. The helicopter bucked and twirled in a circle. The few players still on the soccer pitch fled while the aircraft spun earthward.

It landed with a crunch of metal. Bell saw the pilot lurch forward and spring back when the skids struck the turf. Black smoke poured from the engine as the pilot and another officer climbed out of the helicopter and ran for cover.

Out of breath, Bell lowered Gardy to the ground as Detective Ames raced over to them.

"He's been shot. In the shoulder."

Ames nodded and spoke into her radio, impossible to hear over the clamor.

Gunfire erupted from the forest. Bell held on to a glimmer of hope—the police might flush Meeks away from the creek and force him up the hillside. Toward her.

She raised her gun and pushed through the first line of trees, the hillside cloaked in darkness as her eyes struggled to adjust.

She saw him. A hundred feet away and closing fast. The M82 pointed at her skull.

The rifle fired, but Meeks' aim was poor on the run. The bullet buried into a tree.

Bell ripped off three shots. The first missed wide. The

second blew through the killer's chest and stopped him in his tracks. The third punctured his forehead and dropped Meeks.

The leaf-strewn hillside was treacherously steep. Bell's feet slipped out from under her, and then she flew down the hill and slammed her back against the ground. The hill pulled her down and down, the darkening sky flickering behind the trees.

Then the hill ended, and her head struck the bottom.

CHAPTER SIXTY-SEVEN

Bell could hear Gardy arguing with the nurse before she reached his hospital room. She opted not to go inside yet and waited on a plastic chair outside his door. It was more fun this way, listening to Gardy bleat over the size of the needle before the nurse jabbed it home.

"You might feel a small prick," the nurse said.

This was followed by a sharp yelp that would have been appropriate had the nurse skewered Gardy with a sword. A minute later, the nurse, a rotund woman wearing a scowl which suggested she'd administered one too many shots to prima donna cops over the years, exited with a huff and shook her head. She noticed Bell on the chair.

"Is he really an FBI agent?"

"He is. One of the best."

"You're kidding."

When Bell knocked on the door, Gardy was rubbing the hurt off his uninjured shoulder. The bullet had grazed the other shoulder and excavated a chunk of flesh, but stitches and rest would have him back to full strength soon.

"What are you smiling about?"

Bell plopped down in the bedside chair and tried to erase her grin.

"I'm happy to see your energy is back," she said. "You're rather feisty today."

Except for the strong chest accentuated by the open gown, Gardy looked like a six-year-old boy who didn't want to go to the dentist. Gardy caught her looking and pulled the gown shut. He groaned.

"I *was* fine until Nurse Ratched lanced me with a scimitar."

She started to laugh, then grimaced and reached for the back of her neck.

"You okay, Bell? Maybe it would be a good idea if you had your own room."

"I'm all right. It's a deep bruise, not whiplash."

Gardy strained to sit up.

"What did the doctor say?"

"He gave me the usual advice. Plenty of fluids and lots of rest. Don't head-butt any bad guys for a few weeks."

"Smart doctor."

They fell silent for a spell. Outside the door, the Milanville hospital slumbered with inactivity. A phone rang, a monitor beeped, and two orderlies gossiped in the hall.

The quiet became uncomfortable, and Bell saw Gardy's mind wander down the same dark halls as hers. He'd nearly died. A foot to the right and Meeks' shot would have torn through Gardy's heart.

He cleared his throat, and she glanced up.

"You missed Harrington," said Gardy. "He was here an hour ago."

"Oh?"

"Looks like Ames was onto something about the White Wall after all."

"Hostetler sold Meeks the weapon?"

"Maybe not Hostetler himself, but somebody in the White Wall. Ames hasn't traced the weapon back to them yet, but she will." He frowned. "This William Meeks thing bothers me. Your profile nailed him, but I don't know what good we're doing."

"We stopped him."

"Yeah, after he murdered three people and killed another two at the stadium."

Two dead was two too many, yet Bell couldn't believe Meeks hadn't killed more. They were fortunate only two murders and a few dozen injuries occurred at the soccer match.

"Here's the part that bothers me, and Harrington stressed this too." Gardy stared at the wall. He seemed to look toward an uncertain, frightening future. "There was no warning Meeks would snap. Sure, his business fell apart when the loan officer turned him down, but that's life for a lot of us. Are we to accept that was his trigger? These data points keep the academics employed and reinforce theories. What about practical application? Do we track everyone who grew up in a dysfunctional household and put them under constant surveillance as soon as they experience disappointment?"

Bell's elbows rested on her knees, head tilted at the floor.

"We're like firemen, Gardy. We save lives when the smoke detector goes off and do our best to save the home. But sometimes the fire is out of control before we arrive."

"There has to be a better way. I didn't get into this

racket to mitigate damage."

A female orderly in a ponytail interrupted Bell's reply. It was time to take Gardy's blood pressure. He'd pumped himself up with frustration and seemed to deflate as the test progressed. Bell was surprised his pressure was normal.

"Where to now?" he asked.

"Megan is taking me to some mall in LA. Supposedly they filmed a scene from Melrose Place there."

His eyes dropped to his chest.

"Have fun. But hey, don't hang around California on my account. I know you miss the condo."

"We're a team, Gardy. We leave together. Besides, if it was me in that bed, you'd stay."

He looked at her and nodded.

"Have a good time at the mall. Bring me one of those cinnamon pretzels."

"All that butter?" She tutted. "You'll wreck your exemplary blood pressure."

He grinned, the first real smile she'd seen on him in days.

"Then I'll take a smoothie instead."

She rose off the chair, and trepidation touched his eyes.

"Wait a minute. What about Logan Wolf?"

"Megan's a cop, Gardy. Relax. Nobody's gonna mess with us. Anyhow, I'm starting to doubt I saw him at all. It's like you said. He was in my head after the letter, and my mind saw what it wanted me to see."

Nurse Ratched returned, a one-woman force of nature.

"Don't tell me there are more shots."

335

"Just need to take a little blood."

The syringe looked like a jousting lance from a Renaissance festival.

"A *little* blood? That's ten gallon's worth."

"Calm down, Mr. Gardy. This will only take a minute."

Bell smirked and moved for the door.

"That's my cue to leave. He's in your hands, Nurse."

Ratched grinned.

"I'll return him to you in one piece."

CHAPTER SIXTY-EIGHT

A few hundred people crowded the mall food court where Bell and Megan picked at mediocre sushi. A Gap shopping bag was tucked beneath Megan's chair.

Megan brought a hand to her mouth.

"I can't eat another bite."

"Thank you. I thought it was just me."

"No, this is irrefutably terrible."

They shared a laugh, and Bell tossed the remains in the garbage. Megan grabbed her bag, and they rode the escalator down to the main floor.

A mix of families and teenagers swarmed the corridor, the storefronts filled with bright colors and clothes which made Bell feel self-conscious. When had this happened? Yesterday she'd been a teenager a step ahead of the latest fashion trends, and suddenly she was thirty-two and a fish out of water. Most of the store names were alien to her, and the clothing these kids wore confused her and made her feel old.

Bell's phone buzzed as a text came in. She gave it a glance and felt a hitch when she saw the message was from her mother. Stuffing the phone into her pocket, Bell swallowed the indignation. It settled in her stomach as sorrow.

Megan looked at her with inquisitive concern.

"Everything okay?"

"It's my mother."

Before she knew what she was doing, Bell opened up to Megan about her parents, the fight, and the cold, dead months of silence that withered between them.

"So write her back. You can't fight the ones you love for the rest of your life."

Bell sighed and sat down on a bench. Megan slid beside her.

"I don't know how to start."

"Look, kids put their parents on pedestals and turn them into Gods. We expect them to be infallible, but they're exactly the same as us. Imperfect, insecure, trying to figure things out on the fly. And no matter how much bullshit we face every day, they've dealt with the same issues for a few decades longer. It doesn't mean they're always right, but they do their best."

Bell propped her chin on her palm and watched the shoppers pass in an endless stream, and she wondered if she'd made a terrible mistake. This wasn't about modern women thriving in fields traditionally dominated by men. No, this was about love and worry. To her parents, Bell would always be their little girl.

"Okay, you convinced me. I'll write them tonight."

"Why wait? I'm not going anywhere."

"No, it's better this way. Gives me a chance to get the words right."

They gathered their belongings when Megan giggled.

"I think you found yourself a new boyfriend."

"What?"

"Mr. Dark and Mysterious over there. He's checking you out."

Ice filled Bell's legs. She stood and looked over the crowd.

"What man?"

Megan scrunched her brow.

"That's funny. He was right there a second ago."

Bell scanned the corridor, the sea of shoppers.

When she stood on the bench, Megan's face creased in worry.

"What's wrong, Bell?"

Bell saw the back of his jet black hair a moment before he turned into a store and vanished. Knew the black would match the deep set of his eyes.

She ran to the storefront, Megan trailing behind and firing questions. Bell was too late.

Logan Wolf was gone.

THE BONE WHISPERER

CHAPTER SIXTY-NINE

The old farmhouse juts from the earth on a lonely road outside of Pronti, Kansas. The two-story is more gray than white, its exterior paint chipped and stained by time and the unrelenting wind that scours the prairie. The front steps squeal like a gutted animal, and if you stand too long on the second board, the wood will snap and swallow your ankle.

Above the stairs is a long, warped porch. Most of the balusters are crooked or missing. The filthy windows which front the home are longer than a man is tall and consume all but the strongest midday sun rays. But the sun rarely shines upon this house. The wind blows and blows, and when it does, the chill runs amok through the home's corridors, halls that would scream if they could speak.

The Skinner calls the farmhouse his home. People don't come out this far. Only the mailman, and the box is set along a dirt road which floods when the monstrous spring storms roll across the plains.

The Skinner's real name is Lucas Hunt. He has lived here since the day he was born, two months after his father guzzled a bottle of Jack Daniels and chased it with both barrels of a shotgun. The Skinner's mother was an alcoholic who took to burning young Lucas with a lit cigarette when the boy needed a whooping. She died and left him the farmhouse when Lucas was nineteen. Sixteen years later, he is still here and will never leave.

He walks the long hall from the kitchen to the living room. Slumps into the chair and studies the plaster crumbling off the cracked ceiling. A brown water stain runs across the ceiling toward the corner where it blackens and slumps like a distended beast.

He rubs his knees. The Skinner does this when he is nervous, and he is always anxious before he stalks.

His first victim was a prostitute in Kansas City, Kansas. She was young and brunette, probably not of legal age, he thought at the time. He rarely craved sex and never considered propositioning a hooker, yet he was drawn to the black heels and shapely legs, the pale, alabaster flesh. And the frightened eyes. The eyes of a neophyte in a cold and dangerous world. She was new to this, probably on the run. Lucas promised he'd pay for a hotel room. Instead, he drove the girl to an empty lot behind an abandoned building and choked her until her fish eyes bulged from their sockets.

When he finished, Hunt pulled the girl from the vehicle and beat her with his fists. Bloodied and bruised the young prostitute. He threw her in the trunk and drove around the city until nightfall, when he dumped her body in an alley a block from where he'd picked up the girl. Her street corner. The police arrested the girl's pimp, who eventually walked after the police failed to prove he was the murderer.

Hunt was twenty-three then. He immediately got a taste for killing.

He killed again two years later. Another prostitute, this time in Oklahoma City.

The police believe he murdered eight women over the last five years. They are mistaken. The real number is twenty-three, most of which the authorities never uncovered.

Some he abducted from small towns in Nebraska, Oklahoma, and Texas. He brought them to the farmhouse. Played with them until he grew bored. Afterward, he dumped the bodies on open farmland far from home, places where the bodies might go undetected for weeks. Enough time for the insects and animals to pick the flesh clean.

He likes to keep his trophies near. A few bones are tossed into the hay inside the dilapidated barn. Many more are buried a few feet into the earth where the soil is as soft as a mother's belly. It excites him to keep the remains close.

The newspapers started calling him The Skinner because of his proclivity to butcher his victims. When he is bored, he reads the so-called experts' psychological profiles. To the police, Hunt is an enigma. They search for a discernible pattern, attempt to link the victims and find the overlap in the Venn diagram. There is none. He is undetectable. No man can find him.

Though Hunt never graduated high school, he is of above-average intelligence. Hunt regularly studies serial killers and how they were eventually caught. He kills no one he knows, and to this point, he hasn't murdered a woman from Pronti.

Don't shit where you sleep.

That is about to change.

He knew Marianne Garza was the one the first time he saw her outside Delbert's bar on the east end of town. Caught her scent the way a lion does injured prey upwind. Hunt can't say why she draws him, only that her death at his hands is as inevitable as the setting sun and the icy breath of winter.

The time has come. He walks to the stairway. If hell exists, it surely resides up this flight of stairs. The steps creak as he climbs, one hand running along the dusty, splintered banister. Slashes of window light are harsh across the hallway floor. Inside the master bedroom, the ceiling joists are exposed. Pink insulation bleeds through the joists and makes his throat itch. He has taken to sleeping in his mother's room while he procrastinates the repair.

He grabs his gloves and keys from the nightstand and peers through the window at the old barn. Toward the graveyard of hidden bones. Soon there will be more.

CHAPTER SEVENTY

Special Agent Scarlett Bell was too frightened to stay angry with her partner, Neil Gardy. She felt certain she was lost as darkness settled over the lonely country road, then the sign sprang out of the deadwood and weeds.

Welcome to Pronti, Kansas
Population 726

Why Bell was there was a larger mystery. Gardy's message was vague and only requested she assist him on a case. Funny that no case officially existed. She wondered if Deputy Director Weber knew either of them was here, wherever here was.

The weather was cold for late-October, a different world from the warmth she left behind in Virginia. The clouds hung low and ominous from the airport to the Kansas border, and now the night thickened as a gusting wind rocked the rental car across the road. Something pinged across the windshield as though the heavens hurled pebbles at the vehicle. Sleet.

One traffic light swung at the edge of town. Bell waited at the red light, no sign of another car in either direction. Pronti reminded her of old spaghetti westerns in which the bad guy rode into town on a black horse. A row of brick-faced stores stood off to her right—a five and dime store and a small grocery market. To the left was a barbershop with the iconic red-and-blue striped pole, and next stood a bar called Delbert's.

All of this consumed two short blocks, and then she was out of town and back in God's country.

It wasn't like Gardy to be clandestine and keep her out of the loop. He'd acted strangely since he learned Logan Wolf, the feared at-large serial killer and former Behavior Analysis Unit agent, had obtained Bell's address and sent her a letter. Then a bullet grazed Gardy's shoulder while they took down a shooter outside of Los Angeles, and while he recovered in the hospital, Wolf followed Bell into a shopping mall. Did the current case have something to do with Logan Wolf? Her instinct said this was something huge.

Gardy wasn't supposed to put himself in harm's way while his shoulder healed. All the more reason to keep Weber out of the loop, especially if Logan Wolf was involved. But why would Wolf be in the middle of Kansas?

She bit her tongue. Not knowing made her edgy, half-crazy. Gardy should have told her why she needed to come to Pronti.

The storm intensified as she searched for the motel. Rain and sleet fell in sheets and caused a headache-inducing racket inside the car.

She felt the back end fishtail as the road turned slick. Heart pumping, she turned into the skid and straightened the car. She'd grown up in Virginia, where the rare winter storm meant you holed up indoors until the snow and ice melted a day later. The one time she drove on snow-covered roads, she was visiting family in New York. Bell hit a patch of ice and put the car into a ditch. That split-second of losing control, feeling the car skid toward across the road with no way to stop, never left her. Even driving in the rain made Bell anxious the tires might hydroplane or a tractor-trailer would jackknife in front of her.

She needed to get off this road.

A sheet of paper with the motel's name and address lay on the seat. She reached for the paper, and it fell on the floor.

Bell cursed and brought the car onto the soft shoulder. Rocks peppered the undercarriage as she came to a stop. The storm grew loud while the engine idled. Black night engulfed the plains.

She caught hold of the paper between the tips of her fingers, and as she lifted it, something brushed the window and made her jump. Just tall grass whipped by the wind. The dark and vast nothingness unsettled her, made the world seem too large, too barren. She thought this was a good place to disappear. One could meet her fate on these roads and simply vanish.

The name of the motel was the Pronti Inn, located just outside of town on County Route 36. Which meant she should have passed the inn a mile back. Was this the correct road?

Bell checked her phone but couldn't raise a signal. Google Maps wouldn't save her tonight.

She noticed the voicemail from her mother and tapped the phone on her thigh in consideration. Last week, the doctor removed a tumor from her father's colon, and she'd been on pins-and-needles awaiting the test results. The message had arrived before her plane departed Dulles, and throughout the flight, the fear of not knowing chewed at her gut. She promised herself she'd listen to the message when the plane touched down, but she hadn't. Instead, she stuffed the phone into her bag as it incessantly flashed notification of the waiting message.

Bell swiped to the message and put her finger over the green play icon. Almost pressed play but couldn't.

She threw her head against the seat back and drummed her fingers on the steering wheel.

Then she shoved the phone back into her bag and put off the inevitable.

Damn Gardy and his secrets. She wheeled the car around and headed back to town.

CHAPTER SEVENTY-ONE

The sky took on a bruised look at sunset, an angry color that reminded Marianne Garza of tornadoes. It was too cold for severe thunderstorms, she thought as she went about her chores outside. When the night snuffed out the last bit of daylight, a winter wind screamed across the plains and sent the bluestem into a frenzy.

Marianne couldn't believe how cold it was as she closed the gate on the goat pen and huddled inside her jacket. For goodness' sake, it wasn't yet Halloween. If this was a sign of things to come, this winter would cut to the bone.

She wrapped her arms around her chest and ran with her head lowered until she reached the back door. Inside, she needed to tug against the wind to force the door closed. She could still hear the gale whistling around the eaves as though she'd angered the sky.

Marianne sighed at the mess of plates in the sink. It seemed impossible for one person to dirty this many dishes.

She got the water running and wrote a memo to

herself while the bubbles mushroomed. Scott, who owned the next farm over, had agreed to take care of the goats while Marianne was in Orlando, but Scott was painting the church in Solom and might forget the goats if she didn't remind him.

The hot water made her jump when she reached her hands in. As she whittled away at the backlog of dishes, she caught her reflection in the window. Dark hair tied back in a ponytail, reading glasses perched on top of her head, eyes wary at the thought of seeing her daughter and ex-husband again. It had been five months since she'd last seen them, and that had been a disaster, Marianne drunk and belligerent during the weekend they'd spent in Pronti.

Her lip quivered, and sadness welled into her throat.

She inhaled and held her breath. Closed her eyes as the faucet dripped.

There. That was better.

The window rattled and pulled her back to the present, and the memories of five months ago induced the old cravings. She wandered to the cupboard and stared at the half-empty bottle of Jack Daniels. There were two schools of thought regarding alcoholism. The first school, also known as conventional wisdom, stated all alcohol needed to be purged from the home. Remove temptation. That was great if Marianne locked herself away for days on end. But what happened when she stopped at Delbert's with the after work crew or went to a restaurant? Hell, temptation lived everywhere, and she was smart enough to know you could shun sin and still dance with the devil.

The more controversial ideology allowed for one bottle of alcohol kept on the premises. If you stared the glistening liquid in its golden, alluring eye, you overcame your demon and stole its power. No longer was it capable of following you when you left the perceived safety of your home.

This was the school of thought Marianne subscribed to. She nodded at her adversary and returned to the dishes.

The phone rang as she rinsed the last plate. It was her sister, Melissa, wishing her luck on the trip.

"You sure you don't need me to watch the goats?"

Marianne locked the phone between her cheek and shoulder as she towel-dried the dishes.

"That's too far, kiddo."

"Homer is only thirty minutes away."

"Don't worry. I've got someone keeping an eye on the place. Besides, I'll be back Monday evening. You'll hardly know I was gone."

It was quiet on the other end. She pictured Melissa leaning over with her forehead on her arm, searching for the right words.

"Hey, Sis. Don't let William talk you down. We both know you turned your life around, so don't let the bastard get inside your head."

Marianne plopped down at the kitchen table. This trip was for her daughter. In seven months, Erin would be a teenager. Growing up too fast. And that wasn't counting the rocket ship ride into puberty and, God forbid, boyfriends and dances and first kisses.

If Marianne didn't keep it together, she'd miss out on the years Erin would remember forever.

"I won't."

"Good."

She was off the phone when the wind blew the attic window open and toppled a stack of boxes. Wrenching open the garage door, she fished through the toolbox and removed a hammer and nails, knowing if she didn't nail the pane shut, the wind would blow the faulty window open while she was away and let the rain in.

Marianne was almost to the stairs when she saw the car parked along the shoulder across the road. That was strange as the next nearest residence was a quarter-mile east.

She peeked between the blinds and saw the man cross her lawn.

CHAPTER SEVENTY-TWO

Bell spotted the sleepy Pronti Inn at the edge of town. Her phone rang as she turned into the lot, and she snatched it from her bag, expecting the caller to be her mother again. Instead, Gardy's name and a picture of Muttley the cartoon dog popped up on the screen. If he was inside and impatiently awaiting her arrival, she'd personally thank him for transposing two numbers on the address and sending her into the middle of nowhere.

But Gardy wasn't at the motel.

"There's a convenience store at the corner of Billings and Main called Morgan's. Meet me there."

"Billings…and…Main," she said as she wrote the name and location beneath the motel's address. "What's this about, Gardy? You sent me on a wild goose chase."

"I don't want to say over the phone. Just get here, and don't mention this to anyone at Quantico."

"Yeah, yeah. I got that part. This better be worth it."

She ended the call and tossed the phone onto the passenger seat. Her mother's message flashed and flashed. Bell turned the phone over. Shaking her head, she took one look at the ramshackle motel before turning out of the parking lot. Gardy had booked his share of unfortunate accommodations during her first year with the BAU, but this place took the cake. The roof sagged as though depressed by an invisible weight, and the doors were paper-thin. She didn't want to imagine what the inside looked like.

The windshield wipers worked overtime against the sleet and rain. She almost drove past Morgan's before noticing the sheriff's truck at the front of the lot. After so much darkness, the bright light blazing through the glass made Bell squint.

Gardy and the sheriff stood on the concrete walkway fronting Morgan's. Gardy shifted from foot-to-foot as the wind rippled his jacket, his head ducked inside the coat while his teeth chattered. The sheriff was a haggard-looking man with a horseshoe mustache that reminded Bell of Hulk Hogan, except that he was half Hulk's size, and the horseshoe was brown, not bleach blonde.

When Bell climbed out of the rental, the sheriff took a long drag on a cigarette and blew smoke through his nose. He threw the butt on the sidewalk, stamped it out, and watched as Gardy stepped out to meet her.

"Good. You found the place all right."

"Why the cloak-and-dagger routine? Are you going to tell me what's going on?"

He blew air through his lips and glanced around, then turned his back to the sheriff and lowered his voice so the man couldn't hear.

"Guy working the counter, Alan Bodner, age twenty-seven of Pronti, Kansas, was on shift last night. Claims a guy he recognized entered the store around ten. Bodner couldn't place the face until it hit him this afternoon. Says he saw the man's picture on a crime website. Logan Wolf."

Bell felt a shock run through her body. She glanced over Gardy's shoulder at the rail-thin, pimply man working behind the counter. Bodner's eyes shifted around the store as if they couldn't keep still.

"You think Bodner's claim is legit?"

"We're about to find out. The store saves surveillance footage for forty-eight hours. We're waiting on the manager to arrive so we can take a look."

"Okay, but why are you speaking so the sheriff doesn't hear?"

"Because I don't want him to know we're keeping this quiet until we're sure it's Wolf. I promised him I'm in contact with Quantico and will call in backup."

"And you aren't."

"No. Weber can't know either of us is here until we're certain it's Wolf. Besides, it would be a huge waste of resources to pull additional agents to Pronti when all we have to go on is the testimony of a convenience store clerk who reads too many crime websites. I don't want to sneak around like this, but it's the only way. I haven't been able to get out from under Weber's thumb since the shooting."

"Don't make me defend Weber. But Gardy, you aren't fully healed."

"Getting better every day."

Bell rolled her eyes.

"If it were me, you'd chain me to a chair and make me do desk work."

"Sounds kinky."

"Shut it. So what are you going to tell the sheriff?"

"Nothing yet. Sheriff Lowe would order every deputy

to surround Pronti if he had his way, and that would be a tactical mistake. Wolf doesn't know we're onto him yet."

"Don't be so sure. He's managed to stay ahead of the FBI for five years."

"Fair point. One thing is for certain about Wolf. If the deputies spook him, he'll vanish. I can't risk losing Wolf on the small chance he's in Kansas."

Bell's teeth chattered as she bounced on her feet.

"We won't know if it's him until we look at the footage. Can we go inside now?"

Gardy led Bell to the storefront where the sheriff, who looked perturbed to be out in the cold and taking direction from Gardy, leaned against the glass.

"Sheriff Lowe, this is my partner, Agent Scarlett Bell."

The sheriff removed his hat before offering his hand to Bell.

"A pleasure, little lady."

Little lady?

Lowe fixed his hat and stood a little taller now that Bell was present. He practically beamed.

Gardy cleared his throat.

"Maybe we should go inside."

Thankfully, Morgan's was warm inside. It was a standard convenience store, divided into four evenly matched aisles stocked with jerky, chips, candy bars, overpriced grocery items, OTC medicines, and motor oil. A neon *ice-cold Budweiser* sign was affixed to the back wall. The cooler held beer, soda, fruit juices, and milk, and the recently mopped floor reflected their images.

While they awaited the manager, Bell walked the aisles. Gardy and Lowe were at the counter with an intimidated Bodner. She stared at a pack of Starburst and rummaged for pocket change when the door chimed. A bald man with two greasy strands of hair draped over his head tottered inside. The manager stamped his boots on the mat and assessed Bodner's mopping job before acknowledging Gardy and Lowe.

"We appreciate you coming down on short notice, Mr. Baughman," Lowe said.

Baughman sniffled his nose and barely nodded. Bell joined the others and followed Baughman around the corner. The room holding the recording equipment was too small for more than one person. The manager typed one finger at a time on the keyboard until the video monitor on the counter switched from live to recorded footage.

"What time do you need to see, Sheriff?"

"Mr Bodner says the man came inside around seven last evening. Is that right?"

Bodner glanced furtively between Lowe and the agents. He nodded.

The clerk's estimate was a half-hour off. Baughman replayed the security footage at triple speed. An elderly woman with a cane moved down the aisles and paid at the counter. After she left, the store was empty except for Bodner for a long time.

"You sure it was seven?"

Bodner appeared anxious and confused. Then his eyes brightened.

"He came in after the old lady left. Yeah, I remember now."

The sheriff grumbled under his breath and sidled over to the display of cigarette cartons.

Bell couldn't pull her eyes from the monitor. Logan

Wolf. The serial killer who discovered her address and stalked her to their last case in California. She'd seen his photograph enough times to memorize every crevice and pore on his face, the black and depthless eyes. The possibility he'd walked these aisles in the last twenty-four hours tingled her skin.

On the security footage, the entrance door swung open, and a man with his head lowered turned away from the counter and cut toward the medicine aisle. Until this point, Bell didn't believe Wolf had been here. Bodner had made a mistake, saw someone who looked like the nation's most-feared serial killer. Bell knew it was Wolf though the camera failed to capture his face. The serial killer knew where the camera was and purposely avoided it. She wanted to reach through the screen and grab him before he disappeared.

Gardy stood by her side. He didn't say a word. Just glared at the screen as the man bent to retrieve an item off the shelf. What was it? A bottle of Pepto Bismol, Bell thought. If it wasn't Wolf, it was for damn sure a shrewd criminal. The man approached the counter and stood at an angle so the camera only caught him in side profile, then he kept his head down as he paid.

"Is that our killer?"

Bell jumped at Lowe's voice. He crowded behind them, stinking like an old ashtray.

Bell held her breath. Wolf would need to turn toward the camera when he headed for the door. The alternative was to pirouette and duck low, a move which would snowball suspicion.

Wolf's turn was swift and graceful. In a split-second, he escaped the camera's eye and reached for the door.

"Rewind it," Bell called to Baughman, who'd come out of the room to watch.

He harrumphed and turned back. Gardy followed the manager and instructed him to play the footage as slowly as the recording system allowed. The video quality suffered and appeared blurry when he did so. Bell cursed.

"Stop it. Right there."

Bell bent close to the screen. The monitor hummed and produced a dusty heat smell.

There was no mistaking the man in the picture. Short black hair, black eyes that bore holes into your soul.

Frozen on the screen was the face of Logan Wolf. The face of death.

CHAPTER SEVENTY-THREE

Marianne Garza awakened to the scent of spent fuel and stale cigarettes. Her head hurt. When Marianne moved her jaw, the corners of her mouth tore.

For a moment, she thought she'd fallen asleep on the plane, but the trip to Orlando was tomorrow. Wasn't it? She was tired, bones aching. No, she wasn't on the plane. Had she spent the evening at Delbert's and had too much to drink, and now she paid for her sins with a migraine and a tumultuous stomach? Couldn't be. She didn't drink anymore, refused to let her daughter down again.

Marianne realized her wrists and ankles were bound. Then she remembered. Like a splash of ice water against her face.

There had been a knock on the front door. A man spoke to her through the barrier and said his car broke down. He needed to use her phone. Though Marianne wanted to help, she wouldn't let him in. You couldn't trust anyone these days, and there were countless stories on the news about overly trusting women who were abducted.

So she promised to call the towing garage, and when

she walked away from the door, he…

He…

Marianne's pulse raced as she recalled the window shattering. A black shadow raced across the living room and cut her off from the phone, and as she turned for the door, he grabbed her. Smothered her face with a cloth. A cloyingly sweet scent. Chloroform.

Oh, God.

Her eyes flicked open to the backseat of an old car, too large and noisy to be modern. It was dark. Sleet bounced off the roof and windshield.

The floor mat stank of cigarette smoke and dust. A brown splotch marred the center.

Four thin shreds ran down the back of the driver seat. Four slashes to match a woman's nails.

She might have been inside anyone's car. A rapist, a jilted lover out for revenge.

Marianne couldn't say why *The Skinner* popped into her head. Once the idea formed it spread cancerous panic through her body. Impossible. Not The Skinner.

An old Hank Williams song played through the radio. A throaty roar came out of the engine when the driver pressed the gas. The muffler was on its last legs. She imagined a plume of smoke puffing out of the tailpipe.

Bound on the floor, she made out his sneakers from beneath the seat. Manure coated his sneakers, and that placed him as someone who lived on a farm, not the elusive serial killer who hunted the plains.

Unable to wiggle her wrists, she searched with her fingers for anything to cut the ropes. There was nothing. No ice scraper lodged under the seats. He'd bound her ankles too tightly and cut off the circulation. Pins-and-needles coursed through her feet and spread up her legs as she writhed.

With the gag across her mouth, she couldn't speak. Nevertheless, she moaned and pleaded through the cloth. The engine noise consumed her voice.

An idea occurred to her. If she got the blood flowing in her legs and kicked the door...

Old cars had faulty parts. The door might not latch properly. Yet she didn't know how fast the car traveled. The whir of the tires told her they were moving at highway speeds, too fast to leap from the car.

Torn fabric hung from the roof like a tongue, revealing the metal. Two control panels powered the passenger windows. She guessed he'd locked their use with the master control.

Yet Marianne didn't need to leap from the vehicle. If she fought her way onto the back seat and kicked out the window, there was a fighting chance someone would notice. She prayed this wasn't the only vehicle on this stretch of road.

She battled to get her knees beneath her when the vehicle slowed. The blinker ticked, and then the car's momentum rolled Marianne onto her side as the vehicle swung left. She glanced up at the window and saw nothing but dark sky. A slash of light interrupted the black and left red marks on her eyes. Then more lights.

The car turned again and bucked over a bump in the pavement. She smelled gas before the pumps floated across the windows. A gas station.

The engine cut off and killed the song. Now it was quiet. Just the sound of him breathing and the storm biting at the car.

Feeling him shift around in his seat, she closed her eyes and feigned sleep. She willed herself not to open her eyes. Marianne didn't wish to see his face any more than she wanted him to know she was awake.

There were people here. The store attendant, at least. A chance to escape.

A cold blast of wind ruffled her hair when the door opened. She listened for his footsteps but heard nothing. She sensed him staring at her through the window.

Marianne lay still for what seemed an eternity before his sneakers scuffed the blacktop and moved to the back of the car.

Be patient. Just a little longer.

He unscrewed the gas cap. The vehicle shook when he shoved in the nozzle.

Tick, tick, tick. The meter rolled as gas poured into the tank. Remaining patient, she clamped her eyelids together and stayed motionless. He could easily watch her through the window while he pumped.

After he finished, she was shocked when she heard him step over the island and walk toward the store to pay.

Her eyes popped open. She knew no other cars were at the island. Otherwise, he wouldn't have chosen this gas station.

Several thoughts moved through her head—kicking out a window, testing the door latch, wriggling herself onto the front seat and pressing the horn. She had a minute at most.

She bridged and slid her back across the floor, slowly inching toward the door. When she was close, she reared back and kicked. The door rattled but didn't budge. She tried again and failed.

Marianne battled the bindings and tried to throw herself up to her knees. It took several attempts before she finally got there. By then she was out of breath and sweaty. Crawling onto the back seat without use of her hands proved to be nearly impossible, yet she had no choice. When she successfully rolled onto the seat, she scooted her legs toward the window with growing desperation.

She kicked out and felt the window give. Kicked again, her legs half-numb and unable to generate power.

The back door flew open behind her. She screamed into the gag as he clutched her by the hair.

Marianne saw his face now. A man in his thirties, thin and cord-like, eyes sunken. She thought she recognized him.

"We're almost home. You should rest."

He stuffed the chloroform-laced rag over her nose and mouth. She writhed and tried to hold her breath so the drug wouldn't pull her into the depths of sleep again.

The man was relentless. He filled the open door with his body, shielding anyone from seeing. He remained preternaturally still as he leaned over her body. To the proprietor glancing through the window, it would appear as if nothing out of the ordinary was going on. Just the man grabbing an item from the backseat.

Marianne couldn't hold her breath any longer. She gasped and inhaled, a duck-call gag that made her head swim.

The lights went out for Marianne.

CHAPTER SEVENTY-FOUR

Gardy's room was a pleasant surprise. The fireplace was artificial, nothing more than a space heater with an animated light that looked like a flame if you used your imagination, but Bell couldn't sit close enough while she waited for her body to warm. She wore sweatpants and a George Mason basketball t-shirt, the shirt long enough to cover her knees while she sat cross-legged on the floor.

Gardy slipped his shoes off and lounged on the bed. Beside the nightstand, a potted tree branch reached toward the tall ceiling, lending a rustic vibe to the decor. The walls were white stucco, and logs bordered the ceiling to create the appearance of a log cabin. Gardy, who flicked on the television and found the Ohio State - Oklahoma football game, couldn't be bothered with the decor.

A half-eaten pizza and container of wings lay on the floor. Palatable, but not New York City quality.

Gardy had contacted Quantico and relayed the security cam footage. The technicians were attempting to clean up the image and make a definitive call on whether it was Logan Wolf, but backup was en route to Pronti already. Gardy's proverbial net was about to be cast. The backlash would come when Weber caught wind of the situation and questioned why Gardy was in Kansas without his approval. True, the deputy director of CIRG had tasked Gardy with catching Wolf, but that was before the sniper bullet excavated an inch of flesh from Gardy's shoulder in California.

Bell finally started to warm when her phone buzzed. She reached into her pocket and saw another message from her mother. The dread rushed back at Bell.

"Something wrong?"

Gardy studied her from the bed. He lost focus easily lately, seemed to space out, as though his mind constantly replayed his near-death experience.

"I need to make a call. Do you mind?"

"Of course, not."

He returned to the football game, yet Bell sensed his eyes following as she slipped into the bathroom.

The bathroom was clean but minuscule. Barely enough room existed to stand between the toilet and sink, and the shower was a glorified phone booth with a sprinkler attachment. The fan and light ran off the same wall switch. Though the fan's rattle made it difficult to hear, Bell was thankful the sound cloaked her conversation from Gardy.

She stared at the call screen for a long time. The sensation felt similar to standing on the end of a tall diving board, heart racing as her toes curled over the edge. The longer she waited, the more she wanted to back away and never again try anything so crazy.

Her breath shuddered as she exhaled. Fingers trembling, she placed the call.

The phone rang twice before her mother picked up.

"Scarlett? Where have you been? I tried to call you twice."

"Sorry, Mom. I was in the air the first time, and the service is terrible here."

"Wait, I thought you were on vacation this week. Don't tell me the FBI forced you to work again. Where did they ship you this time?"

"It's not important. I'll be home in a few days, and the vacation time will still be there. I have until January to spend it."

"It just seems like they never let you breathe. It's not healthy, Scarlett. There's more to life than—"

"I know, Mom. Please. We discussed this."

Tammy Bell sighed. Bell could almost hear her mother bite back the next retort.

"You're right, dear. I won't say another word about it." Bell wondered how long the detente would last. "You got my message, I hope."

Bell stammered. She couldn't bring herself to listen.

"Oh, never mind. This isn't the sort of news one wants to hear in a voicemail."

Please, get it over with.

"The tests came back fine. Dr Meehan says it's a polyp. Something called an adenoma, lots of men Dad's age get them."

A thousand pounds fell off Bell's shoulders. Her legs felt weak, and she sat on the edge of the toilet with her head between her knees. The gurgle that came out of her throat was part-laugh, part-sob.

"Scarlett? You still there?"

Bell sniffed.

"Yeah. Right here, Mom."

"You're not crying, are you?"

"I'm just happy Dad is okay. So the doctor said it was benign?"

"Yes. He'll keep an eye on it for a while, make sure nothing changes."

There was a joke in there somewhere—the doctor keeping an eye on her father's colon. Relief left her too drained to laugh.

Small talk filled the rest of the conversation. A new Costco went up a few miles from their house. Mrs Urtz had a new poodle, and the darn thing barked if a leaf fell off the tree.

Bell was surprised they'd spent fifteen minutes talking when the call ended. It was the most amicable exchange she'd had with her mother in weeks.

Gardy had the laptop on the bed when Bell returned. He quickly shut the screen and became interested in the football game again.

"You didn't get sick in my bathroom, did you?"

"I made a phone call." She eyed the laptop suspiciously as he slid it into the case. "Caught you looking at porn again."

"What…no…I never…"

"Uh-huh. You're keeping a lot of secrets lately, Gardy."

His eyes strayed to the laptop, then to the television. "How so?"

"This case, for one. Here I am in the middle of nowhere when I should be on a beach with a piña colada, and up until an hour ago I had no idea why."

"Yes, but I couldn't risk Weber—"

"To hell with Weber. I never would have said a thing to him had you told me you'd picked up Logan Wolf's trail. So come clean about the laptop. What's so important that you won't let me see?"

"Bell, you don't need to see."

"I can handle it, whatever it is."

Gardy shrugged and removed the laptop. When he opened the computer, her breath caught in her throat. The browser was open to a tabloid website called *The Informer*. The headline read, *FBI VIXEN HOT ON WOLF'S TRAIL*. A closeup photograph of Bell took up the majority of the front page.

"Oh, shit."

"Yeah. That's why I didn't want to show you."

"FBI Vixen?"

"Well, they got the FBI part correct."

She slugged him in the shoulder.

"I recognize the picture, Gardy. That's downtown Milanville after Meeks murdered the businessman. Christ, I remember the guy who took the photo."

"Gavin Hayward," Gardy said, clicking on the byline. A smug male with a toothy grin smiled out from the screen. "He made a mint writing about the case after Wolf went rogue. And he seems to know your every move."

Gardy clicked back to the article and scrolled down the page. There was a photograph of Bell in Coral Lake taken from a long distance and blown up. She recognized the Finger Lakes village. In the picture, Bell stared pensively at the water.

"He's following us."

"He's following you, Bell."

"We're a team. You were there, too."

"Ah, but sexy vixens sell tabloids, not middle-aged men."

His eyebrow shot up. If he snickered, she'd make sure he limped for the next month.

"You think there's any way he knows we're in Kansas?"

"How could he? We're off the books, so even if he has an informant inside the FBI—"

"—but if he has my address—"

"That's classified information."

"It didn't stop Wolf from figuring out where I live." A chill ran down her body. "My God, what if Hayward harasses my parents?"

"We'll cross that bridge when we come to it. Look, Hayward isn't dangerous. He's an exploitive sleaze bag, and we need to ensure he doesn't compromise our investigations. My concern is Wolf reads The Informer."

"That explains how Wolf found me in Milanville." A light turned on in her head, and she snapped her finger. "We could flip this around and use Hayward as bait."

Gardy steepled his fingers and rested his chin on the tips.

"Right. Give Hayward bad intel and draw Wolf to a location of our choosing. The trouble is Hayward is a bullshit artist. He'll see through the facade."

Bell crossed her legs and chewed her lip.

"We're so close to catching him this time, Gardy."

CHAPTER SEVENTY-FIVE

Marianne sprung awake when a door closed. She stared up at a filthy water-stained ceiling. A sagging crack ran down the center and branched toward the corner. The room was dim. Ambient light spread from another room.

She tried to lift her head, but it was too heavy, and her head collapsed and sank into a couch cushion which smelled of ancient dust and body odor. The ceiling spun. She wanted to vomit. The gag was removed as were the ropes from her ankles.

Marianne didn't know where she was until her head cleared. She was inside the house of the man who kidnapped her. The sudden realization got her moving, and she swung her legs off the couch and pushed against the cushions. Her body, still under the barbiturate-like influence of the Chloroform, refused to cooperate. The urge to wretch came again, and she clutched the armrest until the room ceased its infernal spinning.

A shadow crept across the floor. The man was outside the room. Listening.

A standing cabinet had been shoved against the front

door. She didn't think she had the strength to move it.

When she glanced back to the floor, the shadow was gone. A glass clinked from the kitchen, then a drawer opened. She pictured the man with a butcher's knife, and her mind leaped to the discovery of dismembered bodies in open farmland. Bled out. A few body parts missing from each victim, taken by The Skinner.

Consciously, Marianne refused to believe this man was The Skinner, but the depths of her mind screamed it had to be him.

A burning scent came from the kitchen. The man was cooking eggs. She could hear the grease splatter and flame hissing.

Quickly, she looked around the room for a weapon, something she could defend herself with. There was nothing. Only two lamps on stands in the sparsely furnished room. No television, no phone. That made her wonder if her own phone was in her pocket. She checked and found her pockets empty. The phone, she recalled, was on the kitchen counter inside her house.

Grabbing hold of the armrest, Marianne pulled herself to her feet. Her knees wobbled, but the cushions blocked her legs and saved her from toppling. Another dizzy spell rocked her back on her heels. After it passed, she stepped toward the entryway.

She waited at the corner, careful to ensure her own shadow wasn't cast upon the floor. The frying sounds continued from the kitchen, the clink of spatula on pan. Somehow this lent her a small measure of comfort knowing he was human and needed to eat. A human could be reasoned with.

Except the other women tried to reason with him,

didn't they? A prickle of fear scuttled down her neck.

A staircase ascended from the hallway. If she couldn't budge the cabinet, she'd take her chances upstairs. Climb through a window or find a place to hide.

His footsteps came quickly down the hallway. She darted back to the couch on cat's paws and sprawled on the cushions. Her eyes closed a moment before he turned the corner.

Goosebumps covered her body. He was watching her. Only a few steps away.

Marianne held her breath until she was certain he was gone. She never heard him leave. It struck her how silently the man moved.

The weakness from the Chloroform lingered like old flu symptoms that clung long after the disease abated. Exhaustion. Confused thoughts. She felt it in her arms and legs, but it resided most in her neck. It took great effort to push herself off the couch again. Her heart did gymnastics as she moved toward the wall. One quick burst was all it would take to get her across the hall and to the stairs. She gambled he wouldn't notice.

The kitchen was quiet now. Too quiet. The vent fan hummed, and the downstairs was thick with the smell of his cooking.

Her neck hairs prickled, and she swung her head around. A man stared through the living room window, but it was too dark to make out features.

Marianne didn't react at first. She thought it was her own reflection before she realized the ghostly figure didn't mirror her own movements.

The scream caught in her throat a moment before The Skinner's hand cupped her mouth.

She yelled and tried to bite down, but his grip was strong. His free hand reached around with the Chloroform-laced rag.

He smothered Marianne's face. Her legs went limp.

CHAPTER SEVENTY-SIX

The phone shocked Bell out of a dream she couldn't remember. The hammering of her heart told her she didn't want to.

Gardy's number lit her screen.

"Bell, were you asleep?"

She rubbed the grit from her eyes and fumbled for the light switch. Damn unfamiliar motel rooms.

"What…what time is it?"

She answered her own question when the clock came into focus. Two in the morning.

"Time to roll. We have a potential abduction."

"Wolf?"

"My gut says yes."

Ten minutes later she stumbled into the cold night, eyes heavy and shying away from the lampposts. Gardy wore a grin as he leaned against his rented Escalade. He held two Styrofoam cups of coffee.

"Wait, how did you manage to get coffee? You just called."

He glanced at his watch.

"With the way Molasses moves, I could have driven to the city and back and gotten us Dunkin." He handed her a cup. "You drink, I'll drive."

Unlike her own bargain basement rental, the Escalade kept the cold at bay and doused the wind. The silence was loud until Gardy fired the engine and turned onto county route 36.

Gardy reached into his bag and handed the iPad to Bell. A driver's license photo appeared on the screen.

"Marianne Garza, age forty-two, of Pronti, Kansas. She was supposed to drive to Oklahoma City and fly to Florida in the morning. A neighbor drove past her house an hour ago and noticed a window was smashed. Knocked on the door, but Garza never answered."

"Any chance she already left?"

"Car was still in the driveway. The sheriff's office is trying to contact family and friends and find out if anyone saw or heard from Garza tonight. Meanwhile, Lowe is on the scene, and he's pissed."

Bell swiped the screen. A map displayed Garza's residence.

"Because we didn't move on Wolf after studyng the security camera footage."

"Right. It'll be my head when he tells Weber."

"But Quantico hasn't determined if it's Wolf in the picture."

"Hard to argue with the evidence, Bell. Bodner swore it was Wolf, and you were pretty sure."

Gardy shook his head and slapped the steering wheel.

"I had a chance to go after Wolf and I froze."

Bell put the iPad away.

"Don't do that to yourself, Gardy. I could look at that

footage a hundred times and never be certain. Besides, a dozen agents couldn't cover an entire town, not even a one-horse burg like this one."

The outskirts of Pronti were devoid of streetlights. The black was so complete Bell worried the sun would never rise.

The lights atop the sheriff cruisers came into view as they turned down a dirt road. The vague suggestion of a silo stood back in a field, and in the dark, it looked like a monstrous beast poised over a sleepy farm.

Red and blue flashers cut the night in front of Marianne Garza's residence, a green, two-story with a small barn and animal pen around the back. The front window was broken.

One deputy, a tall male with a pocked face and sideburns, nudged his partner.

"Well, well, well. If it isn't the government serial killer experts."

The deputy made air quotes around experts and spoke just loud enough for Gardy and Bell to overhear. They sneered and turned back to the scene.

Bell edged closer to Gardy.

"We have our work cut out for us."

"Did you expect a welcoming committee?"

Sheriff Lowe stood beside the porch steps. A woman in sweatpants and a winter coat stood with her arms crossed, bouncing on her feet to stay warm.

Lowe's attention shifted from the woman to the approaching agents. He didn't appear happy to see Bell and Gardy.

"This is Allison Hinchey, Garza's neighbor."

"Hello," Hinchey said, offering her hand to Gardy

and Bell.

"She's the one who saw the broken window and reported Garza missing."

"That's our farm a mile up the road." Hinchey pointed into the night. All Bell saw was darkness on the horizon. "I deliver milk and eggs to Marianne once a week. I usually get here by eight, but I ran late tonight on account of my youngest falling ill and didn't make it here until after midnight. She's got an old cooler out in the barn. I figured the eggs and milk would keep on the porch with it being so cold tonight, but I didn't want to chance it, so I grabbed the flashlight and started around back. The window caught my eye before I got far."

"So you knew Marianne Garza would be gone for the weekend?" Bell asked.

"Yes, and I told Sheriff Lowe. I figured I'd hold the delivery until she got back, but Marianne said to drop it off before she went to bed."

Bell nodded.

"What did you do next?"

"Well, I saw the lights on and figured she was still awake, probably all nervous about the flight, so I knocked. After a while, I started to worry someone broke in and robbed the place, and maybe they were still here. That's when I thought I'd better call Sheriff Lowe."

"Mrs Hinchey, do you know anyone who had reason to harm Marianne Garza or vandalize her property?"

Hinchey scrunched her brow and glanced between the sheriff and agents.

"What? No, not Marianne."

"No jealous ex-boyfriends or someone she argued with?"

"Marianne went through a messy divorce a few years ago."

"Messy how?"

Hinchey's eyes flew among the agents as if she'd said something wrong.

"I didn't want to say nothing because she's a nice lady, always has a kind word for you, but she lost custody of her girl. Husband took the daughter to Florida."

Bell looked at Gardy.

"Is that who she was going to Florida to visit? Her husband and daughter?"

"I assume so."

They thanked Hinchey, who shot furtive glances over her shoulder as she hurried to her pickup.

"Nice lady," Lowe said, bobbing his head at Hinchey. His thumbs curled in his belt loops. "Lots of good folk around here, Agents Gardy and Bell. And you fed them to a shark."

Gardy raised his hands.

"Sheriff, please."

"No, no. It's my turn to speak. You knew Logan Wolf was here and you did nothing. Tell me, agent. If a tornado was about to sweep through Pronti, would you counsel me to keep it quiet so as not to panic everyone?"

"I phoned Quantico. They're sending agents from Kansas City and Oklahoma City as we speak."

"Well, then. I hope they're more helpful than the two of you."

CHAPTER SEVENTY-SEVEN

The wind chewed into Marianne's skin and found her bones. It was the cold that snapped her awake and out of a dream in which she drowned, pulled under by a black and frenzied sea.

She was inside a dilapidated barn. Panicking, she tugged and found her arms bound to a wooden support beam. The timber groaned as she struggled.

Time and neglect had torn the roof. Half the slats were gone, the night sky peeking in at her. The door hung cockeyed from one rusty hinge. Loose planks danced when the wind gusted.

And it was dark. So dark.

She twisted her arms and tugged, but the bindings were strong. Wherever she was, her abductor felt confident her screams wouldn't be heard.

Something moved in the dark. Inside the barn.

Marianne's breath flew in-and-out as the hulking shape shifted and drew closer. A monster sprung out of the dark. A nightmare face oozing pus.

She screamed until she tasted blood on the back of her

throat.

She realized the hideous thing was only a cow. Blisters dotted the cow's head, and a milky substance dripped from its mouth. Marianne had been around farms long enough to recognize foot-and-mouth disease. It wandered forward and back as though stuck in an endless loop.

A stable door created a barrier between Marianne and the cow. The animal made a snorting noise and lay down in the hay.

Marianne had never been so cold, not even when she snowshoed with her ex-husband in the Colorado mountains and became lost after sunset. Or maybe it was fear that raised gooseflesh on her skin and made her quiver uncontrollably.

An assortment of ancient-looking scythes, sickles, and pitchforks hung from the wall. They moved on their own with the wind.

The hay was up to her shins, brown and soiled. Allergens tickled her nose. She stood and listened for a long time but didn't hear the man.

The Skinner.

As much as she tried to bury the thought, it kept crawling out of a shallow grave.

The belief her kidnapper was a serial killer brought the fight out in Marianne. She struggled with the ropes and twisted her arms. The beam made a squealing, crackling noise that ran to the roof. A jagged slat broke off and tumbled down. She ducked before it could gouge her face. It splintered against the ground and crumbled, the wood rotted through. If she wasn't careful, the entire roof would come down on her head.

Nausea from the Chloroform sapped her strength. The exertion roiled her stomach, and Marianne bent over and dry heaved. A long string of spittle connected her lips with the hay.

The cow grunted. Marianne slumped to the ground and sobbed. This wasn't the way she was meant to die.

She closed her eyes and imagined herself in Orlando where her ex-husband had custody of Erin. Exhaustion overcame her, and she fell into a shallow sleep.

"Wake up, Mommy."

Marianne's eyes sprung open. Erin sat before her in the hay, legs crossed. Only it couldn't be her daughter, for Erin was twelve now, and this was the nine-year-old version, complete with wide, searching eyes and braces that glittered despite the darkness. Marianne shook her head, not as a negative but in the way one does when shaking the cobwebs free. The day after tomorrow Marianne was supposed to take Erin to Disney World, their first quality time spent together in three years.

"Why...how did you get here?"

Erin scrunched her brow.

"What do you mean? I've been here the whole time."

"No. You can't be here, honey. You're in Florida."

"You never came like you said you would, so we came to find you. Daddy says you always break your promises."

Marianne glanced over Erin's shoulder but didn't see anyone else inside the barn.

"No...I did my best. I really tried this time."

A branch snapped outside. Marianne's eyes shot to the open doorway.

"You need to run. Run before he comes back."

"Not unless you come with me."

Marianne's head slumped. Too heavy. Her eyelids fluttered, and when she lifted her eyes, she was shocked her daughter was still there. No, this couldn't be Erin. The real Erin hated her, blamed her for the divorce. Explaining why she left Jeremy, who cheated on Marianne, would only drive another wedge between them. Which is why Marianne wanted to spend the day with Erin at Disney, just the two of them. Warm sun and shared laughs.

Marianne had stopped drinking. Six weeks sober, her peace made with God. Someone once told her it took sixty-six days to form a good habit or squash a bad one, and dammit, she was almost there.

"Why don't you get up and come with me, Mommy?"

A tear crawled down Marianne's cheek. Picked up dirt and grime and became gray before it dripped off her chin. She twisted her body so the bindings were visible.

"I can't."

"How did you get all tied up?"

"I don't know. He hurt me, I think."

Erin nodded once. Marianne looked over her shoulder at the infinite darkness. For the first time, Marianne caught a glimpse of a distant light. It only appeared when the wind moved the tree branches. The man's house.

'He's coming, Mommy. You need to get your hands free."

"I'm trying, baby. He tied the ropes too tight." Marianne blinked. "Erin, is Daddy here, too? I need you to run and get Daddy. Tell him I need help."

"Daddy is angry."

"Why? Why is Daddy angry, Erin?"

Then her twelve-year-old daughter knelt before her. The girl's eyes were hard and tinged with derision.

"Because you're a drunk, a monster."

"No. Don't say that."

"And when *he* comes, you'll get what you deserve. You know who he is, Mom."

"You're scaring me."

"You should be scared. Nobody escapes The Skinner."

A frigid mist blew through the slats and wet her face. She brushed the water on her shoulder, and Erin was gone.

Marianne collapsed and hung suspended by the ropes. Her tears wet the hay as a shadow moved past the barn door.

CHAPTER SEVENTY-EIGHT

As Bell expected, Sheriff Lowe pulled a power-play and took over the investigation. They were lucky the sheriff allowed them to search the house after the deputies walked through.

Muffled voices from the deputies and sheriff moaned from behind the closed door as Bell and Gardy entered the foyer. Deputy Keene, the tall man who'd already made clear his distaste for the agents, remained in the house to keep an eye on them.

Glass from the shattered window was sprayed into the dining room. Gardy knelt and pointed at a discoloration in the shag carpet.

"Mud from the front yard."

Bell agreed.

"Deputy Keene," said Gardy. "Have your men check for shoe prints between the window and road. He tracked mud inside, so it stands to reason he picked it up in the yard." The deputy didn't blink. "Please."

Keene gave an exasperated sigh. He slammed the door behind him.

Bell wanted to scream.

"What an asshole."

"He's following Lowe's lead and doesn't know any better," Gardy said.

"How about a little decorum? We're on the same side."

"We won't get it on this case. Keep your head low and your eyes open."

A dining room chair lay on its side. They followed the vague damage path into the living room. A picture frame held a photograph of Garza and a young girl, probably the daughter. No blood, no obvious signs of a struggle.

The faucet dripped in the kitchen, and the dish rack held plates and two glasses.

Gardy folded his arms and leaned against the counter.

"What do you make of the husband winning custody?"

Bell found it curious.

"It's uncommon, but not unheard of. If she abused the daughter, there'd be a record. Lowe would have said something. There must be another reason."

"Drugs?"

"This doesn't look like the home of a drug user."

"No, but it doesn't look like the home of a woman who would lose a custody battle, either."

The upstairs held a bathroom and two bedrooms. The first bedroom had been the daughter's. A twin bed stood lonely in the corner, bare of blanket or sheets. There was a small dresser against the wall and a desk fit for a grade school student. Garza's bedroom was cramped but neat, the bed made and no dirty clothes strewn about the floor. The bare light bulb in the closet didn't work. A modest collection of shirts, pants, and dresses hung from hangers.

The front door opened with a momentary suction of air and closed. Keene was back.

Gardy listened at the bedroom doorway. It was quiet downstairs. He edged the door shut.

"I didn't expect we'd find anything upstairs. I wanted to talk without an audience."

"Okay."

"It's not Wolf," said Gardy.

"What?"

"Think about it. The Logan Wolf murders are all men."

"You're forgetting he killed his wife."

"No, I'm well aware. That pattern never sat right with me. He kills his wife, then murders a bunch of nameless males. Now he decides to murder women again? I feel like we're forcing a square into a circular hole."

"Serial killers shift their patterns. We know this."

Gardy glanced out the window. The pane, blurred by raindrops, offered a nebulous view of the clouds.

"When I joined the BAU, Logan Wolf was a legend. Forget that he was the best profiler the agency had ever seen. Nobody ran an investigation like Wolf. Attention to detail. Visualizing the scene through the killer's eyes."

"Easy to believe since he was a psycho, himself."

"That's beside the point. Many of us thought he'd be Deputy Director. Ironically, Wolf's downfall opened he door for Weber. But I'll tell you this. If the unknown subject left a hint of evidence, Wolf uncovered it." Gardy pointed through the floor toward the broken dining room window. "Which is why I'm not buying this shit-show. A shattered window, a footprint. Wolf wasn't sloppy."

Bell pressed her finger to her lips and put her ear against the door. Nothing.

"Then who did we see on the security footage? In a few hours, there will be more agents than people in this town."

Gardy blew air through his lips. He walked in a circle, hands buried in his pockets until an idea came to him.

"What if it *is* Wolf on the video, but the abductor is someone else? Lowe jumped to the conclusion a serial killer took Marianne Garza. It could be anyone. A jealous ex-boyfriend. A prowler who lost control of the situation. We're shooting in the dark."

The floor groaned at the foot of the stairs.

"Agents? You still up there?"

Gardy poked his head through the doorway.

"Finishing up with pictures. We'll be right down."

Keene grunted and wandered back to the living room. The couch protested when he sat down.

Gardy closed the door.

"You'll say I'm crazy, but I want to throw an idea out there."

"Hurry. Keene's getting suspicious."

His eyes wandered to the ceiling. She could tell his confidence was low, too many perceived missteps following on the heels of being shot.

"What if there are two serial killers?"

"You're fishing. This town is hardly large enough to support two killers. Anyhow, what are the odds of two active serial killers showing up in Pronti?"

"It doesn't have to be by chance. There's an established history of serial killers who worked together. The two guys in Italy."

"Abel and Furlan."

"Right. Not to mention the DC snipers."

"In those cases, the killers worked together from the beginning. They didn't suddenly connect and form a pact."

Gardy shook his head.

"That part bugs me, too. There's a first for everything." He reached for the door and froze. "Oh, that's not a good thought."

"What's that?"

"This is Skinner territory."

Bell's stomach dropped as she recalled the photographs. Bodies dumped in farm country, bloated and crawling with insects. It wasn't likely they'd stumbled upon The Skinner's latest victim by chance, but the location fit.

"This seems like a long shot. What the hell. I trust your instinct. Are you going to tell Lowe?"

"I have to."

"He'll have an aneurysm."

Gardy opened the door and stood in the threshold.

"We have to get this right, Bell. Two serial killers in the same town is a slaughterhouse."

CHAPTER SEVENTY-NINE

Marianne was numb from the cold when something pulled her out of a dream. A noise like footsteps swishing through the hay.

She glanced up and saw the diseased cow watching her over the stall. The gate glistened with mucus. The cow bobbed its head as if acknowledging her, then it paced through the stall's shadows.

In the nightmare, Erin no longer remembered Marianne. Guilt made the dream seem real, and the hurt inside Marianne's chest followed her out of the dream like a vengeful shadow.

She was slumped on the ground with her arms almost stretched to the point of snapping, the tension tearing at her joints.

Except her arms weren't tied to the post. They lay extended behind her with the ropes severed and coiled at the base of the support beam.

This was impossible. She couldn't have pulled the ropes apart on her own.

It hurt to raise her arms, and as she did she heard

another whisper of a footstep on the hay. She swung around and saw nothing but empty barn.

Confused and delusional, Marianne believed Erin truly had been inside the barn and cut her free. She whispered her daughter's name, and the wind answered. Another plank tumbled from the ceiling and narrowly missed her head.

It occurred to Marianne her abductor might have cut the ropes. All part of a sick and twisted game. He wanted to stalk her before he…

Don't think it. He's not The Skinner. Just a sicko pervert.

Yet Marianne knew better. She'd felt the evil pouring out of the man. She knew her fate.

If releasing her was part of his game, she'd give him a fight. Make him regret underestimating her.

Marianne stepped forward and stubbed her toe on something under the hay. The bleach-white bone protruded from the hay like a skeleton rising out of a grave. She covered her mouth with one trembling hand and noticed more bones.

Her survival instincts took over, and she was almost through the barn doors before reality set in. She was alone. Only God knew where. Nobody to help her.

She stopped before she plunged into the meadow. Lights burned inside the house. No movement at the windows. As she crossed the yard, she kept to an area of unkempt field where the grass grew past her shoulders. The grass soaked her through and made the chill worse.

Marianne recognized the living room as she drew even with the farmhouse. When she remembered the ghostly figure outside the window, she knelt down. Had she imagined the man?

Now she saw the road ahead. A dirt road not unlike the farm-to-market road which ran past her house. She searched for a landmark, something she could use to pinpoint her location. Nothing appeared recognizable in the dark.

It didn't matter. The Skinner was nowhere to be seen.

Burgeoned by hope, she willed her stiff legs to move and sprinted for the road, but running made too much noise. The Skinner's face appeared in the living room window.

She heard him wrenching the cabinet away from the door as she broke out of the meadow. A door slammed open as she angled across the yard. All she could see was his shadow when she looked over her shoulder.

Marianne opened her mouth to yell, but the man screamed first. The same death rattle shriek she'd heard when Uncle Darrel's hand caught in the wood chipper.

Something wet and viscous splattered the ground. And she ran like the devil himself was on her heels.

The terrible sounds chased Marianne down the dark and unknown road.

CHAPTER EIGHTY

Earl Grendell had twenty-three years experience driving for Briggan's Trucking, and over those many years he'd never seen the roads this bad at the end of October. And it wasn't just the road. The visibility dropped to a few hundred feet as an unearthly ground mist drew a curtain around the sleet and rain.

He was somewhere on County Route 36, a mile outside of a little town named Pronti, when the weather worsened. Snow grains, sleet, fog, freezing rain. It made him wax nostalgic over ninety-five degree days in July when heat rippled off the pavement and seared your nostrils if you bent too close.

He didn't see the stop sign spring out of the fog until he was right on top of it. The big 18-wheeler slid through the four-way stop at sixty mph and jetted down the road, kicking up sleet and rain.

His heart was a permanent part of his larynx now, fingers bone-white as they clutched the wheel. He muttered silent thanks to the man upstairs that another vehicle hadn't crossed the intersection. People fretted over hurricanes and earthquakes and tornadoes, but for Earl Grendell's money, there was nothing more dangerous than driving on a sheet of ice.

The way forward was a blur of storm and macadam, the road more a suggestion than something tangible. Sometimes the swirling storm almost conned him into driving off the road. At least the land was flat in Kansas. If a bad winter storm caught you in the mountains, the wrong move would take you through a guardrail and down a ravine.

Earl thought back to his second year behind the wheel. Old Harlan Nichols jackknifed outside of Norman at seventy, and that was the end of old Harlan. But that had been freezing rain in the middle of January when you expected the weather to be a bitch. Not in October, for God's sake.

Before the near-accident at the four-way stop, Earl's eyes had grown heavy. Not anymore. He figured he could drive to Dallas on adrenaline alone. He'd be damned if he admitted it aloud because the kind folks at Briggan's would have been more than happy to take him up on his offer. *Our drivers rest every six hours* was written in gentle cursive on the back of the trailer. That was a load of hooey. You stopped every six hours to gas up until you delivered the load, or you found yourself in the unemployment line.

Earl rubbed the murk out of his eyes as he put the sleepy town in his mirrors and entered farm country. For the next twenty miles, it was nothing but silos and the thick scent of manure. He thumbed the power button and scanned the radio for a country station. The old stuff—Johnny Cash and Willie Nelson, not the pop garbage that passed for country today. Hell, if Eminem rapped with twang, they'd call it country.

He was halfway through the dial when a pallid figure darted into the road. It waved its arms and ran toward the grille with a lunatic death wish, and for a second he believed she was a witch or specter. But it was only a woman, he realized. No jacket, just a hooded sweatshirt to shield her from the storm. What the hell was she doing in the middle of the road this far out of town?

Earl pumped the brakes and felt the back end slide. Jesus-on-a-totem-pole, the road was black ice. He turned into the skid and thought about Harlan again and how the windshield had turned the old man's forehead into spaghetti. The cab came around, and Earl screamed like a baby as the truck barreled sideways at highway speeds.

Though she couldn't have heard, Earl bellowed for the woman to get out of the road before the trailer cut her in half. Then the front wheels caught the ditch and threw the trailer past him like a bullwhip. His teeth clicked together, and a horrible squeal sliced holes in the silent night as the tires shredded.

When the truck finally came to rest, Earl panted with his fingers locked around the wheel. A putrid rubber scent mingled with the storm. His heart wouldn't slow. He didn't dare look at what the trailer had done to the crazy woman. Instead, he stared at a distant silo and prayed for an opportunity to go back in time, reverse fate and pretend this never happened. Old Harlan got off easy. This was vehicular manslaughter. He'd do hard time when the sheriff—

The knock on the cab door scared him enough to smack his skull against the headrest. The crazy woman.

For the second time tonight, he closed his eyes and

thanked the man above. A fevered chuckle crawled out of his throat.

You dodged a bullet, a voice seemed to say inside his head.

The woman begged him to open the cab. He did.

CHAPTER EIGHTY-ONE

"Do you expect me to believe Marianne Garza's abduction is the work of another serial killer, potentially The Skinner, when I saw Logan Wolf with my own eyes on the security footage?"

Sheriff Lowe stood bull-legged on Garza's lawn, hands on hips with his hat drawn down to his eyebrows. The grinning deputies stood behind Lowe like jesters to their king.

Bell interjected.

"You have to understand. Wolf's profile doesn't fit—"

"I don't have to understand shit. All this profile mumbo jumbo is academic garbage. Fortunately, law enforcement only requires common sense, and I've got enough common sense to know if someone goes missing when a known serial killer is in town, you make the serial killer your number one suspect."

To Bell's astonishment, Lowe spat on the ground. It was as if she'd stumbled onto the set of a bad western. The deputies nodded and muttered agreement.

"Don't think I don't know what the two of you are up

to. Covering your asses. If we'd gone after Wolf last night, we wouldn't have a missing person on our hands."

The dispatcher's voice came over Lowe's radio. He snatched it off his waist without removing his eyes from the two agents.

"Lowe here."

The sheriff strolled away to keep the conversation private. The deputies looked like a firing squad as they glared at Bell and Gardy. Whatever the conversation was about, the sheriff became animated.

When he was done, Lowe bolted back to them.

"Well, now. Seems the two of you dodged a bullet. Marianne Garza is alive."

Bell glanced at Gardy.

"Local trucker named Earl Grendell nearly ran her over on county route 36. Says Garza claimed she was abducted and taken to a farmhouse a few miles outside of Pronti."

Gardy's hands twitched.

"Does she know the address?"

"No, but our guys made sense out of her statement and narrowed the address down to a residence on Triphammer Road." Lowe tapped his forehead. "And that's what you call good old-fashioned police work. Pay attention, agents. We're about to take down the famous Logan Wolf."

The dashboard clock clicked over to four in the morning as Bell and Gardy followed the parade of trucks and flashing lights through Pronti.

Bell checked the GPS and watched Gardy.

"What do you make of this development?"

"I'm sure of one thing. It's not Wolf's house."

"You think it's The Skinner, don't you?"

Gardy's fingers drummed the wheel. His eyes were slitted, skin pale. He looked like death warmed over.

"I don't know what to believe anymore."

"Trust your instincts. I do."

He looked at her. Their eyes met and held for a second. He nodded.

It took ten minutes to reach the farmhouse. No road sign marked Triphammer Road, and the bulk of the drive was dirt and stone made slick by the storm.

Bell climbed down from the Escalade, and as she took in the farmhouse, she knew they'd found the right place before they set foot on the grounds. The house looked at-once derelict and stoic, an old beast who'd witnessed too much pain and hardship. A sagging porch fronted the house, and the windows flared with light like devils' eyes searching the night.

A commotion came from the front lawn. Deputy Keene and another officer knelt over a dark shape on the ground. Bell ran to catch up to Gardy.

A wiry figure lay in a heap. His throat was slashed, head inside a sack.

Lowe wheezed and pulled up. A triumphant smile curled his lips.

"What did I tell you? That's Logan Wolf's work, if I'm not mistaken."

Keene stared bullets into Bell as he worked the sack off the victim's head. The man was emaciated yet muscular, his eyes lifeless sunken holes. Nothing made sense.

Gardy grabbed Bell's elbow and pulled her away from the others.

"There's no mistaking it anymore. Logan Wolf did

this."

"What about Marianne Garza?"

"For now, all we have to go on is she escaped. This doesn't add up."

Sheriff Lowe directed his deputies to search the property. Two approached the front door while another pair circled around the back.

Bell stuffed her hands into her pockets and hurried over to Lowe while an approaching ambulance blared its siren from the end of the road. Gardy yelled for her not to do this, but Bell was finished playing games with the backwoods sheriff.

"Sheriff, did Garza describe her attacker?"

Lowe laughed without mirth.

"She's asleep at County General, agent. What does it matter? Logan Wolf did this."

"Then who is the dead man?"

Lowe looked flummoxed. He turned and pointed to the farmhouse.

"I reckon he's one Lucas Hunt of Pronti, Kansas. It's his name on the deed."

"Does this make the least bit of sense to you? Logan Wolf kidnapped Marianne Garza?"

"Obviously."

"Then he brought her to an occupied residence and killed the owner while Garza ran into the night."

Lowe shifted uncomfortably.

"Don't confuse the point, ma'am. We'll piece all of it together. Now if you'll excuse me, I have a murderer to catch."

"Wait, Sheriff. Agent Gardy studied Wolf. Wolf doesn't make mistakes. No way he'd let Garza escape."

"Doesn't make mistakes? Then how come his mug showed up on the security camera? Admit it, Agent. You couldn't catch Wolf, and you're jealous that we're about to steal your glory."

Gardy hugged Bell to stop her from going after Lowe. The sheriff waddled up the steps with a gun in his hand. The second step from the top screeched and snapped, and the lawman's leg disappeared through the stairs. Keene rushed over and helped Lowe to his feet. The sheriff had a noticeable limp as he staggered to the front door and leaned against the wall, catching his breath. He glared warily at the broken step as though he'd stepped into a hungry crocodile's jaws.

Bell and Gardy ascended the stairs, keeping to the ends where the steps appeared sturdy. More sirens approached. If Wolf was on Hunt's land, they'd surround him soon.

"Look at this place," Gardy said when they stepped inside.

The stained and cracked ceiling seemed skeletal. The house felt cold to Bell, not in terms of temperature, but demeanor. If walls could talk, she didn't wish to hear what they had to say. Keene and a hobbling Lowe climbed the stairs. Gardy bobbed his head toward the kitchen, and she followed him down the hallway. The kitchen was empty of people. A closed door stood in the corner.

Bell looked back at him.

"The basement?"

"That's my guess."

The door opened with a groan. Dust flickered down from the joists. Gardy led the way with the Glock in one hand and a flashlight in the other. Bell reached up and snagged the pull string to turn on the light.

An ancient water heater leered over one corner. A blue flame puffed beneath. Gardy found the wall switch near the washer and dryer and flooded the cellar with light. Boots on steps brought Bell's head around. Deputy Keene followed them with his own flashlight, ostensibly to keep an eye on the agents.

"If you don't mind me saying so, Deputy," said Bell, "wouldn't it be better to spread out and cover more ground? That is if you intend to capture Wolf."

"Sheriff wants me to check out the basement."

"And if we search the attic, will he want you to—"

Gardy touched her arm.

"Don't. We're better off working together."

Keene brushed past and lowered his shoulder as he bumped into Gardy. Gardy bit his lip.

Bell leaned close to his ear.

"You were saying?"

Though the basement was well-lit, the deputy held the flashlight above shoulder level and aimed the beam at a pile of discarded items in the back of the basement—a musty rag, a pitchfork with a missing tine, two work boots, a dusty coffee maker, and a broken shelf. Bell wondered what Keene was looking for.

She turned and saw another door tucked behind the water heater. She needed to squeeze past and scrape away a cobweb to reach the door.

"Not so fast," Gardy said, blocking the door with his hand. "Take it slow for once."

He reached for the handle, and Bell took a position beside the door. To his credit, Keene drew his own weapon in case something monstrous sprung out of the dark.

The door opened to an alcove. Tacked to the wall were a dozen or more photographs of women. Bell recognized Garza from the picture in her living room.

Keene muscled his way past them and shined his light across the photographs.

"What's all this?"

Bell's head spun.

"Memoirs, trophies. That's Garza on the right."

Keene reached for the photograph but Gardy stopped him. It wasn't a good idea to touch evidence.

"I can't believe Logan Wolf lived under our noses all this time."

Gardy's eyes moved over the pictures. His mind slowly pieced the puzzle together.

"I don't think so. Get Sheriff Lowe, Deputy."

Haunted, Keene fell back against the wall and leaned there.

"Sure…right away."

"He'll want to compare these photographs with the missing persons database and known murder cases. We just discovered the home of The Skinner."

CHAPTER EIGHTY-TWO

The coroner and a slew of crime techs were on the scene when Bell and Gardy descended The Skinner's front steps. A handful of FBI agents had arrived from the Kansas City and Oklahoma City offices. A piece of rope and several bones were uncovered from the old barn behind the house. Lucas Hunt's body left the scene in a bag.

Jerome Tyner, a senior agent and old friend of Gardy, had taken charge of the scene. Lowe resisted initially, but Tyner, who stood several inches taller than Lowe and possessed a commanding, baritone voice that would have led castle raids during Medieval times, quickly persuaded the sheriff he was in over his head.

Dressed in a dark blue FBI jacket, cap, and a pair of oversized eyeglasses, Tyner folded his arms before Gardy.

"The search teams are combing a two-mile radius around the farmhouse in case Wolf is on foot. It's mostly open field and farmland from here back to Pronti, not a lot of cover, so we'll find him if he's out there. In the meantime, the two of you need sleep. I'll have one of my guys—"

"I've got it, Jerome."

"You sure, Bon Jovi?"

Bell cocked an eyebrow.

"Bon Jovi?"

Tyner chuckled and thumped Gardy on the shoulder.

"His nickname since the academy days. What better name for a rock star than Bon Jovi?"

After the levity, the humor left Tyner's eyes, and he squared his shoulders with Gardy.

"You stepped in it big this time, Gardy."

"I'll catch hell back at Quantico."

"Maybe not. I'll give Weber a call later and smooth things over."

"You don't have to do that, Jerome."

"The hell I don't. Do you know how long we've been looking for The Skinner? Here he was right down the road all along. That's a helluva catch."

Gardy looked off to the horizon. The first grays of daylight were spreading out of the land.

"Except I didn't catch him."

"Yeah. About that. Why do you figure Logan Wolf murdered The Skinner?"

"A better question is why he brought Garza here in the first place."

"Maybe Wolf gave her to The Skinner? Some weird gift from one psycho to another."

Gardy's breath puffed little clouds in the cold.

"Whatever the reason, they tied her up and cut her free. I can't wrap my head around it."

"You suppose they were working together and had a falling out?"

Gardy shook his head.

"That doesn't feel right to me, and I don't think Bell is buying it, either."

Tyner studied Bell, the curiosity evident in his eyes. Bell knew her reputation preceded her, the uncanny ability to enter a killer's mind and unravel his darkest secrets, and it always made her uncomfortable. The truth was she was at a loss on this case. She started this case searching for Logan Wolf and never could have guessed the night would end with The Skinner dead on a lonely plot of land in the middle of Kansas.

"Your expert opinion, Agent Bell. Garza didn't escape. The ropes were cut. Why would Wolf or Hunt cut her free and allow her to escape?"

"Could be it was part of the thrill. They wanted to stalk her first."

Yet that didn't feel right, either. The answer felt forced, almost negligent as though she viewed the case through tunnel vision.

Gardy tapped Tyner on the arm.

"I better get Bell back to the motel before she turns into a pumpkin."

"Get some sleep, my friend. We'll need you at full strength this afternoon."

"Thanks for coming out, Jerome."

"You're still the rock star, Gardy. Damn. The Skinner case finally closed, and Logan Wolf next."

Tyner shook his head and grinned as they slogged to the Escalade. Lowe, looking neutered now that Tyner was here, touched the tip of his hat when they walked past.

Gardy said little during the drive into Pronti. The weather cleared and left a gelid glaze on the grass as the sun peaked into the mirrors. A few times Bell opened her mouth to tell Gardy he'd done the best he could and needed to stop being hard on himself, but the angry glare he directed through the windshield told her this wasn't the time. Then the Pronti Inn appeared, and they labored up the steps toward their beds when the rest of the world was waking up.

Bell didn't remember her head touching the pillow. The Sandman took her before she pulled the covers up.

CHAPTER EIGHTY-THREE

Intravenous fluids pumped through little tubes into Marianne Garza's arm as she lay in the hospital bed. She was a pretty woman, Bell thought, but one who'd made unfortunate choices in her life and shouldered the weight of her misdeeds. A tray lay on a stand beside her bed, the chicken dinner half-eaten and the fruit cup untouched.

One of Lowe's crony deputies had been out to interview Garza earlier. He'd barely gotten a description of her abductor. Bell, holding onto the thin hope she'd figure out the connection between Wolf and The Skinner, sat down to question Garza.

"Mrs Garza…"

"Please, call me Marianne."

"Okay, Marianne. Let's start with the kidnapping."

Garza's eyes deviated to her lap. She swallowed.

"Sure."

"What do you remember?"

"My sister called. Melissa. She wanted to wish me luck in Florida. I guess I won't need that luck anymore."

"You'll be out of here soon, Marianne."

Garza's eyes were glassy. She nodded once without responding.

"Is that when the man who abducted you came to your house?"

No response.

"Marianne?"

She snapped into focus.

"Yes, after...after the phone call."

"Where were you in the house?"

"Um, by the stairs, I think. Yes, I was going upstairs and saw the car parked alongside my property."

The woman recounted how the man lied about his car, then broke the dining-room window. She didn't recall much after he drugged her. It was a big vehicle, Garza said. Something old, but she only described its color and shape.

"Did you get a good look at his face?"

"No. Only glimpses now-and-then, like at the gas station."

Bell noticed Gardy perk up. If the camera caught the abductor, they'd have an additional evidence trail on Logan Wolf.

"What gas station was it, do you know?"

"Carter's, I think."

"You sure?"

"No, but it's the only station between Pronti and Triphammer Road."

"What was the approximate time?"

Garza's lips moved in silent thought.

"It was dark. Before midnight, I guess."

"Do you recall what time your sister called?"

"Yes. Around dusk."

"That would be a little after six," Gardy said.

He rose from his chair and left the room with his phone. The odds strongly favored Wolf stopped at the gas station after kidnapping Garza.

Gardy's voice carried back to them as he told Tyner to send an agent out to Carter's.

"How good a look did you get of the kidnapper at the gas station, Marianne?"

"Not very good."

"Do you think you would recognize him from a picture?"

"Maybe. I'll try."

Bell slid several photographs out of a folder and passed them to Marianne one-at-a-time. The first two photographs were of convicted serial killers unrelated to the case. Garza shook her head at both.

Bell's stomach clenched. The next photo was of Logan Wolf.

When Bell handed Garza the picture of Wolf, Garza studied it for several seconds.

"It's not him."

Bell leaned forward, eye-to-eye with Garza.

"Please, look again."

Garza dutifully scanned the picture and shook her head.

"No. That's not the man who abducted me."

"Did you see that man last night?"

Confused, Garza glanced between the photograph and Bell.

"No, I've never seen him before. Should I have?"

The energy drained out of Bell. She wanted to drip through the chair and puddle on the floor. Garza studied two more photographs before she stopped on the picture of

Hunt. Her fingers trembled.

"That's him. That's the man who kidnapped me."

Bell angled the photo toward the light as if doing so would change Hunt into Wolf.

Gardy was back, the phone pocketed.

"Tyner sent one of his KC agents to Carter's. We should have confirmation soon."

"Perfect. We'll have a good picture of Lucas Hunt."

"Huh?"

Bell shook her head and gathered the photographs.

The ride back to the search site was somber. It had been The Skinner, Lucas Hunt, and not Logan Wolf, who abducted Marianne Garza. As far as either knew, Wolf had nothing to do with the case except he happened to be in town and butchered Hunt. Why? Bell smacked the passenger window with the side of her fist.

"Hey, now," Gardy said. "Easy on the rental."

"This is a Skinner case, one hundred percent. So what the hell was Wolf doing at his house?"

Whatever answer Gardy intended, it died on his tongue. They crisscrossed from one farm-to-market road to the next, the land plots looking the same, until they reconvened at Hunt's residence. Tyner was waiting for them when they arrived, and a K-9 search team fanned out through the countryside. The confidence that had been on Tyner's face at dawn was long gone. A thumping noise came from the far end of the prairie as a helicopter flew over.

"You'll hear it again soon," Tyner said, walking them toward the back of the property where the old barn stood. "We've got a chopper in the air. Thing is, if Wolf was here at all, he's long gone by now."

"Come on, Jerome," Gardy said, lifting a tree limb so the others could duck under. "Wolf was here. We have the video evidence from the convenience store, plus a man with his throat slashed and a bag over his head."

"No murder weapon, no evidence Wolf killed Hunt."

"That's his signature. Don't pretend it's not."

"It's his signature, but a grainy photograph and an unsolved murder won't convince our bosses to throw more bodies at this case. Face it, Gardy. Wolf is gone, and we'll never know why he came here."

"Shit."

"Yep."

"By the way, where the hell are we going?"

Tyner glanced over his broad shoulder at Bell.

"The K-9's found something while you were interviewing the Garza woman. Brace yourself. You aren't gonna like it."

Gardy looked back at Bell. She plunged her hands into her pockets and trudged through the overgrown grass.

The day's last light burned through the missing slats and drew sharp lines across the hay. A hole eight-feet-long by two-feet-deep lay along the ground. A diseased cow roamed the barn's perimeter.

But no one was looking at the cow. They all stared at the mountain of blanched human bones.

CHAPTER EIGHTY-FOUR

A plane buzzed over Hunt's land and left a trail of smoke. The search crew blossomed as the FBI, sheriff's department, and police out of Wichita combed the countryside for Logan Wolf. Another helicopter dipped toward the horizon, and Bell realized it wasn't one of theirs.

"Looks like the media found out."

Bell removed the binoculars from her eyes and entered the barn. A clear sheet of plastic was affixed over the door to keep the wind at bay, but the elements found their way inside through holes in the barn walls.

She stepped aside for Dr Bartholomew, a heavyset, bearded man who wheezed when he spoke. Acquiring Bartholomew had been a stroke of luck. The Texas State forensic archaeologist was giving a speech in Lawrence when the FBI unearthed the shallow graves.

He mumbled under his breath about the FBI's sloppy excavation techniques as he knelt on creaking knees. He held a brush and tweezers. A shovel lay beside him. The doctor chewed the inside of his cheek as he watched a female crime tech named Neander dig around another bone.

Bending over the hole, Bartholomew used measured strokes to sweep a layer of sediment away. Another bone, a femur, glared under the spotlight.

Five minutes later, he picked the femur out of the soil and placed it on a tarp. Bartholomew clutched his lower back and groaned when he rose. A necropolis of bones covered the tarp, which curled at the corners when the wind blew. A complete skull lay among the human remains.

"Are they all female?"

Bartholomew glanced at Bell. He removed his glasses and cleaned the lenses on his shirt collar.

"No way to be certain without more tests, but the skull is clearly female."

"How can you be sure?"

It took effort for the doctor to kneel again. Bell cringed when his knees popped. Bartholomew used the brush to paint an invisible line across the skull's forehead.

"Notice the rounded appearance. A male forehead is less round, and the ridge along the brow is sharper."

The doctor moved a finger along his brow as way of demonstration.

"Also, note the circular shapes to the victim's eye sockets and how they conclude at sharp points near the top. Again, distinctly female."

Bell nodded as he shifted his attention to the femur bone.

"We can discern the difference with the femur, as well. This particular femur is angled more than one would expect to find in a male, hence my belief it belongs to a female."

So much death. Bell's heart ached as she considered the number of families ripped apart by this maniac. It was clear The Skinner had murdered far more victims than the FBI believed.

The plastic crinkled as Gardy entered the barn. The defeat was clear from his slumped shoulders and long face.

Bell glanced up at Gardy, who ran his gaze over the growing pile of bones.

"Anything?"

"Nothing. Wolf's gone."

Gardy held a ham-and-cheese sandwich. He offered her half, and she shook her head.

"No thanks. I can't eat after looking at all of this."

He cocked his head as if to say, *more for me, then.*

"There are sandwiches in the truck if you change your mind." He nodded at the bones. "How many bodies do you estimate we found?"

Bartholomew struggled back to his feet with labored breath.

"As far as I can tell, the majority of these bones belonged to different people. I won't know for sure until I get them back to the lab, but if I had to guess, I'd estimate twenty to twenty-five."

A pained sound came from Gardy's chest. Bell walked toward the back of the barn. A stocky woman was leading the cow to a trailer as Gardy got Bell beyond earshot of the others.

"I don't get it, Gardy. Wolf followed me to California, and for all I know he led us here. Obviously, he wants my attention."

"And now that he has it, he disappears."

"Right."

"You think he had anything to do with these bodies?"

Bell peeked through the stalls. She couldn't look at the bone pile for more than a few seconds.

"No. This is The Skinner's work. No evidence exists that Wolf dismembered and buried his victims."

"Doesn't mean he didn't."

She considered the possibility. Gardy had taken the lead on tracking Logan Wolf to this point, and as much as she respected her partner's experience and opinion, they were no closer to finding the serial killer.

"With your permission, I'd like to get more involved with the Wolf case."

Gardy picked at a loose chunk of wood on the stall.

"You're my partner, and I don't want you getting too close to Wolf. He's made it personal."

"But Gardy—"

He straightened his jacket and glanced through the doorway. The day grew late, and the shadows stretched long across The Skinner's property.

"We'll talk about it later."

CHAPTER EIGHTY-FIVE

A handful of couples sat in booths at Reggie's Diner as an overworked waitress with curly, red hair hustled from one table to the next. The diner smelled of fried hamburgers and onions, and a country song thumped from the jukebox.

"Y'all sit where you like," the waitress said.

Bell settled into a booth in the back of the diner and peeled off her jacket. The weather had broken, the evening not as cold as last, yet the two-block walk from the hotel had left her chilled. She pulled a menu from behind the napkin dispenser and paged through the choices. The strawberry pancakes looked good, as did the milkshakes. She couldn't stomach greasy food after the macabre excavation.

The waitress set a glass of water on the table.

"I'll be right back for your order, hon."

"Thank you. Take your time."

She tore the paper off the straw when Jerome Tyner slid into the seat across the table.

"This seat taken?"

"No. It's all yours."

He grinned and picked up a menu.

"So what looks good tonight?"

"I'm leaning toward breakfast for dinner."

"Hmm. Can't go wrong with second breakfast."

Noticing Bell had company, the waitress dropped another water on the table. Tyner smiled and winked at the waitress, who stopped when she saw the FBI emblem on his windbreaker.

"FBI? We've been watching the news all day. Terrible business, all those bodies."

Bell glanced at the television in the corner. She'd purposely avoided the news to this point. Footage of the barn from the helicopter segued to a photograph of Lucas Hunt. The text at the bottom of the screen read, *Horror in Kansas: Dozens of bodies discovered.*

The waitress's lips went tight.

"I can't believe one of our own was The Skinner."

Tyner rubbed the weariness from his eyes.

"We never truly know our neighbors."

The waitress pushed through a pair of double doors that led into the kitchen. A man at the counter wearing a CAT hat looked in their direction, then lowered his eyes to his food.

Tyner sipped his water.

"Just you? I expected to see your rock star partner."

"You mean Bon Jovi?"

Tyner's laugh was deep and straight from the chest. It attracted a few curious stares.

"Glad to see the nickname will stick. He's in your hands now." When she didn't share his laugh, Tyner looked at Bell over the top of the glass. "You look like someone kicked you in the gut, Agent Bell."

"Long day. Long couple of months, actually."

"I followed your work on the Hodge case."

"Please tell me you didn't read it in *The Informer*."

"No, but I confess to grabbing a copy off the newsstand now-and-then."

"Intellectual curiosity?"

"Bathroom reading."

"Fitting."

He took a second to get her joke, and he laughed again.

"Seriously, you do good work. Also on the Longo and Meeks cases. Most dangerous LDSK I can remember since the DC snipers, and from what I hear, you took him down single-handedly."

"I hardly think that's accurate. Sounds like something Gavin Hayward would write."

"Three cases of national significance closed in a matter of months. You're going places, Agent Bell. Don't give me the *aw-shucks* routine. But something is on your mind. What's bothering you?"

She realized she'd been shredding her napkin while Tyner talked. She swept the pieces into her hand before he noticed.

"It's our rock star friend."

"Gardy?"

"He's been in a funk since California. Sullen, negative. When I first joined the BAU and learned I'd be paired with Neil Gardy, I almost quit." Tyner raised his eyebrows. "It was his reputation. The former golden boy, now senior agent, on the fast track to Deputy Director. After that, the sky would be the limit."

Tyner nodded.

"You were intimidated."

"In a sense, yes. How do you live up to the expectations of Neil Gardy? I imagined what working with Gardy would be like. Stuffy, by the book, eyes always on my back."

"And none of that turned out to be true."

Bell grinned and bit her hand, remembering the laughs they shared.

"No one is more personable. And he always has this smirk behind his eyes like he's in on a joke you haven't gotten yet."

"I know that look. And believe me, I was usually the butt of the joke. So what's the problem?"

Bell leaned back against the cushioned seat back and let out a breath of air. Her shoulders sagged.

"The shooting changed him. He doesn't laugh anymore, or when he does, it seems forced. Like he's the proverbial third wheel at the party and trying to fit in."

Tyner folded his arms, and the gleam in his eyes told Bell he'd been through this before.

"Post-Traumatic Stress Disorder. It's to be expected. Several inches in either direction and the bullet doesn't graze his shoulder. It goes straight between the eyes or catches him in the heart or stomach. He got off lucky."

"He doesn't act like he did."

Tyner itched at his chin.

"You know, he probably feels like he isn't doing his job when a rookie agent saves his life." Tyner saw Bell's posture switch to defensive. He held up his hands in placation. "It's not a man-woman thing. Hell, it's not even that he views you as a rookie. You're way too advanced to be labeled as such. This comes down to Gardy second-guessing himself, wondering if the rock star superhero still has it."

"That's ridiculous."

"To you and me, it is. But not to Gardy. I hope you never walk in those shoes. I grew up in Brooklyn and used to play hoops with a kid named Irvin Robinson. We all knew we'd watch him on TV someday. NBA finals, running the court with LeBron. Irvin got a full-ride to Seton Hall. First season, he scores twenty per game and gets named to the all-conference rookie team. Then that summer, he's driving on the GW and a school bus hydroplanes in front of him. Now, Irvin did the right thing. He stayed calm and evaded the wreck. The lady in the next lane slammed her brakes, a big no-no in heavy rain. She went headfirst into the bus. Wasn't wearing her seatbelt and died on impact."

Tyner ran a hand over his head and stared at the table.

"Irvin saw the whole thing. He saved his life that day, but the legend died. Sophomore season, the kid can't hit a free throw. Ridiculous, right? He had a career three-point percentage above forty, but he couldn't make a free throw with everyone looking at him and expecting him to fail. He quit before his junior season. Said he couldn't deal with the pressure."

He thumped his finger on his forehead.

"That's how your mind turns on you. I trust Gardy is going through counseling."

"It's mandatory," said Bell. "He doesn't have a choice."

"Good."

"I wish I could do more to help."

"Stay on Gardy about his appointments. Make sure he does more than the bare minimum. Anyone can show up and put in his sixty minutes. He needs to remain open to the process."

"I'll keep an eye on him."

"Of course, you will. That's what a good partner does. In the meantime, don't be so hard on the guy. Give him time. He'll come around."

Tyner and Bell stopped talking when the waitress returned. They both ordered the super stack of strawberry pancakes. After the waitress moved on to the counter, Tyner leaned over the table.

"Nobody knows better than you, Agent Bell, what the human mind is capable of after a shock event. Consider Derek Longo and Alan Hodge. I'm not a big believer in good versus evil. They probably started off as ordinary people. Life experiences turned them bad."

Bell dug her nails into her thighs. She didn't want to think about all the Longos and Hodges stalking the shadows.

"What about Logan Wolf?"

The blood drained from Tyner's face.

"That's a different situation."

"How so?"

"He's the devil incarnate."

***

The pancakes sat at the bottom of Bell's stomach like a bowling ball as she climbed the steps of the Pronti Inn. She wished she'd brought antacids. Good luck finding an open drugstore at this time of night.

It was after dark, the lampposts throwing off circumferences of refuge that the night slowly devoured. A neon light flashed down the road outside of Delbert's. The rest of Pronti had gone to the grave. Her sneakers scuffed and clonked on the stairs, an unsettling sound amid the quiet.

There was an abandoned cart of sheets, blankets, and cleaning supplies at the end of the walkway. Odd. Housecleaning typically finished before three.

Gardy's room sat in darkness beside hers. She considered knocking and thought better of it. Let him rest.

The key card didn't work on the first two passes. She swung the bag over her shoulder and tried again, and a green light flashed indicating success.

She pushed the door open and sensed something was wrong. Pulling the Glock-22 from her hip, she aimed the gun into the black. She listened for a moment. Nothing.

Using the wall as a shield, she slipped her arm around the entryway and flicked on the light.

The room was empty.

Brightly lit, it no longer carried the burden of dread. Bell felt a little silly for scaring herself. After today's horrors, it was easy to imagine The Skinner dragging himself out of the morgue and hunting her down. She made a mental note to take a break from horror movies for a while, at least until the memory of the bones lost its bite.

Tossing her bag onto the bed, she fluffed the pillow and turned down the covers. The bed looked heavenly, but she needed a shower almost as much as she needed eight hours of uninterrupted sleep.

She reached for the bathroom light when the motel room went dark.

"Hello, Scarlett."

CHAPTER EIGHTY-SIX

A thump on the wall brought Gardy awake. Thinking he was at home in bed, he reached for his nightstand and touched the motel telephone. He remembered.

He flicked the light switch and squinted at the infernal brightness. The clock read eleven. His body and mind drained from the grisly discoveries in Pronti, he'd fallen asleep before nine. Now he was wide awake, a sheaf of frayed nerves. He glanced up at the ceiling, then behind him to the neighboring wall, and uttered an oath to hunt down the idiot who woke him up.

Gardy pointed the remote at the television and watched the sports scores. When that didn't make him drowsy, he muted the volume and stared at his mobile phone. Bell kept sleeping pills. They didn't prevent her nightmares, but they helped her get back to sleep after a bad dream. He felt sleazy asking Bell to share prescription medication, and heaven knew she needed them more than he did, but he'd be up all night and no good to the search crews tomorrow on two hours of rest.

As though they had a prayer of capturing Logan

Wolf. The search was a dead end.

He picked up the phone. Bell was probably still awake. He moved his thumb over the call button and stopped himself. This was stupid. If he woke her up, they'd both be zombies tomorrow.

To hell with it.

He pressed call and the phone rang.

After several seconds, her message started. Bell kept her ringer on, so she should have answered. He called again, worrying this call would yank her out of a deep sleep, and then she'd really be pissed. Again, the call ended with her message.

He pocketed the phone and padded to the window. Pinching the blinds open, he looked into the parking lot and saw her rental beside the Escalade. She hadn't gone out. Regardless, Bell would have taken her phone with her.

Gardy sent her a quick text and waited at the window. Any minute now, he expected to hear Bell's door open and close, then a frustrated sniff before she pounded on his door. She never came.

As the hockey highlights played, Gardy dragged his sweatpants on and pulled a jacket over his t-shirt. After a moment's consideration, he grabbed his ID badge and put the Glock on his hip. He looked ready to go to war if it wasn't for the Tampa Bay Rays sweatpants.

He turned the key card in his hand as he leaned an arm on the wall and tried to talk himself out of this foolishness.

She was a deep sleeper, wasn't she? Not that deep.

That's when the creeping sensation that something was terribly wrong came over him. He hadn't felt this way since…

Since when?

Not since the moment before the sniper's bullet almost took his head off.

Gardy pulled the door open and stepped into the crisp night. The orange-tinted moon was full, its face screaming down on Pronti as he cupped his elbows and stepped barefoot to her door.

He knocked quietly at first, and when that didn't rouse her, he pounded on the door.

No response. Not even the whisper of feet crossing the carpet.

He took a deep breath and let it out before checking his phone one last time.

Gardy descended the stairs two-at-a-time and followed the walkway to the welcome desk. A bleary-eyed college kid with a face full of scruff hopped out of his chair when the door opened and pretended he hadn't been asleep.

"Can I help you, sir?"

Gardy flashed his badge.

"I need you to open room 203."

The kid stammered and glanced around the office as though the answer lay on the desk.

"I…don't think I can…who did you say you were again?"

"Agent Neil Gardy, FBI."

"Don't you need a warrant or something?"

"Look, nobody's in trouble. My partner is in there. She's not answering her phone and didn't respond when I knocked."

"Maybe she went out."

"She didn't go out. Her car is in the parking lot."

The kid wrung his hands and spun toward the phone.
"I better call the manager."

Gardy leaned over the desk. His jacket slumped off his hip and exposed his gun. The kid's eyes widened.

"No, there's no time for that." Gardy cocked his head and whispered conspiratorially. "Between you and me, this is about all the bodies they dug up outside of town."

The worker's face turned pale.

"I thought the killer was dead."

"Yeah, but who killed the killer?"

Gardy lifted an eyebrow and invited a response.

"Oh, damn. You don't think the other killer came here and—"

"I won't know anything for certain until I get a look inside the room and ensure my partner is all right."

Conflicting emotions warred on the kid's face. Finally, he nodded.

"Okay. But I have to be there when you go inside."

As they climbed the stairs, the worker shot worried glances over his shoulder. He knocked on Bell's door and gave her several seconds to answer while Gardy tapped his hand impatiently on the wall. The kid checked the walkway and made sure no one watched, then he slipped the master key card into the slot.

Bell's door opened to an empty room. The bed covers were turned down, the bathroom light on and the fan buzzing. Gardy aimed the Glock-22 as he slipped around corners. The kid watched from the doorway, afraid to cross the threshold. The bathroom was empty, the tub and towel dry.

His eyes fixed on her bag. It was tucked under the bed, which is why he hadn't seen it before. Gardy sifted through the contents and closed on her wallet. The key card to her room lay beside her ID badge on the nightstand. No phone. She must have taken the phone and left her wallet, and that didn't sound like Bell. Nor was she prone to forgetting her room key.

Where the hell was she?

"Was the killer here?"

Gardy turned to the kid.

"I don't know. This stays between the two of us, got it?"

The kid nodded.

Gardy pulled out his phone and called the only other person he trusted in Pronti—Jerome Tyner.

CHAPTER EIGHTY-SEVEN

Bell opened her eyes to the interior of a long, dark room. Rows of shelves and boxes. The bitter, metallic scent of heavy machinery.

Seated on a folding chair, she blinked once, twice, tried to make sense of things. The memory from the motel room flashed like lightning across her mind. Her muscles went rigid. Heart hammered.

She wasn't alone in the room.

She pulled her hands up and expected them to be bound by ropes. They weren't. Nor were her legs, which she slid forward to work out the numbness.

Instinctively, she reached for the Glock-22 and found it missing, along with her phone. Of course.

"I trust you are well rested."

His voice seemed to come from everywhere. It reverberated off the walls and through the dark corridors, yet she knew he was close.

Logan Wolf. Who else could it be?

"Where am I?"

"You are safe, Scarlett. No need to panic."

He stepped out from the shadow and faced her from down the row. He appeared as a black silhouette, rigid and statue-like.

"What did you do with my gun?"

He chuckled. Edged a little closer.

"You'll have your weapon in due time. Exercise patience, please."

Right. He'd hand the Glock to Bell after he slit her throat and threw a bag over her head.

"You're...Logan Wolf, I assume."

Another chuckle.

"In the flesh. We finally meet in person. I awaited this day for many months."

She was weaponless, but if he thought she couldn't defend herself, he was in for a rude awakening. She shifted forward on the seat, a subtle change in position which would allow her to spring at Wolf when he came closer.

"I wouldn't do that if I were you."

His voice was eerily persuasive, eloquent and compelling. It scuttled up her spine and whispered at her brain stem. Bell assumed he held a gun, probably her Glock, and would cut her down the second she leaped from the chair. Why not shoot her now and be done with it? Why the games?

"Or what? You'll murder me? Slice my throat open and bag my head as you did to your wife?"

He froze. She imagined his face twitching.

"I...did not murder my wife."

Bell smiled. Good. She'd hit a sore spot. What other buttons could she press?

"You claim you waited a long time to meet me, yet you ran when I saw you at the mall."

"It was neither the time nor place for us to talk."

"Seems to me you were scared."

Wolf smiled. She caught the gleam of his teeth reflecting in a thin shaft of moonlight.

"I have no reason to fear you, Scarlett."

He took another step forward. Part of his cat-and-mouse game. Wolf wanted her scared before he swept the blade across her neck. In a moment, he'd be on top of her. There was no hope in fighting a trained male agent with a weapon, but she wouldn't sit still and be butchered.

She shot off the chair and angled down the next row with no idea where the exit was or where she headed. The shadow form leaped after her, and she heard his shoes pounding the floor as he closed the distance between them.

At the end of the row, she swiveled, unsure which direction to run. The moment of indecision cost her.

Wolf pressed Bell against the wall and covered her mouth with his hand. She bit down. He cursed and drove his forearm into her chest, pinning her against the wall. She saw his eyes now. The black irises and pupils blended together without beginning or end as though he carried the night sky. To Bell, he appeared sick, a man who'd lost a lot of weight in a short period of time. The skin didn't fit over his bones.

"Don't fight me, Scarlett."

She pushed against him, but he was too strong. He held the Glock-22 when she glanced down. That struck her as peculiar. Wolf murdered with a knife, never a gun. Was this a show of respect? Admittance he needed the gun against a BAU agent?

She relented, her breath coming quick and hard as he glared into her eyes.

Tyner's words came back to her. *He's the devil incarnate.*

Something in his coat pocket brushed against her hip. Another gun? The knife? A crazy idea came into her head —pick his pocket.

Wolf observed every move she made. If he caught her, she'd die. Hoping to deflect his attention, she lowered her shoulder and shoved him off the wall. When he pushed her backward, she reached inside his pocket and closed her fingers over the object.

She lifted it and spun the item into her own pocket before her mind processed what it was. Not a weapon. Her phone.

"Now, I will bring you back to the chair so you are comfortable, and we will cease these ridiculous games."

"What difference does it make? You'll kill me anyway."

"Murder you? Is that what you think this is about? Dear Scarlett, had I desired to murder you, I would have done so already. There were opportunities, were there not? In Milanville. The motel room."

"You couldn't kill me there. Someone would hear me scream. That's why you brought me here." She ran her gaze over the warehouse. "Wherever *here* is."

"Fair enough," he said, releasing his grip. He still held the gun on her. "If you are convinced I mean to murder you tonight, then you have nothing to lose by hearing me out."

"Why would I believe anything you say?"

He tutted.

"You don't have to believe. I only require you listen."

Bell's eyes strayed down the next row. A rectangular

box jutted off the shelf and blocked her view, yet orange light slid around the edges. An exit sign.

She averted her eyes before he figured it out.

"Okay, Mr Wolf. Lead the way."

CHAPTER EIGHTY-EIGHT

The Jeep's motor announced Jerome Tyner's arrival before Gardy saw the headlights sweep across the window. Having changed into jeans, Gardy double-checked for his gun and badge and closed the motel room door.

"So you last saw her at the diner?"

Tyner checked his watch.

"We left at a little after seven."

"Dammit, Jerome. Didn't you offer her a ride back?"

The big man sighed.

"That partner of yours is as stubborn as a mule. She refused." Tyner saw Gardy heating up and raised a hand. "Now, you know me, Gardy. I wasn't about to let her walk in the dark by herself. I trailed her to the motel, stayed back a few hundred feet so she didn't get the drop on me. Even waited until she was safely inside her room."

Gardy thumped the Escalade's trunk.

"Yeah, I knew you would. Besides, I already knew she made it back. Like I told you on the phone, her key card and wallet are inside."

"You think someone took her?"

435

The thought had scrabbled around inside Gardy's head since he awoke. Hearing Tyner speak the words aloud hit him with a fresh wave of panic.

"Or lured her out of the room. I don't know." Gardy ran his gaze over the lonely town. "Christ, Jerome. What if it's Wolf?"

"Don't jump to conclusions."

"It makes sense. He figured out Bell's address and stalked her to California."

"You said Agent Bell took her phone with her?"

"I think so. It's not in the room."

"All right, then. Let's track the phone. I'll call my people."

Gardy climbed into the Escalade.

"Better yet, call Quantico. If anyone can locate a phone, it's Harold. Hop in. We're going after her."

They stopped at Reggie's Diner on their first pass through Pronti. The same waitress was on, and she recognized Tyner when he stepped inside. No, Bell never returned, though the waitress wished to thank her for the generous tip. Trips to the gas station, convenience store, and Delbert's bar, the only establishments open at this time of night, came up empty.

Harold's voice spoke through the Escalade's speakers.

"The last location on Agent Bell's phone is the Pronti Inn."

Gardy gritted his teeth.

"We know that, Harold. Tell me where it is now."

They heard him punching keys at his computer terminal. An exasperated huff, followed by more typing.

"I'm not getting a signal. Could be her battery died."

Was he to believe Bell left her motel in the middle of

the night without her wallet and key card, and the phone battery was dead?

"Keep trying to reach her."

"It's possible she's out of cell range or turned off the phone. I'll call you as soon as I locate the signal."

The farm plots and ramshackle houses looked the same as they crisscrossed the checkerboard of connecting roads. Gardy didn't know what he was looking for. He only knew he couldn't sit inside his hotel room and assume Bell would show up. Memories of The Skinner's graveyard came back to Gardy, and he felt nauseous. He needed to search Hunt's property on the off chance Wolf took Bell to the scene of his last murder. Gardy didn't want to know what they'd find.

Tyner was in contact with his FBI crew and the sheriff. Additional vehicles searched for Bell through Pronti. Gardy didn't expect Lowe's department to lend a hand, but Tyner held sway over the sheriff.

"Stay calm, Gardy. We'll find her soon."

Gardy didn't think he could live with himself if they didn't. They turned toward Hunt's farmhouse when Lowe's voice came over Tyner's radio.

"We took a call from a resident at the Pronti Inn. Herbert Miller, room 217. Says he saw a guy in a black coat and pants enter Agent Bell's motel room a little after sunset. Sent a cruiser out to get a better description and see if anyone saw a vehicle."

Tyner looked at Gardy.

"Sounds like Wolf."

Until that point, only in Gardy's darkest thoughts did he truly believe Wolf took Bell. He'd constructed walls around his fears and fortified them well with logical explanations for his partner's disappearance, but Lowe's news tore those walls down and left him isolated and afraid.

Gardy pressed the accelerator. Harold needed to find the signal before time ran out.

CHAPTER EIGHTY-NINE

Water droplets echoed through the warehouse. The roof was leaking.

Bell swiveled her eyes down the aisles as Logan Wolf led her back to the chair. When the moment came to run, she wanted to know the precise path to the exit doors. No missteps or mistakes. She hoped the doors weren't chained.

"Sit."

Bell slid into the seat. Her back ached from slumbering on the uncomfortable chair, and bruises throbbed along her neck. Though she didn't recall the attack inside the motel room, she ascertained he'd clutched her from behind and cut off her carotid artery. A choke hold meant to put the victim to sleep.

"How did you get into my motel room?"

"A second-rate motel key card reader wouldn't stop an ingenious ten-year-old, Scarlett, let alone a BAU agent."

"You're not a BAU agent anymore."

His face changed. Anger? Pain? It was difficult to tell in the dark.

"No, I am not. Tell me, Scarlett. Do you believe in

your skill as a profiler, or is it all hocus-pocus? A parlor trick?"

"I don't know what you mean."

"Your ability to step into the mind of a psychopath. That is how you find them, is it not? Alan Hodge, for instance. A nasty individual if there ever was one. Murdering young girls right under the sheriff's nose. He'd still be at it if you hadn't found him."

"My partner was as much responsible for apprehending Hodge as I was."

She felt the phone in her pocket. It would take only a few seconds to locate the power button, but Wolf watched her every move.

"Ah, your partner, a fine agent. How is Neil Gardy these days? I trust he is well and recovered from the gunshot. If the chips fall in his favor, he will run the FBI before his career comes to a triumphant conclusion." Wolf paused. "But it was you who did the dirty work and rooted out the killer. Gardy merely took the credit."

"If you say so."

"I do say so. Good police work and evidence gathering might explain how you caught Hodge and the others. Was it a key piece of evidence or the proverbial smoking gun which led you to one of the most feared serial killers of the last decade? Or was it your skill as a profiler? The magic trick."

Bell's eyes slid toward the escape route.

"There is no need to run, dear Scarlett."

"Why not? You'll murder me, anyway. What if I refuse to answer your questions?"

Wolf bent so his face was even with Bell's. She noted he kept his weight on the balls of his feet, ready to lunge if she tried to escape.

"I swear I will not kill you. I don't intend to harm the famous Agent Bell."

"What do you want from me?"

"Only the truth. Did your profiles lead you to Hodge and Longo?"

She nodded after a moment, and he straightened.

"A curious claim. There are many who assert profiling as nothing more than sleight of hand. In 2002, a study conducted by Kocsis, Hayes, and Irwin demonstrated a group of profilers—"

"Failed to outperform police work. Yes, I am aware of the study. The profilers' accuracy also fell short of chemistry students, though questions exist regarding the test methodology."

Wolf grinned, a smile which displayed too many teeth.

"Very, very good. Though I'm not surprised you are well-read on the subject. Do you agree with their assessment?"

"No. A number of BAU agents are sufficiently skilled in delivering accurate profiles."

"Sadly, not everyone has the ability."

Bell bit her tongue. She didn't want to speak badly of her coworkers, but what Wolf said was true.

"No, not everyone does."

"You do."

Wolf circled Bell. The hairs stood on her neck when he passed behind. She imagined the blade sliding free of its sheath. A quick swipe across her throat. She slid her hand inside her pocket in an attempt to turn on the phone, but he rounded the chair too quickly.

"Academics forever seek to discredit rather than further the science."

He passed behind again, and Bell shifted her weight. If she was quick enough, she could stand and kick the chair into his groin. Buy herself a few steps toward the exit doors before he recovered.

"And yet forensic evidence and police work failed to produce Renee's murderer," said Wolf. His wife. She needed to be careful. Say the wrong thing, and Wolf would snap. "Demonstrate your profiling ability. Humor me."

"How?"

"What's your profile of the elusive Logan Wolf? Tell me something no one else could possibly know."

Bell squirmed. In the year she'd spent brainstorming psychological profiles, she couldn't get a firm grasp on Wolf. The belief she lacked a crucial bit of information always muddied the picture.

"I'm…not sure."

"Come now, Scarlett. You can do better than that."

Her tongue ran along her teeth. A picture popped into her mind as she glared at Wolf. She felt certain she was right. But the truth might push him over the edge.

"Your wife." She saw Wolf's spine go rigid. A dangerous look flashed in his eyes. "You don't carry a picture of her. Not in your wallet or on your phone."

Wolf's teeth clenched.

"Why?"

Bell swallowed.

"Because you don't want her around when you commit murder. It's like she can see you if her picture is nearby."

Wolf shifted. He looked like a beast unleashed in the

darkness.

"Most impressive. But I will warn you not to use my wife's name again when you profile me. A confession. I never doubted your ability, only wished to confirm you believed, too."

"For what purpose?"

"Because, Scarlett. I want you to catch a killer."

Wolf grinned, and Bell returned his smile.

"Then put out your hands, and I'll take you to Gardy now."

Wolf laughed, a sound like old parchment paper burning.

"You have a sense of humor. I can appreciate that. Renee had a wonderful sense of humor."

"You're wasting time, Wolf. We both know how tonight will end. Be done with it."

"You misunderstand my intentions. What if I told you, dear Scarlett, that you will leave the warehouse on your own accord with your phone and weapon?"

"I wouldn't believe you."

"I meant what I told you. I want you to catch a killer for me. My wife's killer."

Bell read his eyes. If Wolf was lying, he had a helluva poker face.

"Explain."

"What I am about to say will shock you. Keep an open mind. As a token of good faith, here is your weapon. I took the liberty of removing the magazine, you understand."

"Then the gun is hardly a token of faith."

"You will have the magazine soon."

She quivered as Wolf reached down and slid the

Glock into her holster.

He turned from her and strolled into the shadows, his hands clasped behind his back as if unsure how to begin. The water continued to drip from the ceiling.

Bell slipped her hand into her pocket. A moment of panic followed when she couldn't find the power button. The phone was upside down. Her fingers skimmed the edges until she found it.

Bell pressed it down as he turned.

Hoping the dark cloaked her hands, she slowly edged them from her pocket. He was close to her now.

"On July 21 of the year 2013, I returned home after a trip to Houston. The Brindisi case. You may have read about it."

"Yes. You thwarted a mob hit."

"It was after ten when I arrived at my doorstep. And when I entered the kitchen…"

His voice went dry. To Bell's astonishment, he sniffled.

"I…found her on the kitchen floor with her…"

His shoulders rose and fell as he struggled to compose himself.

Bell instinctively touched the gun though it was no use to her. Wolf was losing control.

Come on Gardy, she prayed. I sent you a homing beacon.

"I did not murder my wife."

"If you didn't murder Renee, who did? "

In the dark, she saw red in his eyes. His face glistened with tears.

"I don't know who murdered my wife. If I did, I would track him to the four corners of the earth."

"You fled the scene."

"Because the so-called experts at the FBI concluded I was the killer, though the only forensic evidence tying me to the murder can be explained by my having lived in the house for ten years. It's almost enough to make you believe someone at the BAU wanted me out of the way. You don't believe me, do you? Amend your profile, Scarlett."

Bell slid to the edge of her seat. The next time he turned, she'd make a run for the exit.

"You murdered your wife on the night of July 21, 2013. Slit her throat. Placed a bag over the head, most likely so you wouldn't have to see her eyes. Her accusation. Since that time, you've relived the fantasy repeatedly by murdering—"

"Men?"

This was the snag neither Bell nor Gardy unraveled. Why switch to killing men?

"Yes."

"Does that make sense to you?"

"No." Wolf began to nod, but Bell cut him off. "But then again, I'm not a psychopathic killer."

He growled and slammed his fist against a metal rack. A box tumbled over the side and spilled its contents on the floor.

"Nor am I."

"The FBI tied you to multiple murders over the last five years. Witnesses saw you near the crime scenes. Can you look me in the eye and claim you're not a murderer?"

The walls seemed to shift inward. Wolf stalked closer, and for the first time, Bell appreciated how strong and imposing he was.

"Yes, I killed those men, And for that, you should

thank me."

A siren rang out over Pronti, at least a mile away but approaching quickly. Wolf squinted at her. His hands moved to his pocket. When he found it empty, he leaned his head back and laughed.

"Well played, Scarlett. It seems you got one over on me. But you made a grave mistake—"

Bell made her move. She was out of the chair when Wolf shot into her path and blocked her. This was it. He would kill her now.

He clutched her by the shoulders. His grip was firm. No chance to power free.

"What more can I do to earn your trust? Still, you betray me. You have your phone and gun. Go now before there is trouble."

"You lied to me, Wolf. The gun is useless without the magazine."

"You have everything you need, Scarlett. I know who murdered Jillian. I can find him for you."

Bell's throat hitched. The psychopath who killed her childhood friend was never identified.

Wolf vanished down the rows and into the shadows. The door edged open, letting in a sliver of light from the lamppost. Then he was gone.

You have everything you need.

The approaching siren was joined by two more as she pondered what he meant.

She reached for the Glock. The magazine had been inside the gun the entire time.

CHAPTER NINETY

She was a zombie walking. No more alive than the bones excavated from The Skinner's barn.

Flashing lights blinded Bell as she stumbled with Gardy's assistance to the ambulance. When she arrived, Gardy and a male paramedic with facial stubble and a buzz cut sat her down outside the vehicle. The paramedic shined a light into her eyes. She didn't blink.

"Can you tell me your name?"

"Scarlett Bell."

"Do you know where you are?"

"Yes, we're in Kansas."

He asked her for the date, and she answered correctly. They ran a battery of tests, checked her reflexes and blood pressure. Bell was in perfect health.

Except she was dead inside.

The paramedic wanted her to ride in the ambulance to the hospital, but she refused. Gardy glanced at the man and shrugged. There didn't seem to be anything wrong with her.

A small group of deputies and FBI agents massed

outside the warehouse. Tyner barked orders into his radio as the cruisers canvassed the area. It didn't matter. Wolf had disappeared by now. They wouldn't find him.

"What happened in the warehouse? Bell?"

She slowly turned her head toward Gardy. His face was drawn. He looked as if he'd aged ten years tonight.

"Did he hurt you?"

She slumped forward and shook her head, her blonde hair sweaty and veiling her face.

"No."

A look of confusion contorted Gardy's face.

"What did he—"

"He told me he knew who killed Jillian."

"Bell...you don't believe him, do you?"

How could she tell Gardy that she believed Wolf? She chewed her lip and kept the truth to herself.

"Bell, it's what he does. He's playing mind games with you."

Gardy brushed the hair from her face and flinched when he saw the rekindled fire in her eyes.

"Is he, Gardy? He could have killed me at any point. In the motel room, while I was unconscious, when I tried to escape. All he did was ask for help."

Gardy narrowed his eyes.

"What did he ask you to do?"

"He wants a profile, I think."

"A profile of who?"

"The man who killed his wife."

Gardy dropped his head and stared at the pavement. His hands rubbed at the back of his neck. She knew what he thought. This was another one of Logan Wolf's twisted games. But to what end?

"Quid pro quo, Gardy. I give him Renee Wolf's killer, and he hands me the man who murdered Jillian."

"For God's sake, Bell. Listen to yourself. Logan Wolf murdered his wife, and he's left a trail of bodies across the country for five years running. Don't let him inside your head."

"That's what I don't understand."

"What?"

"He admitted to all the murders except his wife's."

Gardy took a deep breath. Over his shoulder, she saw Keene and Lowe watching.

"He's either lying or guilt-ridden. The human mind uses defensive mechanisms to conceal ugly truths. You see it every day. Five years is a long time. He may have convinced himself he wasn't capable of taking the life of a loved one, but the evidence is clear."

"No, the evidence is circumstantial."

"Bell, please don't say you believe him."

"I don't trust him, but we're not seeing the whole picture, Gardy. Until we do, we'll never catch him."

Gardy rose to his feet and buttoned his jacket against the cold.

"I'll catch him, Bell."

Bell looked at him for a while, shivering. Her mind drifted among the past days' haunts. The scare over her father's tumor, discovering The Skinner beheaded, the barn, the warehouse. Seeing Gardy revitalized and back on the hunt grounded her, pulled her back to the present.

She nodded.

"Then I want to be there when you do."

Scarlett Bell Books 1-5

DEAD
RINGERS

CHAPTER NINETY-ONE

Special Agent Scarlett Bell wished she could bottle this moment and keep it forever.

She leaned her head on Lucas's shoulder and closed her eyes as a cool spray blew off Chesapeake Bay. Overhead, a pair of seagulls squawked and circled.

He cupped her hip with his hand and nudged her closer, and she sighed contentedly as the Virginia sun, mild for the first week of January, slid over her body. The warmth lent the sensation that they were cheating winter, a season which turned raw and cruel along the coast. Weather like this wouldn't become commonplace for another three months, yet here it was during the coldest month of the year. Summer trapped in a bottle. Their time together was short and would soon end.

"You should tell them you're sick," he said. "Play hooky."

She touched his lips to quiet him and ran a hand through his sandy-brown hair. Thirty-years-old, Lucas

Crawford was two years younger than Bell. She'd met the software developer while jogging along the beach on the first morning of November, when the mornings turned crisp and the wind off the ocean peppered her legs with goosebumps. On the verge of financial independence, Lucas lived in a quaint little beach house a half-mile south of Bell's apartment. He'd invited her over for dinner every week since, where they grilled fresh-caught fish and ate on the deck while the naval ships crawled across distant waters.

There was a long island in the kitchen which carried the scent of cut lime, and he'd nailed a fishing net to the living room wall and adorned it with blue and red starfish. She found joy in his playful collection of seashells which he laid out on an ocean blue tarp in the den.

More than anything, Bell wanted to stay with Lucas for the next week and forget work. She watched the tide pull the sand out to sea and deposit sediment in its place. Perpetual motion. Life in balance. She leaned her back against his chest, and he hugged her close.

"I wish I could. Not this time. The case is too serious."

"It's the murders in Florida, right? Everyone's talking about them. The pictures are all over the news."

The pictures.

Imagining the crime scene photographs turned her stomach. As an agent with the FBI's Behavior Analysis Unit, hunting murderers was Bell's specialty. She'd witnessed too much death, too much evil over the last several months, including her near-death encounter with Logan Wolf, a former BAU agent and the nation's most wanted serial killer. The reports about the stabbing were all over the television. It was the second woman murdered in Palm Dunes, Florida, in the last two weeks.

Another serial killer.

Instinct told her this one was more dangerous than most, a phantom haunting the beach town.

"Can we not talk about it? It'll be my life for the next week, or at least until we catch him."

"Sure, of course. Promise me you'll text and keep me up to date."

"I'll do you one better than that."

"Sexy selfies?"

She tutted.

"I meant I'd call...but I'll take the suggestion under consideration."

He knelt in the shallows, scraped at the sand, and came up with a blanched, V-shaped shell that fit in the palm of his hand. Wiping the hair from her face, she leaned over to study the finding.

"That's a weird looking shell," she said.

"It's not a shell. That's a shark tooth. Hammerhead or bull. Something big, anyhow."

"I didn't think Chesapeake Bay had sharks that large."

"They're rare, but they swim through from time-to-time. Great whites, too. You want the tooth?"

She shook her head, and he hurled the tooth over the waves. Frigid as it was during winter, the Atlantic was beautiful, soothing. And dangerous. The shark's tooth served as a reminder that danger lurked where the light didn't touch.

From the corner of her eye, she saw a shadow approach. Bell turned and saw her partner, Neil Gardy, struggling down the beach in his suit and dress shoes. Was it time to leave? No, Gardy was early as usual. He kept his head down while he walked, navigating sand hills which sought to swallow his shoes.

He was out of breath when he caught up to them. Bell moved a half-step from Lucas and waved.

"You could have called from the apartment."

Gardy smiled.

"I thought a nice walk on the beach would do me good." He glanced at his shoes, scuffed and gritty with sand. "Guess this wasn't such a good idea."

Gardy and Lucas met with their eyes, and there was an uncomfortable moment of silence before Bell broke in.

"Lucas, this is my partner, Special Agent Neil Gardy."

They nodded, but no handshake followed. Closing the space, Lucas edged toward Bell and moved his hand back to her hip.

Gardy cleared his throat.

"So Bell tells me you're into computers."

"A born coder," Lucas said, smiling, and this chipped the ice away. "Got my start on the PC when I was twelve and never looked back."

"My parents bought me a used Commodore 64 back in the eighties," Gardy said, staring at the sea and remembering. "I started out playing games, and I figured out a lot of them were written in BASIC. Took me a few days of trial and error, but I hacked the code on a movie monster game and made my fire breathing lizard unbeatable."

"It wasn't Rampage, was it?"

"No, but I played that game in the arcade until I ran

out of quarters and my fingertips went numb."

They laughed. Gardy and Lucas had gone from distant to amiable in a matter of seconds over retro gaming, and she became the third wheel.

The grin on Gardy's face waned, and he shot a look back at the apartment where the morning sun turned the exterior golden.

"Yeah. I know, Gardy," Bell said. "Time to go."

"Sorry."

She squinted up at Lucas.

"Why don't you walk back with us? Hang out while I pack. You guys can talk about…Mario Kart or something."

"I'll take a rain check and head back to the house. I've got a conference call at eleven." Lucas checked his phone. "And I'm totally unprepared."

"You sure you can't come?"

"I can't. I'll see you when you get back."

Lucas kissed her on the forehead and shared a nod with Gardy, then he trudged toward the beach house, following the footprints they'd made earlier when the sun crawled out of the sea with the day's first light. A lump formed in her throat. It was only a week, yet she already missed him.

Gardy apologized again. They didn't talk during the walk to Bell's apartment complex. He sat on the porch overlooking the beach and thumbed through a magazine while she packed. He lifted the radio to his ear and issued a command. Bell couldn't hear through the glass, but she knew he'd given the all-clear to the agent parked in front of the apartment and sent him home. The FBI put Bell on 24-hour surveillance after Logan Wolf kidnapped her, believing the serial killer would come after her again.

Bell was almost out the door when she remembered her appointment with Dr Morford, her therapist. The nightmares had become vivid and intense since the abduction. Swiping through her contact list, she found Morford's phone number and rescheduled the session.

While Bell waited in the doorway with her belongings, Gardy checked the windows and the sliding glass door to the deck. It was pointless. A locked door never stopped Wolf.

"Everything sealed tight?"

He nodded.

"We should go. The plane leaves Dulles in ninety minutes."

They pulled out of the lot and followed a long and weaving access road that cut through marshland and undeveloped meadow. Through the window, she saw the top of Lucas's beach house peaking up from behind a grass covered dune. Then she couldn't see it anymore, and the vehicle hurtled toward the interstate.

CHAPTER NINETY-TWO

The jet ride into Tampa International Airport was smooth and didn't aggravate Gardy's motion sickness. By the time the plane landed, it was five o'clock, the palm shadows lengthening across the heat-baked parking lot as they wheeled their bags to the rental. The temperature was a pleasant seventy-five degrees, the sky a deep cerulean blue that you could swim in, and Bell felt a pang in her chest when she thought of her seaside apartment. She checked her texts and found nothing new. Lucas was probably fishing on the coast, planning a sunset dinner on the porch.

Gardy noticed Bell lost in an alternate reality.

"He's nice."

His voice brought her back to the present.

"What?"

"Lucas. He seems like a nice guy."

"I suppose so."

"That's a ringing endorsement if I ever heard one. What do you tell people about me?"

Bell winked.

"You don't want to know."

Gardy pressed the key fob, and the rental SUV honked and flashed its lights. He loaded Bell's bag into the trunk despite her protests, and then they were on the highway, cruising south with the salty tang of the gulf pouring through the open windows. This wouldn't be so bad if they were here for a pleasure trip. If only that was the case.

He patted the case folder on the seat between them.

"How much do you know about the murders?"

"Only what I saw on CNN and read in the papers. Two young women stabbed in their homes in the last two weeks. Killer used a glass cutter on the patio door the first time. Second murder, he lifted himself onto a roof overhang and crawled in through the attic. Violent stabbings."

"Similar to the Hodge case in New York."

"Similar, yes, but not teenage girls. These women were upwardly mobile, single, career oriented. Both lived in upscale homes, new developments. Not likely you'd need a handyman like Hodge when everything is new and working."

"So here's the timeline. Cheryl Morris, age twenty-seven, murdered in her home on December twentieth. The latest, Lori Tannehill, age twenty-five, killed last evening."

Bell opened the folder and cringed at the grisly pictures.

"Those are deep wounds."

"Which suggests he's a big man, or at least strong. Tannehill must have heard him coming out of the attic. She locked the bedroom door, but the killer snapped the lock and forced the door open. Local PD is working under the assumption the killer knew both women, and I agree."

He glanced over at Bell as he weaved through rush hour traffic.

"But you don't think so."

She shook her head.

"It doesn't feel right. He knew them, yes, but not intimately."

"Explain."

"It's possible he was an acquaintance, a co-worker or someone who crossed paths with both women now-and-then. This isn't a case of a jilted lover exacting revenge."

The traffic glut cleared, and Gardy accelerated. The first road sign for Palm Dunes appeared off the shoulder. Another seven miles. Peering over a coastal development, Bell spied the gulf, the water a fiery red that left imprints on her eyes.

Gardy cleared his throat.

"Hey, there's something else you should know."

"Okay."

"The point on this investigation, our contact, is Detective Jay Phalen of the Palm Dunes Police Department."

"Why do I know that name?"

"Formerly of the BAU. Phalen was well before your time, but you might have heard his name. He worked during the Wolf years."

Bell squirmed.

"We came through the academy together," Gardy said. "Good cop, hard worker, but he flamed out with the BAU. Phalen never cut it as a profiler and quit after a few years."

She glanced across the vehicle. Gardy chewed his

lower lip as he gripped the steering wheel.

"Why do I get the impression this is a problem?"

"Because he doesn't buy into profiling. Claims it's theoretical bullshit that doesn't fly in practice."

"So why are we here?"

"Because the Chief of Police sees things differently. Unfortunately, he put the investigation in Detective Phalen's hands. We'll get good cop work out of Phalen. He'll hustle and shoot straight with you. Don't be put off if he comes off as caustic."

"You know me."

Gardy maneuvered around a tractor trailer.

"You bet I do. He says the wrong thing, and you'll bite his head off."

"I won't. Scout's honor."

"Bell."

"I'll behave."

Gardy sighed.

"I remember how much you love office politics, but you need to be careful with Phalen. He'll push you. Anyhow, we have just enough time to check into the hotel and grab a bite to eat before we meet him at the station."

Palm Dunes was as Bell envisioned — sprawling homes and condominiums along the beach, gated communities with brick roadways, and pastel storefronts which blended with the tropical flora. Their hotel, the Palm Dunes Garden Inn, was a white Victorian property with ruby red shingles and a gable roof. Bell whistled when she stepped into the air-conditioned lobby where three children giggled and chased each other in a circle. The front desk gleamed with fresh polish, and a replica cage elevator ascended from the center of the room and carried guests a dozen floors into the Florida sky.

"You outdid yourself this time, Gardy. This is hardly the Pronti, Kansas Inn."

"Don't thank me. The Holiday Inn was overbooked."

"Alas, fate is on my side for once."

After checking in, they made their way to the elevator. Gardy opened his hand expectantly.

"What?"

"Your room key."

Bell huffed and handed it over. Gardy's rules forbidding Bell from staying alone were in effect again. She thought they were past this point, but the threat of Logan Wolf had Gardy on high alert.

"You're acting ridiculous. This place reminds me of Disney World. You can't believe Wolf will stride in here unnoticed and try to kidnap me."

A bell dinged, and the door opened.

"Better safe than sorry. Besides, we make good roomies. Just try to keep your side of the room clean this time."

She followed him into the elevator with one fist cocked and loaded. He snickered as the doors closed.

The third-floor room was spacious and included a modern kitchenette with a two-burner stove. A balcony overlooked the gulf, dark now and frothing against the beach.

Gardy pulled out the bed on the sleeper sofa before she could claim it.

"The bed is yours."

"You gave me the bed in Milanville. It's your turn to sleep in style."

He fluffed the pillow and patted the mattress.

"I prefer the sofa bed. Good for the old back."

She muttered doubtfully and unpacked.

Bell wondered what Lucas would say if he learned about their living arrangement. She'd dated him for less than two months, not long enough to build lasting trust and loyalty. Hell, she had no idea how long the relationship would last or if either of them wanted to move beyond the casual stage. She checked her phone and found his message waiting.

Did you arrive safely? How's the weather?

She thumbed her response.

Arrived fine and the weather is great. Gotta unpack and head to police department. Will text you after.

The sending indicator spun while the hotel WIFI struggled. Finally, a *delivered* icon appeared beside the message. She finished unpacking and watched Gardy smooth the sheets on the pullout bed.

This felt like a betrayal.

CHAPTER NINETY-THREE

The Palm Dunes Police Department looked more like a swanky car dealership than a headquarters for law enforcement. A black and white American flag flew on a mast towering above the parking lot with the classic Thin Blue Line running parallel to the stripes. The front of the building was blue-shaded glass, the windows reflecting the parking lot lights. Palms lined a concrete walkway to the doors.

Bell and Gardy flashed their badges at the front, and a male officer pointed them toward the stairs. The lobby was busy for an evening. A group of officers stood in a circle beside the stairway. Their laughter ended when the tallest member of the group noticed Bell and Gardy. Bell felt their eyes follow her up the steps.

They found Jay Phalen's office at the end of the hall. Gardy knocked on the open door. The detective greeted the agents without lifting his eyes from the case notes.

"Agent Gardy. I could have saved you the trouble. We've got all the manpower we need on this case." Phalen issued a tired sigh and ran his hand through a tuft of brown, thinning hair. Then he dropped his pen and lifted his head. "Glad to have you, regardless."

Phalen rounded the desk and shook Gardy's hand.

"Good to see you again, Jay. What's it been? Five years?"

"Time flies even when you aren't having fun."

The detective wore a white short sleeve Polo that accentuated strong arms and his deep Florida tan. In his younger years, Bell reasoned, Phalen was the boy who inspired clandestine entries into teenage girls' diaries, but he was older now and fighting a losing battle against time.

"I expected you'd be running the place by now," said Phalen, leaning against the desk. "Tell you one thing, when I heard Don Weber got Deputy Director of CIRG, I thanked my lucky stars I got the hell out of there. Damn shame. Everyone and their mother had you pegged for the job."

Gardy coughed into his hand and glanced around the office.

"You're doing okay for yourself. This has to be the most spectacular law enforcement building I've set foot in."

"The taxpayers aren't impressed."

Gardy remembered Bell was in the room.

"Sorry, I lost my head for a second. Jay, this is Special Agent Bell. She'll take the lead developing the profile."

One corner of the detective's mouth curled into a forced smile.

"Yes, I know about Agent Bell. Her reputation precedes her."

Bell met Gardy's eyes. He shrugged.

Phalen rolled open his desk drawer, pulled out a folded newspaper, and slapped it on the desk. To Bell's horror, she saw it was a recent issue of *The Informer,* the tabloid that made a mint exploiting her. The lead reporter, Gavin Hayward, had tracked Bell to numerous manhunts across the country in the last year. On one memorable occasion, Hayward broke through a police barricade in California to get a quote and snap Bell's picture.

Bell rolled her eyes.

"Hopefully, you don't take anything Gavin Hayward writes seriously."

"I wouldn't wipe my ass with *The Informer* or any of these crime rags stacked at the grocery store checkout line. But I'm concerned. The sleaze ball has a knack for tracking you to crime scenes, and I can see it becoming a problem."

"We'll handle Hayward," Gardy said.

"You do that. With a serial killer on our hands, we can't afford distractions."

Bell opened her mouth to respond, and Gardy cut her off.

"I've read the notes, but I want your take on the murders."

Assuaged, Phalen gestured at two chairs fronting his desk. Gardy and Bell slid into the seats as Phalen circled around to his chair.

"Based on the ME's estimations, both murders occurred during the late evening hours, most likely after seven but before midnight."

Bell opened a notepad.

"That suggests the unknown subject works during the day."

Phalen chewed on a pen as he nodded across the desk at Bell.

"Makes sense. He leaves the office in the late

afternoon and has time to plan the murder, gather supplies. Gets home early enough to make it into work the next morning. Yes, we figured that much. Little good that does us if he works hours typical of the general population."

"And the women?"

"Both of the killings took place in affluent homes, but again, that doesn't narrow the search much. Palm Dunes is bursting at the seams with money."

"The victims will lead us to the killer."

Phalen folded his arms over his chest and rocked disinterestedly in his chair.

"How so?"

"Both were young adults and successful. The photographs show each had blonde hair. That could be a coincidence, but often serial killers target a certain type. If you have them, I'd like to examine recent photographs of Morris and Tannehill."

Detective Phalen glared at Bell for a moment before he removed two pictures of the women from his folder. The photograph of Cheryl Morris appeared taken at a company party or gala. An older, inebriated man had his arm around her shoulder. Morris wore an uncomfortable smile. Bell tapped her finger on his face.

"Who's the guy?"

"Lionel Rhinehurst, her boss."

"Looks like he's all over Morris."

"He's a scumbag, but not the killer. He was at a conference in San Diego the night of the murder. We checked."

Bell drew the photographs closer together. Though the two women wouldn't be mistaken as sisters, there were similarities. Their hair was beige blonde, not silvery, a

466

subtlety not indicated in the crime scene pictures. The camera flash blew out the details in those photographs. Both women possessed high cheekbones and would stand out among their friends as one of the prettiest in the crowd. Pretty but not glamorous. Soft, trusting eyes. The girl next door.

"Hard to imagine either relying on a dating website to find companionship," Gardy said. "I expect both had boyfriends."

"She was single," Phalen said, tapping Morris's picture. "Based on the depth of the stab wounds and the busted door lock, we can rule out the killer being a woman. We have a lead though."

"Oh?"

"Matt Doss, Tannehill's boyfriend. Guy got charged with assault in Tampa two years ago for a road rage incident, and his last girlfriend..." Phalen shuffled through the case notes. "Ah, here it is. Kendra Moore, age twenty-seven. She claims Doss roofied her at a party last May and took her upstairs, but the hospital didn't find evidence of a sexual assault. One of Morris's friends figured out what was happening and told Doss she'd call the police if he didn't open the door."

"Does he have an alibi on the night of the murder?"

"He says he was asleep by nine, but nobody can verify. Claims he had a migraine. As of now, we don't have evidence tying him to the scene."

"What else do we know?"

"He's a strong guy. Athlete. Ran the Florida Marathon last year and finished in the top third."

"Strong enough to create these wounds?"

She pointed at the deep knife wounds on Morris and

Tannehill.

"Yes, I think so." Phalen glanced at his watch. "Anything else I can tell you?"

"I want to see the houses," Bell said.

"I have the floor plans and pictures of the residence."

"No, a full walk-through of the Tannehill home. And the Morris home if possible."

The detective sat back with his hands behind his head, eyes narrowed.

"Let me guess. So you can see things as the killer did."

"Something like that."

Phalen glanced at his desk calendar.

"Well, I'm free tomorrow between ten and noon if the two of you want to meet me at Tannehill's."

"Why not now?"

The detective met Gardy's eyes as though he expected his old workmate to intervene. It was obvious Phalen was ready to head home for the day.

"I'm not here to inconvenience you, detective," Bell said, leaning forward but careful not to rest her arms on Phalen's desk and invade his space. This was a man who defended his territory with impunity. "Gardy and I can handle the walk-through ourselves. Go home to your wife and dog. Enjoy your evening."

Phalen blinked.

"How did you know I have a dog?"

She didn't want to tell him his slacks were spotted with dog hair.

"A good guess. That, and you have kind eyes. A dog lover's eyes."

Phalen looked at Bell skeptically, then nodded.

"No skin off my back if you want to walk around in a dark house. I'll get you the keys, but you won't learn anything our guys didn't already figure out."

CHAPTER NINETY-FOUR

He shouldn't be here. It's too soon.

Yet he can't help himself. He feels compelled as though his arms and legs dangle from marionette strings.

The bruised sky of dusk has burned out, and all that remains is black and a sprinkling of stars. The car window is open to a crack. Enough to alleviate the stench of sweat. He hasn't showered. There wasn't time to change after work, not if he wanted to see the house again and rekindle the memory.

The sports car, a Camaro, rests several doors away from Tannehill's home. He chose a spot under a bald cypress, far from the nearest street lamp. A long and leafy branch extends over the Camaro like the arm of a loving mother. It holds him in its shadow.

The lights are off inside the Craftsman bungalow. No crime techs skittering inside the property, no concerned neighbors gossiping curbside as they cast nervous glances at the home.

Did you know her?

No, but I saw her every morning around seven climbing

into the Audi with a thermos of coffee.

Such a tragedy. Who would do such a thing?

A jealous boyfriend, I bet.

Yes, I heard something about the boyfriend.

What?

He beat his old girlfriend.

Oh, my.

Yes, I was surprised Ms Tannehill would date a boy like that. But it's none of my business.

I just hope they catch him if he did it.

He attended Cheryl Morris's funeral and sat at the back of the church a dozen pews behind the mourners. He felt nothing. Their sniffs echoed around the capacious interior like bats in a cavern. Before the ceremony's conclusion, he slipped into the restroom and waited until the church emptied. Then, amid the mottled slashes of light and dark, he approached the hanging cross of Jesus and knelt. No regret, no guilt. If God wished him dead, he would have struck him down for sullying this holy place. As he grinned at the plaster Christ, powerless and perpetually affixed to the cross, he understood nothing could stop him. Not in this life or the next.

His eyes slide along the properties. As he waits in silence, he decides he will visit Tannehill's grave after she is laid to rest. Lean against the headstone with the sun on his face and remember what he did. Close to her again.

Porch lights shine from every home, standing guard against the night and its terrors. But not against him.

Outside a sea-blue Cape Cod, a young man and woman huddle close on the top step of a porch. The man's arm is around the woman's waist, and her neck lolls against his shoulder. Now-and-again, their eyes drift to Tannehill's bungalow and glance away. The entire neighborhood is fearful because of him. Because of what he did to her.

Blood thrumming in his head, he touches the door handle and stalls. The compulsion grows. A part of his subconscious believes he will recapture the ecstasy if he approaches the bungalow. The logical part of his brain knows better, understands he's taking an incredible risk. Yet the urge grows and refuses to be quiet.

He waits for a car to pass. The headlights burn in his mirrors and blind him. He slides below the steering wheel when the other vehicle is close, and after it passes, he emerges from hiding like a shark fin cutting through breakers.

Certain the road is empty, he edges the door open and steps onto the blacktop. The road holds the day's heat. The tarry warmth puffs at his shins as he clicks the door shut.

A baseball cap is pulled down to his eyes. His hands plunge into his pockets as he steps over the shoulder and reaches the sidewalk. His head hangs low, eyes fixed on the concrete blocks. He skips over the cracks and mumbles the childhood mantra about breaking his mother's back. It's enough to make him chuckle. He swallows the laugh before he attracts unwanted attention. Already he senses the man and woman watching him from the Cape Cod, wondering who he is and what business he has in the neighborhood.

This is enemy territory. Sentries are everywhere.

Beneath a weeping willow, he vanishes and becomes a silhouette. Then he wades through another pool of light under a street lamp.

The bungalow is two houses away, the windows dark and dead to the world. Eternal sleep. The anticipation dries his mouth and pumps his heart.

Before he reaches Tannehill's home, headlights flare and catch his chest. He turns his shoulder before the beams sweep across his face. The vehicle, an SUV of some sort, swings to the curb. Quickly, he crosses the street as the doors open. Out of the corner of his eye, he watches the man and woman climb from the vehicle and stroll up the bungalow's walkway.

Cops?

His heart races. Puts dizzying butterflies in his head. What were the odds the authorities would arrive the second he returned to the scene? It might be a trap. He doesn't think so, but the coincidence freezes ice on his spine. They climb up the steps, and the man inserts a key into the lock.

They don't look like cops. Christ, they're feds. The FBI knows about him now. It was inevitable for the FBI to get involved, but he believed it would only happen after many killings.

Looking over his shoulder, he confirms he isn't being followed. The couple outside the Cape Cod can't see him from this angle. As the agents struggle with the lock, he slips behind a hedge and peers through an opening. Confident he hasn't drawn their attention, he settles into the shadow and exhales.

Until the female agent swings around and stares in his direction.

The man unlocks the door and pushes it open, then stands in the threshold, following the woman's gaze. They lean their heads close and speak. It isn't possible they saw him, yet the two agents stare at the hedge as though they sense him. Like a cold pool in tropical waters.

Another vehicle approaches, a truck with a growling

engine. The headlights glide across the agents' faces.

And he sees her.

The female agent's shoulder-length blonde hair reminds him of Morris and Tannehill. The woman is alluring. A dead ringer for the other women. His palms go sweaty as he inches closer to the hedge.

No longer spooked by his presence, the two agents enter the bungalow and close the door.

This is his chance to flee. To run to the car before the agents return.

He can't leave. The drumming of his heart confirms her fate.

A cloud passes over the moon and cloaks the street in darkness. He slips out of the hedge and approaches the bungalow.

CHAPTER NINETY-FIVE

Bell looked over her shoulder as Gardy entered Lori Tannehill's house. Someone was across the street behind the hedgerow. The possibility it was the killer didn't occur to her, her mind settling on the likelihood of kids or a curious neighbor. Still, the shadow figure unnerved Bell and increased her paranoia.

Gardy flicked the wall switch. With the lights on, the bungalow wasn't as creepy. The floor was strand bamboo hardwood and shining from a recent polish. The first floor was an open concept, a dining room with a cherry wood table off to the right, a sparsely furnished living room to the left with a computer room nestled behind it. Windows let in ample sunshine during the day. Night pressed against the glass now.

"Easy to watch her through the windows," she said as they stepped into the living room.

Stepping through a victim's house always sent a shiver up Bell's spine. The lights were too bright, the shadows unexpected and deeper than she imagined.

A kitchen and a sitting room took up the rear of the

first floor, and a sliding glass door off the sitting room opened to the backyard.

Gardy touched the pane and ran his eyes along the vulnerable entry point.

"So the unknown subject used a glass cutter at Morris's house."

"Right."

"So why not here?"

Bell studied her reflection in the window. After dark, Tannehill wouldn't be able to see her attacker in the backyard.

"Because she was downstairs. He couldn't cut the glass without her noticing, and if he broke the pane, she'd have time to dial 911." Bell retraced her footsteps to the center of the bungalow. A wooden staircase led to the second floor. Craning her neck as she looked up, she spotted another flight of stairs leading to the attic door. "Instead, he climbed up the side of the house using the roof overhang on the back porch."

Gardy followed her to the staircase.

"So Tannehill is downstairs, maybe watching television and doesn't hear him break into the attic."

"Until he opens the door."

A thought seized her, and Bell took the stairs two at a time with Gardy racing to keep pace. As she had with the Alan Hodge case in New York, Bell formed a vague picture of the killer.

"Slow down."

She passed the second floor and ascended to the attic door. The knob was warm, holding the heat of the attic. Turning the knob, she listened for any noise that might give the killer away. It twisted in her hand. Then the door drifted open with an excruciating groan that reminded her of a horror movie sound effect.

"She would have heard the door drift open from downstairs," said Gardy, nodding.

"So she comes upstairs to inspect the noise, thinking the wind blew the door open and never imagined it was an intruder."

"And by the time she sees him, it's too late to reach her phone. That's when she locks herself inside the bedroom."

Their shoes thumped on the staircase as they descended. The master bedroom was at the end of the hall, past a large bathroom and an empty spare room. The door, a classic paneled mahogany, splintered along the edge where the knob broke.

Bell knelt and examined the knob. It hung at an oblique angle like a broken limb. She thought back to the photograph of Lionel Rhinehurst, Morris's boss. No way a wiry man pushing seventy could have done this. And what connection would he have to Lori Tannehill? Even without the alibi, Bell knew Rhinehurst wasn't the killer.

"Phalen didn't say if Doss was a big guy, did he?" Bell asked.

"No. Phalen only said he was athletic."

"This is a well-constructed door. Not easy to break through."

Gardy dropped beside Bell and shined a flashlight at the knob.

"The knob is the weakest link in the chain. Anyone with a bobby pin and know-how can pick an interior lock. Or, if you're in a hurry, you smash it until the bolt disengages."

The warped hinge made a squealing sound when Bell pushed the door open. A posted queen-size bed was the focal point to Tannehill's bedroom, but the dark blotch marring the white pile carpet drew Bell's eyes. This was where he murdered Lori Tannehill. Multiple stab wounds to the chest. Deep. An unwanted memory returned to Bell —Kacy Deering's blood staining the floorboards in Coral Lake. Torn drapes hung at the window, the rod bent at the center like narrowed eyebrows. Panicking, Tannehill had run for the window and ripped at the drapes as she searched for the latch.

Bell padded into the room, careful to step around the stain, and looked out the window. It was a long drop to the grass, no ledge to climb upon.

Blood splatter spread across the carpet and blackened the bedspread and walls.

The flash on Gardy's camera lit the room in brief bursts. He moved around the room and photographed the murder scene from multiple angles. When he finished, he took pictures of the door.

"We should check the attic," Gardy said.

Bell led the way up the stairs. The air inside the attic was hot and stuffy and made her throat itch. The roof slope forced them to bend over. Pink insulation filled the lower joists. A vinyl gable vent accepted air on one end of the attic, and the opposite side featured a window, open a crack.

Gardy reached above his head for a string and pulled. A bare bulb threw a small circumference of light over the attic. They filled in the rest with their flashlights.

A buzzing sound whistled past Bell's ear, and Gardy cursed and ducked as a wasp darted against the upper joists.

"Careful," he said, aiming the beam at the ceiling.

"Did it get you?"

"Hell, yes."

Gardy rubbed at his cheek, the red blemish swollen. An umbrella-shaped wasp nest hung off the ceiling. Dozens of wasps with black and yellow stripes crawled over hexagonal cells.

"You allergic?"

"Not that I'm aware. But then again I haven't gotten stung since I was a kid."

Bell grinned.

"That surprises me."

"How so?"

"Bees and wasps love the sweet stuff."

"Har-har."

"Hey, you could date someone. A lot of women would be interested."

"No time," Gardy said, flashing the beam along the joists. His face had a sheepish, sad-dog look.

"What do you do in your free time?"

He shrugged.

"Hit the gym, read."

"Yeah, and it's only dudes at your gym. Come on, Gardy. You're a good-looking guy. Fun to be around. For the most part."

"For the most part?"

"It was a joke."

"No, tell me. You don't think I've been fun to be around lately."

Bell exhaled. She wasn't ready for this conversation.

"Listen, I get it. The shooting in California affected

you. It would anybody. But you can't let it define who you are. You can talk to me, you know?"

His back to her, Gardy moved further down the joists. It took effort to keep up, and she kept losing her balance.

"I made a mistake. If I'd positioned myself properly —"

"Then the bullet would have passed over your head and hit me instead. You took a bullet *for me*, Gardy. Did you ever consider that?"

A sneaker-sized indentation marked a strip of insulation. Gardy bent to examine it. He kept his face averted, and Bell got the distinct impression he was crying.

"He tried to walk across the joists and stepped on a bag of insulation," Gardy said. "That's a tough balancing act."

Bell pictured the maniac walking a tightrope across the thin piece of board through the darkness, Lori Tannehill downstairs and unaware. Her own struggles confirmed it was impossible to walk along the joists without stumbling. Instinctively, she reached up and held the upper joists for support. Her fingertips were gritty with cobwebs and ages of dust. Gardy stood and reached for the ceiling.

"Don't touch anything."

Confusion crossed his face.

"What's the matter?"

"It's like you said. A tough balancing act. I bet he grabbed the ceiling to keep from falling. And it's nothing but grime and dust."

Gardy snapped his fingers.

"So there should be a fingerprint."

"Damn straight."

He wore a smile now, his eyes lost in the shadows. Gardy straightened and aimed the beam along the ceiling. He almost tripped, and Bell hurried to reach him.

"Here," she said, one knee on the board, her shoulder offered for support.

"Should I hum a bar from *Lean on Me*?"

"Just get on with it. This board is killing my knee."

He had one hand on her shoulder, the other moving the flashlight along the dusty ceiling. The grit and insulation played havoc with her sinuses as if tiny spiders crawled in-and-out of her nostrils. She sneezed into the crook of her arm, and he lost his footing and fell. Gardy's upper body sloped across her back, his arms wrapped around her shoulders. In the awkward silence, he steadied himself.

"Sorry about that."

"I didn't know you cared," she said, smirking.

"You're full of it tonight."

As Gardy climbed to his feet, Bell thought about Lucas and ached with guilt again. Nothing had happened, but in a matter of hours she'd be sleeping a few steps away from Gardy, and she couldn't ignore how she felt right now with the agent's arms around her. It felt *right*, comforting. She shook the thought from her head and braced herself as he placed his hand on her shoulder. She'd turned off her own flashlight, and her eyes started to adjust to the dim light when Gardy whistled.

"I'll be damned. He left a thumbprint."

That was when something thumped against the sliding glass door.

CHAPTER NINETY-SIX

Bell edged down the staircase behind Gardy. The agents moved on cats' paws, not making a sound as they descended from the second-floor landing. The wall shielded them, but when they rounded the banister, they'd be exposed to whoever snooped outside the house.

It was then Bell recalled the shadowed figure watching from across the street and thought of the killer. Had he returned to relive the crime so soon? She slipped the Glock-22 off her hip.

A scraping noise came from behind the house. It sounded like someone bumped into a patio chair and nudged it across concrete.

Gardy held up his hand and brought them to a stop. He pointed at the wall switch at the bottom of the stairway. Throwing it would plunge the lower floor into darkness and make them invisible, allowing the agents to see outside. His gun was in his hand as Gardy reached along the wall and flicked the switch. It was as if night swallowed the downstairs.

They waited several seconds for their eyes to adjust,

listening. For all Bell knew, it might have been a raccoon pawing at the glass and waddling around the patio, but she didn't think so. The hairs on the back of her neck told her she was being watched.

Gardy swung around the wall first, and Bell followed with her weapon aimed into the living room. The concrete patio was visible beyond the glass, one chair pushed at an angle. The front door was locked, no face at the window.

"You don't think it's PD snooping around," Bell whispered.

"No reason to. Not unless someone wanted to keep an eye on us, and I can't see Jay—"

Another thump, this time along the back of the house.

Gardy slipped toward the glass and motioned Bell toward the front door. She nodded, knowing she was to circle around the house and cut off the intruder after Gardy swept him out of hiding. A clicking noise came from behind the house. Damn, it sounded like someone cocked a gun.

She moved outside into the warm Florida night. Shrubs lined the bungalow's perimeter. Too many hiding places.

Bell rounded the house and crept toward the backyard, using the wall as a shield. The clicking sound came again, and her heart jumped into her throat.

Then Gardy shouted, "FBI, freeze!"

Running footsteps. Whoever was out there, she'd meet him at the corner of the house.

The shadow figure crashed into view.

"FBI!" The man's face came up in alarm. "Stay where you are. Hands above your head where I can see them."

She turned her flashlight on the figure, a middle-aged,

balding, dumpy man with glasses. Gavin Hayward, the lead reporter for *The Informer*.

"Don't shoot, don't shoot. I'm unarmed."

"Hold still."

She kept the gun fixed on the reporter, his eyes rolling like marbles as Gardy patted him down.

"He's clean."

Bell harrumphed.

"Jesus, Hayward. What the hell are you doing out here?"

"Pictures, just pictures," he said, raising the camera.

The camera hung from a strap around his neck. The zoom lens looked like a miniature telescope. Bell guessed he could have photographed the house from a few hundred feet away if he had a clear sight line.

Gardy reached for the camera, and Hayward snatched it away.

"You can't take my camera. I know my rights."

"You're trespassing on private property," said Gardy, gripping the reporter by the arm.

"Who will press charges? Lori Tannehill is dead."

"Don't give me that shit, Hayward. Trespassing is trespassing."

"Good luck getting the charges to stick. Wait until you hear from our lawyers."

"Yeah, yeah. It's out of our hands now. You'll have to sic your big city lawyers on the Palm Dunes Police Department."

Gardy reached for his phone.

"Is that necessary? Come on, guys."

But Gardy was already speaking to dispatch, one eye fixed on Hayward. The reporter shuffled his feet.

"Stay where you are, Hayward," Bell said. "The police will want to talk to you."

"Listen, Agent Bell, it was just a few pictures. Nobody got hurt. I didn't try to go inside the house."

"Quiet."

"We can work something out, you and me. I came here for you."

"Excuse me?"

Hayward grinned. One of his top incisors was fake. It looked silver in the moonlight.

"Don't you get it? You're a star, Agent Bell. Whatever the FBI pays you, we can double it. I'm talking an exclusive interview."

"You're insane."

"Am I? The world is fascinated with serial killers and the agents who track them. Nobody captured more serial killers than you in the last year. Meeks, Hodge, Longo, for God's sake, The Skinner."

Bell kept the light fixed on Hayward's face. She nudged the beam until he squinted and shielded his eyes.

"Not interested. *The Informer* is exploitative trash."

"Tell me about this guy. This new killer. Is he like Longo?" Bell sighed and shook her head. "Come on, Agent Bell. Give me something. One hand washes the other. I swear I'll make this worth your while. Is it true Logan Wolf kidnapped you and you escaped? Christ, do you know how much that story is worth? Think of the book and movie rights. You'd be set for life. You could move your parents into—"

"Don't you go anywhere near my parents, Hayward," she said, gesturing with the Glock.

"Hey, hey. No need to get excited. I'm just saying

Bealton, Virginia isn't as safe as it was thirty years ago, so maybe if you allowed me to interview them—"

"Say one more word and I'll shut your trap permanently."

Hayward opened his mouth to protest as the red and blue lights flashed curbside.

"That was quick," said Bell, lowering the flashlight.

Rubbing the glare out of his eyes, Hayward gave her a desperate, defeated look.

Gardy clutched Hayward's arm.

"Come with me. There are people who want to meet you."

CHAPTER NINETY-SEVEN

Neither Phalen nor the crime scene techs seemed overjoyed to analyze the bungalow after nine, and Phalen was perturbed to see Gavin Hayward in the back of a cruiser. Regardless, the detective gave Gardy an atta-boy pat on the back for good police work.

"Told you Hayward is a distraction."

"He's all yours, Jay. Throw the book at him."

Phalen glanced over his shoulder at the cruiser and shrugged.

"Not much we can do, to be honest. He didn't damage the property. Best we can do is hit the louse with a fine, and even then *The Informer* will pay it. You have any idea what he photographed?"

"I caught him taking shots behind the house. He tried to document how the killer climbed up to the attic."

"Scumbag."

"That's the world we live in. Hold him as long as you can, Jay. Make him uncomfortable."

"The lawyers will spring him inside of an hour. I'll put the fear of God into him, but I doubt it will do much good." Phalen waved his finger at them. "No more distractions from Hayward. Keep him out of our hair."

"Easier said than done."

A crime scene tech wearing a white suit and dust mask shuffled up the front steps. Phalen cocked his head at him.

"To hell with *The Informer*. Good work spotting the print. I don't know how we missed it the first time."

"Don't congratulate me. Bell was the one who figured out the killer grabbed the ceiling joist."

Phalen nodded and gave Bell a cautious, undecided smile.

It was eleven when Bell and Gardy made it back to the Palm Dunes Garden Inn. Neither had eaten since the plane ride, and that meal had been a gnat-sized pack of honey-roasted peanuts. The poolside cabana was still serving food, and Bell grabbed a haddock sandwich, while Gardy chose a questionable looking barbecue meal. Bell cocked an eyebrow. She wouldn't forgive him if he was up late with stomach issues.

Two women, a blonde and a redhead, shared a stool at the end of the counter. The redhead dipped her straw into a fruity cocktail and gave Gardy a sly grin. She wore a sundress that kissed the tops of her tanned thighs.

Bell elbowed Gardy.

"What?"

"You should go talk to her?"

"Uh..."

"Come on, she's checking you out."

Gardy's face turned crimson. He focused on his food, which consisted of ninety percent barbecue sauce and bread and ten percent mystery meat.

"We should go—"

"Too late. They're coming over."

The blonde locked arms with the redhead who'd lost her sea legs. Gardy stood as they approached and backed against the counter. The redhead laid a hand on his chest and ran a finger to his navel.

"You're a cute one."

Bell turned her head and bit her cheek to keep from laughing.

"I'd hit that in a second if I was into guys."

Then the two women kissed, and the redhead fell into the blonde laughing. A moment later, they stumbled together toward the resort. Gardy's mouth hung agape. He shook his head as if clearing cobwebs.

"Thanks a lot," Gardy said, taking a monstrous bite out of his food.

Bell raised her hands, a contrite smirk on her face.

"Sorry. I thought she liked you."

"Yeah? Maybe she was looking at *you*."

Bell cut her laughter off, her cheeks rosy.

They grabbed their food and found a bench on the boardwalk. The walkway remained active with walkers and bicyclists, the temperature comfortable despite the cool breeze. Bell couldn't see the gulf, only the waves as they crested against the sand. Beyond that lay the deep of night and pure imagination, a darkness that swallowed the world.

"Oh my God, this is so good," Bell said, dabbing tartar sauce off the corner of her mouth. Given her famished state, a gas station hot dog would have tasted like nirvana.

A roller skater cruised past, and Bell brought her legs

in to give him room. A good looking man in cargo shorts sat cross-legged on another bench and sipped on a soda.

"The barbecue is amazing, too."

"You sure? You can't identify the ingredients."

"Pork, I think they said. And no, I'm not sure, but I'd maul a boar with a steak knife if one galloped down the boardwalk."

Bell was eating too fast. Fries came with the sandwich, a bad idea this late, but the salty, greasy treat tempted her with its delectable scents. In between bites, she took a breath and closed her eyes. She could have drifted into a peaceful sleep on the bench. She wondered if the nightmares would follow her to the boardwalk.

"I'm not buying our sleeping arrangement, Gardy."

"Well, too bad, because I'm not changing my mind."

"We're paying for two rooms in a luxury resort hotel and only using one. Talk about fleecing the American taxpayer."

"There's no helping it. I can't cancel your room without everyone thinking we...you know."

"What? You make it sound like we're having an affair."

Gardy choked on his food.

"Don't even say that. The FBI will fire both of us. Point is it would look bad if anyone found out. I won't risk leaving you alone. Not after what happened in Pronti."

A young couple walked past holding hands. The boardwalk traffic had thinned, the resort guests retiring to their rooms or wandering into seaside pubs.

"You can't guard me all the time, Gardy. You don't hide in the bushes when I'm inside my apartment, do you? Wait, don't answer that."

Gardy snickered.

"I don't need to. Remember, the FBI has round-the-clock detail outside your apartment when you're home."

"Comforting," she said.

Logan Wolf and the overprotective FBI killed the quiet privacy of her beach apartment. Would they put Gardy's house under constant surveillance if Wolf stalked him, or was this a male-female thing? She chewed her lip as the light from a distant ship pass across the horizon.

"So here's what I think about our unknown subject," she said.

"Go."

"He's hedonistic but organized."

"What do you base that on?"

"That he's choosing a certain type points to him being a lust killer, yet all we have to go on is one fingerprint in a dusty attic."

"And the fingerprint won't help us catch him," Gardy said, dipping a fry into the barbecue sauce. "Not unless he has a record. What else?"

"He's upscale enough to fit into both Tannehill's and Morris's neighborhoods. Otherwise, someone would have spotted him."

"A sad commentary on society, but I agree."

Bell drummed her fingers on her thigh.

"It wasn't the boyfriend, Doss."

"I can buy that." A man in tattered clothing walked past holding a saxophone. Gardy dug into his wallet and handed the man a five-dollar bill. "But with the boyfriend's history of violence, it wouldn't be prudent to rule him out yet."

"I'm keeping my mind open," she said. Gardy

491

glanced at Bell, then looked away. "What?"

"Nothing."

"Tell me. There's tartar sauce on my face, isn't there?"

"No. It's just that..." He groaned. "You realize you resemble both Morris and Tannehill, I hope."

"I'd hardly say I resemble them."

"Close enough. I won't preach, but with you in the limelight now, all thanks to our friend at *The Informer*, the killer will notice the FBI agent tasked with tracking him fits his type."

"So he'll try to murder me next? Pretty brazen."

"He probably won't. But it pays to keep our eyes open and for you to watch your back."

She studied Gardy from the corner of her eye.

"Given any more thought to Wolf? He's been unusually quiet, not a single sighting since Kansas."

"He'll resurface soon, and when he does, I'll be waiting."

She gave a noncommittal nod and picked the sandwich up from her lap.

"You still believe he killed his wife?"

"Absolutely, and I hope you do. The evidence points in his direction."

"But most of the evidence is circumstantial."

Gardy put his food on the bench and gave her a level stare.

"Logan Wolf is a cold-blooded killer. We only know about the bodies we've found. Only God knows how many other's he's murdered. Wolf's gotten inside your head, Bell. Recognize it before he takes up permanent residence."

Bell peered over the ocean. The ship, just a pinprick of light flickering in the distance, was almost out of sight.

"What if he disappeared because he's sick? I told you he looked thin. Emaciated. Remember the store footage? He risked appearing on camera to buy a bottle of Pepto Bismol."

"I remember. That's how we'll find him — one day he'll wander into a hospital and someone will recognize him. But I can't depend on luck. I'll track him down. Nobody targets my partner."

Gardy's face looked sour as he tossed the rest of his food into the garbage.

"You're finished?"

"This Wolf talk made me lose my appetite. Let's go."

Still hungry, Bell gathered up her sandwich and fries and followed Gardy into the resort.

CHAPTER NINETY-EIGHT

The families and couples walking the boardwalk give him a wide berth. He's dressed like one of them—cargo shorts, running sneakers, an ocean-green t-shirt with a surfboard on the front. Yet he is not one of them, and on a reactive, instinctual level they recognize the danger though they wouldn't be able to explain why if asked.

Full dark has set upon the boardwalk. Regularly spaced lamp posts drive back the night. To his right is the roaring surf, to his left the endless commercial ligature of bars, hotels, and food stands. A cover band performs a drunken version of an old Jimmy Buffett song. He stops at a bench and sits, one ankle balanced upon the opposite knee, and nods at a passing bicyclist as he sips at his soda. He slips the phone from his pocket and turns on the camera function. Ensuring the flash is off, he feigns texting and zooms in on the FBI agent sitting kitty-corner on a nearby bench.

She is beautiful, he thinks. So much like his two victims. His *selected*. Shoulder-length blonde hair, green eyes, slim and shapely. He knows he walks a tightrope, much as he did when he revisited the bungalow so soon after the murder. And it almost got him caught. He feels the urge to toss the soda into the trashcan and leave.

Yet the woman draws him.

The man beside her is middle-aged, a few flecks of gray in his dark hair, but strong. And armed. The male agent will be a problem.

When the male agent tosses his food into the garbage, he rises from his bench and follows the two agents from several paces back. A mother and father with two young girls fall in behind the agents. The girls, overtired and sullen, complain their feet hurt as the mother prods them to walk. Finally, the parents comply, and each parent hoists a sniffling child into their arms. The distraction allows him to follow the agents unnoticed, a ghostly shadow moving up a winding brick walkway toward the resort.

The female agent stops and fishes the key card from her bag. She slides the card into the slot, and the hotel doors open.

He slows his pace while the mother struggles to retrieve her own card. When she fumbles the card with an exasperated groan, he hurries forward and retrieves it.

"Let me," he says.

The parents smile and utter thanks, too busy with their insolent children to give him a second thought. He slides the card into the reader, and the doors open. Then he hands the card to the mother, who snatches it between her fingers and thanks him again as he holds the doors.

Now inside, the same prickle of excitement he experienced upon entering the women's homes runs through his flesh. Invasion of privacy. No boundaries to hold him back. He held the ultimate power over them. Life or death.

The lobby is sparsely populated, half as busy as during peak hours. He blends in with his surroundings. A chameleon.

Across the room, the family enters a cage elevator with the two agents. No need to hurry. He takes a seat on a cushioned chair and thumbs through a gardening magazine, one eye following the elevator's ascent. It stops on the third floor, and the male and female agents exit. The open design leaves them vulnerable, unshielded, and he watches until they stop in front of room 335.

Interesting. They share the same room. This new piece of information throws a wrench in the works. It won't be easy to catch her alone. No problem. He is stronger than her. Stronger than the man, too. Without their weapons, they are puny, weak.

He enters the room number into his phone and wanders back to the boardwalk.

He will have her soon.

CHAPTER NINETY-NINE

Bell awoke after the best night of sleep she'd experienced in months. She couldn't recall her head hitting the pillow before midnight, only a nebulous recollection of slipping off her clothes and sliding under the covers, and no monsters or child abductors invaded her dreams. It was after nine. The Florida sun cut between the drapes and slashed a hot white streak across the television.

Water ran in the bathroom. Gardy was in the shower.

Bell thought of Lucas, one of the few solid foundations upon which her life rested. She checked her phone and found a message waiting. He'd written her at midnight to ask how the case was going, and now he probably wondered why she'd ignored him. She typed a response and promised she'd write again soon when there was more time. Then she hit send and stared at the ceiling pattern, guilty. Why? This was her job.

But what did sharing a hotel room with Gardy have to do with tracking serial killers?

She hurried into her sweatpants as Gardy finished. They exchanged sheepish nods outside the bathroom, Bell on her way in, Gardy dripping wet with a towel around his hips.

Bell locked the door and stepped into the shower, running it sufficiently hot to work up a steam. The bathroom became a foggy morning on the Moors, and she felt at ease, safe, as though she'd walled away her problems. And maybe she had. Multiple walls and locked doors stood between her and Logan Wolf who, for all she knew, was a thousand miles away. A warm shower helped her relax and freed her mind, and the more she worked the case over inside her head, her conviction grew that Doss couldn't be the killer. How did the killer find his victims? Random chance? Perhaps he spotted Morris and Tannehill in public and became fixated. That fit the hedonistic, sexual predator profile. Yet this killer was unlike Hodge and Longo. Those murderers were impotent in a social setting, men who lowered their eyes when women stared. The Palm Dunes killer was bolder, confident.

A chill touched the back of Bell's neck upon recalling the shadowed man across the street from the bungalow. She'd theorized the man was a nosy neighbor or Gavin Hayward. But Hayward was short and soft-bellied. The man across the street had appeared strong and fit. She considered the depths of the victims' knife wounds. She cut the water off and dried.

Dressed and seated on a lounge chair, Gardy dropped the tourism pamphlet when she opened the door.

"Ready for breakfast?"

"Before we eat you need to call Detective Phalen."

He narrowed his eyes.

"What's up?"

"The man across the street from Tannehill's. I think it

was the killer."

Gardy phoned Phalen from the elevator. The sudden realization the brazen killer might have returned to the scene turned Bell paranoid, and she scanned the lobby. Instead, she saw only vacationing families, children darting among parents' legs. A young couple in swimsuits carried boogie boards toward the doorway to the boardwalk, and Bell wished she was here with Lucas on vacation. No murderers, no evidence trail leading to a bloody finale.

Smelling of hotcakes and syrup, the hotel restaurant offered indoor and patio seating. They chose the patio where they ate breakfast with an unobstructed view of the gulf waters. Several sunbathers lay beside the water.

"So Jay wants us to check with the neighbor," Gardy said between bites of french toast.

"Where we saw the guy in the bushes?"

"Yeah. He's sending two uniforms to search for evidence in case it was the killer. We're to talk to the neighbor first and make sure it wasn't him or her watching from the yard."

Bell nodded. She pointed her fork at Gardy.

"What did Phalen say about Hayward?"

"It's like we figured. The Palm Dunes Police Department got a call from The Informer's law firm before Hayward made it into the interrogation room. He walked out the door an hour later."

"Son of a bitch."

"Hopefully, the arrest encourages him to be more cautious."

"Why? Last night proved we can't touch him. Unless Hayward picks up a machete and aids the killer, there's nothing we can do to keep him out of our hair. Well, my hair."

Gardy picked up a spoon and viewed his reflection.

"Not my hair? I'm insulted."

Bell smirked.

"There's one upside to sharing a room with you."

"What's that?"

"I'm gonna find that bottle of Just For Men."

Gardy coughed into his hand, and a long-haired man in a Hawaiian shirt offered to perform the Heimlich maneuver.

CHAPTER ONE HUNDRED

Lynn Thomas shielded her eyes and leaned through the doorway, the top third of her back permanently hunched over. Bell guessed Thomas was closer to the century mark than ninety as the woman chewed her gums and gave them suspicious stares.

"You could have gotten that out of a cereal box," Thomas said, eyeing the ID badge Gardy flashed.

"I assure you, we're FBI."

"And her?" Thomas swung a pointy nose at Bell. "She FBI, too?"

"Yes, we're with the Behavior Analysis Unit."

"Never heard of it." Thomas studied the badges for another moment, then nodded. "Can't be too careful these days. With the Internet and those printers the kids use, anyone can make a fake badge and pretend to be the cops."

"Ma'am, is your husband home?"

Thomas shot Gardy a *you-must-be-an-idiot* look.

"Now that would be a story for the police." She pronounced it *poh-lease*. "My Dean passed twenty years ago."

"My apology."

"No need to apologize. You didn't kill him."

"Last evening," Bell said, shuffling through the case photographs. "Did you have anyone over at your house? Family, a neighbor?"

"No, it was only me, and I was asleep with Jared by seven o'clock."

"Jared?"

"Why, yes," Thomas said, as though the answer was obvious. "My Persian cat."

"Oh." Bell couldn't think of a better cat name than Jared. Except for Mitch. "So no one was in your yard after sunset?"

"Not that I'm aware. But then again I was asleep." A realization crossed her face, and she jolted. "It wasn't the murderer, the man who killed the young girl across the street, was it?"

"There's no reason to jump to that conclusion," said Bell. She didn't want to alarm Thomas, but they'd need to ask permission to search the property.

Thomas's breathing slowed.

"Thank goodness. I hope you catch the monster. Fifty years ago, we felt comfortable leaving the doors unlocked. Now, you need a security system to protect your home."

"Do you own a security system, Mrs Thomas? A security camera, perchance?"

"No," Thomas said, shaking her head. "But maybe I should get one installed."

A police cruiser pulled behind Gardy's rental, and two male officers, one middle-aged and one young, climbed out of the vehicle. The older officer touched the tip of his cap and nodded at the agents as they followed a brick walkway to the porch stoop.

"Mrs Thomas," Gardy said, introducing the officers. "May these officers search your front yard?"

She fretted with her hands and looked between the two policemen.

"Oh, all right. But don't trample my flowers."

The officers examined the yard between Thomas's house and a tall, wooden privacy fence. Gardy and Bell bee-lined to the hedges where they'd witnessed the shadow figure. It didn't take long before Gardy whistled between his fingers and drew the group to his position.

Gardy glanced at Bell.

"That's a sneaker print. Our guy."

The partial print in the loamy soil was intact. The weather had remained dry the last few days. During the stormy summer and fall months, the print would wash away, but it had been dry for most of January. Bell bent closer to examine the print, marked by a pattern of hexagons and perpendicular lines.

"Any idea what brand of sneaker?"

"That's a Nike running sneaker." They turned to Adames, the younger of the two officers. "I'm going to say it's the 5.0 Free Flyknit."

Haggleston, the older officer, crinkled a heavily lined brow. His confusion made the officer look like a Shar Pei.

Adames shrugged.

"What? I'm into sneakers."

Gardy looked up at Adames.

"Is that a sneaker the average Joe wears around town?"

"They're affordable, especially in this neighborhood, but they're running sneakers. Even in Florida I'd want to protect them. Save them for jogging and wear a walking sneaker the rest of the day. No sense wearing out the treads while you pick up groceries."

"I didn't know you were so into sneakers," Haggleston said, itching his forehead.

"I've got a closet shelf of Air Jordan's, mint condition. Stop by sometime and check them out."

"Uh, I'll pass."

"Hey," Gardy said. "Tannehill's boyfriend is a runner."

The officers exchanged unsure looks.

Bell nodded, a flicker of excitement in her eyes.

"Detective Phalen said he ran marathons."

"That's right, and he didn't have an alibi."

"Let me borrow the folder for a second." Bell took the folder and headed up the walkway. "Be right back."

Lynn Thomas had the door open when Bell climbed the stoop. She'd been watching them through the window.

"You didn't trample my flowers, I hope."

"Mrs Thomas, I want to show you a picture. Have you seen this man in the neighborhood?"

"Hold a second." Thomas slipped on glasses and looked down her nose at the photograph. "Yes, I recognize that man."

"Where have you seen him?"

"He was the Tannehill girl's friend. Boyfriend, I guess, but I mind my own business."

"Did he visit Tannehill often?"

"Yes, at least once a week."

"Did you see this man the night Lori Tannehill was murdered?"

Thomas thought for a moment, and then her eyes

widened.

"Oh, dear lord. Yes. The police asked me if I saw anyone outside her house, and I said I didn't. What have I done?"

"You've done nothing wrong, Mrs Thomas. In fact, you're helping a great deal."

The elderly woman wiped at a tear with a finger gnarled by arthritis and age spots. She reached out with a quivering hand and gave the photo back to Bell as if desperate to rid herself of its filth.

"I should have remembered the first time they asked."

"What time did the man arrive?"

"I don't recall the time. It must have been before sunset because it was still light outside. But he didn't go into her house. He sat in his car right where the police are parked."

Thomas pointed at the police cruiser past the hedges.

"Did you see him leave?"

"Well...no. I went back to the living room and fell asleep with Jared. I woke up later on account of the sirens and lights."

"So it's possible the man in the photograph entered Tannehill's house after you fell asleep."

"I suppose he might have. Did I make a mess of things?"

"No, not at all. You helped a great deal."

The woman's tear-streaked face brightened a shade. Bell darkened. Not only did Matt Doss lack an alibi, a witness put him at the crime scene within hours of the murder.

CHAPTER ONE HUNDRED ONE

This was too good.

Gavin Hayward aimed the Canon lens out the car window and focused on the pretty FBI agent. The 400 millimeter lens was cumbersome, but it allowed him to photograph celebrities from a football field's length away and capture their faces in perfect detail. The 30-mega-pixel camera's resolution was high enough for him to crop the image and blow the picture up several times without degrading the quality, and now he had Scarlett Bell centered in the frame.

Hayward knew the public was fixated with serial killers, true crime, and sex, and Scarlett Bell was all those things rolled into one luscious package. Pure money.

She bent to analyze something on the ground, and he pressed the shutter release button and captured a string of images in a split second. The male agent, the one who'd harassed him and called the police, knelt beside her, while two male cops looked over their shoulders. One picture captured Gardy in side profile. Hayward didn't care if he didn't get a good shot of Neil Gardy. The public wanted

Scarlett Bell, and he'd damn well feed her to the people.

Hayward knew he was a hack. It didn't bother him. He'd paid his dues, spent the better part of two decades bouncing between small town rags, forever waiting for *The Times* or *The Post* to call. He'd attended a good school, graduated with honors from Northwestern, and landed an internship with *The Chicago Sun Times*. The world was his for the taking.

Until he realized he was the one being taken.

You didn't get ahead through hard work and a strong resume. You got there through contacts—networking, they called it these days—and a pretty face. He owned neither.

When Hayward felt inspired, his writing was every bit as eloquent as that of the national reporters, and his ability to research and ferret out difficult to acquire information put the competition to shame. He took the job with *The Informer* fifteen years ago and ascended from the back pages to the headlines, his salary growing five-fold. Sure, he'd stepped on a few people on his way up the ladder. They would have done the same to him, but he was the alpha predator now. Nobody could deny him power and glory. It didn't take long before he became *The Informer's* go-to reporter for crime and murder stories, and the more Hayward dominated the byline, the larger the tabloid grew. They ranked number one in the western world, and the Alan Hodge murders in New York set records for papers sold and online subscriber growth.

Hayward grinned. Scarlett Bell was closing in on Logan Wolf...or was Wolf closing in on Bell?...and when she captured him Hayward intended to be there. The elite press corps wouldn't be able to deny him any longer. He could sell his story to the highest bidder, leave the rat race, and purchase a small island somewhere. Hell, he might buy *The Informer*. Logan Wolf's capture would be the crime story of the century.

Bell stood and slipped on a pair of sunglasses. The wind whipped her blonde hair around, stressing her beauty. Hayward zoomed back and discovered an interesting composition—the sidewalk darting into the horizon and rimmed by lush flora and palms, Scarlett Bell peering into the distance as though the murderer's identity lay on the wind. The perfect picture for his next spread. A sports car passed through the picture, and a man biked along the curb. He didn't mind. These elements drew readers into the picture.

Hayward panned the lens and saw Bell staring at him. Dammit, she'd spotted him.

Though he broke no laws and had every right to be there, he turned the ignition and checked his mirrors. No cars coming. The officers walked in his direction.

When he looked through the viewfinder, Bell raised her middle finger at him.

CHAPTER ONE HUNDRED TWO

Gardy grabbed hold of Bell and kept her from running after Hayward.

"He's not doing anything illegal."

She stopped fighting, not because she couldn't break free but because Hayward's CRV was halfway to the end of the block and drifting out of sight.

"The man's a menace and should be shot on sight."

Officer Haggleston spoke into his radio. Great. Wait until Detective Phalen hears Hayward photographed the investigation. When Haggleston held the radio out for Bell, she knew Phalen was angry.

"For you."

"Wonderful. I'll take a walk."

Bell wandered to a palm and pressed her back against the trunk. The others watched her, Gardy faking interest in the hedges. She put on a sarcastic smile as if Phalen could see her through the radio.

"Hayward is turning into a bigger problem. What are you going to do about this, Agent Bell?"

"He's within his rights provided he photographs from

the street, and as you found out last night, he'll walk on a simple trespassing charge."

She imagined the detective's hands balled into fists, face red.

"Any idea how he found you?"

"The media know the murder sites, so it's no surprise he's scoping out the neighborhoods and waiting for us to arrive."

"Waiting for *you* to arrive and perform your profiling voodoo."

"My apologies, detective, but that's not fair."

He sighed through the speaker.

"No, it's not. But we can handle the evidence gathering with our own men without attracting Hayward's attention. We don't need the BAU. Your presence is only exasperating the—"

"That's for you and the chief to debate."

She heard him shuffle papers on his desk as he brought his temper under control.

"So tell me about the shoe print."

"It's a running sneaker. Officer Adames identified it as a Nike Free Flyknit."

"Doss was a runner."

"And we have a witness who claims Doss was in front of Tannehill's house on the evening of the murder."

"Dammit, it has to be the boyfriend. I'm bringing him in."

Bell glanced over her shoulder. Gardy was holding court with the officers. A man walked his dog on the other side of the street.

"Okay. It's hard to argue with the evidence."

"Yet that's what you're doing. You don't think Doss

killed her."

She didn't. Bell bit her tongue. The last thing she wanted to do was further alienate Phalen.

"I don't know. His build fits the profile, and one witness places him at the scene, though her testimony won't stand up in court. I doubt she can see past her mailbox, let alone identify Doss inside a dark car from fifty feet away."

He clicked a pen repeatedly.

"That's a problem."

"Listen, whether it's the boyfriend or someone else, the killer can't control his compulsion to revisit the kill scenes. He only lasted one day before he returned to Tannehill's, and I'd bet good money he's been to Morris's home multiple times."

"Shit."

"But that's how we'll catch him. Stake out the houses. Put one crew on Morris's home and another on Tannehill's."

"Yes, that makes sense. I'll set it up with the chief now."

"And Detective Phalen?"

"Yeah?"

"I want to be part of the team watching Tannehill's house. He'll come back tonight."

"Okay, Agent Bell. I'll work out the logistics and get back to you."

"Let's talk at the office. We're coming in as soon as we wrap up the scene."

Phalen agreed.

But when they arrived at the station, the police had a suspect in custody.

CHAPTER ONE HUNDRED THREE

Reporters and a slew of uniformed officers trying to hold them back crowded the front entrance to the Palm Dunes Police Department. Someone lowered a shoulder into Bell as she and Gardy waded through the crowd. A female reporter with enormous, shiny teeth and a sanctimonious smile recognized Bell and shouted questions targeting Logan Wolf and the serial killers they'd captured in recent months.

Holding his ID badge aloft, Gardy guided Bell to the front doors, where a young, alarmed officer put his hand up to stop them before he recognized the agents. Then they shoved through the doors and into the bright lobby, the reporters' shouts muffled by the windows. Gardy turned back to the officer and grabbed his arm.

"What the hell is going on?"

"The killer is in lockup. They're starting the interrogation soon."

"What do you mean the killer is in lockup? I spoke with Detective Phalen an hour ago."

Bell and Gardy had stopped for lunch on the way into

the office and hadn't heard from the Palm Dunes Police Department.

"Didn't he contact you?"

"No."

Gardy huffed and pushed on, Bell right behind him as he took the stairs two-at-a-time. Phalen stood talking to a female officer with dark hair at the end of the hall. He held a clipboard and an iPad as he nodded at her questions. When Phalen glanced up and saw them coming, he touched her arm and shared a look, and she disappeared into an office and closed the door.

"Agents Gardy and Bell."

"Save the salutations, Jay. You caught the killer and didn't bother to notify us?"

Gardy was a second from throwing the detective against the wall. Bell considered intervening and decided Phalen deserved what was coming to him.

Phalen held up his hands.

"Slow down. It's not how you think."

"Then illuminate me."

"We didn't catch him. The bastard walked right through the front door and confessed the murders to the officer manning the front desk. This all happened less than an hour ago."

Gardy caught Bell's eye. The unknown subject was confident, brazen. He wouldn't succumb to guilt and confess.

"Every reporter in the city knows, Jay. You could have radioed me."

"I know, and I'm sorry. It wasn't me that leaked the arrest to the press. I haven't had a second to breathe, and now we're setting up for interrogation. Come on. Walk with me."

Phalen talked over his shoulder as they descended the stairs and returned to the lobby.

"The perp's name is Randall McVay, twenty-six-years-old, Palm Dunes resident."

Turning down a hallway, Bell raised her voice above the clamor.

"Detective Phalen, we're looking for a young, athletic male, good looking and upscale. A confident risk taker."

"No offense, agent, but we're past the point of needing a profile."

"At least tell me McVay is a strong guy. You saw the stab wounds."

Phalen stopped at the door and exhaled.

"Strong enough. Now if you'll excuse me.."

"Wait. Aren't you going to allow us to take part in the interrogation?"

"What's the need? McVay will sign the confession and that will be that. Cheer up, Agent Bell. Your theory about the boyfriend being innocent was correct. See you after the interview."

The door closed. Phalen was a desperate man and needed to close this case despite evidence contrary to the supposed confession. You could sway your mind to ignore a house's creaks as signs of a crumbling foundation, but eventually the structure collapsed.

Bell stared icepicks into Gardy.

"Don't blame me," he said. "I want to be in there as much as you."

"So make it happen, Gardy. What on earth are we doing in Florida? Phalen has shut us out from the minute we arrived."

"Agents Bell and Gardy?" They turned and saw a graying man in a suit approach. He spoke into his cell phone and slipped it into his pocket. "Lee Rimmer, Chief of Police."

He slipped a folder beneath his arm and shook their hands.

"Sorry it took so long to cross paths. I've been up to my eyeballs in cases. We were due a lucky break. Hell of a thing, the killer confessing, but I'm happy you agreed to help us."

"Not much we contributed, to be honest," said Gardy, glancing sidelong at the closed door. Bell felt the same anxiousness to get inside the interrogation room.

"Not true. The fingerprint in the attic, the sneaker print across the street. Crucial pieces of evidence. Say, aren't you participating in the interrogation?"

Gardy opened his mouth, and Bell jumped in.

"We're no longer in the loop."

"Nonsense, Agent Bell. The entire department owes you a debt of gratitude for lending your expertise. We value your opinion."

"I'm sorry to say this, sir, but Detective Phalen stated we weren't to be part of the interrogation."

Gardy rolled his eyes and fell back against the wall.

Rimmer tilted his head toward Bell the way someone does when they're certain they misheard.

"That doesn't sound like Detective Phalen..." Rimmer trailed off, locked in thought. Then his face altered, the look a disappointed parent saves for a misbehaving child. "Wait here."

Rimmer stepped inside the room and shut the door. It was impossible to eavesdrop on the conversation, but Bell

515

heard raised voices.

"You shouldn't have done that."

Bell looked up at Gardy.

"There wasn't any other way. Phalen left us no choice."

"Bell, you can't throw people under the bus. What happens when word gets around that Agents Gardy and Bell go over detectives' heads when they don't get what they want? We'll end up with uncooperative law enforcement everywhere we go."

"And that is different how? Sheriff Lowe in Kansas, Lerner in New York. They stood in our way and stabbed us in the back. Now we're having a pissing contest with a jealous detective who couldn't—"

"Don't say it."

"Who couldn't make it with the BAU. He wasn't good enough, Gardy. And you know why he failed? It wasn't because he didn't have the skill. He's power hungry, more interested in garnering the spotlight than closing cases, and he's about to convict an innocent man. McVay's fingerprint won't match the one they took out of the attic."

"But he confessed—"

The door opening stopped Gardy's retort. Chief Rimmer eyed them both, considering. Then he held the door for them.

"The Palm Dunes Police Department requests the BAU's expertise during this interrogation."

"Thank you, Chief," said Gardy. "Bell?"

Bell followed Gardy inside, and Rimmer closed the door behind them. Phalen wore a tight-lipped smile.

"Now that everyone is here, we'll continue."

Gardy and Bell took seats across the table from

Randall McVay, a gangly, disheveled looking man whose eyes refused to rest. McVay wore torn blue jeans and a red t-shirt with a skull on the front. Red pinpricks marked his arms. Drug use? He swung his gaze between the two agents and Chief Rimmer, who sat on the other side of Gardy, and to Detective Phalen at the end of the table.

"Detective Phalen," Rimmer said, shooting the detective a glare of warning. "Please bring the FBI up to speed on this afternoon's developments."

Phalen recounted McVay's arrival and confession, then gave the grim and gory details of the two murders as described by McVay.

During this, McVay kept moving his eyes to the table whenever Bell looked in his direction. The young man looked intimidated. Afraid.

Phalen clicked the papers together and set them on the tabletop.

"Since we're on the same page, does the FBI have questions for Mr McVay?"

Gardy nodded at Bell, who flipped the notepad open to a blank page and clicked her pen. She looked across the table at McVay. The man shifted in his seat.

"Mr McVay, may I call you Randall?" He nodded. Bell softened her eyes and held her gaze. "Good. Randall, tell me about December 20, the night you murdered Cheryl Morris."

Something clicked in McVay's throat. He swallowed, and Phalen poured water into a plastic cup and handed it to McVay. McVay took a long sip.

"I told the detective. I got off work at five and drove to her house."

"To Cheryl Morris's house."

"Yes."

"Did you park in front?"

"No, I parked down the street so no one would notice my car. I had to wait a long time, at least an hour before it got dark."

"And how did you meet Cheryl Morris?"

McVay shrugged.

"I just seen her around is all."

"So you didn't know her."

"No."

"Where did you see Cheryl Morris first?"

The man turned silent for a moment, his lips moving as he considered his answer.

"Downtown at a club. The Sunset Grill, I think. Yeah, it was there."

"And how did you learn Morris's identity?"

"I f—followed her home and copied the address, then I looked it up on the Internet."

Bell scribbled McVay's answers and set the pen on the table.

"So back to the night of December 20. How did you break inside Morris's home? Were the doors locked?"

McVay glanced around the table. Chief Rimmer's chin rested on his palm, eyes squinted in thought. Phalen rocked back in his chair.

"Sure. I mean, I think so."

"You don't remember if the door was locked when you turned the handle?"

Bell fought not to bite her lip. The killer used a glass cutter on the sliding glass door behind the house.

"I think it was unlocked...no, wait. It was locked, so I sneaked around the back of the house and came in through the patio door."

"Was the patio door unlocked?"

"No, I used a glass cutter."

Bell cursed inside. Phalen wore a smug grin.

"Then what did you do?"

As Bell copied McVay's admissions, the man told them he stalked Morris from room-to-room before he attacked. Again, McVay seemed too cautious and unsure of himself. Not how she envisioned the real killer. True, McVay claimed he cut through the sliding glass door, but that detail made the news and counted as public knowledge.

"We can go over the Tannehill murder if it pleases the agents," Phalen said, drumming his fingers on the desk. "But Mr McVay answered our questions."

"Just a few more minutes," said Bell.

Phalen looked imploringly at Rimmer. The chief shook his head.

Bell shut the notepad and clicked off the pen.

"As I'm certain you can appreciate, Randall, we didn't release all the details of the murders due to the...insensitive nature of the attack."

McVay reached for the water. The cup jiggled in his hands.

"Of course."

"Can you describe how you murdered Cheryl Morris?"

"I st—stabbed her."

"Stabbed her where?"

"In the chest."

Bell's heart quickened as her confidence faded.

"Which killed her."

"Yes."

Fighting not to drop McVay's gaze, she rolled the dice. Went for broke.

"Help me understand what you did next. For the record. And so we may learn from you."

"Will you tell the news?"

"What do you mean?"

"The news. You'll tell them, won't you?"

"Only if you want me to. Shall I?"

"Yes."

"After you murdered Cheryl Morris, you used knives to spike her wrists above her head, then you proceeded to have sexual intercourse with her." McVay stared at the table again, took another long sip of water. "Randall, look at me. I realize details of the murder may embarrass you if I recount them in front of the officers, but I need to understand your actions. Are my facts correct?"

McVay lifted his eyes.

"Yes."

Phalen tossed his pen on the table and buried his face in his hands. Rimmer looked like he wanted to throw up as Gardy worked to suppress a grin.

"Did you do the same to Lori Tannehill on the night of January 6? Spiked her wrists and raped her after the murder?"

"Yes...yes, I did. I couldn't help myself."

Rimmer took the folder from Phalen and snapped it shut.

CHAPTER ONE HUNDRED FOUR

Detective Phalen didn't utter a word on his way out of the interrogation room, just peered straight ahead as he marched toward the stairs.

"Good call on McVay, but you should have handled the argument more tactfully," Gardy said, his stare following Phalen.

"If I didn't speak up, an innocent man would have taken the fall."

"The way you treated Jay was unwarranted."

She prepared to argue, and Gardy held up a preemptive hand.

"You were right, he was wrong, but you need to learn you get more bees with honey."

Rimmer was last to leave the room after a uniformed officer escorted McVay out. The chief exhaled, shoulders slumped as though a horse kicked him in the gut.

"How did you know it wasn't McVay?"

McVay was in the lobby now. Camera flashbulbs strobed like lightning through the glass.

"McVay doesn't fit the profile," Bell said. "He's too

thin and sickly. Our killer is strong, and I doubt McVay is a runner."

"But why confess to a crime he didn't commit? He was looking at a long prison sentence, maybe life."

"Narcissistic fantasy," Gardy said, folding his arms over his chest. "If you check McVay's background, you'll find he's insecure and unnoticed, a guy who wants attention but doesn't know how to get it. So he lies about his life, concocts stories to make himself seem important."

"Why not pretend he's a multimillionaire or a rock star? A serial killer?"

"Who knows? The more I work these cases, the less I understand the human mind. Let's face it. This media circus made the killer bigger than a rock star."

Nonplussed by the altercation with Phalen, Bell struggled not to drop her eyes as she questioned Rimmer.

"What will happen to McVay?"

Rimmer rubbed at his scalp.

"Jesus, what a shit-show. Lying to the police is a serious offense, particularly considering the implications. He perjured himself. Still, I can't see the city throwing the book at him. The district attorney is overrun."

"McVay needs help."

"And he'll get it. So what now? I suppose the focus turns back to the boyfriend."

"It's possible Doss is the killer," Bell said, flipping open the notebook and scanning her thoughts.

"But you don't believe it's him."

"In some ways, Doss fits the bill. We know he's athletic and runs marathons, and the sneaker print across the street belonged to a runner. He has a history of violence."

"And yet?"

Bell fussed with a loose thread on her shirt. Despite recognizing McVay as a sham, she felt inadequate.

"Doss was Tannehill's boyfriend, but I don't see a connection with Cheryl Morris."

"A serial killer doesn't need a connection. He kills types, right?"

"Sometimes the killer targets people he knows," Gardy said, keeping his voice low as a group of officers milled in the hallway. "But it's unusual for a serial killer to mix and match victims. Either he murders women he knows on an intimate level, typically crimes of passion, or he stalks strangers who remind him of someone from his past. Now, I can see Doss murdering Tannehill first because of their relationship, then branching out after he gets a taste for killing. But the other way around? I'm not saying it's impossible. Just unlikely."

"And details about the Tannehill murder make little sense if Doss is our main suspect," said Bell. Rimmer turned his head as the two agents volleyed theories. "Consider this. You hear a noise and go upstairs to check things out. If Tannehill sees Doss, her first impression is to wonder why her boyfriend is inside the house. She isn't likely to panic. Perhaps he has a key and was napping while she was at work. Instead, she ran straight for the bedroom and locked the door. That points to the killer being a stranger."

"Unless Doss came out of the attic brandishing a knife," Rimmer offered.

"True, except Doss would have kept the knife hidden before he attacked. Why give her a chance to run?"

Rimmer sighed and shook his head. His eyes held the

redness of a man who hadn't slept well in days.

"We're back to square one."

"Bell believes the killer needs to revisit the murder scene," said Gardy. "She's right."

"Detective Phalen relayed your interest in staking out the Morris and Tannehill homes."

"It's a good idea. The sneaker print suggests he returned last night."

"Okay. I'll throw a team together and procure a location."

After Rimmer left, Bell eyed the officers at the end of the hall. They stared in her direction, an unfriendly glare that expressed their displeasure with how she'd handled Phalen.

"Apparently, I'm persona non grata."

Gardy looked in their direction and moved beside her.

"Don't say I didn't warn you. Loyalty is important inside a police department. You ready to get back to work?"

She chewed her lip.

"Yeah. There has to be a connection between Morris and Hill. I don't think this guy is picking women randomly. He knew them."

"Phalen's team crosschecked work relationships, boyfriends. No common threads."

"Social media contacts?"

"I didn't notice anything in the report. Never hurts to check."

Despite Gardy's insistence they take the back stairwell, Bell strode past the officers. She felt their eyes burn the back of her neck and caught a whisper of something derisive. The computer lab was on the far side of the lobby. A male police technician with blonde hair and glasses typed code into a terminal when they entered the room. His name tag read Yarborough. Officer Yarborough stood, a tad awestruck by their FBI badges.

"Agents, what can I do for you?"

His cordial nature told Bell the Phalen incident hadn't reached his ears. As far as she could tell, the technicians worked outside of the daily bustle and didn't have regular contact with the other officers unless someone needed a computer search performed. Every office in the building had a computer with access to CODIS and VICAP, but the heavy lifting happened in this room.

Yarborough glanced at Bell over the top of his glasses as he typed.

"What's the deal with the confession?"

"False confession. McVay didn't do it."

"I bet that made Phalen's day."

The unveiled sarcasm made Bell think Phalen had crossed Yarborough. At the very least, Phalen didn't impress the police technician. Gardy shook his head to dissuade Bell from piling on Phalen.

Yarborough entered a string of keystrokes and sat back in his chair.

"There you go. Cheryl Morris."

Bell leaned over his shoulder. Morris's Twitter profile was a selfie taken from the stands at a crowded Tampa Bay Buccaneers game.

"Can you build a printable list of her connections?"

"Sure."

He called up a second terminal window and ran a script. A few seconds later, Morris's followers appeared listed in alphabetical order inside a spreadsheet.

"Perfect. Now call up Lori Tannehill's profile."

"You're looking for common connections."

"You got it."

Yarborough wrinkled his brow and stared at the screen. Bell stepped closer.

"Something wrong?"

"It doesn't appear Tannehill has a Twitter account. I'll try Facebook and Instagram."

The rapid fire click-clack of terminal keys filled the room. A puzzled expression came over the young technician's face.

"Either Tannehill used a fake screen name or she swore off social media, because I can't find her anywhere."

Bell slumped into a chair and rubbed her temples.

"Every path is a dead end."

Yarborough rocked back in his chair and locked his fingers behind his neck.

"So he didn't find them through social media. People send pictures through text messages all the time. You're the experts, but there's a mutual acquaintance in there somewhere."

CHAPTER ONE HUNDRED FIVE

Should he laugh or succumb to the building fury tightening his muscles and sending tremors down his arms?

The Florida sun blares through the windshield and douses his face with blistering fire. Though it is unlikely anyone will pay him attention, he keeps the motor off, no air conditioning, and sits at the back of the parking lot away from the converging flock. The vulture media shoves its way up the steps toward the human wall of police officers who stand stone-faced, refusing to answer the reporters' inane questions.

The media reported the confession on the radio, and he didn't know how to react. Who took credit for his murders? Across town at the time, he wheeled the car around and pressed the accelerator, knowing the press would scuttle to the police department. And that's where he'd find the agent, the woman who so reminded him of his victims.

A fat man with a bald head snaps photographs and shouts questions from the bottom step. He knows who the man is—Gavin Hayward, a scumbag reporter for *The Informer*. Sometimes he pages through the tabloid in the grocery market checkout line, amusing himself over presidential affairs and alien conspiracies. Now he realizes Hayward is a mobile beacon who will draw him to the agent. Provided he keeps tabs on Hayward, who is too stupid to realize someone is following him, he can find the woman.

His heart thumps when the doors open and the female agent emerges. Scarlett Bell. He knows her name from Hayward's tabloid. A trickle of excitement swims through his body. His next *selected* is a national celebrity. Her murder will make him famous. Children will utter his name in the dead of night as they do *Bloody Mary* and *Candyman*.

Attached to her hip as always, the male agent descends the steps beside Bell. Neil Gardy. He learned Gardy's name from *The Informer*, too.

The reporters shout questions at the two agents as they push through the crowd. Hayward, the shark he is, beelines for Bell, but the throng cuts him off. A pair of uniformed officers impede the media and allow the agents to pass, but tension exists between the police and the BAU. He can smell it like fresh chum floating in the gulf.

His eyes follow the agents toward the park, and when he risks losing sight of them, he flips the ignition and brings the car out of hiding. Drifts across the lot, the black shadow of a vulture tracking his prey. From the front of the lot, he can see them again. A vagrant plays the guitar in front of a cafe, and Gardy drops a dollar into his cup. Soon Gardy will be in his grasp, wide-eyed and helpless as he squeezes until the brittle agent's spine snaps. He will do this in front of Scarlett. Show her what real power is before he consumes her.

The agents stop inside a park in the center of town and sit beside a gurgling fountain. He considers moving the car closer to the park before a commotion on the steps claims his attention. More shouting from the reporters as the police assume their position blocking entry to the building. Cautiously, he opens the door and listens. Can't make out their words.

A young, leggy brunette in heels hustles toward the parking lot while a fat man hoisting a television camera follows. Their news van, he realizes, sits two parking spaces away from him.

"Hey there," he says. "What's the excitement about?"

Her eyes take him in. His athletic physique and clothing—cargo shorts, a Nike t-shirt, and sandals—make him look like an off-duty cop. She cocks an eyebrow, and he discerns the tip of her tongue running greedily over her lips.

"Don't you know? The shoe is on the other foot now, me delivering the inside story to you."

His smile puts her at ease.

"I'm off today. Just coming in to grab my paycheck."

"You don't have one of those radio thingies to keep you up to date?"

"I do, but I learned a long time ago not to take my work home with me. The downtime keeps me young."

She stares at the angry red blotch on his forehead, and he self-consciously touches the wound.

"You bumped your head."

"It's nothing. Just an insect bite."

"Must have been a helluva bug."

"Well, they grow them big in Florida."

Her eyes move down his chest to his hips. Linger there. A discernible heat passes between them. She narrows her eyes, reconsidering.

"Jennie Reyser, Channel 8 News."

"Detective Brent Hilliard, Palm Dunes Police Department."

"Detective, eh? Well, then. If you can't trust a detective, who can you trust? Turns out the guy who confessed to the murders was bullshitting the department."

"He didn't do it?"

"Nope." She sends the cameraman a pithy look, and he acknowledges her with an almost imperceptible wink before slipping into the truck. The female reporter edges closer. "I need to learn who the true killer is. Perhaps, after you grab your paycheck, you might snoop around and learn who the department suspects murdered those women."

"You're asking me to obtain classified information. I could lose my job."

He smells her perfume, a flowery scent that brings to mind nature hikes during the humid monsoon season. She touches his chest, runs her finger to his abdominals.

"You won't lose your job. I can keep a secret."

He glances conspiratorially around the lot. Nobody watches.

"Tell you what. Let me poke around and get that information for you." He touches her arm. "Then maybe we can go somewhere and discuss who the suspect is. I don't want anyone to think I'm a mole."

"Sure, we can do that. I'll wait for you, Detective Hilliard."

A moment's hesitation when he realizes he's walking into a trap. He'll never get past the cops guarding the front door.

"I don't know, Jennie. My partner is across the street right now. What if he sees us talking?"

"He won't."

"You're asking me to risk too much. I could lose my job."

She pouts, lips locked in a cartoon purse, arms folded.

"I need this story."

"Then work with me," he says, brushing the hair away from her eyes.

This elicits a giggle. She's persistent.

"What work shall we do, Detective?"

"Hmm, nothing salacious. There's a community park in the middle of the shopping district."

"Sure, I visit the park often."

"Meet me by the fountain in fifteen minutes."

"Okay. Should I go now?"

"Yes, before my partner notices us together."

She locks eyes with the cameraman in the news van, and the engine turns over. The cameraman understands the routine and knows when to vanish. As the van turns out of the parking lot and merges with traffic, the faux detective turns to watch the newsgirl walk away. Her hips swim from side-to-side. Though she is not what he seeks, he concedes she is beautiful. He will enjoy their time alone.

Two in one night.

A cold smile twists his face.

CHAPTER ONE HUNDRED SIX

It wasn't more than fifteen minutes before Rimmer got back to Gardy and Bell. Hoping to avoid the vitriolic glares of the officers who'd heard what happened between Bell and Phalen, the agents walked to the park at the edge of downtown and traded political wrangling for a thin slice of tropical peace. Bell's mind kept straying to McVay. How sad must your life be to confess to being a serial killer?

Gardy tossed popcorn at a flock of seagulls massing around a water fountain when Rimmer rang his phone. The discussion lasted only a minute, Gardy nodding and jotting down an address. He snapped his finger and pointed to the note, then gave a thumbs up. Bell picked the pad off his lap and recognized Levydale Avenue. Tannehill's street.

"Perfect. We'll be there." Gardy ended the call and slipped the phone into his pocket. "We're set. There's a blue Colonial next door to Lori Tannehill's residence. The owner has a brother across town and told Rimmer we're welcome to use the house. Drew Sowell is the guy's name."

"He'll stay with the brother?"

"Apparently."

"Huh. That's generous of him."

"You could say that," Gardy said, crossing one leg over the other and resting against a stone wall girding the fountain. "The way Sowell sees it, we're doing him a favor. Every time he hears a noise at night he worries the killer is back."

"He may be right."

"If that's the case, we'll catch the guy tonight." Gardy checked his watch, then squinted up at the sun. "Looks like we're pulling a late night shift. Not a bad idea to catch a few hours of sleep."

"What time does Rimmer want us at Sowell's house?"

"Six o'clock. Phalen and another officer will relieve us after two."

Bell groaned at the mention of Phalen. She worried the detective might cause a scene at shift change.

"I could never be a cop, Gardy."

"How's that?"

"The shift work. Staying up late was easy when I was in college. Not so much now."

"But we've done overnight stakeouts."

"That's only one night. I can't imagine doing it five days in a row every month. I'd turn into a vampire."

Gardy popped a piece of gum into his mouth and offered her the pack. She shook her head.

"Nah, you'd get used to it."

Out of the corner of her eye, Bell spied a reporter who hounded them on the way out of the police department. A young brunette in heels.

"Oh, shit."

"What?"

"Don't look to your left. It's a reporter."

Gardy automatically looked left, invoking a harrumph from Bell. He ducked his head, but the reporter spotted them. The woman moved in their direction before a good looking man entered the square and stole her attention. She moved to him, and Bell wondered if the man dated the reporter. There was something familiar about him. She'd seen the man. Where? He dressed casual and exuded neatness. A welt on his forehead drew Bell's attention, and she believed he was a cop who'd taken a punch in the line of duty, and now he was giving the inside scoop on the McVay fiasco to the female reporter.

Before she could decide if she knew the man—and how was that possible? This was her first trip to Palm Dunes—he put his arm around the reporter's shoulder and led her toward the clothing shops. Bell swore the man glanced back at her. No, he wasn't a cop. More likely he was a reporter, too. Thank goodness neither bothered to harass Bell and Gardy with case questions.

"You know that guy?"

Gardy's voice pulled Bell out of her thoughts.

"No...I thought I recognized him from somewhere, but I don't think so."

"Really? Because you were checking him out."

Her cheeks bloomed.

"Don't be ridiculous."

"Nothing to be ashamed of. He's a young, good looking guy."

"Sounds like you're the interested one."

A laugh crept to her chest and died there. Something was wrong about the man, something that raised a red flag in the back of her mind.

She considered following them. Then the reality of a long, late night reared its ugly head, and she put the man and woman out of her mind.

CHAPTER ONE HUNDRED SEVEN

The water is bloody with the coming sunset. Waves slam against the shore and tear chunks of sand from the beach, pulling the grains out to the dark and deep sea.

From inside the cool, shadowed parking garage, he can see the surf. The boardwalk is busy as it always is near sunset, but the garage is empty except for them.

He clicks the key fob, and the car flashes its lights in response. Weaving with the erratic gait of the inebriated, Jennie Reyser stumbles against his car and leans on the hood, laughing.

"You won't get me drunk and take advantage of me, will you, Detective Hilliard?"

He hides his initial confusion, having forgotten the name he fed her. They'd spent the last few hours at a seaside tiki bar. Reyser accepted his offer to buy her margaritas. He didn't drink, for he was the designated driver.

"Now, why would you think that of me? An officer of the law must uphold an image."

Her eyes are slitted, glassy. A perpetual smirk twists

her lips. The slit in her skirt reveals tanned, bare leg. His mouth waters.

"You sound like a boy scout."

The words come out slurred, and she bursts into laughter and almost topples before he catches her. He smells the sweet perfume on the nape of her neck.

Reyser jiggles with new bouts of laughter. As he supports her limp body, he grabs hold of the handle and pulls the door open. She slumps into the car and watches him hungrily as one eye peeks out from behind a forest of mussed hair.

"Take me to your leader," she says, laughing again.

He closes the door. Locks her inside. He can't hear her over the distant surf. Rounding the car, he slides into the front seat and starts the engine. An old Van Halen song is on the radio, the line about junior's grades accentuating the classic guitar riff as she sags between the seat and door with growing incognizance to the world.

He shoots one look over his shoulder and backs up the car. Nobody watches. Good, very good.

Before he shifts into drive, he places his hand on top of her head and shoves down, causing Reyser to slump between the dash and seat. When he turns out of the garage, he appears to be alone in the car.

She doesn't awaken during the half-hour drive into the tropical wilderness. He knows this glade well. Cypress trees cloak a deep pond. The waters teem with mosquitoes and dragonflies. And gators. The largest he's seen outside of a zoo.

When he opens the passenger door, she spills onto the soft shoulder. The jolt sobers Reyser, shifts her eyes from lurid to confused.

"Where...where are we?"

She shields her eyes and looks up at him. The dying sun is at his back, rendering him as a black shadow.

"Detective Hilliard? Is something wrong with the car?"

He doesn't speak. Reality and fear haven't set in yet for Reyser, but they will. Soon.

"I don't understand. Why won't you answer me?"

The first spidery sensations of danger touch the back of her mind. He can see it in the rigidness of her spine, the way she draws her legs protectively inward. The doubt spreads to her eyes, and he can smell her fear the way the wolf does a rabbit's.

He steps forward.

"No. Stay away from me."

She scrambles along the car to the rear wheels. He follows, ears attuned to the road. They are alone here, a full mile from the main route on a lonely access road once used by hikers and nature enthusiasts before disuse allowed nature to swallow the trails whole.

Reyser grasps the gravity of her predicament, and her breath comes in stilted pants.

"Oh, God. Don't touch me or I'll scream."

He pounces on her, drives the air from her lungs. She pushes and struggles against him, but he is a mountain of strength, she an insignificant, wilted flower dying in his shadow.

As she opens her lips to scream, he clamps a powerful hand over her mouth. From his back pocket, he removes the knife.

Her eyes are full moons of panic, body thrashing helplessly beneath him.

And as he glares at Reyser, he sees the face of Scarlett Bell.

CHAPTER ONE HUNDRED EIGHT

The monster ran amok in her dreams again. Scarlett Bell was nine-years-old, alone and frightened as she fled along the neighborhood creek with Jillian's murderer somewhere behind her in the fog. Always just out of sight, yet close enough that she could hear the breath huff out of his chest like the big bad wolf roaring out of a storybook nightmare. He grabbed her shoulder and spun her around, and in the throes of panic she saw the killer was faceless. A smooth patch of skin where the nose and mouth should be.

The scream pulled her out of the dream. Had she yelled inside the hotel room? No reaction came from the neighboring rooms.

The lateness of the day surprised Bell when her eyes focused. The shower babbled. Gardy banged around in the tub and spilled the gratis bottles of soap and shampoo. She suppressed a laugh and checked the clock. It was after 5:30, the curtains drawn and the room dark. A red trickle of late day sun purled through the split.

Gardy's bed was a jumble of blankets, and she felt guilty again for taking the bed. The remorse lasted until the shock of forgetting to write Lucas slammed her. She fumbled in the dark for the lamp and knocked her phone off the table. Cursing, she pulled up yesterday's messages and wrote a hurried, apologetic response.

Sorry. Got caught up in this insane case and forgot to write.

She waited for a response. Lucas wasn't the type to keep his phone close at all hours of the day. Still, her anxiety ratcheted up when no reply came.

Miss you and walks on the beach. Will send you a picture of the gulf. We should come here together.

He was away from his phone. Or at least she hoped that was the case. Before she blew off another promise, she pulled on her clothes and padded to the balcony doors and pulled open the curtains. The sun kissed the water, and the brightness blinded her. When her eyes adjusted, she stepped out to the cool, salty breeze. Focused the camera phone on the red orb falling toward its watery grave. Clicked the shutter and admired the colorful image on the screen.

Lucas would want to see the boardwalk, she thought, as she changed the angle to capture the boardwalk and sandy beach. She pictured a warm spring night, no FBI case hanging over her head, just the two of them walking hand-in-hand along the boardwalk and stopping for candy apples or ice cream.

She froze.

Almost fumbled the phone over the rail.

Bell scanned the walkway for familiar faces and recognized no one. Families. Roller skaters. Bicyclists.

She knew where she'd seen the man on the reporter's arm. He'd sat kitty corner to them on a bench last evening.

The killer. It had to be.

The cold truth coursed through her veins. The bump on his head wasn't an injury. Why hadn't she noticed before? It was an insect sting. A wasp sting. She called Gardy's name as she stumbled through the curtains.

It didn't take long before the skepticism on her partner's face melted away. He'd learned to trust her intuition. Gardy checked his Glock-22 and ensured the weapon was ready, and Bell did the same.

They rode the elevator to the lobby. The killer's face was burned into her memory now. It seemed impossible the killer had been here. This was a well-lit, highly trafficked vacation paradise. If he dared to stalk her here, he knew no fear, no boundaries.

Bell didn't pocket her Glock until they entered the rental, and even then she checked the backseat and trunk before they pulled away. Halfway to Tannehill's house, they lost the sun.

Parked at a red light, Gardy glanced over at her.

"Look, I can call Rimmer and put a uniform in your place."

"Don't. I'm not afraid of him, Gardy."

A boy wearing headphones crossed in front of the vehicle, distracting them. Dusk painted the sky and spread a chill over the land as he drummed his fingers on the steering wheel.

"Maybe you should be. He's targeting you now, Bell. It wouldn't hurt to spend the shift at dispatch surrounded by police."

The boy reached the other curb. The crosswalk counted the final seconds before the light turned.

"I don't think I'm wanted at the police department,

and I'm not running away from this guy."

Gardy sighed.

"I didn't expect you would."

"I know his face. He's coming tonight, Gardy. And when he does, we'll take him down."

CHAPTER ONE HUNDRED NINE

Drew Sowell's powder-blue colonial, a massive residential home with 7000-square feet of living space, butted up against Tannehill's property like a castle guarding its kingdom. Five arched windows on the first and second floors offered ample views of Tannehill's bungalow, as did the humongous den and recreation rooms set off to either side of the main floor. Twin chimneys sprung up from opposite sides of the colonial though Bell didn't think there was much need for fireplaces along coastal Florida.

Gardy finished his phone conversation with Detective Phalen as he climbed the front steps. They'd experienced a sudden break in the case. A cameraman for the Channel 8 News team had called to report a missing reporter, Jennie Reyser. She'd last been seen across the street from the Palm Dunes Police Department with a man who claimed to be a police detective but didn't fit the description of anyone in the department, and the man's physical description matched that of the man Bell had seen at the park and on the boardwalk, including the welt above his brow.

"Yeah. Dark hair, cut short. Male, between twenty-five and thirty-five, athletic build." He nodded as he fitted the key into the lock. "That's right. Insect sting on his forehead."

The door swung open and released a puff of cool wind. The air conditioning ran.

"Ask him what they found in the phones," Bell said, glad she wasn't on the phone with the detective.

Gardy asked. After a moment's hesitation, he shook his head at Bell.

"They examined over five hundred photographs," Gardy said after he hung up with Phalen. "Nobody who fit the killer's description, no common people show up on both phones."

"Dammit, Gardy. Seems like everybody has seen this guy in the last few days, and nobody knows who he is."

Though Bell wanted to flick the wall switch and throw light across the room, they kept the downstairs dark. They'd risked giving themselves away when they entered the colonial and couldn't afford to advertise their presence.

Despite the window coverage on the lower floors, Gardy was more interested in the finished attic. They climbed the wooden staircase, the shoes making hollow, lonely thuds in the vacant home. The next riser ended at the attic door.

Windows on all four sides of the attic gained them bird's-eye views of the front, back, and side of the bungalow. Only the far side of Tannehill's house hid from view, and Officers Adames and Haggleston, plain-clothed and hidden in the back of a nondescript van, covered that angle. Black, tinted windows concealed the officers from prying eyes.

Had she not been scanning the shadowed yards for a psychopathic killer, Bell might have marveled at Sowell's attic. New white oak hardwood covered the floor. A red leather couch sat in the corner near the stairs, and a made guest bed took up the left side of the room. A desk with a computer overlooked the street.

Gardy pulled the chair out from the desk and carried it to a side window overlooking the Bungalow. He put his hand out, a gesture for Bell to settle beside him in the neighboring chair. She accepted his offer with reservation. Her body trembled with tension and wanted to move. Although they could see the neighborhood, the dark attic hid them from sight. Nobody knew they were up here. A touch of voyeuristic excitement raised goosebumps on her skin.

"So this is how the other side lives," Gardy said, crossing his extended legs at the ankles. "I've stayed in apartments half the size of this attic."

He snickered, and the strain left her body.

"Now what do we do?"

"We wait. Hungry?" He unraveled a plastic grocery bag of snacks. "Caramel corn, Doritos, and Sun Chips. Take your pick."

"More like *pick your poison*."

"Would you prefer sushi?"

"Actually, yes."

She reached for the Sun Chips. At least they were whole grain.

The crunching sounds were loud inside the attic. On the sidewalk, a man and woman walked hand-in-hand under a stand of palms. Gardy picked up the two-way radio.

"Adames, Haggleston. You guys got anything?"

The radio was quiet, then the older officer answered.

"Two kids throwing a football in the dark. Ball banged off the back of the van and scared the shit out of Adames."

Adames's colorful protest made it clear Haggleston had exaggerated the reaction.

"Do your best to stay alert. Could be a long night."

"Not my first rodeo, Agent Gardy. I'll let you know when the bad guy shows up. You two relax and try to behave up there."

Gardy smiled through a wince and set the radio in his lap. Bell reached for another chip, a mechanical, involuntary action to thwart the uncomfortable silence.

"I almost became a cop," he said, adjusting the volume knob.

"Why didn't you?"

"The FBI called first. It's like a major league team offering a contract when you're hoping to break into the minors. Not that I consider police departments to be minor leagues. It's a different job." He gestured toward the van, a rectangular silhouette at the end of the block. "I hope they appreciate what they have. There's camaraderie. Stakeouts together. A place in the community you're defending. We're like ghosts, here one day and gone the next."

"I don't know. I'd say there's camaraderie in what we do."

He studied her in the dark.

"Yeah, there is. Wouldn't have it any other way."

The backyards were pitch black. Night had settled over the neighborhood. A white picket fence glowed behind the bungalow. Large flowering plants groped at the fence and appeared as people from this distance. Bell glanced at the vacant macadam between the bungalow's front steps and the surveillance van. The night was quiet with its secrets.

Her phone buzzed. Lucas? She reached into her pocket and bobbled the phone onto the floor. It smacked hard, enough to dislodge the protective case. Retrieving the phone, she swiped the screen and felt relieved it functioned.

"Thank goodness for the case—"

Movement in the dark caught her eye. Subtle, yet she'd seen it.

"What?"

Bell didn't speak. She pointed toward a southern live oak behind Sowell's colonial. The branches sprouted from a low spot on the trunk and lent shelter from spying eyes. Together, Gardy and Bell shifted to a window overlooking the backyard. Anxious to determine who was out there, she moved too close to the glass. Gardy pulled her back into the shadows.

He squinted at the tree, then shook his head to indicate he saw nothing.

Bell pointed again, and a dark form moved between the branches.

CHAPTER ONE HUNDRED TEN

Every nerve in Bell's body stood on high alert. The shadow shape behind Drew Sowell's house stalked closer, clinging to the dark. The figure made a beeline toward the colonial's back door. As if it was coming after them.

Gardy brought the radio to his mouth.

"Haggleston, come in."

A burst of static.

"Haggleston here. The two of you want me to order a pizza?"

"I got movement in the backyard. Behind Sowell's house."

The officer's tone shifted to serious. Bell imagined Haggleston and Adames shifting toward the front of the van to gain a better angle. She didn't think they could see behind the Colonial from their position.

"You want one of us to check it out?"

"Negative. Stay put for now."

Gardy raised his binoculars. Too dark. He handed the binoculars to Bell.

The shape was closer now. Past the flower garden and

halfway to the back door.

As Gardy picked up the radio, ready to call for backup, the man in the backyard passed through a sliver of moonlight.

Gardy cursed.

"Stand by, Haggleston. It's Gavin Hayward."

"Shit...okay. You want me to radio another cruiser to the scene? We've got a pair of officers two blocks away."

"No. Sit tight for a second. If our target is nearby, we'll lose him for sure."

"Copied."

Revealed by the moon, the reporter hid beside a shrub. Gardy lowered the radio and cursed again. He raised himself out of a crouch and started for the door. Bell swung around.

"What are you going to do?"

"Hayward will blow our cover. I'll take him."

"I'll come with you."

"Don't. Stay here and keep an eye on the bungalow. I'll be right back."

She heard him quietly move down the stairs. His footsteps shifted to a higher pitch when he reached the first floor. Then she heard nothing except the night breeze riding over the roof.

The radio crackled.

"Gardy?"

She picked it up and replied to Haggleston.

"This is Bell."

A hesitation.

"Where's Agent Gardy? Everything okay up there?"

"He's gonna grab Hayward."

"Sweet Jesus. What the hell is he planning?"

Bell peered over the window ledge. The night seemed darker as though a black veil cloaked the moon.

"Your guess is as good as mine."

The back door clicked shut. Footsteps, too many for one person, swished through the kitchen and into the dining room. A muffled yelp, the sound of someone gagged.

Bell's hand crept to her hip. Removed the Glock-22.

She abandoned her post and slid toward the attic door. Back against the wall as she peeked around the corner.

Bell released her breath as Gardy led Hayward up the stairs, one hand cupped over the reporter's mouth. They reached the second floor when Gardy cried out and shoved Hayward against the wall. Bell burst down the stairs, the gun fixed on the reporter.

"The son of a bitch bit me."

Hayward's face scrunched against the wall, lips puckered and petulant.

"I couldn't breathe, dammit. You can't do this. I know my rights."

"Right now I don't give a rat's ass about your rights. If you blow our cover and the killer gets away, I'll make your life a living hell, Hayward."

"I'd like to see you try."

Hayward's laugh morphed into a pained yelp when Gardy shoved his head against the wall.

"Easy, Gardy." Bell spoke into the radio. "We've got Hayward."

Bell holstered her weapon and grabbed the agent's arm. Ignoring her, Gardy pressed harder.

"How would you like an FBI agent to trail you

everywhere you go? Try nailing an undercover story with a shadow behind you."

"That's harassment. Our lawyers—"

"Screw your lawyers. Two women dead. I'll hold your ass responsible if you scared the killer off."

As Bell moved between the two men, an idea occurred to her.

"Wait a second," Bell said, pulling harder on her partner's arm. "How did you know we were here?"

Hayward twisted his head toward Bell.

"How the hell do you think?"

"Christ, Hayward. You're stalking us."

Hayward wheezed out a laugh and cursed when Gardy twisted Hayward's arm behind his back.

"Stalking is such an ugly word. I'm a reporter, Agent Bell, and you are news. And I'm well within my rights."

"Except you trespassed again," Gardy said. "A second offense in two nights won't look good."

Hayward shrugged.

"Like a horse flicking away flies. You can't make the charge stick."

"Let him go," Bell told Gardy.

"Why?"

"Hayward's not going anywhere. He can help us."

Both men shot her cautious glares. Gardy released Hayward, who clutched his arm and winced.

"Save it," Gardy said. "If I wanted to break your arm, I would have."

Gardy snapped his fingers in front of Hayward's face. The reporter cringed.

Bell shifted in front of Gardy and stared daggers into Hayward. The fat man took an involuntary step backward.

"How long have you been following me?" No answer. "I spotted you this afternoon. Did you stalk me to the hotel, too?"

"I don't have to tell you anything."

She reached for the camera, and he snatched it away.

"If I check your photographs, what will I see? Me gathering evidence across the street. The boardwalk. The park near the police department. Give me the camera."

Slowly, Gardy discovered the angle to Bell's line of questioning.

"Not without a warrant," Hayward said.

Bell stepped closer. Nose-to-nose with Hayward. He butted up against the wall, trapped.

"You're a fool. A fool who's lucky to be alive. You see, Hayward, you're not the only one stalking me."

Hayward glanced between the two agents for clarification. The horror dawned on his face.

"The killer?"

Bell nodded.

"I want those pictures, Hayward."

Her demand shook away his trepidation.

"Never. I captured the photographs legally."

"You know the killer is in your camera. Somewhere. Think, Hayward. You could help us catch a serial killer. How's that for a headline?"

Hayward's grin turned wolfish. As quickly as it appeared, it faded.

"Or what if I keep the photos for myself and show the world why I'm the best investigative reporter in the business? I caught the murderer on camera days before you figured out his identity."

Gardy turned away before he did something he'd

regret. Bell's internal fire turned into gray coals. Hayward seemed impenetrable. There was one choice. She could rip the camera from his hands and peruse the images while Gardy restrained the reporter. A dark and risky path fraught with eventual lawsuits. The move would save lives. And harm their careers.

Another choice existed. Bell chewed on it. She felt nauseous, hollow.

Hayward swung the camera strap over his shoulder and straightened his back.

"I'm leaving now. You can't force me to stay."

The reporter moved toward the stairs. Bell lowered her eyes to the floor.

"Don't leave yet, Hayward. I have a proposal."

CHAPTER ONE HUNDRED ELEVEN

Haggleston scowled at the 32-ounce orange cola he'd snagged at the mini-mart before the stakeout. The human body didn't require this much soft drink even though orange pop qualified as the nectar of the gods. With amusement, Adames watched Haggleston squirm between the front and back seats as if constant motion would empty the older officer's bladder through cosmic osmosis.

"Dude, if you gotta go, you gotta go."

"Thanks, Einstein. Where?"

Haggleston was stuck inside a surveillance van with the nearest gas station bathroom a mile away, and Adames grinned at him. Crumbs littered the carpet, and a bag of barbecue potato chips lay on its side with half the contents spilled across the van's floor.

"The bushes."

Adames bobbed his head at a tiny park nestled between sprawling homes. No. This wasn't reasonable police behavior. Public urination where children play during the day?

Haggleston groaned, and a wave sloshed inside his

555

abdomen. This was going from bad to worse.

"Just go. I'll keep an eye on the bungalow. It's not like the killer is gonna show in the next five minutes."

"I can't."

Adames huffed and waved his hand in front of his face.

"You're polluting the van, Haggleston. I'll make you a deal. Slip out of the van and make a dash for the park, and I'll watch your back."

"This is a terrible idea."

"What's the alternative? You wanna drive back to the mini-mart while I stakeout the neighborhood behind a hydrangea?"

"Fine. I'll do it. But if word gets out..."

Adames raised his hand in the air—scout's honor.

The air turned cool when Haggleston slipped out of the van, typical of January when temperatures sometimes dropped into the forties. He'd grown up in Michigan and knew what real cold was, and this wasn't it. But two decades working in Florida turned you cold-blooded, and his skin rippled and contracted from the wind snaking down the lane.

Haggleston stood at the back of the van and peered around the corner. Avoiding the street lamp, he dashed for the curb and stepped through dew-laden grass, his bladder squealing in protest.

The park was a dark mystery of shapes and shadows. He didn't notice the swing set until he walked face-first into a chain. A jumbled figure several feet away appeared to be playground equipment, a curling elephantine slide, metal stairs leading up to a tower.

He kept walking past the playground, his legs glued

together so he didn't empty his bladder prematurely. Wouldn't Adames love that? Haggleston would never live it down.

Somewhere a dog barked. The faraway purr of thoroughfare motors rode the breeze.

A man-sized bush sprouted near the chain-link fence. Dancing with desperation, he shot a last second glance over his shoulder.

Haggleston unzipped his pants and relieved himself behind the bush. He moaned from the pain of holding his bladder too long. It made him cringe to think a kid might play here tomorrow. What if the child picked leaves off the bush and...

He altered his aim away from the bush and onto the fence. Not that this was better. Kids climbed fences.

It took a full minute before he finished. He smiled up at the moon and gave thanks to the heavens. There was still the matter of his upset stomach, but emptying his bladder had gone a long way toward settling his tummy.

Haggleston hopped as he yanked up on the zipper. Buttoned his pants and glanced around again. He thought his eyes would have adjusted to the dark by now. They hadn't. The park became its own universe, a black abyss set apart from the well-lit street.

He started toward the van when a branch cracked. The noise stopped him in his tracks. Automatically, he thought of Adames playing a joke. That didn't jibe. Adames was a cutthroat prankster, but he wouldn't abandon his post.

Weaving through the grass toward the hulking playground tower, Haggleston reached for his hip and remembered the radio was inside the van. From here, the street seemed a million miles away. Footsteps in the grass brought him to another stop.

"Anyone there?"

The crickets sang back at him. Haggleston grabbed his flashlight and waved the beam over the equipment.

"Palm Dunes Police. The park's closed after dark."

He swept the beam along the fence and saw nothing.

Not wishing to draw attention to himself, Haggleston flicked off the light. He picked up his pace and didn't perceive the footsteps swishing through the grass behind him.

The assailant's flashlight clubbed the officer's head and dropped him to his knees. A powerful hand gripped Haggleston's mouth and stifled his cry for help before the business end of the flashlight rained down on the back of his neck.

The man ripped him off the ground. Python arms encircled his ribs and squeezed. Drove the air from his lungs.

He beat his arms against the man's face as the shadowed figure hoisted him higher. Crushed his back and spine.

Haggleston screamed for Adames. All that came from his mouth was a jet of spittle and a dying wheeze.

Then something snapped along Haggleston's spine.

And the officer stopped feeling.

CHAPTER ONE HUNDRED TWELVE

Bell leaned forward on the chair with her palms supporting her aching head, elbows on knees.

"You can't be serious," Gardy said. "Forget the career implications. This will ruin your life."

Hayward wore a shark's grin as he stood beside the attic window. A slice of moonlight drew a glowing border between the reporter and the two agents.

Ignoring her partner, Bell motioned Hayward forward.

"You know the deal," Hayward said, pulling the camera back.

"And you have my word."

Gardy swore and turned his back to them. His fingers interlocked atop of his head, eyes squinted shut. It was hard to see the agent amid the darkness, but Bell sensed his fury just the same.

Hayward handed the camera to Bell and showed her how to access the images.

"The computer, Gardy."

"What?"

"We need the computer."

Gardy snatched his laptop bag off the floor and brought it to her.

"I hope you gave this enough thought."

"Yes, I did. I'm stopping a lunatic before he kills again. That's what matters."

"If you say so. Take this miscreant with you while I sign on."

While Bell wandered to the window and peered into the night, Gardy started the laptop and entered his password.

"You'll need this," Hayward said as he handed Gardy a cable.

The glare Gardy gave Hayward forced the reporter back a step. The computer churned, then the screen filled with images.

"Okay, you're in," Gardy told Bell. "I'll keep an eye on Tannehill's house."

Bell traded places with Gardy. Hayward followed Bell like a bad habit.

Bell felt as if a pair of slimy eels clung to her neck as she stepped through the photographs. One candid shot after another. Here she was entering the Palm Dunes Police Department for the first time, the sun recently set and the sky full of stars. Now climbing the front steps with Gardy at Tannehill's. Several low angle images aimed at the roof overhang and attic window to capture the killer's path into the bungalow.

A normal man would have become embarrassed and stepped away. Hayward leered over Bell's shoulder, proud of his intrusion into her life.

Flipping through the pictures, Bell searched for a

common thread—a car parked along the curb, the man she saw at the boardwalk and in the park. She found nothing.

She'd examined over a hundred pictures before one stopped her heart. There she was with Gardy in Lynn Thomas's yard, Haggleston and Adames kneeling in the grass, as a sports car passed through the frame. A red Camaro. But it wasn't the car she fixed on. It was the man behind the wheel, caught in side profile. The man she sought.

"I got him, Gardy."

Gardy hustled to Bell. Hayward tried to squeeze between them, but Bell shoved him back. It was a stroke of luck. Hayward had clicked the shutter at the right moment and rendered the driver from the side.

"Look at the mirror," Gardy said, pointing at the rear-view mirror, which captured the killer's face from his forehead to his nose.

"That's him. That's the guy from the boardwalk and the park."

Gardy jumped on the phone with Phalen as he uploaded the image to the police department's server.

"Wait, I've seen that guy."

Bell glanced at Hayward, who squinted and rubbed a grubby finger on the unknown man's face.

"Where?"

"Yesterday around lunchtime, a few hours before I took this picture. I stopped at Vinnie's Diner on Sunset for a burger. The bastard was one booth across from me."

"Told you he was following you, Hayward. You're lucky you didn't end up like Morris and Tannehill."

Hayward's throat made a clicking noise.

Bell clicked the next picture and fumbled the laptop.

"Jesus, Gardy. The license plate."

Gardy told Phalen to hold and lowered the phone. He craned his neck over Bell's shoulder and repeated her curse. The Camaro shimmered with motion blur, but as Bell drew a box around the bumper and zoomed in on the highlighted area, the Florida license plate leaped out of the screen.

"Okay, Jay. It's a red Camaro, Florida license plate. Ready for the number?"

As Bell lowered the laptop, the silhouette of a man crossed through Tannehill's backyard.

CHAPTER ONE HUNDRED THIRTEEN

"Adames. Haggleston."

Gardy pocketed the radio, flustered and increasingly skittish. The backyards were moonlit and desolate, no sign of the man who crossed behind the Bungalow. Beyond a stand of trees, she saw the surveillance van at the end of the block. The lights were off, no movement within the van. That was to be expected. The officers were discreet.

Why didn't the officers answer?

"What do you think?"

Bell glanced at Gardy and shook her head.

"Maybe their radio died."

"I've seen one too many horror movies to pass this off as happenstance. I'm calling Jay again."

Gardy didn't need to place the call. His phone rang as he flicked the screen to life.

As Gardy drifted into the dark corners of the attic, Hayward shuffled forward to take his place. Bell sensed fear cutting through his smug demeanor.

"I should take my things and leave."

"Those pictures are evidence, Hayward. You aren't

going anywhere."

The expected protest didn't come, and Hayward moved obediently to a chair and sat in the shadows.

"We got a name," Gardy said, rolling the phone in his hand. His eyes were ablaze with the confidence they'd catch the man now. "Warren Schuler, 14 Prescott Avenue in Palm Dunes. Two cars are on their way there now. And get this. He's a wireless phone salesman. Morris and Tannehill bought their phones at his shop."

"So that's how Schuler found the women."

The window drew Bell. Levydale Avenue took on a crypt-like appearance at night. No neighbors conversing on the sidewalk. No traffic. Everything colored in dead winter blues by the moon.

"They know his mobile number. As long as Schuler has the phone on him they can track his location."

A flicker of hope. Yet it didn't explain why Adames and Haggleston were MIA. Gardy read the doubt on her face.

"I requested two more cruisers. One to park at the end of Levydale. If the killer makes a dash for the highway, that's the way he'll go. Another to swing past the van and check things out."

"Hopefully without blowing their cover."

"That's my concern, too." Gardy touched her arm. "Listen, you and Jay are at each other's throats, but I gave him your number in case he locates Schuler."

"Wait, where are you going?"

"Nowhere. Just downstairs. I don't want anyone to sneak past the front door." He handed her the police radio. "If you see anything, radio it in and call my phone."

Bell steeled herself, straightened her shoulders. This

case unsettled her, the sense of dread reminiscent of taking a walk through a graveyard at midnight. Not that she wasn't a trained agent capable of defending herself, but she hated splitting up, especially since she needed to keep an eye on Hayward. Before she could protest, Gardy disappeared around the corner and descended the stairs.

The bungalow next door looked dead. No silhouettes crept toward its doors. The person she'd seen was likely a neighbor, perhaps a teenager cutting through the yard.

She thumbed the radio's call button. Neither Adames nor Haggleston answered. Dammit, the van was only a two-minute walk, one minute if she jogged. They could solve this mystery in a hurry if one of them risked running to the van.

Her phone rang, and she jumped. Hayward moved to the edge of his seat, and for the first time he wasn't probing for a scoop. The reporter's nerves were piano-wire-tight.

"Bell."

"Phalen here." Bell braced herself, but the expected antagonism didn't come. "I wanted to confirm your phone number and get our ducks in order before we locate Schuler."

"Anything new on our target?"

"We're trying to locate his position now. You'll hear from me if we get a hit. Shouldn't take more than a few minutes."

Bell switched the phone to her other ear as she traveled to the front window. This gave her the best view of the van.

"I still can't get Adames and Haggleson on the radio. When will the cruiser get to them?"

Phalen lowered the phone and requested an update.

A female voice answered.

"Don't look for a police vehicle. We sent an unmarked car so we don't blow the operation. Should arrive in five minutes."

An SUV crawled along Levydale, the first vehicle she'd seen in a long time. Anxiety gripped her heart when it slowed outside the bungalow. Then it took off toward the interstate.

"Hey, Detective? About what happened with the interrogation."

"Not now, Agent Bell."

The line went dead.

Shit. She knew she'd gone overboard this afternoon. It was too soon to expect reconciliation. What could she have done differently to prevent an innocent man from taking the rap?

Hayward watched her from the gloom.

She felt like a rat in a maze.

CHAPTER ONE HUNDRED FOURTEEN

Years of stakeouts had taught Gardy never to let his guard down. The old adage, *the quiet before the storm,* was a cliche, but when the action began, it always happened fast.

He pawed through the darkened downstairs, careful not to use his flashlight or phone for lighting. The entire downstairs was hardwood though an area rug in the living room silenced his footsteps as he cut between two sofas and a glass table. A piano sat at the front of the room beside the window. He turned and checked the den, then the dining room and kitchen.

Arched windows everywhere, some almost as long as the walls were tall. He couldn't recall the last time he was this unsettled during a case.

He felt watched. Exposed.

Instinctively, his hand drifted to the Glock as he crossed a pool of moonlight in the kitchen.

The air carried a fecund, humid scent unlike the rest of the downstairs. The wind touched his face. Someone had cut a piece of glass out of the deck door.

Gardy swung his body against the wall, the gun in his

hand.

"Jesus, Bell," Gardy whispered before the butt end of the flashlight smashed against his head.

***

A thud downstairs brought Bell away from her post at the window. She moved to the attic doorway and listened. The house was silent again.

"Gardy?"

She meant her whisper to carry downstairs, but no reply came. Hayward started in her direction.

"Stay there, Hayward."

"What was that noise?"

She shook her head and listened. A cavernous whistle came from downstairs as if someone edged a window open and let the wind inside the house.

"Gardy?"

This time the quiet unraveled her self-assurance, and as she removed the gun from her holster, the growing trepidation in Hayward's eyes set her on edge. Someone was downstairs.

Back to the wall, she peered around the door frame and ran her vision to the living room. It was too dark to see if anyone was coming up the stairs. Bell contemplated flicking the wall switch and flooding the house with light. She didn't want to make another mistake today and blow the stakeout.

She swung past the doorway and shot Hayward a warning glare.

"Get back in the chair."

"Hell, no. You're not leaving me up here alone."

"Stay in the attic, or I swear to God I'll put a bullet in your kneecap."

The reporter raised his hands in acceptance and backed away.

Bell tried to convinced herself Gardy was outside, patrolling the backyard perimeter. Something was terribly wrong. Screw this. She decided to call Phalen and demand the detective send backup. To heck with being discreet. The operation had spun out of control. The phone shrilled in her hand. Glancing down, she recognized Phalen's number. Thank goodness.

"Phalen, I can't find Gardy—"

"Agent Bell, we tracked Schuler's phone. He's inside the house."

For a frozen moment, Bell thought Phalen had messed up and traced her own phone. Then she saw the shadow creep past the bedroom door. Schuler's face materialized out of the gloom, and she saw the insanity, the crazed obsession in his eyes.

The blunt object clipped the side of her head and sent her reeling against the wall. A club? No, a flashlight. The phone flew out of her hand and smashed at the bottom of the stairs. Gunfire exploded, deafening in close quarters. The errant shot blew a hole in the plastered ceiling.

Click of the Glock as she racked the slide forward, and Schuler's fists hammered her arms. The muzzle flashed as the gun blew another hole in the plaster. The dark stairway dusty. Gun out of her hands now. Somewhere on the floor as she groped blindly with the madman atop her.

Two powerful hands gripped her neck and choked. She grasped his wrists and pulled, but he was much too strong. Her legs flailed as he lifted Bell off her feet and slid her up the wall.

She smashed her palm into his nose. Bones cracked. He released his grip and stumbled backward.

Schuler touched his ruined nose, and his hand came away with blood.

Enraged, the madman bellowed and threw his shoulder into Bell's stomach and drove her against the wall. Everything broke inside her. Ribs crushed, oxygen ripped from her lungs. Schuler kicked at her head and bashed her neck backward with a geyser of blood.

She lay in the dark. His footsteps thundered on the floorboards. He drew the knife and plodded toward her.

Bell drew her knees toward her chest and kicked out. Clipped him in the groin and backed him up a step. The pain only infuriated Schuler, and he came at her again with the knife raised above his head like a nightmare maniac from a horror movie.

She twisted out of the way as the knife plunged at her chest, driving her palm into his nose again as she spun onto her side. He fell to his hands and knees, the knife still gripped.

Another shadow passed through the hallway as she teetered on the edge of consciousness. Schuler scrambled to his feet, stunned by the intruder. As Bell watched, the second figure brandished his own knife. He slashed and jabbed at the maniac and forced him toward the stairwell. Gardy's skill with a blade shocked her. She'd known he was an expert in close combat, a lethal weapon with his hands. Schuler was no match with the knife and vied to knock the blade from Gardy's grip.

Only it wasn't Gardy.

Bell struggled up to her elbows and collapsed from

the pain. Dragging herself through the hallway, she saw Logan Wolf duck under Schuler's knife and drive the blade into the maniac's side. Wolf was a shadow among shadows, black coat and pants, black gloves. A stunned look came over Schuler's face. He clutched at his side and backed away from Wolf, who rolled the knife hilt in his hand and followed.

"Get up, Scarlett." Wolf's voice.

Pain froze her in place as if dozens of tiny daggers pierced her ribcage.

"I can't."

"You can, and you will."

Quick as a cobra, Wolf lashed out with the knife and flipped the blade out of Schuler's hand. Stunned, the killer glared at Wolf.

Wolf circled around Schuler, and when he was close enough, the nation's most wanted fugitive knelt and retrieved Schuler's knife. He tossed both knives toward Bell. The blades clanged against the hardwood and slid to a stop.

Bell tried to rise. Pushing through the agony, she fought up to her knees and stood. The hallway wobbled, then the dizzy spell passed.

The fear melted off Schuler's face. He eyed the smaller man before him.

Wolf turned his head toward her. His eyes were black holes with no beginning or end.

"Kill him, Scarlett."

Her breath hitched at the sound of his voice.

"He murdered three women and meant to make you his fourth victim. You'll find the female reporter in a glade five miles south of Palm Dunes off county route 24."

"What are you doing, Wolf? Where's Gardy?"

"He's not here to help you. This is up to you, Scarlett." When she didn't react, he glared between Schuler and Bell. "He stalked you, meant to murder you. How does it make you feel?"

"I don't feel anything, Wolf. It's my job to stop him."

Schuler shifted closer to Wolf. It wasn't until then that Bell realized how much larger the Palm Dunes killer was.

"Do not lie, Scarlett. I can see it in your face. End him."

"Stop saying that."

"You're ten times the killer he is."

The look of derision Wolf gave Schuler rekindled the murderer's rage, and as he lunged at Wolf, a sudden need to defend the fugitive gripped Bell.

What happened next Bell wouldn't fully recall. Schuler springing at Wolf, who remained a defenseless statue. A sudden, desperate need for Bell to protect Wolf, who stood motionless as though waiting for the younger killer to eviscerate him. Bell racing between the two killers and stopping Schuler in his tracks with a jump kick. The shadowed hallway tinged red by her fury.

The kick knocked Schuler backward, but the killer recovered and came at Bell. She dropped to the floor and swung her legs at his shins. Knocked Schuler off his feet. As he crashed forward, she clamped her legs around his neck and twisted. The break was instantaneous.

A horrible cracking sound.

Schuler went limp.

Bell lay prone, the fight drained from her. The sound of thunder she heard was the beating of her heart. Schuler's arms splayed across her legs, and she kicked them off with a shudder.

It was then she remembered Wolf was behind her. She twisted to her stomach and spun up to a crouch. The hallway was empty.

Bell sprang for the fallen Glock and swept the weapon from the stairway to the end of the hall. A whisper of breathing came from behind, and she spun around to Gavin Hayward. He yelped and threw up his hands as she touched the trigger.

The reporter slumped to the floor, legs splayed like doll parts.

Bell lowered the weapon. Wolf was gone.

CHAPTER ONE HUNDRED FIFTEEN

Bell located Gardy's body hidden in the den. Somebody had dragged the agent from the kitchen, a red smear of blood marking his journey. It made her wonder who'd relocated her partner—Schuler or Wolf? Perhaps Schuler put Gardy there with the intention of finishing the agent off after he murdered Bell. But if it was Wolf...

That possibility made her head swim. Why did Wolf pull Gardy out of harm's way?

Gardy's eyes looked glazed and unfocused, and he took several seconds before he sat up and responded to her questions.

Her phone was a puzzle of plastic pieces set inside a zipped evidence baggie. She'd used the police radio to contact Phalen. It had only been a few minutes, but the red and blue lights streaking over the window told Bell the police had arrived.

The first officer on the scene, a tall male she recognized from the first night they visited the police department, joined a female EMT who worked on Gardy. Several minutes later, Phalen arrived, grim faced and pallid.

"You okay, Agent Bell?"

She barely had enough energy to nod. The bright lights flooding the downstairs drove railroad spikes through her forehead.

He followed a team of officers upstairs. Another male officer hissed through his teeth. When Phalen returned, he stared at Bell the way he might a strange and undocumented animal who'd straggled into the room. The detective escorted the whey-faced reporter, who tottered out the door and into the night. A flashbulb flared. The media's cameras pointed at Hayward now.

Several minutes later, they were both under the stars near the whirling lights of an ambulance as the police backed away a growing mass of reporters. The female EMT pointed a light into Bell's eyes while her partner, a mustached male wearing an overabundance of cologne, bandaged Gardy's head.

Gardy's eyes flicked to her when he didn't think Bell was looking, but she noticed. She recognized the expression, something between confusion and horror. It was the same look Phalen had given her.

"Bell, you know what happened to Haggleston?"

She lowered her head and glared at a crushed cigarette butt flattened against the blacktop. Yes, she'd heard the other officers talking. Adames was on his way to the hospital with a bloody gash on his forehead where the killer had clubbed him when the officer slipped out of the van to search for Haggleston. He was fortunate to be alive.

Against their better judgment, Bell and Gardy conceded to an ambulance ride to the hospital. Both underwent MRI exams and answered a battery of questions aimed at diagnosing concussions. To the surprise of the attending physicians, both agents passed their tests and stumbled out of County General at three in the morning.

CHAPTER ONE HUNDRED SIXTEEN

Bell sat on the beach in Capri pants, a blanket thrown around her shoulders to stave off the wind, feet buried in the sand. The temperature had cooled on Chesapeake Bay, and the sharp bite blowing in from the Atlantic portended winter's return. Gardy removed his sneakers and dug his toes into the beach. Promising to watch over Bell, Gardy had told the agent charged with guarding the property to grab a late lunch.

She eyed the time. Lucas was due to arrive home from work soon. She'd tell him what she could of the Schuler case, and when she worked up the courage, she'd explain why she shared a room with her partner. To this point, Bell had avoided discussion of Logan Wolf around Lucas. With the impending release of Hayward's new article detailing Wolf's connection to Bell, Lucas would learn soon enough. Best he heard it from her first.

"There's still time," Gardy said. "One phone call from the FBI will put the article on hold."

Bell grinned inwardly. Gardy had read her thoughts.

"No. I'm true to my word, even with a snake like

Hayward."

"But the consequences."

"I'll cross that bridge when I get there."

In exchange for the pictures which identified Schuler, Bell had granted Hayward an exclusive interview about the serial killers they'd tracked in the last year—why ordinary men became murderers and how the BAU caught them. For the first time, she revealed to the world her reason for becoming a BAU agent: the abduction and murder of her childhood friend.

The article had reached the Deputy Director's desk, and she'd done her best to avoid Weber in the office yesterday. In due time, Weber would order a closed door meeting. An embarrassing feature in *The Informer* wasn't enough to lose Bell her job, but the glass ceiling over her head was lower now.

"When are you going to tell me what happened in Sowell's house?"

She glanced at him, then moved her attention to a pair of gulls dodging the tide.

"It's in the report."

"Save the bogus information for Weber. This is your partner you're talking to."

"What are you suggesting?"

"Schuler had multiple stab wounds from his abdomen to his ribcage."

"As I've told you countless times, he knocked the gun from my hand. I had to defend myself. What did you expect me to do—call a timeout so I could pick up the gun?"

"Cute, but you're not escaping with jokes this time. How did you get the knife?"

The wind whipped sand at Bell's face. She rubbed the grains out of her eyes and leaned back on her hands.

"It belonged to Schuler. He had two knives and dropped one."

Gardy's lips were tight, teeth grinding.

"Forensics didn't find Schuler's prints on that knife. As a matter of fact, they didn't find any prints. Not even yours. You weren't wearing gloves, so I need you to explain this to me."

A figure approached from the far end of the beach. Lucas. Bell waved her arms over her head, and Lucas swerved in their direction.

"Bell?"

"I can't tell you why they missed the print, Gardy. Probably for the same reason they missed an obvious thumb print in Lori Tannehill's attic."

He stood and brushed the sand off his pants, offered his hand and helped Bell to her feet.

"So the theory we're going with is bad police work."

Bell shrugged.

"Does it matter at this point? We caught Schuler. He's dead. That's what we were there to do."

Lucas was closer now. Gardy gave the man a half-hearted wave and gathered up his sneakers.

"You don't have to leave, Gardy. Join us for dinner."

"Nah. You know what they say. Three's a crowd."

Before she could reply, Gardy started away. He trudged up and over a sand drift, then she only saw beach grass and the top of his head.

The wind turned a shade colder as Lucas approached. Bell fretted with her hands.

It was time she told him the truth.

***

Lucas didn't take the news well. He held an understanding smile as she spoke, but it looked forced, painted on. The kiss he planted on her cheek was without passion, the kiss he'd give his niece on her birthday. Then he left her with an ambiguous promise to get together and talk more. When? Soon, whenever that was.

A tear pushed at her eye. She squeezed the lids shut before it could show itself. When she forced herself to look, he was halfway to the beach house. Something cold and heavy was on the wind.

Her phone rang and startled her. Bell's first thought was Lucas had called to make amends, but his back was to her and he showed no sign of slowing. She didn't recognize the number. After a moment of contemplation, she answered.

The caller was silent for several seconds. The line crackled like distant lightning.

"Scarlett."

A shiver rolled through her body. She jumped to her feet, feeling exposed on the empty beach.

"How did you get this number, Wolf?"

"You disappoint me, Scarlett. Why did you reveal your secrets to a devil like Gavin Hayward? I trust you won't disclose our relationship."

She switched the phone to her other ear and paced toward the surf.

"We don't have a relationship."

A moment of quiet, then—

"I saved your life."

"I didn't ask you to."

"You needn't ask. That is what friends are for, no?"

"Get one thing straight. We aren't friends, we aren't accomplices. You're a deranged killer, and the only thing we have in common is you're a fugitive and I will find you."

Bell wished Lucas was still here. Or better yet, Gardy. Someone to run a trace on Wolf's number. The phone was a burner. Wolf wasn't a fool. But at least they'd have a shot at pinpointing his location.

"Don't be so hasty. You need a friend. And I dare say young Lucas proved he wasn't your friend when he turned his back on you."

Bell spun. Searched the beach. She saw no one except Lucas, and he was but a pinprick on the horizon.

"Are you watching me?"

"He'll come for you now, Bell."

"What the hell do you mean?"

"Remember what I told you in Kansas? I found the man who destroyed your childhood, your life. I know who killed Jillian."

Bell's throat was too dry for her to reply.

"He hasn't killed in a long time, Scarlett. But the need is always there. He's awake now, and he's more dangerous than ever."

She hadn't considered the possibility Jillian's murderer was still alive. In her mind, he always seemed older. A quick calculation in her head—if the murderer was in his mid-twenties when he abducted Jillian, he would only be in his late-forties now. The realization turned her cold.

"He's seen *The Informer* and knows who you are now.

You claim you can enter the mind of a killer. What is our target's motivation?"

Bell turned again. Saw the beach grass waving like laughing children.

"I don't know."

"Yes, you do. He's ready to hunt again, and you're the one who got away, Scarlett. Find my wife's killer, and I'll deliver Jillian's murderer to you. His name, his address. Even his head on a platter if you so desire."

"I won't work for you, Wolf."

"Then we have nothing else to discuss. Good luck, dear Scarlett. Watch your back."

The line went dead. And winter returned.

***

Ready for the next Scarlett Bell thriller?

Please grab the next book in the series on Amazon today.

Scarlett Bell Books 1-5

Let the Party Begin!

I'm a pretty nice guy once you look past the grisly images in my head. Most of all, I love connecting with kickass readers like you.

Join the party and be part of my exclusive VIP Readers Group at:

WWW.DANPADAVONA.COM

Are You a Super Fan?

How would you like to contribute ideas for my next story? Want to read my novels weeks before they are released on Amazon?

Join me on Patreon at https://www.patreon.com/danpadavona for exclusive stories, interviews, video blogs, and general nonsense.

Be a part of my inner circle and team!

Scarlett Bell Books 1-5

Show Your Support for Indie Thriller Authors

Did you enjoy this book? If so, please let other thriller fans know by leaving a short review. Positive reviews help spread the word about independent authors and their novels. Thank you.

Scarlett Bell Books 1-5

Author's Acknowledgment

Mind of a Killer would not be possible without the encouragement, support, and efforts from my patrons.

Tim Feely
Lisa Forlow
Steve Gracin
Dawn Spengler

I value each one of you more than I can express.
Thank you for believing in me.

To find out how you can become a patron, please visit me at:

https://www.patreon.com/danpadavona

Scarlett Bell Books 1-5

Why Novellas?

The world of entertainment has changed. While I enjoy movies, I watch Netflix series and comparable programming more frequently. Movies are too short to match the story and character arcs of a well-written series, and that's why I favor a long series of novellas over a few novels.

I prefer a long series which I can lose myself in, but broken up into smaller, manageable episodes that don't take up my entire evening.

In short, I'm writing the types of stories I enjoy and composing them into forms I find preferable.

I sincerely hope you enjoy the Scarlett Bell series as much as I love writing it.

How many episodes can you expect? Provided the series is well-received by readers, I don't foresee a definite end and would prefer to expand on the characters and plot lines for the foreseeable future. I still have plenty of devious ideas for upcoming stories.

Stay tuned!

Scarlett Bell Books 1-5

About the Author

Dan Padavona is the author of the The Scarlett Bell thriller series, Severity, The Dark Vanishings series, Camp Slasher, Quilt, Crawlspace, The Face of Midnight, Storberry, Shadow Witch, and the horror anthology, The Island. He lives in upstate New York with his beautiful wife, Terri, and their children, Joe, and Julia. Dan is a meteorologist with NOAA's National Weather Service. Besides writing, he enjoys visiting amusement parks, beach vacations, Renaissance fairs, gardening, playing with the family dogs, and eating ice cream.

Visit Dan at: www.danpadavona.com

Scarlett Bell Books 1-5

Scarlett Bell Books 1-5

Printed in Great Britain
by Amazon

48505028R10352